W9-AQO-375

PRAISE FOR
## *The Story Keeper*

"*The Story Keeper* is a novel of remarkable depth and power. Not since *To Kill a Mockingbird* has a story impacted me like this. You will want to read it and reread it, then pass it along to everyone you know."

COLLEEN COBLE, AUTHOR OF *SEAGRASS PIER* AND THE HOPE BEACH SERIES

"A kaleidoscope of past and present, *The Story Keeper* finds the soft spot of our souls where who we were stands face-to-face with who we are. Can we go home again? Faith, courage, and the power of story are the backbone of generations of the Appalachian women you'll meet in these stories. I was captivated by this story and can't wait to share it with my customers. Lisa Wingate, you rock!"

KAREN SCHWETTMAN, CO-OWNER, FOXTALE BOOK SHOPPE, WOODSTOCK, GA.

"Moving to New York City doesn't break the strong ties to her Appalachian heritage the way Jen Gibbs hopes it will. She finds her ancestors beckoning her when an anonymous manuscript mysteriously appears on her desk. *The Story Keeper* mixes soul-deep darkness with the possibility of redemption. Lisa's writing is as lovely as the mountains, and as with all of Lisa's books, at the end I want more!"

GEE GEE ROSELL, OWNER, BUXTON VILLAGE BOOKS, HATTERAS ISLAND, NC

"Ideal for anyone who enjoys books by master storytellers such as Adriana Trigiani or Karen White. *The Story Keeper* is an inspirational tale about a complex heroine who has managed to survive by navigating around her scars. Set in the captivating world of rural Appalachia, the mountains play a powerful role in this lyrical tale that transports readers across time through a magical and beautiful journey."

JULIE CANTRELL, *NEW YORK TIMES* AND *USA TODAY* BESTSELLING AUTHOR OF *INTO THE FREE*

"Fans of both historical and contemporary fiction will delight in Lisa Wingate's latest tale. *The Story Keeper* is a modern-day quest that beckons readers into the Appalachian lore of yesteryear. The story threads wind and curl in unexpected directions, ultimately weaving an exquisite tapestry. Simply put, *The Story Keeper* is enchanting, inspiring, and beautifully told."

DENISE HUNTER, BESTSELLING AUTHOR OF *DANCING WITH FIREFLIES*

"Lisa Wingate is a master storyteller. *The Story Keeper* is just that—a keeper. A story of hope and redemption that will inspire your heart."

RACHEL HAUCK, BESTSELLING AUTHOR OF *PRINCESS EVER AFTER*

"I am a huge fan of Lisa Wingate. *The Story Keeper* is her best yet. This stunning narrative is exactly what a novel should be: beautifully written with real characters that come to life on the page, a captivating plot with a behind-the-scenes peek into the world of book publishing, and an intriguing and emotional element of mystery to keep you hooked. I have once again fallen in love with this talented author's work."

KELLIE COATES GILBERT, AUTHOR OF *A WOMAN OF FORTUNE* AND *MOTHER OF PEARL*

"Wingate masterfully weaves a haunting tale with the story of a regretful past and sweeps readers along like a mountain stream. The secrets of the eastern hills will linger in your memory long after the last page."

LYNNE GENTRY, AUTHOR OF *HEALER OF CARTHAGE*

the

Story

KEEPER

# LISA WINGATE

*Tyndale House Publishers, Inc.*
*Carol Stream, Illinois*

Visit Tyndale online at www.tyndale.com.

Visit Lisa Wingate's website at www.lisawingate.com.

*TYNDALE* and Tyndale's quill logo are registered trademarks of Tyndale House Publishers, Inc.

Designed by Stephen Vosloo

Edited by Sarah Mason

Published in association with Folio Literary Management, LLC, 630 9th Avenue, Suite 1101, New York, NY 10036.

Scripture quotations are taken from the *Holy Bible*, King James Version.

**Library of Congress Cataloging-in-Publication Data**

Wingate, Lisa.
  The story keeper / Lisa Wingate.
     p. cm
  ISBN 978-1-4143-8826-7 (hc) — ISBN 978-1-4143-8689-8 (sc)  1. Unfinished books—Fiction. 2. Authorship—Fiction. 3. Memories—Fiction. 4. Psychological fiction. I. Title.
  PS3573.I53165S76 2014
  813'.54—dc23                                                2014015243

Printed in the United States of America

| 20 | 19 | 18 | 17 | 16 | 15 | 14 |
|----|----|----|----|----|----|----|
| 7  | 6  | 5  | 4  | 3  | 2  | 1  |

*To the readers*
*who take these journeys with me:*
*thank you for inspiring me*
*always to seek another story*
*that will connect us*
*to one another.*

# Acknowledgments

*The Story Keeper* began as a dream. I suppose all stories do, but in the case of this story, the description applies in the most basic sense. On a morning in September, I literally woke having dreamed this story. Scenes were still scrolling through my mind as I opened my eyes.

It was magical. An unexpected gift.

But even stories that begin in mysterious ways don't fall onto the page and travel to the hands of readers without hours of work and the contributions of many people. The final product becomes a communal effort. Many friends, neighbors, colleagues, and benevolent strangers have contributed to the creation of *The Story Keeper*, and now you, dear reader, are the golden clasp that binds the story circle.

As always, I am grateful for my loving, supportive family. Thank you to my mother for being an awesome assistant and first cheerleader, who can aptly critique a manuscript but will still tell me to eat my vegetables. Thank you to my sweet mother-in-law for helping with address lists and still feeding these big-boy children at the Nanny in Pajamas Café whenever they're home. Thanks also to relatives and friends far and near for everything you do to make me feel loved and nurtured, and for stopping people in the checkout line and at the doctor's office to talk about books. I'm grateful to my favorite digital designer, Teresa Loman, for beautiful graphics work, to Ed Stevens for constant encouragement and help with all things technical, and to my wonderful aunt Sandy (also known as Sandy of Sandy's Seashell Shop) for help proofreading and for contributing with beautiful sea glass jewelry for book giveaways and gifts. Thanks also to my friends and fellow Southern gal bloggers at www.SouthernBelleView. com, and especially to talented author friend Julie Cantrell for taking time to do an early critique of the manuscript.

In terms of print and paper, my undying gratitude goes out to the talented folks at Tyndale House Publishers. To Karen Watson, Jan Stob, Sarah Mason, Maggie Rowe, and Cheryl Kerwin, thank you for being a fabulous publishing team. To the crew in marketing, publicity, design, and sales, thank you for using your talents so well. Without your vision and hard work, books would be loose-leaf pages in black and white and would never reach the hands of readers. To my agent, Claudia Cross at Folio Literary, thanks again for all that you do.

Last, but not least, I'm so grateful to reader friends everywhere, who give these books such good homes and by doing so give me the inspiration to tell more stories. Thank you for sharing the books with friends, recommending them to book clubs, and taking time to send little notes of encouragement my way via e-mail, Facebook, and SouthernBelleView. I'm incredibly grateful to all of you who read these stories and to the booksellers who sell them with such devotion. You are the fulfillment of the hope my first grade teacher sparked in me when she wrote on my report card, "Keep that pencil moving with that great imagination. I'll see your name in a magazine one day." God has grown that dream in so many wonderful ways, not the least of which being that it has connected me to you as you hold this book.

# Chapter 1

*This is the glory hour. This is the place the magic happens.*

The thought fell quietly into place, like a photographer's backdrop unfurling behind the subject of a portrait. Its shimmering folds caught my attention, bringing to mind a bit of advice from Wilda Culp, the person without whom I would've ended up somewhere completely different. Someplace tragic.

It's strange how one person and a handful of stories can alter a life.

*The trick, Jennia Beth Gibbs, is to turn your face to the glory hours as they come.* I heard it again, her deep-raspy Carolina drawl playing the unexpected music of a bygone day. *The saddest thing in life is to see them only as they flit away.*

*They're always a passing thing. . . .*

My first afternoon in the war room at Vida House Publishing was a glory hour. I felt it, had an inexplicable knowing of it, even before George Vida shuffled in the door and took his place at the head of the table to begin the weekly pub board meeting—my first at Vida House. This meeting would be different from all other such gatherings I'd attended over the past ten years at a half-dozen companies, in a half-dozen skyscrapers, in and about Manhattan.

There was magic in the air here.

George Vida braced his hands on the table before taking his seat, his gaze strafing the room with the discernment of a leathery old goat sniffing for something to nibble on. His survey paused momentarily on the pile of aging envelopes, manuscript boxes, and rubber band–wrapped papers at the far end of the conference room. The odd conglomeration, among so many other things, was Vida House's claim to fame—a curiosity I'd only heard about until today. One of the few remaining actual slush piles in all of New York City, perhaps in all of publishing. In the age of e-mail communication, paper-and-print slush piles had quietly gone the way of the dinosaurs. Digital slush is smaller, easier to manage, more efficient. Invisible. It gathers no dust, never achieves a patina like the slowly fading fragments in George Vida's relic.

*Behold . . . Slush Mountain,* the young intern who'd taken me on the new-employee tour had said, adding a grandiose hand flourish. *It's practically a tourist attraction.* He'd leaned closer then. *And FYI, don't call it that in front of the big boss. George Vida loves this thing. Nobody, but nobody, touches it. Nobody asks why it's still taking up space in the conference area. We all just pretend it's not there . . . like the elephant in the room.*

Slush Mountain was an impressive elephant. It consumed a remarkable amount of territory, considering that real estate in Manhattan is always at a premium. Its peak stretched almost to the antique tin ceiling. From there, the collection slowly fanned outward toward the base, confining the conference table and chairs to the remaining three-quarters of the room.

The intern's information wasn't new. George Vida (I'd noticed that everyone here referred to him by both names, never one or the other) kept his mountain to remind the youngsters, hatched into an e-publishing generation, of two things: *one*, that unreturnable manuscripts are unreturnable because someone didn't mind their p's and q's in terms of submission guidelines, and *two*, that success in publishing is about leaving no page unturned and no envelope unopened. Slush Mountain stood as a reminder that publishing is a labor of love, emphasis on *labor*. It's no small struggle to climb to a level where you might discover the next great American bestseller . . . and actually get credit for it when you do.

"Is it everything you imagined?" Roger leaned in from the next chair, surreptitiously indicating Slush Mountain. Roger and I had been coworkers ten years ago, starting out at a publishing house that practically had its own zip code. He was straight out of Princeton, streetwise and sharp even back then, a Long Island golden boy who had publishing in his blood, while I was the doe-eyed, dark-haired newbie who looked more like an extra from *Coal Miner's Daughter* than a New Yorker in the making.

I nodded but focused on George Vida. I wasn't about to be lured into talking in pub board meeting on my very first day . . . or ogling Slush Mountain. I'd never been quite sure whether Roger was a friend or the competition. Maybe that was just me being jealous. I'd been pigeonholed in nonfiction and memoir for years, while Roger had managed to float from acquiring non-fiction to fiction, and back again, seemingly at will.

At thirty-one, I was starving for something . . . new. Some variety.

My cell phone chimed as a text came in, and I scrambled to silence it.

Not soon enough. Every eye turned my way. The moment seemed to last much longer than it probably did, my heart suddenly in my throat and beating at ten times the normal rate, my instinctive response to shrink, duck, back away before a hand could snake out and grab my arm, compress flesh into bone. Some habits die hard, even years after you've left the place and the people behind.

I turned the sound off under the table. "Sorry. I usually leave it in my office during meetings, but I haven't unpacked yet." The excuse felt woefully inadequate. Doubtless, George Vida's cell phone had never busted a meeting.

A sudden shuffling, rustling, and muffled groaning circled the table, everyone seeming to prepare for something. A horrifying thought raced past. *What if cell phones in a meeting are a firing offense?* Silly, no doubt, but I'd left my previous job, my apartment rent was due in a week, and over the past few years, I had sent my savings, what little there was of it, to a place where it would only prolong a bad situation.

"Box." George Vida pointed to the upturned lid of a printer-paper carton. Andrew, the intern who had given me the tour, snapped to his feet, grabbed the container, and sent it around the table. BlackBerrys, iPhones, and Droids were gently but reluctantly relinquished. No one complained, but body language speaks volumes. I was the class dunce.

*Perfect way to meet the rest of the coworkers. Brilliant. They'll never forget you now.* On the upside, they'd probably get a laugh out of it, and it never hurt to make people laugh.

Across the table, the intern swiveled his palms up when George Vida wasn't looking. He grinned ruefully, giving me what was probably a twenty-two-year-old's idea of a flirtatious wink.

I sneered back at him in a way that hopefully said, *Forget it, buddy. You're just a baby, and aside from that, I won't date anybody I work with.*

Ever. Again.

The meeting got started then. The usual power play went on—editors with pull getting support for the bigger deals, the better deals, the deals with real potential. Various editorial team members stepped up in support of one another's projects, their alliances showing. The sales and marketing gurus leaned forward for some pitches, reclined in their chairs during others. I took note of all the dynamics, mapping the lay of the land at the foot of Slush Mountain and, quite wisely, keeping my mouth shut. Stacked in front of me, and in my office, were company catalogs, manuscripts, an iPad, and a laptop that would help bring me up to speed. I hadn't gotten that far yet, but I would. As quickly as possible. Once the day wound down and the building cleared out this evening, I could dig in uninterrupted, making serious headway before drowsy eyes and a growling stomach forced me to the subway, where I would read some more on the way home.

Short night, early morning. Lather. Rinse. Repeat. By the end of the week, I'd be functional. Mostly. In next Monday's pub board meeting, I could begin to contribute, a little at a time. Carefully. George Vida did not appreciate braggadocio—I'd done my homework. Buying projects and getting the support to make them fly off the shelves rather than *fall* off the shelves was a matter of gaining the favor of the old lion.

"Hollis, if you will introduce us to the newest member of the Vida House family, we'll adjourn this meeting," he requested, and suddenly I was the center of attention again.

George Vida's secretary, Hollis—picture Jane Hathaway from *The Beverly Hillbillies*, but a couple decades older—rose from her chair, behind her boss and slightly to the right, her close-cropped gray hair making her thin face more angular and imposing. I'd heard she had been with George Vida since 1967 when he took over the family newspaper business and began building it into the multimillion-dollar operation it was today.

Hollis's long, thin fingers braced in backward arcs on the tabletop, her expression as stoic and seemingly detached as it had been that morning when she'd looked over the folder of contracts and paperwork I'd signed.

Her gaze swept the room. "Jen Gibbs comes to us from the nonfiction arm of Stanislaus International. She brings ten years of experience in memoir and historical nonfiction. Her gradu-ate work was completed at NYU, where she was the recipient of the Aberdeen Fellowship of Arts and Letters and the Steinbeck Fellowship. We are pleased to welcome her to the team." Her regard settled on me, though she looked neither pleased nor unhappy. "If you will share a few facts about yourself that are not on the dossier, Jen, we will begin the process of getting to know you."

"Thank you." I did a split-second mental debate on whether to sit or stand, then decided standing made more sense, as I could see the whole table that way, and making connections with coworkers is the first critical step to success in a new house.

I recapped my publishing history, all the while backhandedly thumbing for something else interesting to say—something that wouldn't make it sound like my life was all about work. It was, and I liked it that way. If you love what you do, you don't mind devoting yourself to it. But at times like this, I did wish I had something more colorful to share. Kids, house, a classy hobby like antique rose gardening or something. A childhood anecdote about where my love of stories began. Something having to do with bedtime tales and that one treasured book received as a birthday present.

It was nice to imagine, but it didn't solve the problem. When your past is a locked box, introductions are . . . complicated.

I finally settled for a quick recounting of a wild trip to a mountaintop in Colorado to persuade Tom Brandon to sign his celebrity memoir deal with Stanislaus, during an auction between several publishing houses. It was one of the greatest coups of my career, but also the closest I had ever come to plummeting to my death.

"You haven't really lived until you've slid off a mountain on a snowmobile and spent twenty-four hours huddled against a blizzard," I added, knowing that my new coworkers would assume I'd been desperately out of my element that night in the mountains, which couldn't have been farther from the truth. After that experience, Tom Brandon knew things about me no one else in my adult life had ever known, but to his credit, he never revealed any of it during the interviews and hoopla surrounding the book. By mutual agreement, we'd kept one another's secrets. Action hero Tom Brandon was a babe in the woods. And I was a backwoods girl in hiding.

"The search and rescue made for great publicity for the project, though, even if that was one seriously bone-cold night in the woods," I finished, and my coworkers laughed—all except Roger. I'd forgotten until now that he was working for a competitor during that bidding war. I'd beaten him out.

He sidled close again as the meeting broke up. "I've never quite forgiven you for that Tom Brandon deal. That was sheer brilliance."

"Oh, come on, Roger. You know it's not often that I actually win one of our little battles." It was the usual love-hate interplay. In a competitive business, colleagues tend to be like siblings who can't stand one another half the time and play nice the other half.

Roger pulled me into a momentary shoulder hug. "It all worked out. Losing that deal was what convinced me to pursue more fiction."

*Quick little stab-stab there. Oh, that hurt.* He knew I'd always had stories in my blood—that fiction was my real dream—but when you're successful in one arena and you've got bills to pay, it's hard to take a chance on foreign territory.

Roger caught me stealing a glance at the slush pile. "Fascinating, isn't it?" His breath brushed across my ear, minty fresh. Too close for comfort.

"Yes, it is."

"Stay away from Slush Mountain. It's the old man's masterpiece." A quick warning, and then he was gone.

I considered waiting around for a chance to casually tell the boss how thrilled I was to be here, but he and Hollis were enwrapped in conversation at the end of the table, so I gathered my things and started toward the door.

"North Carolina," George Vida said just before I reached the exit. I stopped short, turned around.

The boss had paused to look at me, but Hollis was still sifting through papers, seeming slightly frustrated by the delay.

A thick, stubby, old-man finger crooked in my direction. "That's what I was hearing." He tapped the side of his face. "Reporter's ear. I can usually pick up accents. I remember now. You're a Clemson grad. It was somewhere in the paperwork, or Hollis may have mentioned it."

"Must have been in the paperwork," Hollis contributed dryly.

The boss smiled at me, his round cheeks lifting into an expression that reminded me of Vito Corleone in *The Godfather*. "You North Carolina girls should find some time to catch up. There are no memories like those of the old home place." Still smiling, he returned to his paperwork, not noticing that neither Hollis nor I jumped on the home place conversation.

Somehow, I had a feeling we wouldn't be sitting down for a sweet-tea-and-magnolia chat anytime soon.

# Chapter 2

From my first day in New York, when I'd arrived to a graduate school fellowship, a part-time editorial assistant's job, and no place to live, I'd loved the feel of early morning. There's something special about the city as the night people fade into their lairs and the streets wake to a new day. Shopkeepers open storefronts and breakfast carts roll to sidewalks, smoothie stands offering cornucopias of fresh fruit, yogurt, and protein powders.

Jamie eyed me suspiciously as we walked together from the subway and emerged onto the street, then ducked into a bagelry to grab the usual.

"You look ridiculously happy," she assessed on the way out, taking a sip of the protein smoothie she would drink exactly one-fourth of before dropping it into a trash can—her form of calorie counting. As fashion editor for an upscale glossy, she had to look good. Today, her mid-thigh dress, trendy boots, and swing coat formed a perfect autumn-in-New-York ensemble. She'd managed a cross between Audrey Hepburn and a Paris runway model.

"Sorry," I said, but I wasn't really. So far, other than the pub board cell phone gaffe, my first week at Vida House had gone phenomenally well. I'd worked like a banshee, catching up on reading for next Monday's meeting, and I had disseminated my updated contact information to various literary agents who consistently brought good projects my way. New proposals were beginning to come in. George Vida might have been both an enigma and a dinosaur in the industry, but the house had a reputation for finding manuscripts that had been flying under the radar, then developing those properties into the next big thing. My contacts were excited about the move.

"Well, stop it, okay? You're making me depressed about my own life." Only a best friend can be that honest and get away with it. Jamie and I had been close since the NYU years. I knew all about the disintegrating conditions at her workplace. With the rise of e-publishing and fashion blogging, her future at the magazine was a massive question mark.

"Sorry. I'll try to look appropriately glum. But it is Friday." I heard something in the last word of the sentence. The faintest stretching of the *i* in *Friday*. The hint of an Appalachian twang I thought I'd expunged years ago.

I'd been listening since George Vida's startling observation. It bothered me that he'd picked up on it so quickly. Had anyone else over the years? Maybe just not said anything?

I could've asked Jamie, but that would have opened the door between the two worlds that I had worked all my adult life to separate. Between *before* and *after*.

The great thing about moving far from the place that began you is that it's a chance to rewrite your history, wrinkle up and throw away entire pages of the past and pretend that they never were.

"I'm happy for you," she promised, tossing the rest of her smoothie in a trash can as we stopped in front of her building. "I am, really, Jen. I can't wait for you to discover the next book that goes crazy wild. When it debuts on the *Times* list, I'm going to buy a hundred copies of the newspaper and send them to that wicked ex-boss of yours. Along with a hundred copies of the book. I will *never* forgive her for taking so much of the credit on the Tom Brandon thing after you brought it in."

I hugged her, still clinging to my smoothie, which I intended to consume to the fullest before finally slurping the bottom dry. I'd learned early in life not to waste food. "You're such a brute, but I love you. Try to have a great day, okay?"

"Do my best. Catch a show this weekend?"

"I've got a date with a pile of proposals and manuscripts. You wouldn't believe how much paper they still shuffle around that place. George Vida doesn't think you can really get the feel from e-material. It's primeval, but in a nice way. My desk came with a stapler that looks like it's been knocking around the building since about 1920. And I have a three-hole punch. I haven't been close to one of those since high school English class, I think."

Jamie rolled her eyes. "Okay, okay. Now, you're just making me jealous. Once you get all settled in there, you have *got* to sneak me in and show me the famous slush pile. Is it true that Vida found the stuff stuck in the corner of the basement and had it moved to the board room?"

"That's what Roger tells me. And it's *George Vida*, sort of like all one name—just so you'll have it right when you come to visit."

Jamie walked backward up the steps of her building, her

bottom lip pooching into a frown. "I'd stay away from Roger, if I were you. He's always had a thing for you, you know?"

"*Pppffff!* Roger's got a thing for anyone under fifty in a skirt."

We shared the look of rueful understanding that passes between single girls in the city, equally unlucky in love. All of a sudden, Jamie was deeply bothered by that. Maybe it was crossing the big *three-oh* mark, or maybe it was all the magazine stories about wedding fashions, or perhaps her sister's recent engagement, but she had it in mind lately. When Jamie finally did plan a wedding, it would be a gorgeous, lavish affair filled with loved ones and paid for by the bride's family. That kind of thing was as far from possible for me as the earth from the moon. If you know something isn't going to happen, it's easier to just arrange your life so there's no need for it. The secret to happiness is to love where you are, and it's hard not to love autumn in New York, especially when you've finally landed your dream job.

I was floating about six inches off the ground when I walked into Vida House. So far, I'd felt that way every day as I scanned my key card at the front door and circumvented the reception desk, still empty this early in the morning. Beyond the lobby, I walked down the marble entry hall past rows of office doors and oodles of cover art from books that had made careers and started hot trends that were quickly chased by a horde of scrambling copycats. Rounding the corner, humming under my breath and in full stride, I slid across the tile like an ice-skater, did a YouTube-worthy scramble, and caught myself on a half-height partition in the customer service area, barely saving my smoothie.

"That's wet, sha." Russell, the cleaning guy, emerged from a nearby office, pushing a mop bucket. Russell and I had become acquainted over the past few days. He was at least six and a half feet tall, lamppost thin, and not entirely pleased to have someone disturbing his usual morning routine by coming in so early. He'd been cleaning the building since the sixties and had an apartment in the basement, so it was definitely his domain.

"Sorry." I backtracked across the freshly mopped floor, my pumps leaving little tracks in the sheen of water. "You'd think I would've learned to watch by now."

He lifted the mop from the dingy bucket and plopped it into the wringer. "I got it. Boss man don' like his flo' track up at the beginnin' a the day. Like a clean start." His slow Southern drawl ran in direct contrast to the three quick, efficient swipes that cleared the floor. Russell was a hard person to read. I hadn't quite decided if he liked his job here or liked me, or if he was simply resigned to both as a reality of life.

I wanted Russell to like me. He seemed like a guy with a story, and I'd always been fascinated by stories. That was the first thing Wilda Culp had noticed about me all those years ago, after she caught me pilfering from her orchard. To pay back the damage, I became her Wednesday help around the old family farm she'd moved home to after retiring from Clemson and taking up writing full-time. She'd noticed immediately that I understood the lure of a good story. Sometimes a world that doesn't exist is the only escape from the one that does.

Russell's silvery eyes narrowed, age wrinkles squeezing in. He was an interesting man to look at, his skin a warm brown, his cheeks burnished to a lighter color with an almost-unnatural shine, like the face of a carving lovingly touched many times by the hand of its maker.

"Guess you betta get'a work, sha." Leaning on his mop handle, he sidestepped to let me by, his gaze ricocheting across the open area toward the semicircle of soft light shining from George Vida's office. No matter how late I stayed at work or how early I came in, George Vida was always there, occupying his space. Amazingly, nothing went out of Vida House that hadn't traveled through his hands.

That scared me a little, as I contemplated acquiring new manuscripts here. What if I got it wrong? What if my instincts ran counter to the big boss's liking?

*A woman must be confident!* Wilda's gruff reminder was the snap of a rubber band. A quick, sharp rebuke. *When the negative comes against her, she must B-E-A-T. Be, expand, arise, triumph. Be all that she was designed to be. Expand her vision of what is possible. Arise from every challenge stronger than before. Triumph over her own insecurity. This is what I always told my students.*

*You, Jennia Beth Gibbs, have greatness in you if you want it.*

I felt Russell watching me as I continued down the hall and slipped into my office at the end, where new editors began their careers, no matter how many years of prior experience they brought to the job. At Vida House, you started at the bottom and worked your way up. It wasn't so bad, really. Being at the fringe of the nonfiction hall meant having a corner space. My office was in a three-sided turret, which made it quirky and interesting. Even though the skyscraper next door blocked both the sunshine and the view, I liked the place.

The fluorescent light flickered stubbornly overhead when I flipped the switch, the room bright, then dark, then bright, then dark.

"Oh, come *on*." I slipped off the burnt-orange silk coat I loved during the fall months. It would've been an indulgence, given the designer label, but it had been a gift from Jamie, a bribe to get me to stand in for a last-minute magazine shoot, in which she promised I would be carrying an umbrella, and no one would know who I was. *Please, please, please, I need mid-length dark hair, and skinny legs, and you can have the coat afterward.* My short modeling career was worth it. I treasured the coat, partially because the color called up memories of my favorite sugar maple tree growing up, the one I often climbed as a hiding place. The coat was a secret reminder of the Blue Ridge, a small piece that wasn't painful to relive.

The overhead fixture clicked softly, teasing me. I tried the switch again. Up. Down. Up. Down. No luck. Finally there was no choice but to surrender and use the ancient gooseneck lamp that had come with the desk. The lamp's cast-iron base was rusty, and the built-in inkwell was of no use, but I liked it all the same. It hovered like an all-seeing eye and gave the place a feeling of journalistic authenticity. I imagined it hunched above a reporter, monitoring the progress of stories about the spread of Hitler's forces or the first words spoken on the moon or the sad sight of little John-John Kennedy saluting his father's coffin.

*Someone's been messing with things on my desk.*

The thought wound past my momentary romance with the gooseneck lamp. I squinted at the arrangement of things. The next three reads in my queue, which I always stacked and placed just left of center at the end of the day, were dead center now. The pencil I had left lying atop them had rolled onto the desk.

*Who would've come in here overnight? Russell, maybe . . . cleaning?*

Nothing else seemed out of place.

And then I noticed it. Another detail that hadn't been the same yesterday. A brown craft-paper envelope, the crease along its edge sun-washed white as if it had been sitting long near a window. It rested on the corner of my desk, slightly cockeyed. The department admin hadn't put any fresh material in my in-box or on the credenza by the door. Had someone left the packet here accidentally while passing through my office? Who? And passing through my office for what reason? My little cubby wasn't on the way to anywhere.

The envelope was crisp to the touch. The upper corner had been torn off at some time in the past. No return address. Dust clung along the feathered edge so that it drew a jagged brown line against the paper peeking through from beneath. The underlying sheet was aquamarine, a vibrant color beside the brown. The juxtaposition made me stop, admire the random art of everyday life.

Inside, the small stack of pages had yellowed around the edges, but the aquamarine cover sheet was bright. A handwritten swirl of ink lay just beyond my thumb.

An odd sixth sense tightened the corridors of curiosity in my brain, brought a wariness that warned me to leave the papers inside. The postmark—what I could read of it—said *June 7, 1993.*

Was this thing from George Vida's famous slush pile? The one *nobody* was supposed to touch?

Outside my door, the building was silent, yet I had the eerie feeling of being watched. Leaving the envelope on the desk, I walked down the hall, checking for signs of life in the other offices—a coat hanging over a chair, a fresh cup of coffee, a pair of comfortable tennis shoes tucked in a corner after a coworker changed into heels.

Nothing.

Who would take part of Slush Mountain and leave it in my office? Why?

A mistake? Hazing the new girl? Or was someone trying to—I hated to even think it—set me up? Had I made an enemy here without realizing it? Maybe a colleague was insecure about the new addition to the team? Publishing could be a cutthroat business. . . .

Was this a test to see if I could be trusted? To see if I'd return the envelope to its place or look at the contents?

Not this girl. I had plenty to do without toying with a loaded weapon. Whatever this was, it belonged in the war room, and the time to take it there was now, while the office was empty. No one would be the wiser. In the future, I'd watch my back, just in case. If this was a joke, the joke would be on somebody else once the package was quietly returned to its original resting place.

In under a minute, I was out the door with the forbidden fruit innocuously tucked in a folder. Unfortunately, Roger was just around the corner at the coffee credenza, preparing his morning mug of brew.

"At it early again?" He smiled, toasting me with his cup and seeming amiable enough. "You're making the rest of us look bad, you know."

"You're here too." I tried to sound casual, but I felt like I had a package bomb squeezed to my chest. I just wanted to get rid of it before it blew.

Yet in the back of my mind, there was that bit of aquamarine paper, the swirl of ink, the niggle of curiosity . . .

"I have an author and an agent coming in for an early meeting in the boardroom," Roger offered.

Was it my imagination, or was he casting an eye toward the folder in my double-armed embrace? Maybe I looked guilty. Or maybe he knew what was inside. Maybe he'd put it on my desk.

"Well, have a good meeting, then." I turned on my heel and headed back to my office. My trip to Slush Mountain would have to wait.

The folder seemed to grow heavier and hotter as I walked down the hall. A part of me was saying, *Just tuck it in the desk drawer where no one will see it, then return it after they all leave this evening.* But another part of me, the part that had led me around more than one blind corner in my life, was saying, *Well, if you're stuck with the thing for a while, why not take a peek?*

That whisper of mischief, the one my father and the men of Lane's Hill Church of the Brethren Saints had so vehemently tried to beat out of me as a child, always brought about one of two things: incredible adventure or unmitigated disaster.

I was sliding my fingers over the forbidden treasure before I rounded the corner into my office and shut the door. The glue on the bottom flap clung for a moment, seeming determined to keep whatever secrets lay hidden inside, then the tension released, and the contents, perhaps fifty sheets in total, came loose in my hand, the blue-green piece on top. A pen-and-ink drawing inched into view—a sketch of what looked like a thick cord holding six oval-shaped beads and a rectangular pendant of some sort, all ornately carved.

The artwork was nicely done.

Below the drawing, three words had been hand-inscribed in graceful, curving script that seemed fit for an ancient scroll in some long-hidden chest.

*The Story Keeper.*

# Chapter 3

## The Story Keeper

### CHAPTER ONE

If they caught Sarra here listenin', she'd get a beatin'. Each day that passed by, Brown Horne Drigger grew a little bolder, a little more sure that Sarra's daddy wasn't comin' back for her. Could be he was dead in the river or tumbled off a rockslide on his mule or got by a black bear or shot for the money pouch he toted for Brown Drigger. Mighta been any of them things, or some other.

The thought was a quilt of light and dark, worrisome in one way, freein' in another. If her daddy was no more for this world, she could run, and there was scarce a thing she wanted more than to bolt off down the holler and fly far as her legs would carry her. But there was sin in bringin' about the killin' of the man who sired you, the man your mama must've loved sometime long past. And though she never knew much of him—he'd come and went from Aginisi's small farm as he'd chose to over the years—Sarra knew sure as dayrise that he was the one who'd made her.

There was no gettin' by that truth, much as she wished it sometimes. As she'd rounded from knobby-legged girl into a womanish body these last few seasons, *his* favors were the ones she saw in the cloudy, oval-shaped mirror over Aginisi's dresser. His high cheekbones and wide, thick mouth. His straight brows that cast a hard, heavy shadow. His long, lean frame. But Mama's stark blue eyes and rope-crimp black hair and hickory-nut skin. At sixteen, there was no mistakin' Sarra's kin, and for that reason Brown Drigger had thought twicet about takin' her to secure the debt agin his money pouch until her daddy's returning.

Brown Drigger was afraid to end up keepin' her . . . but then again, he *wanted* her. She'd found that out quick. He'd come round at night, touchin' while she lay curled into herself like winter possum, playin' sleep. He'd do no more while he waited for her daddy to show hisself here, but time was runnin' out for her either way.

She'd heard it said to Brown Drigger—there was money in a girl that hadn't been made a woman yet.

Sarra wanted nothin' of Brown Drigger, nor her daddy, nor any man. Aginisi had warned her of it, and Mama'd taught the lesson by doin', time and time again. Her daddy's coming brung sweetness and bobbles and sour mash whiskey to the little dugout behind Aginisi and Gran-dey's log house. And then come hurt. Mama, simpleminded as she was, never seemed to have a knowin' of it ahead, but Aginisi did, and Gran-dey did when he was still livin'. The three of them warred inside Sarra, even from the grave. There was Aginisi's tellin' that her daddy was no good, and Gran-dey's warnin' there wasn't no trustin' the man, and Mama's believin' there was some good that hadn't been found out yet. There was the bond of blood ties, the last she held on this earth.

If the man was still livin', after all.

If not, she knew the mountains well enough. She'd got friendly with Brown Drigger's dogs—the ones he'd promised would track her down and tear flesh from bone if she tried runnin' off.

Even as the thought henpecked, Sarra crept past the low-slung cabin wall, shinnied under the edge in the wet leaf litter where stone piers held the split joists up off the mountainside. Smothering a hand over her mouth, she tipped an ear up to listen. It was one of the new-comers she was wonderin' about just now. The younger man who'd come up the trail to Brown Drigger's store, ridin' a rawboned gray behind the muleteer's wagon.

Muleteers, she'd seen a time or two here, come to trade goods and haul off pelts, silver coin, and sour mash whiskey. But the young man was a new thing, and strange to the mountains. His clothes made him out for a Jasper plain enough, but it showed most in how he watched ever'thing while the muleteer and Brown Drigger chewed words as traders do. The young man studied the world in the way of a winter colt finally let out to spring pastures and catchin' sight of the big, wide world, first time ever.

When he snatched off his fine felt hat to follow inside, his hair fell straw-colored and soft, close-cropped behind his neck and curly. His face was shaved bare, too smooth and young for the tall, lankish way of him. But he'd moved toward Brown Drigger's cabin with a sure stride. Just before steppin' up the porch, he seemed to look her way, toward the smokehouse, where she'd been cleanin' the boil pot to ready for a sausage makin'. This morn, Brown Drigger's men had kilt three hogs took in trade for moonshine. Their fat carcasses hung behind the cabin, split and gutted, the blood draining off into the ground, the last of it slow and thick like honey.

Brown Drigger and the newcomers had been inside hours now as the carcasses cooled and Sarra worked to wash and prepare the intestines for casing up the sausage. She'd done the same many a time with Aginisi, her small hands workin' beside her grandmother's to turn the guts wrong-out and rinse water through before carefully scrapin' off the tiny fingers that moved waste along the animal's insides when it was livin'. She knew how to wash gut, was good at it even, and she knew she'd best not stop when Brown Drigger hollered for his woman to come in the cabin.

Pegleg Molly left behind a threat before she headed off. "You git 'em done while I's seein' to the mens." She backhanded Sarra on the way by, catching an ear so that Sarra's head rang before she blinked the pain off.

She didn't answer, and Molly left to do for the men, who'd likely worked up an appetite while gamblin' and dealin' in thin mash and goods.

It was the change in the sounds of the cabin that'd finally pulled Sarra from the crock of petal-white membranes. The careless laughter and loud talk had took to quietin' in a worrisome way, and so she crawled under the cabin to hear. Could be they'd brought news of her daddy. Bad news.

Settling her fingertips on the tree litter and mud, she peeked up through a gap in the floor near the stone hearth where she'd found broken hours of sleep for nearly a month now, folded in the wool blanket Aginisi'd wove with her own gentle hands—one of the few things Sarra'd carried from the little log house before leavin' on a mule behind her daddy.

The men in Brown Drigger's store sat gathered round the table. Six, maybe seven in all were there now. Either Brown Drigger's men had got back while she worked in the smokehouse or others'd rode in lookin' for a drink, a place to sleep, or trade for goods.

"My horse!" The words rattled out in Brown Drigger's liquored slur. "You ain't leavin' here with my horse. Double or nothin.'"

Silence. Sarra stopped her breath along with it. Brown Drigger was as prideful of the palomino stud as of his own left hand. He'd sooner lose one as the other.

"We've gambled enough." The voice had a dangerous sober to it, and Sarra knew the voice too—the man with the pockmarked face, the one Brown Drigger had made uneasy trades with three weeks before, not long past the time Sarra'd been left here. "Take my advice, old man. Quit before I figure there's anythin' else here I got a hanker for. Believe I'll be ridin' on now."

Overhead, chairs shifted and bodies moved. Pegleg Molly's wooden foot dragged the cabin floor, her heavy steps moving toward the door. "Git gone with you'uns now."

"Not with my horse, they ain't!" Brown Drigger come desperate then. "I give a gold bag fer the beast, and come spring he'll earn it back in breedin'. He ain't leavin' this place, less'n it's with a bullet in 'im." A pistol cocked, and Sarra reached for the tiny carved-bone box that hung at her neck—the other thing she'd brought from Aginisi's when her daddy led her off. Long as she could remember, she knew it'd be hers when Aginisi shed this world for heaven.

"Ain't no reasonin' with a fool, now is there?" The man with the scars again. "Yer woman best put down that gun and be friendly-like, friend. You trade me outta that horse if'n you want 'im. Ain't seen much else here I got me a need of, but ya want the horse back, I'll trade 'im for the girl. The one with them blue eyes. She yourn, ain't she?"

Air caught in Sarra's throat. Turned solid.

"Ain't yet. Not for four more days yan, leastwise. Her pap left 'er for promise agin a money pouch. He don't clamber back with my goods, I'll keep the girl, let Molly make a little business outta her. They's plenty come by here who'd pay to get under the blanket with somethin' looks like her."

"Guessin' you got yerself some decidin' to do. The horse stayin' here when we shuck off . . . or the girl? It's one or t'other."

A fist slammed the table. "I give my word a the man. Ain't no livin' soul can say Brown Horne Drigger ain't good as his word. 'Sides, the girl's daddy, he's copperhead mean. Man'd as soon gut ya like them hogs out back as look at ya. Ain't bound to cross 'im."

A chair slid over the well-worn floor, and dust mist sifted through the planks, catching the long rays of afternoon light, beautiful against the ugly. "I be takin' the horse and gone then, reckon. Make it back this way again, mayhap I'll stop and see what I missed out'a with the girl." Footfalls crossed the floor, the sound heavy and unhurried, the boards groaning neath the giant of a man.

"Wait." Brown Drigger's protest stopped the walking. "You leave the horse. Hist yerself by here four days yander—the bargain be up then. Girl's yourn if her pappy ain't showed hisself yet."

A shifting, a turning, a curtain of dust against light, and then the striking of a bargain. "Reckon I'll take 'er now and make sure the man don't show his face nowheres n'more."

## CHAPTER TWO

Rand Champlain whistled to himself as he wandered upward from the creek toward Brown Horne Drigger's cabin. He riffled through his field notebook as he walked, checking his sketches against the leaves in the underbrush alongside the path. It was one of his purposes during this year of wanderings to catalog the flora and fauna of the Blue Ridge Mountains and points beyond, as well as the customs, languages, and cultural variations of the peoples he found. He was by no means a professional—as an artist, a naturalist, or a student of the anthropological disciplines—but the pursuit of scientific knowledge had been one of his justifications for leaving behind Charleston, and the expectations of family, for this singular year in the wild.

He intended to return home, having preserved much of it by way of his sketches and his Hüttig & Sohn folding camera. With the dawning of a new century just over a decade away, and railroad tracks spreading in all directions like climbing vine, he suspected that the days of untraveled lands were numbered. He intended to see them, discover all he could of the unspoiled places, before they were gone. These months traversing the Appalachian wilderness were the beginning of a journey westward from which he eventually planned to return by waterway and steam train.

His toe struck a stone in the path, and he stumbled before catching himself near a growth of hemlock. This pest he had learned of when the muleteer had assured him that by merely touching the hemlock in order to preserve a leaf between the pages of his pressing form, Rand had condemned himself to certain and agonizing death. It was all for the sake of a joke on the muleteer's part, but the ruse had continued for hours while Rand waited for the first signs of death by hemlock to occur. Ira Nelson had proven to be a disagreeable, if competent, mountain guide.

A soft, slight jingling caught Rand's ear as he squatted on the path, observing what appeared to be a small patch of low-growing alpine pennycress just beginning to show autumn bloom. It shouldn't have been there. Pennycress hadn't been known to grow east of the Rockies, but he'd seen it in the mountains of Europe while on holiday, and this looked for all the world like it.

He was so taken by it, as he reached for a leaf to see if tearing it would produce the familiar, noxious odor, thus confirming its identity, that the jingling failed to capture his focus until it was directly overhead on the rough, rutted wagon trail that had brought him to the Drigger store. He recognized the sound quite suddenly as what it was: the mule-teer's wagon moving away . . . without him. The mules were tracking at a good pace, causing the brass buckles to ring against the tugs.

What in heaven's name?

His heart paused a beat before he snatched a leaf from the penny-cress, then abandoned the path and dashed uphill toward the wagon road, leaping stands of huckleberry and tumbles of rock. Tree trunks flashed by, his feet sliding in the damp blanket of forest moss. For-tunately, he was both fast and agile, a champion in the young men's footrace at preparatory academy not so many months before.

Perhaps this business of the wagon leaving was just another of the muleteer's pranks, but an uneasy feeling had niggled Rand for a time now. With the arrival of the scar-faced man and his two companions, the business inside Brown Horne Drigger's outpost had turned dis-tasteful enough that Rand had excused himself to walk to the creek. He was more than happy to leave the stench of the rough cabin store behind. He'd had no idea of how long Ira's dealings here would carry on, but he hadn't minded it either. There were things to see, and Rand had dried beef in his field pack, should he gain an appetite before they made evening camp nearby. Wandering along the creek, he'd enjoyed both the solitude and the discovery.

Now he feared that his original impressions as to the potential of homemade liquor, illegal activities, and immoral men were correct. The muleteer was clearly in a hurry, the team's hooves sliding and the steel-rimmed wheels bouncing over the stones and watersheds in the rush downhill.

As Rand cleared the brush and made the wagon road, the lead mule, Curly, spooked and balked, testing the traces and struggling to stop the inertia of the wagon.

"Bleedin' fool!" Ira managed the reins and the wagon brake, finally bringing the load to rest just after Rand leapt to the side of the path to avoid being run down. "You'll send us both edge-over. How many times I gotta tell you not ta be runnin' out, spookin' my mules?"

"I heard the wagon moving," Rand gasped, somewhat winded.

"Git on your saddle horse, boy. We're leavin' out." Ira cast an impatient nod over his shoulder.

"Leaving?" Puddinhead, the mount Rand had purchased after disembarking the new rail line in Murphy, was tied behind the wagon, walleyed at the end of the lead line, as usual. Puddinhead's name was as much an incongruity as the Murphy liveryman's assurance that the gelding was a competent mountain horse. In reality, the animal feared most of what he saw and intensely disliked the rest. "I thought we'd planned to camp overnight nearby Drigger's outpost." Not that Rand was looking forward to more time in the company of Brown Horne Drigger and Pegleg Molly, but he had intended to study the surrounding area thoroughly while he waited.

"They's bad business afoot here. Don't need none of it." Ira was nervous—more so than Rand had ever seen him. "Man's gonna survive in hither parts, he's gotta know when to git his mud hooks a-movin'. Gotta know not to wander off too. You's s'posed to be down to the crick crossin'. Lucky you ain't been left fer bear bait. I ain't yer nursemaid, boy."

The crack of a rifle shot echoed from the direction of Brown Drigger's cabin, the sound rushing through the trees and startling birds to flight. Rand whirled toward the noise as Ira stood against the reins, holding the mules from bolting. Behind the wagon, Puddinhead scrambled up the hillside, staggering over loose rock and sapling hickories.

"Never mind the horse. He's tied on good." Ira swiveled, casting a wide-eyed look. "Clamber on up in the wagon, boy. Less'n you're a-gonna stay here. Take yer choice. This rig and me are leavin' out. Now!"

In two quick steps, Rand grabbed the side rail, planted a boot on the wheel, and swung himself upward. The rim rolled before his foot left it, and he landed in a tangle, bouncing upside down and sideways on the canvas that covered Ira's trade goods.

The wagon was splashing through the creek by the time Rand had righted himself and crawled to the seat. Behind, Puddinhead rose on hind legs, testing the lead, blowing and snorting as if he fully expected the water to rise up and swallow him whole. The gelding jumped, stiff kneed, landed in the stream, and jumped again, raising an infernal ruckus as he went.

"Git'up, Curly! Git'up, Luke!" Ira laid the whip hard on the team as they struggled to tug through a bog along the opposite bank.

"Give them time, man," Rand protested. He'd never found it tolerable to watch the abuse of something helpless. The beasts were doing all they could.

"We ain't *got* time. That horse a yourn don't stop pullin' on my rig,

31

I'll shoot 'im and cut 'im loose. Had my fill a that critter. He's draggin'
my mules down. Git on up, Luke! Git on, Curly. Git! Git! Git!" The
wagon rolled backward into the mud, and Ira went harder with the
black snake, snapping it against sweat-slickened hides, drawing blood.

Rand reached for it, the action almost an involuntary response.
"There's no need of—"

An elbow caught him hard in the ribs, stealing his breath and rolling him sideways on the seat so that he hung bent over the edge and
clinging on, the mud oozing against the wheel beneath him.

"You'll stay 'ere, ya know what's good fer ya. Git on, Luke! Git on,
Curly!"

The wagon lurched, the mud releasing with a great sucking
sound, and then they were rolling up the hill, Rand grimacing as he
righted himself. At six foot four and consistently taller than his contemporaries, he'd always thought of himself as competent in physical
combat. But the truth was, because of his height and the fact that
he'd grown up among youths who were raised to become gentlemen,
physical combat had never become necessary for him, other than the
harmless play of boys.

But this world, this mountain kingdom of questionable men and
unforgiving landscape, was ruled by the play of life and death. A completely different game.

He pondered this as he caught his breath. Beside him, Ira pushed
the team hard for quite some distance before allowing them to settle,
puffing and foaming, into a somewhat-slower pace. The white specks
on the mules' backs were pinked with blood.

Rand didn't apologize for going after the whip. "What was the trouble back there?"

"Doin's come ugly in the card game after while." The old man's eyes narrowed beneath a split leather hat that had seen better days. "The other fella won that pallermina stud horse Brown Horne's so proud'a."

Rand quickly formed an image of the confrontation. "That's a fine animal." Actually, there had been three good horses in Brown Drigger's corral. Rand had been tempted to try a trade for Puddinhead. "So they went to gunplay over it?"

"Nosir. Fella swapped the horse back to Brown Horne fer the girl. But when Pegleg Molly hist out to git 'er, she'd done scat off. Gone. Fella figured Brown Horne's at some trick. Says if 'n Drigger don't find the girl, he's takin' the stud horse and stringin' Drigger up next'a them hogs. Right 'bout then, I got my wagon and got gone while they's lookin' fer her."

Rand's impressions grew dark and murky. "What girl?"

"The one was back by the smokehouse when we rolled in. Skinny, but a looksome thing. Black hair, blue eyes. Worth more'n that pallermina stud, if 'n a fella don' mind what she is. You didn't git a look at 'er?"

*If 'n a fella don' mind what she is.* What could possibly be the meaning of that? "But this . . . this is practically the dawn of the new century. Women can't be . . . traded for horseflesh." Morality aside, such things were not legal and had not been since the ending of the War of Secession, some eight years before Rand's birth.

"Not much but a girl, truth be tolt. Fifteen, sixteen, might be."

A queasiness awoke in Rand's stomach, tasting of acid. Lucinda, the eldest of his three sisters, was just fifteen, preparing to make her debut into Charleston society. Her face appeared in his mind, and he swiveled in the seat. "We must go back, then." But miles had been covered in their wild flight, and darkness had begun to descend. In truth, it was surprising that Ira hadn't stopped to make camp. He was pushing hard to gain distance tonight.

The muleteer cast a look Rand's way, and before Rand could react, a pistol had been drawn from Ira's boot and laid across the man's lap, aimed in Rand's general direction. "You sit right there, boy, and thank ol' Ira fer savin' yer life this day. Don't be gettin' no wild ideas. Ain't havin' you bring them men down on me. Don't want no part of it."

Rand's mind bolted ahead. "The law. How far to an authority of some kind who could . . . ?"

"Ain't none a that sort up here. You oughta figured that out b'now. And if'n they was, wouldn't be nothin' done 'bout one like her."

"She's a *human being*, for heaven's sake. Decency aside, she has rights under the law."

Ira shook his head, kept the pistol aimed, but relaxed his finger and laid it over the trigger guard. "You got a hankerin' t'know 'bout the mountains, young'un, they's things you gotta learn. That girl ain't got no rights. She's a Melung."

"A what?"

"A *Melungeon*. She ain't white, she ain't colored, she ain't Injun. Ain't any one a them three kinds would claim her. Ain't just any fool'd take a chance on her, neither. Them Melungeons been hidin' up in these mountains long's anyone can remember. Got a certain look to 'em, like her—dark skin, but not red like a Injun. Black hair, and them cold blue eyes. Them eyes bewitch a man, send 'im to his grave. 'Cut yer throat and breathe the ghost wind into ya while yer sleepin',' my mama used'a say. Got six fingers on each hand. Take out a man's heart while it's still beatin', and do the bad magic with it. A Melungeon's meaner than a timber rattler and wickeder by twicet. Got the devil in 'em. Call up the wind and the weather and the walkin' trees and the haints from they restin' places. Send 'em agin ya."

A chill teased Rand's skin, and he slid a hand over his throat, felt the fine growth of a day's beard that needed shaving. His gaze drifted again over his shoulder. In his mind now, the girl took life, even though he had not laid eyes upon her. Never before, in fact, had he seen a Melungeon in the flesh. He'd doubted their very existence, categorized them in the make-believe realm of fairies, moon men, and Rougarou—the beast rumored to haunt the sloughs and bayous of Louisiana.

To his mind, Melungeons were a figment used to frighten children from going into the forest alone. *Don't wander off afield. The Melungeons'll git ya.* Old Hast, the downstairs maid of his growing-up years, had threatened this fate quite often. She had little patience with the folly and pranks of children. His own grandfather had teased him thusly of the Melungeons during hunting trips when he was young. He'd fallen asleep many a night with the bedroll pulled over his head, just in case it should be so, but in all reality, he'd never believed there were such people.

Until this very moment.

"Don't do nothin' foolish," Ira warned again.

Rand felt the weight of the pistol, its muzzle eyeing him. Who or what was the creature back there? The one he'd passed by without noticing as he'd observed the nature of the land and the interplay of the men? Surely not ghost or haint or wood fairy, for he knew there were no such things. No creature existed in this world but by the grace and hand of the Almighty.

The girl was flesh and bone. Real enough.

And now, with a pistol trained his way, all he could do was pray that the Almighty would watch over the poor wretch, as he watched over each of his children.

# Chapter 4

The knock at my office door seemed distant at first, as if it were slipping through the trees, echoing along the hollow, following ragged rock curves and edges as mountain sounds did, the origins hidden in the mist.

The door handle jiggled, and I jerked to attention, slapped the folder shut, and looked up as Roger poked his nose in. "E-mail system's down. Editorial team powwow at eleven thirty to line up the nonfiction attack for pub board Monday, just in case you didn't get the message."

"Thanks, I didn't." The words were slightly breathless. I felt strangely out of body, not at all myself. My heart hammered against my chest, caught in the instinctive flight response that an uncertain upbringing leaves behind. I felt like Sarra, crouched beneath the cabin floor, afraid I'd be beaten if caught.

Roger cast a quizzical glance toward my laptop case, the

computer still tucked inside. Pretty obvious that no e-mail had been checked this morning. "Dark in here. Grabbing a nap?"

"Got caught up in something." *Caught up* was a mild description. In reality, I was dying to open the folder again, read the rest, find out if Sarra escaped Brown Drigger and his dogs.

"Anything good?" Roger pushed the door open wider and advanced a half step into my office.

"Oh, who knows." The folder suddenly felt like a bomb again. I slid my hands over it almost unconsciously, felt the ticking beneath my fingers. *Tick, tick, tick.* "Overhead light wouldn't come on when I got here. But I kind of like using the gooseneck lamp, anyway. It gives the place an authentic feel."

"You always were an old-fashioned type."

"Compared to you, everyone's old-fashioned." I rolled my eyes, trying to let the comments slide off. Roger considered anyone with morals, sexual or otherwise, old-fashioned. It still amazed me that he didn't find life under George Vida's old-school system way too confining. I'd always had the impression of George Vida as a highly moral man, principled in the way of 1950s print journalism, but then again, I only knew his public image.

Maybe there were reasons why Roger was so comfortable here, but I hoped not.

A smooth grin answered. "Don't miss Mitch's meeting. She doesn't like it when people miss her meetings."

Despite the source, I didn't doubt the validity of the advice. The head of our nonfiction editorial team, Mitchell Lee, was a matter-of-fact woman with little tolerance for incompetents or slough-offs. The fiction team, under Chris Singer, was a looser group. They went out for drinks, attended book launch parties if the venue and the schmoozing were good, and sometimes even vacationed together. I'd been invited to tag along last night but hadn't gone. I didn't want to give Mitch the impression that I was sniffing after other opportunities. For now, I needed to concentrate my efforts where I was.

Looking back at the folder on my desk, I considered its possible origins. It was fiction, but something about it felt so very real. The description of Brown Horne Drigger's home, the details of butchering hogs and making sausage by hand, the mention of Sarra's Melungeon ancestry, even her use of *Aginisi*, a Cherokee word for *grandmother*, brought Rand and Sarra to life. Eerily so. There was a familiarity to the piece, and I couldn't decide if it was just that the subject matter scratched old memories or if something in the author's voice or style strummed a tune I'd heard before. I wanted to put a finger on it, and it seemed that I should be able to, yet I couldn't. That taunted me almost as much as the mystery of the manuscript itself. No author's name, no header or footer on the pages, the return address torn from the envelope, the postmark faded almost beyond reading. No submission letter. If there had been one, it'd long since been lost.

What *was* this thing?

The questions played a tantalizing game, like voices calling from behind moss-covered rocks and deep mountain hollows, as ours once had when we slipped away to play games of fox and hen or anty over around the old barn.

*Anty.*

*Over.*

*Over she comes . . .*

The calls of my sisters whispered now, their high-pitched laughter painting a mist of light and dark, the murky shades of regret.

The whispering stopped as I put the envelope in my desk

drawer, a decision made. I could've slipped it into my pile of in-process manuscripts and summaries for the editorial team meeting, could've been the first one to arrive, surreptitiously dropping the package onto Slush Mountain, then walking away. Even if George Vida noticed that it was out of place, no one would know I was responsible.

No one . . . except the person who had anonymously left it on my desk. And how could anybody reveal that without being in as much trouble as I would be in for having it?

Scratching a fingernail across the aging brass pull, I contemplated my own foolishness. The manuscript was over twenty years old, a relic from well before my time. By now, it had either been published, left for dead in some writer's closet, or trashed. Maybe this stray fifty-page partial was all that remained of the effort.

Forgetting it made sense. Putting it back without burning up the time to read the rest made sense. In fact, it was the *only* thing that made sense.

But the meeting wasn't for a few more hours. Enough time to think about it, maybe talk some sense into myself.

Or not.

As I worked through the morning, sifting through summaries of nonfiction projects that would be presented at the pub board next Monday, Rand and Sarra remained where they were. When I gathered my things to leave, the contraband stayed behind. Snatching the key from beneath my in-box, I locked the desk before heading for the war room.

Slush Mountain loomed larger than before when I arrived at the team meeting. Basking in the sunlight of a beautiful autumn morning, it seemed to watch me accusingly as I took a seat—purposely at the other end of the table. I wanted to search the uneven surface for the faded outline of a nine-by-twelve envelope. But I didn't. Just in case someone was watching. If the guilty party was nearby, let him or her think I hadn't even noticed the surprise on my desk or that I hadn't opened it. If this was a joke, two could play that game.

Five minutes into Mitch's meeting, I figured out that, while distracting myself with *The Story Keeper* earlier, I had screwed up. Royally. Via e-mail that morning Mitch had sent around material for a submission she wanted to push through the upcoming pub board meeting. We'd been given summary, proposal material, and sample chapters via attachment. Since I hadn't checked e-mail before the system went down, and the system still wasn't working, I'd missed the memo.

It was clear enough that Mitch's project was the intended primary topic of today's session. She wanted each of us to be familiar with the story—the memoir of a World War II soldier who had fallen in love with a Japanese girl behind enemy lines. We were here to brainstorm sales points and build a united front for pub board, where sales, marketing, and other departments would be invited to throw any and all possible darts at our presentation. I was clueless. Unlike everyone else on the team, I didn't even have Mitch's material with me. Consequently, I felt like an idiot and knew that, soon enough, I was bound to look like one too.

It wasn't long before Mitch noted the lack of her last-minute material in the stack I'd brought with me. "Didn't get the e-mail?" She was somewhere between surprised and peeved. Probably more toward the second option.

"No, sorry. I got caught up in something this morning and hadn't checked before my in-box went down. I'll read the material as soon as the system's back up and be ready for pub board on Monday, I promise." What else was there to say, really?

Mitch's lips pressed together in a thin line intended to remind everyone *whose* interests came first. I'd just stumbled dangerously close to making myself look too mercenary—caring only about finding and acquiring my own projects, rather than supporting the projects of others, *especially* others higher up the ladder than me. On the other hand, Mitch was aware of the hours I'd been putting in the past week. She knew I was dedicated.

"All right. Here's the situation." She eyeballed the group from behind unfashionably thick glasses with heavy black frames. "I *want* this one, and I want it *bad*. I don't just want on the short list this week. I want on *the* list. I want agreement on a potential marketing plan, an advance in the low sixes, and some viable thoughts on packaging and placement that I can take to the author's agent."

Across the table, Roger leaned back, angled his body away slightly, hooked an arm over the back of his chair. He wasn't sure of this acquisition, and it showed. Interesting.

Mitch didn't look his way but instead centered her pitch on the three female editors clustered at the end of the table. Also interesting. "I realize at the outset that this one sounds like material that's been done before—soldier meets war bride, love triumphs against all odds. But this story is unique, and we are *not* the only house pursuing it. I have it from the agent that she's expecting other offers to come in over the next few weeks. Our advantage to the author, as I see it, is that we're smaller, faster, nimbler. We can put this thing out in nine months and manage a first-rate job of it. What we have to do now is convince George Vida that this one is worth going after, and going after big."

"Jump on the bandwagon for whatever project his niece brings to the table next week," Roger advised casually. "Throw her a little love. He can never resist that. She has him wrapped around her little finger." Was it my imagination, or did Roger's lip curl a bit on that last one? It was no secret that George Vida was smitten by the talents of his niece and hoped to one day relinquish Vida House into her hands.

"I disagree. I think we just go right out with it," Hillary Vecchio offered matter-of-factly, her words as crisp and slick as her appearance—hair neatly flat-ironed, lipstick perfect, figure a size two, if that. We'd chatted by the coffee credenza a couple times. I liked her. "It's a good proposal. It's everything you said it was and more. Nonfiction, but it reads like fiction. I say we bring it up alongside books like *Seabiscuit* or *Truman*. If we can convince him that this book has the same potential, he won't be able to stand *not* going for it." She punctuated with a nod, pleased with herself.

The remaining three members of the team chimed in with ideas, which left me the one voiceless body at the table.

Of course, Mitch turned my way next. I was hoping she wouldn't, but it didn't surprise me. "Ideas? You've undoubtedly run into situations like this in the past, given your years in publishing, at much *larger* houses." It was hard to say what the emphasis meant—whether Mitch was trying to espouse my qualifications or backhandedly swat at the fact that I'd missed the memo, despite having cut my teeth at big conglomerates.

I shifted forward in my seat. "I think there's a point to be made in the lasting social value of the piece—the fact that it is not just the story of one man and one woman falling in love; it's the story of a historical period, an hour of American triumph. A time of sacrifice for the greater good. Yet even amid the nobility of the cause, there are still the smaller human struggles—love and hate, jealousy and altruism. It wasn't an easy life for these couples if they chose to marry against Army regulations and cultural prejudices. They faced all sorts of difficulties, even if they did finally make it to the States together."

A correlation formed in my mind. The personal side of history had drawn me toward memoirs long before my first editing job. "I remember interviewing a woman from Kobe, Japan, years ago for a journalism class. She married an American soldier after the war and came to Georgia. She'd just found out she was pregnant when she happened to visit a dentist to have a tooth fixed. The dentist told her she should end the pregnancy because the mixing of the races would cause genetic problems. Her child would never be born normal. And this was a *medical* professional—can you imagine?"

Across the table, Hillary widened her eyes and shook her head, clearly horrified but fascinated at the same time, her reaction much like mine had been the first time I heard the story.

"The doctor offered to connect her with someone who could do the procedure. She got as far as arranging a ride to some back-alley clinic before she broke down and told the whole story to an Atlanta socialite she cleaned house for. The woman was so mad, she drove to the dentist's office and ended up slugging the man in the nose, then writing a letter to the editor of the city paper. The society ladies tried to run her out of town. She became an activist after that."

Across the table, Roger was scratching his head. "And your point is? Not that it's not a great story but . . ." He wheeled a hand as in, *Get to the meat of it, Jen.*

"My point is, that story about the dentist might have taken a minute or two to tell, but everyone leaned in and listened. Nobody interrupted me." Which didn't happen all that often in editorial meetings, where the conversational floor was more like a pinball trapped in an electrical surge. "Chances are, each one of us can relate to that story in some way. We all care about the human element, the part that's timeless. But we also care about those turning points in history, those social mores that we can't believe were accepted just a generation ago. We want to believe we would never have stood for it ourselves, had we been there. The generation that *lived* the stories of that time is dying out. And they're dying with their stories untold. There's a media hook in that, and media sells books. There's nothing better than a story that would be unbelievable if you read it as fiction, but you *have* to believe it because it's true."

Mitch blew through tightened lips, the airstream whistling around the end of her pen. "Okay, I like that. Make sure you read the proposal ASAP and get back to me with any more thoughts."

"Of course."

"I want you to repeat that whole thing in pub board on Monday." Mitch scribbled furiously in her notebook, and then the meeting went on. Before we dispersed, the pitch plan was as slick as a newborn kitten, and I had a half-hour break in which to check out Mitch's proposal before a late lunch with an agent who was shopping a couple of projects around, looking for interest.

Even so, as I sat down to speed-read Mitch's project, the words calling to me most were the ones hidden in my desk. Locked in the darkness, *The Story Keeper* beckoned, seeming to have an understanding of its power.

It whispered unrelentingly as the day continued, presenting one sidetrack and then another—Mitch's proposal, the agent meeting, phone calls, a consult with Hillary. Meanwhile, Rand and Sarra flickered through my thoughts like leaf shadows against a window, parting, then thickening, then parting again, stealing my attention.

By the end of the day, the temptation was so strong I could barely focus. A last-minute mini meeting to go through Mitch's proposal for the war bride story felt more like torture than a chance to bond with my new boss. The meeting ended at five fifteen, and I returned to my office, a musty remembered scent teasing my senses as I walked through the door.

I was underneath the cabin again, hidden with that young girl, listening to the conversations of dangerous men. But there was a memory intertwined also. One I hadn't uncovered until now—the feeling of hiding, hearing, then running for freedom, my bare feet landing in rock and sticker brush, brambles and branches tearing at my clothes and my skin, soft moss and the glitter of mica flakes among stones catching the last of the sunlight.

The surface of the desk faded away, and I saw thin, bare legs beneath the hem of a rose-colored dress, old scars healing while new wounds bled into the cool water of Honey Creek.

What day was that memory tied to? Perhaps the morning I'd learned that my mother was gone? Was that it? Hard to say. So much of the time that included my mother I'd either given up freely or had strangled out of me. When she left, we'd been warned never to speak of her again.

Something else tripped a memory too. That long, strange word that Rand Champlain had pondered.

*Melungeon.*

The recalling was sudden and oddly clear, a misted mirror swept clean by the palm of a hand.

*You run off in them woods again when you got chores to do, Jennia Beth, I'll let the Melungeons come 'n' git'cha.* My grandmother's voice ground out a warning, a wooden spoon shaking in her hand. I knew what the spoon was for. Not for whipping up something tasty, but for dealing out a whipping. *Them Melungeons'll come after ya in the night. You can thank it that I been prayin' 'em away. Come round after dark, lookin' for the bad uns, like yer mama. Take yer soul off to the devil, you don't walk in the good way, girl. You hear me talkin' at'cha?*

"I hate you, you witch." The words came aloud, in the voice of a woman. The voice of *now*. I would never have said them then.

Like Rand Champlain in the story, I'd thought that the Melungeons were a made-up thing, like the black-eyed children who came to you seeking help, their faces hidden in their cloaks until you agreed to let them in. Only then did you see that there were no eyes, just hollows of darkness where the eyes should be. If the Melungeons didn't spirit us off into the woods and steal our souls, Momaw Leena promised, the black-eyed children would. We were none of us worthy of salvation because our mama wasn't worthy.

I hadn't thought about that in years, hadn't allowed Momaw Leena and her meanness into my life—not even long enough to consider how incredibly wrong it was to heap misery on kids who were already struggling to survive. Whose mother had gone missing and whose father demanded that even his smallest commands be scurried after, or else.

Slipping into my desk chair, I opened the computer, typed the word into Google.

*Melungeon.*

One stroke of the key and there were hundreds of links to choose from. Unlike Rand Champlain, I had endless information at my fingertips almost instantly.

*. . . a term traditionally used to describe one of several tri-racial isolate groups in the Southeastern US. Historically, Melungeons were considered a dangerous oddity due to their isolative natures and peculiar . . .*

*. . . "Myth or Genetic Mystery: DNA Study Chases Melungeon*

*Origins." For generations, diverse and sometimes-outlandish stories have been told about the dark-skinned, blue-eyed Indians of the Appalachian . . .*

*. . . comprise a group of mixed-race people originating from the Cumberland Gap region. Melungeons were thought to be offspring of intermarriage between shipwrecked Portugese or Turkish sailors, escaped slaves, and native populations. . . .*

*. . . or from the Afro-Portuguese word* melungo, *meaning "ship-mate." But in reality, no one has the faintest notion of where the name came from or what Melungeons' cultural origins might have been. . . .*

*. . . Melungeon populations, who migrated from western North Carolina to the mountains of eastern Tennessee and southern Virginia to escape the persecution of incoming populations. Deemed . . .*

*. . . possibly descendants of the ill-fated Lost Colonists, left on Roanoke Island in 1585. The first English and French to later explore North Carolina's mountains reported blue-eyed Indians, living in houses. The Melungeons . . .*

*. . . and folks left them be, because they were queer and devil-fired, witchy. If a man was fool enough to go into Melungeon country and come back without getting shot, he was sure to later wizen away or get some ailment nobody could . . .*

Even from my cave-like space at the far reaches of the hall, as I clicked through pages, wildly taking in a frenzy of information, I sensed the day ending and evening settling. Sounds pressed through—doors closing, arms swishing into jacket sleeves, backpacks and laptop cases zipping, the faint hum of passing conversations about weekend plans.

My favorite intern stopped by. Andrew, the sweet but flirty one. "Friday night. Fiction team is headed down to Blockers to grab a drink, peruse some happy hour goodies, and watch the

Knicks game. Good way to get to know people. Wanna come? You can join the dog pile, even though you're not fiction."

The dog pile image made me laugh. Aside from a cute face and baby-blue eyes, this kid had a wry sense of humor about the publishing world. In the lunchroom one day, as we waited for microwave meals to heat, he'd shared his impression of editorial team meetings as great big sessions of *Does this manuscript make me look fat?*

I liked Andrew, but—I was afraid—not in the way he wanted me to. He was a small-town Iowa boy, all alone in the big city now. The first thing a displaced small-town kid usually does is desperately try to create an instant family, emphasis on *desperately*. I'd learned that the hard way after coming here.

"Too much work to do, but thanks for asking."

"All work and no play . . ."

"If you haven't figured out by now that I really *am* a dull girl, I might as well let you in on the secret."

Andrew offered that sweet smile his mama back home undoubtedly loved and missed. She was probably horrified that her boy had taken off to pursue his dreams far away. She probably called him every night to make sure he was eating okay, to ask if he'd *met anyone* yet. Andrew had all the hallmarks of a kid well loved and carefully raised. Well supported by an adoring family.

For a moment, I was a little jealous. I wished he were ten, maybe twelve, years older—still single for whatever reason and looking for just the right girl to take home to his wonderful family. Silly, of course. But even when you love everything else about your life, sometimes there's a part of you that still wrestles with the instinctive desire for home and hearth and family bonds that don't feel more like family bondage.

"Next week maybe." I shouldn't have said it. It was wrong to encourage him.

"Cool." He hesitated in the doorway as if there was something more he wanted to talk about. "Well, have a good weekend, anyway. See you Monday."

"See you Monday, Andrew. Thanks for helping me settle in. I appreciate it."

"No problem. Anytime. Totally." The kid was going to have to learn to quit using words like *cool* and *totally* if he wanted to be taken seriously in this business. Bless his little heart.

After he was gone, I debated either digging into the Google research some more or packing things up and taking my work home with me, where I wouldn't have to look over my shoulder as I opened *The Story Keeper* again.

A floor machine came on somewhere down the hall and made the decision for me. A belt squealed high and long as the brushes rotated. Maybe it was *The Story Keeper* that brought the association to mind, but it sounded like a baby pig being grabbed by the foot and dragged from its mother to become suckling pork.

I packed everything in the rolling briefcase I had learned to carry on weekends when the transport load was heavier, then stood for a moment considering the risk of actually taking the forbidden bit of manuscript home.

*You could probably sneak over to Slush Mountain and return it now. Almost everyone's gone. . . .*

But I knew I wouldn't. Even before I unlocked the desk drawer and took out the envelope, I was already slipping back to the world of Sarra and Rand. Stepping into the Blue Ridge—not into the places the tourists love, but the dirt roads and backwater settlements and hidden valleys where civilization had been far away at the turn of the twentieth century when Rand Champlain traveled there, and in some cases still was.

On the way out, I passed Russell and the massive floor polisher. He'd stopped the thing and was looking underneath the hood now.

"Loose belt," I said.

Russell glanced up, surprised. "Believe dat's it, all righ'." He paused to eyeball me a moment. "Goin' home earlier dis evenin'?"

"Yes, I am." I wondered if anyone else, like George Vida, or possibly Mitch, would notice that I wasn't the last one leaving the editorial halls tonight. After the screwup in this morning's meeting, it would've been smart to be seen hanging around, but right now, playing it safe was the farthest thing from my mind. "Got something I have to do."

# Chapter 5

My apartment was shadowy and dim, quiet except for the sound of Friday snoring in his makeshift doggy bed. Friday was a holdover from the era of Brian and me. We'd found him stuck in a Dumpster while walking back from dinner one evening, a skinny and scruffy Chihuahua mix, wary of people.

It had been Brian's idea to take the dog back to my apartment, keep it a week or so and put up flyers in case someone was looking. Having grown up in nice neighborhoods, Brian had a perspective that was sweetly innocent about some things. It never occurred to him that people would throw out a living creature on purpose.

"You should take him to your place," I'd protested as we stood at the end of the alley trying to decide what to do next. "He likes you better than he likes me."

"Oh yeah, that's obvious." Brian had the animal in a defensive choke hold. With its ears tucked against its head, bug eyes, and sharp, pointed teeth, it looked like something from *Alien*. "I don't have time to take care of a dog, Jen."

"Like *I* do?" Sometimes Brian forgot we worked at the same place. His department was sales; mine was editorial. We both had careers that demanded a lot of our time. We'd been dating on the down-low off and on for a year and a half—on the down-low because the company had a no-fraternization policy, off and on because we couldn't seem to figure out whether our relationship was going anywhere or where it could go.

The dog whipped its head, biting air in a pint-size show of bravado. I couldn't help it. I laughed. "Good thing it's not a pit bull."

The argument ended where all of our arguments ended: with me giving in. Brian managed to calm the dog, and the two of them gave me puppy eyes side by side, and I couldn't say no. "Okay, but just until next Friday."

Almost three years of *next Fridays*, and one final breakup, had come and gone since then. The dog lasted longer than the relationship and the job did.

I wasn't even sure why I hadn't gotten rid of Friday. Maybe because, with his personality and looks, I figured he wouldn't find a home. Maybe just because he was low maintenance and really wasn't hurting anything here. The space went mostly unused anyway, and I could pay the kids down the hall a few bucks to walk him. Their mom was single and they needed the money.

He yawned and rolled a look my way as I parked my briefcase by the small, two-person table that served mostly as a desk, then set the rest of my things on the kitchen counter, which also served mostly as a desk.

"Beat anybody up in the dog park today?" Friday was known

for threatening animals four times his size. The little girls who walked him thought it was funny.

He rose and stretched one leg at a time, then circle-sniffed and plopped down again with his rear facing my way and his nose pointing toward the empty butter tub that served as a food dish. As usual, he was an expert, if not tactful, communicator.

"Great to see you too, Friday. Tough day at work?"

He didn't answer of course, but I helped him with his end of the conversation. "Oh, not so bad, Jen. Sat in the windowsill. Held down the sofa awhile. Drained the water dish dry. Made a few more enemies at the dog park. Normal day."

He yawned, sighed, then sneezed in a way that said, *Puh-lease, that is so yesterday. Get a new routine, Jen Gibbs.*

It seemed like, if you were going to pay a dog's bills, he ought to at least wag or something, but with Friday, you had to use your imagination. "My day? Well, thank you for asking. It was interesting. Good and bad. I botched an editorial team meeting, but something really curious did happen. Bizarre, actually. What do you make of this?"

Leaning over my briefcase, I unzipped the front flap and extracted the old envelope. "It just showed up on my desk out of nowhere. First thing this morning. And based on the postmark date, about the only place this could've come from is . . . Slush Mountain."

When I looked, Friday was sitting up in his bed, watching me. His gaze moved then, focused over my shoulder as if he'd seen something there. He growled, and a cold sensation feathered my skin.

Was someone in here? I wheeled around to check, surveying

the open-concept studio. Nobody. Nothing out of the ordinary, other than Friday's behavior.

"Stop that." I flipped on the overhead light. The bulbs flickered and threatened to fail, creating a creepy moment of déjà vu.

Just as suddenly, everything was normal again. The lights came on. Friday flopped over on his side. A siren wailed on the street below. I looked down at the envelope. With the fluorescent glow overhead, I could almost make out the rest of the postmark.

I moved to the center of the room, held it closer to the light, squinted.

Two letters: *NC*. This story wasn't only set somewhere in the Blue Ridge; it had been written there. In North Carolina. The home state I'd long ago left behind.

The cold feeling washed over me again—a brew of fear, fascination, and uncertainty. How could all of this be coincidence? Who'd left this thing on my desk, and with what intention?

# Chapter 6

## The Story Keeper

### CHAPTER THREE

"What'n foddershocks you doin', boy?" Ira thundered up the hill, lugging a bucket in a heavy-legged run. "Quieten that ruckus! The sound runnin' these hollers the way it do, any man in ten-mile yander's gonna figure where we's holt up. Why you reckon I ain't lit us no fire agin the cold t'night?"

Rand drew back slightly, looking at the mouth harp he'd purchased in a mining settlement that wasn't much more than two buildings clinging to the side of the hill. He'd seen instruments such as this being played during his three weeks of travels with Ira and had become fascinated with the native music of the mountain folk.

"You'll git the both a us put on the wrong side a the dirt." Ira hung his pail near the mules' picket line. For the most part, they watered the mules and the saddle horse as they went, but tonight, Ira had pressed through every crossing without so much as a pause.

"Surely they've gone on their way by now." The sharp edge of guilt traced along Rand's skin again, cutting in. So much was wrong in this. Very wrong.

The girl. Yes, he had committed prayer to the issue as he and Ira fled the area, but surely there was more he could have done, even to the point of going back and . . . he wasn't certain what exactly, considering Ira's loaded pistol pointed his way, but he wanted to believe he would have done something, given the opportunity.

He had taken out the mouth harp as a distraction, but it hadn't worked. *Conscience is a formidable and determined adversary. By nature, it strikes the weakest point in a man's reasoning.* His father or grandfather had told him that at some time past, during one of their many mission journeys to spread the gospel to the unenlightened corners of the known world. As bishop of the diocese of South Carolina, the oversight of such things had been among his grandfather's jurisdictions. Having traveled often with both men, Rand had learned much before death had taken his grandfather and then his father. Indeed, those recent losses were partially responsible for Rand's determination to experience the wilderness while he could.

Ira returned to the center of their camp, the place where the fire pit would have been, had they started one. "You listen at me, boy." He leaned close, releasing the scents of liquor and tobacco and rotting teeth. "They's gonna be either a killin' or a blood feud or both on this mountain before all's been said. Folks make up they minds you got a part in it, you gonna find that pearly hide a yourn peeled and strung on a tree somewheres t'show ever'body what be done to a feller that gits on the wrong side a the wrong man."

A dark tingle started under Rand's ribs and traveled his body end to end, but despite the presence of fear, his hackles rose. "A man who doesn't stand for what is right dies his own death well before it happens." This, again, from his father, a man of great, God-given courage, both on the battlefield and off.

Ira tossed back his head, laughing into the night, the sound falling louder than any note from the mouth harp. "A fella what minds his bidness, keeps his bidness. And his hide." He reached for the poke he'd carried off the wagon before going to the spring for water. "Ye'll thank me I learnt ya that, some yan day, young'un. Just like ya can thank me for gettin' us this 'ere loaf a Pegleg Molly's bread 'fore things gone bad up'n there." He tore off a chunk and threw it to Rand. "That high moralsome thinkin' ain't ruint yer appetite, reckon?"

Rand took the bread but only sat with it, looking into the lantern's flame and watching the wick burn.

"Let it lay, boy. Ya look like someone done shot yer mule. You git past it, mark my word. Mountain's breakin' ya in the way she do ever' man. Hard life up'n here. *Man's* life, not a boy's. Here, jus' livin' and dyin', that's all they is." He bit off a hunk of bread, then circled the remainder of the loaf in the air, spitting chunks as he offered up another thought. "Tell me some more a them tales 'bout lions and g'raffes and convertin' them mangy savages in Afr'ca. That oughta shine yer mood some."

Rand didn't oblige. For two weeks now, he'd been sharing those stories with Ira and people they met along their travels, in hopes of turning eyes to the Almighty. So far, it seemed, he'd done little more than entertain. The people here were as hard and set in their ways as the mountains themselves.

Yet where there is life, there is hope, and he had not yet given up hope that, over the course of the time he expected to spend with Ira, the man could yet be educated in the ways of the faith.

Such an accomplishment would validate this trip as the thing Rand had reported it to be, in order to win both his family's agreement and financial backing. In the technical sense, this trip was a mission. A good work. Even though he'd never been convinced that he was particularly suited for clergy life, he was expected to accept a pastorate once he was sufficiently trained and of appropriate age.

Such was the family business, and though he had often rejected the notion of it, a homesickness settled over him as he stared into the lantern flame, lost himself in it for a time. His mind was back in Charleston, at La Belle, the family home on South Battery, with its beautiful polished floors and welcoming hearths. For a few moments, he sat curled in a chair before a crackling flame, a cup of Old Hast's special cocoa in his hand. He was enjoying a good book rather than facing a long, cold night in the mountains with no flame to burn away the gathering chill and ward off predators that wandered the forest.

He didn't, at first, see Ira reach for the rifle and rise to his haunches. "Who be out there nigh'way? You friend 'r foe?"

The words caught Rand's attention, startled away his daydream. He shifted to rise, realizing he'd left his pistol in the saddle pack—a foolish oversight, given Ira's warnings.

"Whoever ya is, better git talkin.'"

Ira's threat was met by the click of another gun.

"Jus' leave it be where it lay." The voice pressed from the darkness, and after it, the steps of a man, his boots compacting the carpet of leaves.

Ira stiffened, let the rifle rest, index finger still circling the trigger guard.

"Shuck yer hand off'n it, friend."

Rand caught a familiar tone in the voice, and the pulse in his neck bolted. The man from Brown Drigger's store—the one with the pockmarked face? He hoped it wasn't so, but the thing Ira had feared seemed to be coming to pass.

The intruder materialized at the edge of the lantern light, his ready pistol solidifying Rand's fears.

Ira rested his elbows on his knees, turning his palms up and squinting over his shoulder, attempting to see behind himself. "No need'n that. Yer welcome to come set-along, if'n you got a mind." The words were cordial, even relaxed, but the muleteer's face told another story. His gaze shifted rapidly from the gun to the wagon. "Ain't offerin' no troublesomeness. Just holt up fer the night here, then be headin' on down to Whistler Holler by morn. Keep'ta my own bidness."

The scar-faced man entered camp, circled, and stood left of the lantern, so as to keep a bead on both of them.

Rand's breath shuddered inward. Many times his father had told stories of having experienced situations like this during the War of Secession, but Rand had never been involved in anything of the nature.

Now his mind raced. He imagined the consequences of his choices, pictured his dear, sweet mother standing over his grave, wailing alongside his young sisters and his grandmother, the family irreparably broken by an ill-fated decision upon which he'd stubbornly insisted. Or worse yet, his family never knowing his fate at all—his resting place an unfound, unmarked corner of these mountains, his bones scattered by the wind and the weather and whatever creatures would come after these men departed the area.

"When a feller lights off not sayin' his far'-thee-wells, can't help to wonderin' where he might be headed, and who he's headin' t'see." The intruder squinted at Ira over the barrel of the pistol.

*What would a bullet feel like?* Rand wondered. What would be the sensation as it tore through flesh and bone?

"Ain't goin' to see no-some-ever person. Nosir. Be quittin' in the country, is all. Ain't one to git twixt things. Want no part of it."

The pockmarked man tasted his bottom lip, thoughtfully savoring the salt of his own skin. Sweat beaded there despite the cold. "I'd reckon such a feller might be goin' to warn some'un. Let the gal's daddy know I be watchin' out fer 'im. Maybe git some a her people to come on me whenevers I ain't lookin'. Rise a blood feud."

"Said I don' want no hand in it." Ira's voice rose, insistent or desperate or both. "Don' be knowin' her people. Wouldn't have nary'thing to do with it if'n I did. Girl's a Melungeon. I keep clear a them six-fingered devils, what's left of 'em round these parts. Give me the all-overs just thinkin' of 'em."

"That so, is it?" The man swung his pistol in Rand's direction, wiggled the barrel. "And what a this here young sap? Don' seem he got him much to say of it."

"He don' know nothin'. Ain't none but a kid come up from Charleston-town. A Jasper wantin' to git a look at the mountain. He ain't got none t'say." Ira delivered a glare Rand's way, cautioning him not to enter the discussion. But Rand could feel the words building inside him, pressing upward, gaining strength, eclipsing even the wild hammer strikes of his heart and the pounding of blood in his ears.

The pockmarked man caught the exchange of silent warning. "Might be you done tolt 'im to mind his lippin'. Might be he's afraid he'd give ya away. Could be he got some plans a his own."

"He ain't got nary a one." Again Ira raised his voice.

The man swung the pistol in the trader's direction. "He ain't got no tongue, neither, do he?"

"I've got a tongue." Rand's temper thundered now, so much so that he expected his voice to shake with it, but the sound was steady.

The man appraised him silently, head cocking back. "That be good. 'Cause we gon'ta settle here the night long, have us'ns some jaw together. Me and the boys, we need us a mite a convincin' you'uns ain't got plans agin us. That be fine at you, young Jasper?"

Rand clenched his fist at his side, willed himself not to react in the impulsive way he might've had any man offered such a threat to him in a place governed by law and order. "Don't suppose I have much choice in the matter."

"Don't s'pose you do."

Men emerged and then horses. Two men. Four horses. Another

sound followed as the horses stilled. Chain rattling, a man's growl, a woman's gasp, her outcry of pain.

Rand stiffened, drew up, began rising to his feet. The men's attentions were focused on the woods. Their backs were to him. He outsized all but Jep, but three with guns and another still out of sight? What were his chances?

His mind churned. Grab the lantern? Throw it hard enough to splinter it, spread fuel and flame over the men, hope for enough panic and distraction? Or rise silently to his feet, steal toward the wagon, toward the pistol in his saddle pack? Or bolt toward it and hope he could reach cover before someone turned his way and took deadly aim?

He imagined himself bleeding out on the leaf litter, his life wasted, the girl still no better off.

"Be still 'ere, pup." The pockmarked man seemed to sense his thoughts. "Revi? What you doin' out'n them trees? You be usin' her, I'll skin yer body'n wrap yer neck in it. Woman's mine. Troublesome as she been, I'm gonna carve my brand on 'er, right off, t'night. Don' mean I ain't got mind t' share, but she gonna know whose she is now."

Rand could only picture his darling sister Lucinda, trapped in such a gruesome predicament. The horror turned his stomach, pushed bile into his throat. He looked to Ira. The old man shook his head and dropped his gaze to the lantern, elbows still resting on his knees. He made no move toward his weapon.

"I got 'er," Revi yelled from the woods. "She done tried scattin' off again. Good that Brown Drigger hanged the chain on 'er." Revi materialized from the shadows, a ghost in the dim light at first, then a lanky, half-grown youth as he entered the lantern's circle. He'd tossed the girl over his shoulder. Her hair hung in blue-black waves, catching both the lantern light and the illumination of a full moon that had finally risen high enough to find lea of their camp.

The girl fell hard as Revi tossed her to the ground. She landed in a heap, the heavy chain clinking link by link as it settled around the irons clamped to her wrists and ankles. Rand recognized the abomination as what it was. Slave irons still hung in carriage houses and cellars in and around Charleston, the relics of a world that no longer existed.

"Ain't a-havin' me no more t'do with 'er, Jep." Revi stepped away, dusting his hands in the air, ridding himself of any remaining contact. "Heared 'er talk hoodoo out 'ere in the dark. Speakin' spells and devilment lang'edge. Ain't havin' me no more doin's with her."

"Yeah, you is." Jep's tobacco-stained smile lifted his scarred face, reflecting his anticipation as well as his confidence in his mastery of the group. "We all a us is. Her kin come agin us, ain't gonna be none of you'uns can say you done nothin' at the gal."

Revi's eyes widened almost imperceptibly. The captive began to drag herself from the ground and Revi stepped away, lifting his hands higher.

Jep's laugh drifted upward into the night. "Ain'tcha a spookish thang, cousin? Think she gonna rise somethin' from the dust that'll git'cha? She can't do nothin' in irons. They can't call up spirits when they's bound in chains. And I got this'ere key, right'n my boot. She can't git'cha. But she'd like to now, wouldn' she? Don' look in them eyes, boy. She'll draw the life out'n ya."

Jep laughed again as the girl threw back her head, tossing the length of thick hair over her shoulder. A bruise had swollen one eye shut, and a mat of dried blood lay crusted and peeling near a split lip. But she was beautiful even so, Rand realized. Almost otherworldly, her uninjured eye a bright, silvery blue against dark lashes, her hair as black as the night shadows deep in the hollows.

She seemed a piece of the mountains themselves, pressed into human form, her skin the smooth olive-brown of drying leaves. For a moment, he wondered if the things they'd said about her were true. Out of instinct, Rand's fingers traveled to the gold cross in his pocket—the one that had seen his father and grandfather through travels to many lands. He touched it through the fabric, cast off the heathenism of Jep and his men. This battered creature had been formed by God, not the forest. Though she knew nothing of the Almighty, the Almighty knew of her.

*Somehow you must stop this.* The conviction was instant, all that he knew was right, and sane. This evening's events could not reach their intended end. Quite simply, he could not live with it. Could not live with himself if he allowed it.

Force was not a viable option. He was outnumbered and weaponless. He must think of something. Quickly.

He slipped the holy cross free of his pocket as the men turned their attention temporarily to the question of pitching their horse picket. Opening his palm, Rand studied the treasure, this thing that had remained with his family, given from one generation to another since even before the first Champlains reached the New World by way of Charleston Harbor. The cross had ridden heavy in his pocket, mile upon mile, these past weeks, reminding him that he had not been entirely honest about his reasons for this trip.

"That thang ain't gonna protect ya. Don't go gittin' no fool ideas," Ira hissed under his breath. The sound caught the notice of Jep, and Rand closed his fingers over the cross again.

Jep returned to the area near the lantern, his gaze traveling to the girl and back to Rand. "She lookin' at'cha, young sap. She lookin' at'cha like she *know* who you *be*. You a friend a this gal's people?"

Rand hazarded a glance at her. She was watching him, true, and clutching some form of pendant—a small, rectangular locket, shaped from bone or ivory. The bauble hung with several carved beads and shiny bits of wampum shell on a leather cord around her neck. A bit of something misty and blue dangled over her thumb, and though he could not identify it for certain, it looked much like the salt glass occasionally found along the shores near Charleston.

"I do not know the girl." Inside, cold fear chilled the heat of indignation, threatened to abort the plan forming in his mind.

"She lookin' like she knowed 'im!" one of the other men called from beyond the lantern arc. "She look to be waitin' on 'im fer somethin'."

"I do not know the girl," Rand insisted.

Jep squinted at him, then moved to his captive, grabbed her hair, and pulled back her head so that she glared at him with the one good eye. "He one a yer people, is he?"

"I have never seen the girl." Rand's words came rushed, a bit desperate now, but he forced himself not to move, not to rise.

Somewhere in the trees, an owl called. Rand thought of Peter denying the Christ three times.

Jep released the girl, propelled her with the sole of one boot, and she fell in a heap once more. Rand didn't look her way again. Around him, the party of men went about making their camp and, at Ira's uneasy invitation, pillaging the mule wagon for stores. Rand waited for them to satisfy themselves with food and alcohol, to become sated around a newly lit fire and not so well within their faculties before he set about his plan.

"She be lookin' at'cha again, young sap," Jep observed finally, and Rand knew his time had come. There would be no other opportunity. Jep was rising to his feet, intent on the girl again. "And you be lookin' her way. Mayhaps you ain't knowed her people. Mayhaps you be waitin' fer a chance to try'n take me. That it, pup?"

Rand's temper came surprisingly short, and with it a hasty response pressed his lips, the response of a boy who had always towered confidently above his contemporaries. He bit back the words and smiled a tight smile instead. "I would like to purchase the girl." The offer came too fast, a bit unleveled and uncertain. He clutched the cross more tightly, steeled himself. This was not a boy's game. This was a game for men. A game of life and death.

Jep looked deeply into him, narrow, piggish eyes giving no hint of the man's thoughts. If there was a soul in this man, anything but evil, it lay well hidden.

Around the camp, the others turned their heads drunkenly. The girl only watched without moving. Rand wondered if, perhaps, she did not even speak English. There were those in the mountains who only knew the old languages. Cherokee, Catawba, French, Scotch.

"Undamaged," Rand added.

"She done witched 'im, that's what she done!" one of the men stammered, the words blending together. "She been holdin' that thang round 'er neck, and he done look in her eye. You's a fool, boy. Don' never gander a Melungeon in the eye. She's turned ya spellish now."

Rand rose slowly to his feet, stood himself straight, regarded Jep from only slightly below the other man's height. "I can assure you, I am not bewitched. Nor do I have any fear of whatever she may be. I am a Christian, sir. I put no stock in such things."

Jep blinked once, again, struggling to regain a greater measure of sobriety, and for the first time, Rand saw a sense of concern in him. "You be a preacher man, young sap?"

Rand opened the hand with the holy cross in it. "Preparing to be." It was not, precisely, an untruth, he hoped, lest these be his last moments on earth. "This was given me by my grandfather, carried by many generations of my family as they brought the gospel to the darkest corners of the globe."

Jep staggered backward a step. "I ain't offerin' her fer sellin'. Not yet, leastwise." He took another swig of Ira's mash liquor, wiped his mouth with the back of his hand, and stretched the jug toward Rand. When the gesture was refused, Jep reached toward the cross as if he meant to take it, then pulled his hand away again, said instead, "But might be I done decided to go soft on you, boy. Might be I let you live to learn a few thangs. Might be . . . *not*."

"Jep, you can't go killin' no preacher man," one of the others warned. "Could be he's why the witchin' spirits and haints ain't flew agin us a'ready."

Ira climbed to his feet cautiously, seizing the opportunity now that liquor had dulled minds and loosened the conversation. "Preachin' do run pow'rful thick wit' this'un. He ain't stopped talkin' 'bout it since I brung him outta Murphy. You go on and kill him, you be havin' the *unseen* a-comin' on ya from above *and* below all at oncet. That be why the girl been lookin' at 'im. She scared'a his magic."

"That so?" Jep's lips parted into a brown-stained smile and he turned his regard to Ira. "Might be I just gut *you*, then."

"Leave him as he is." Rand's pulse was rapping like a beggar at the door, but his thoughts were acute, precise. He sensed the balance slowly turning. He could feel, for the first time in his life, the power of good against evil.

Jep backed three crooked strides toward the girl. She drew away, tried to scramble out of reach, but the man caught her by a handful of her brown woolen dress and her hair, dragged her upward as buttons popped and stitches tore.

"You ain't nothin.'" The words ground low, and then Jep threw the girl forward. Encumbered by the chains, she fell facedown in the dirt at Rand's feet.

He resisted the urge to help her. This was a delicate game of cards they were playing. He could not risk revealing his hand.

On the ground, she gathered herself to her knees, wrapped both hands over the carved amulet strung around her neck, and began murmuring in some tongue that he'd neither heard before nor understood.

"It be the devil talk!" The other men backed away, putting the wagon between themselves and the girl.

"You fix 'er," Jep commanded, spreading his feet to catch his balance before pointing at the girl and then at Rand. "Git the devil outta 'er. I'll put my brand on 'er then, and she might be worth keepin'."

"Do it, boy," Ira commanded. It was impossible to tell whether he believed such a thing to be possible, but it hardly mattered now.

Rand pretended to consider the request, to assess what sort of procedure might be needed. The girl's murmurings grew louder, the language strange and guttural, almost familiar in some way, but he couldn't isolate it.

The flame flared and popped. Both Rand and Jep jerked toward it.

A strangeness slid through Rand then, a current of doubt, a sudden lacking of faith. He banished it quickly, narrowed his focus, let the doxologies whisper through his mind. "I'll need my saddle pack that I might retrieve the Bible from it." He angled toward the wagon, but no sooner had he taken a step than Jep's pistol was trained his way.

"Hack, bring 'im his book."

"I ain't touchin' it!"

"Bring his whole pack, then!" Jep took another swig of whiskey, swung the pistol toward the wagon, fired off a shot that struck the dirt and sent the mules skittering on their tethers. Puddinhead sat back on his lead, trying for all he was worth to pull down the tree to which Rand had secured him.

"Now!" Jep demanded, turning the weapon toward the girl. "I want 'er fixed."

At the wagon, the men elected Revi to deliver the pack. Rand waited anxiously, counting each step until the pack was safely in his hand. The pistol lay within it, but what now? He was a fine shot, and quick, but Jep's weapon was already drawn.

He took out the Bible first, the old brown leather-bound that had been given him by his father. A family heirloom that had seen the pulpit in many a church. Turning the pages, he envisioned childhood days when he'd stood at altars in empty sanctuaries and pretended to preach the sermon. He'd put on convincing performances back then.

Letting the book lie flat in one broad palm, he allowed the night air to tease the pages, noting that Jep, his men, Revi, even the girl, seemed momentarily transfixed by the movement.

And a moment was all he needed.

Before Jep could react, Rand had drawn the pistol, aimed, and sighted it. Jep's bleary gaze met his at the end of the barrel, the realization dawning slowly.

Ira grabbed his gun as the others scrambled for their weapons. "You'uns jus' quieten over there. Believe we's about to be havin' us a diff'rnt kinda conversation, now ain't we? Now, ya done et my food and stolt goods off'n my wagon. I don' care none 'bout the girl. You gimme back all's mine and you take 'er and git. We gonna figure this'ere bidness be done with and we gonna part ways. Ain't got no more twixt us, savvy?"

Skirting the lantern, Rand stepped backward so he had the whole of the group in his sights, including Ira. "We're leaving," he informed them. "And we're taking the girl with us."

# Chapter 7

It was nine thirty at night when I finally called Jamie. By then, I'd read through the three chapters of the manuscript at least a half-dozen times. I'd tried Google searches on the title of the story, the characters' names, and other key phrases, looking for publication information, but come up dry.

The manuscript, as far as I could tell, had never been in print. Once that was established, I scanned the piece like a code breaker trying to ferret out its secrets, understand its power. Why did it seem as though something lay hidden just beneath the surface . . . something I was missing? Why did the manuscript compel me so? I'd never bought anything tied to Appalachia. In fact, I'd avoided such projects when agents pitched them to me. Too real. Too close to parts of myself I wanted to forget.

But this story had me by the throat. I needed to know why.

Jamie was the only one I could call. A best friend will come over at nine thirty on a Friday night when you can't explain the reason, and if she happens to be brilliant as well, so much the better.

Friday leapt from his chair and went ballistic when I let Jamie in the door. The little Napoleon didn't cotton to visitors generally. He barely allowed me to live here.

Jamie curled her lip and growled back at him. "You know, Friday, I'm totally an animal person, but you are seriously obnoxious. Maybe you should consider therapy." She unwound a fashionable scarf and dropped it with her designer coat. She had on a little black dress and ridiculously high heels with a platform sole under the toe. No doubt she'd been out with her roommates.

"Great shoes. Can I borrow those sometime?"

"Yeah, if you'd ever go out with us. It's like that thing with Brian ruined you for good. You know, just because he turned out to be a schmuck-ola doesn't mean every guy you meet is a loser." Bracing her hands on her hips, she tipped her head to one side. "So what's with the big phone call?"

I picked up the envelope, the packet reassembled exactly as I'd found it. I wanted Jamie to get the full effect. "Look at this. It was on my desk this morning at work."

"You dragged me over here for a *submission*? Seriously?"

"It's not a submission. I mean, it wasn't delivered to my in-box *or* my pile. I'm saying that I *found* it on the corner of my desk this morning. No explanation."

Jamie teetered on one foot while she unbuckled a shoe, then switched to unbuckle the other and finally kicked both off by the door. "Ohhh, my toes."

She crossed the room to the kitchen, skirting Friday, now back in his night-night chair, and proceeded to the refrigerator, where she began sifting through the takeout until she found a container of egg drop soup. "Will I get food poisoning from this?"

"Ninety percent chance, no."

"Thanks, that's comforting." Helping herself to the microwave, she stood there twirling the spoon in the air. "So the new mail service at Vida House is sloppy, is what you're saying?"

"No. This thing is over twenty years old. My guess is that it came off Slush Mountain."

The microwave's chime punctuated the sentence, but Jamie didn't reach for the button. "You *stole* something off Slush Mountain? As in, the stuff you were never supposed to touch? That *nobody* is supposed to touch?"

"No, follow me here. I'm saying it appeared on my desk overnight."

Suddenly the soup and the microwave lost all importance. Jamie abandoned them, crossed the kitchen, and reached for the manuscript. I knew she would. "And you kept it? You should be ashamed of yourself." Settling her fingers over the envelope, she withdrew the contents and slipped into a chair.

By the time she finished reading the pages, she was hunched over the table with her feet tucked and her blonde hair stuffed behind her ears. She sat staring at the last page for a minute before laying it on the stack. Her soup was cold, even though I'd put a spoon in it and set it beside her.

"Well . . . ," she said finally. "I definitely wish I had more. I used to love it when that happened . . . back when I was working in fiction, I mean." Jamie's chance to move over to the magazine had come along out of the blue, years ago. She knew someone who knew someone. "I would've requested the rest of it. Good pacing and a nice sense of voice. I was right there under that cabin with the girl in the opening scene. And now I'm wondering if they get away from the Huns here or not."

Flipping the manuscript over, she looked at the aquamarine title sheet, then thumbed through a few of the pages behind it. "Gruesomely amateurish presentation, though. A cover page with someone's hand-done illustration on it? And colored paper? Who does that? You learn better the first time you go to a writers' group at a local library. This poor doofus was obviously living in a cave, which is probably why the material feels like such an organic experience. Wonder who opened this first and what they did with it. There's no author name on the pages, no query letter . . ."

"I'd love to know the answer to that, but I can't exactly *ask* anyone." Jamie's excitement fanned the flame of my own. "And yes, it's amateurish, especially the whole title page thing, although the artwork isn't bad. But it's the voice that's been bothering me. Something about it rings a bell . . . like I should *know* who wrote it. But why would I? It's way before my time." I turned the envelope over on the table, pointed. "There's a postmark date, but the rest is too faded to read."

Jamie lifted the envelope and brought it close to her face. "Something . . . North Carolina. Got any kind of magnifying glass around here?"

"No. Well . . . Wait. Hang on a minute, maybe I do."

I hurried across the room and around the willow-branch screen that divided off the bedroom area. The corner was thick with shadows, but the cylindrical box with its wooden spool handle and unimpressive painting of sweet gum leaves was still where I had tucked it when I'd moved into the apartment. I worked the lid free and dumped the contents on the bed.

"There's one here in my sewing kit."

"You have a sewing kit? Do you know how to use it?"

At times like these I realized what an impostor I really was. I'd spent half my childhood sewing and patching up clothes. "Yes, I know how to use it."

"So I've been paying for things to be hemmed or taken in at the cleaners all these years, and I could've just brought them to you? Why have you never told me this?"

"I haven't opened this thing in forever." But the antique magnifying glass was exactly where I'd kept it hidden since the day Wilda let me take it home from her place on Honey Creek. She'd found me trying to sneak it into my pocket after working in her greenhouse. The frame was beautiful and ornate, filigreed silver with colored gems in the handle. It seemed a shame that something so lovely was left lying on a windowsill with discarded nuts, bolts, and garden tags. I'd told myself she would never notice it was gone.

*All you need do is ask, Jennia Beth Gibbs. No sense making a thief of yourself, now is there? You keep it . . . and remember that no matter how many wrong choices we've made in the past, we can always decide to make the right ones today. The past need not determine one moment of the future.*

The memory covered me as I handed Jamie the magnifying glass and she leaned close to the envelope, attempting to decipher more of the postmark while elbowing me out of the way. "Cut it . . . out . . . Stop . . . You're in my light. Shoot. I can't . . . Just wait a . . . Do you have . . . a flashlight or a little lamp?"

I grabbed my phone and turned it on. "Flashlight app."

"Clever." We leaned together again, like a pair of Alices peering down the rabbit hole.

"Try putting the flashlight inside it. Sometimes when the

light shines through, you can see the pigments that are still down in the paper. I read that in a novel somewhere."

"That was on *Pawn Stars* last month, you goofus. We watched it together, remember?" Jamie reminded me.

"Oh . . . maybe it was." TV shows featuring all manner of undiscovered and rediscovered antiques were my weakness. Somewhere on my bucket list was, *Travel around the world looking for lost treasures.*

Jamie carefully lifted the envelope and I slid the phone in.

"See anything?" No doubt her eyes were better than mine. I'd been half-blind in elementary school, until a teacher discovered I needed glasses and the Lions Club provided some in secondhand frames. LASIK had finally helped bring me closer to normal a few years ago.

"*E* . . . something," Jamie mused. "It's two words. *Emerald Isle*, maybe? That's in North Carolina. We went there a couple times on vacation when I was a kid. It's south of the Outer Banks. No, wait, it's three words, and that's not an *E*. That's an *L*. . . . *Look* . . . something. That's a *G* on the second word . . . and an *O* or . . . or maybe a *G* on the third."

"Looking Glass Gap."

"You can make that out?" Jamie leaned back, then forward again. "Why does that sound so familiar, though? Is that on the beach somewhere? Maybe I've been there."

"It's not on the beach. It's in the mountains." The only reason I could decipher those words was because they were so close to home. Our high school played Looking Glass Gap in football. I'd never been to a game, but I'd desperately wanted to go to the ones in Looking Glass Gap because . . .

A thought struck so suddenly that I tore the seam of the envelope pulling away. "Holy cow! Oh . . . oh . . . Whoa . . . That can't be. There's no way that . . ." Connections rushed together like raindrops racing down a window, meeting, combining, gaining speed, the pathways so clear that I couldn't believe I hadn't seen them before now. Grabbing the manuscript, I turned it over, started leafing through the pages, reading passages, looking for proof.

"What? What, what, *what*?" Jamie's hands flailed. "Holy cow . . . *what*?"

Across the room, Friday growled, protesting the interruption of his beauty sleep.

"Grab my computer. It's in my . . . Wait, oh. Here it is." I was on such a wild ride that I'd forgotten it wasn't still in my briefcase. I'd already been on it this evening, trying to figure out the mystery of *The Story Keeper*, but the answer was right under my nose all along.

So incredibly close to home.

I brought up a webpage, clicked backward through the books listed on it, looked at a sample chapter.

Jamie moved into position behind me. "Are you going to tell me the deal, or do I have to keep guessing? *Why* are you on the Evercrest Books website, on the Time Shifters page? Are we thinking there's, like, some kind of alien abduction involved in this manuscript? Or has your taste in literature changed?"

I tapped the screen. "I think *he's* the one who wrote this. Evan Hall." There was an author photo on the press pack, probably an old one by now. Evan Hall hadn't penned a new book in ten years. Not since his Time Shifters series took off overnight, generating a movie franchise and a cult of crazed followers who wanted to believe that there really were alien time-travel portals hidden in the Blue Ridge Mountains.

In the jacket photo from the first Time Shifters novel, he

brooded for the camera, his dark hair swirling over eyes that were deep blue and eerily intense. He was probably only eighteen or nineteen then, ridiculously young to have hit on such massive success. That was one of the media hooks the publisher had used to push the book. It made for a great story—*Unknown engineering student sits down and writes blockbuster book one day, out of the clear blue. . . .*

He'd generated a flurry of teenage sci-fi Cinderella fantasies, grabbing hearts everywhere. Including mine. I'd sneaked the first book home from the school library when I was thirteen and tucked it in the old springhouse downwater from my grandparents' home. Fetching the hanging meat and crock vegetables stored there had always been my job. That book was the first rebellious thing I'd ever attempted. Reading it amounted to both a protest and a survival mechanism—an escape. My mother had recently vanished in the night, and with her, the gossamer-thin protective layer between my father, my grandparents, and us kids. Suddenly I had become what my mother was. A barrier stretching and tearing and binding up before being punctured again.

"Evan Hall?" Jamie's voice seemed to rise out of the blue. "Oh, come *on.*"

"No, just listen." I turned the manuscript around, slid it into the space next to the computer. "Look at the phrases here. Some of the pet words. Every author has them. And the postmark—Looking Glass Gap? That's right where the Time Shifters books are set. That's where he's *from.*"

Jamie sucked in a breath. "Oh, I know that place. I bought a feature piece on movie-inspired fashions a couple years ago—remember that time I guested and did the little fashion-show spot on *The View*? Part of the article was about Time Shifters and the people who are, like, crazy into it. They make pilgrimages to

Looking Glass Lake, dress up in clothes from different time periods. Some of them even carry antique weapons and money and wander around the mountains *looking* for time portals. Personally, the background material from that piece freaked me out just a wee bit." She slanted an appraising look at the manuscript. "But this isn't sci-fi. It wouldn't be Evan Hall's kind of thing."

"What if it *used* to be his kind of thing? He came out of nowhere with the time-travel books. According to his bio, he'd never written before that. He just had the idea for Time Shifters one day when he was sitting in a physics class. What if that was some clever spin-doctoring—to add a little author mystique when the first book came out? 'Future aerospace engineer falls off the turnip truck and writes blockbuster book' is a great hook, but the truth could be that he'd been writing and trying to get published for a while."

Jamie drummed a nice manicure job against the table, considering it. "Well . . . that'd be interesting. The whole phenomenon made a lot of people a lot of money. He left a bunch of people hanging when he quit, that's for sure. It's any publisher's worst nightmare."

I looked at the manuscript again, turned a few pages, studied Evan Hall's image on the computer screen. "This could turn the Time Shifters franchise on its ear."

"And the fans. What if they find out Evan Hall wasn't some kind of time-traveling genius with a miraculous vision? What if they find out he was just another aspiring author looking for a story that would sell?"

Across the room, Friday barked as a garbage truck rattled along the street outside. Jamie and I jumped like thieves caught in the act, then looked at each other and laughed.

"What do you plan to do with it?" Jamie leaned over as I

moved to the computer again. "It's not like you can walk into the office on Monday and tell everybody. And it's not like you can call the author. Evan Hall doesn't talk to his fans, reporters, editors, or anyone else—I know because we tried when we did the movie fashions segment. He's been locked away on his mountain ever since he quit writing and went through the lawsuit with his publisher. Even if this manuscript were his, it'd be tied up by the option clauses in his contracts. You'd never be able to make a bid on it. Where do you go from here?"

I didn't have a good answer. No telling what would happen next, but this felt like the night I found myself trapped on a snowy mountain with Tom Brandon. This was big. "I'm not sure, but the first step is to find out where he is now and who's managing his business."

# Chapter 8

The trouble with obsessions is that by the time you know you've got one, it already has you by the throat. Chasing Evan Hall was like chasing a ghost. His publicist no longer had anything to do with him and he'd broken all ties with his agent years ago. The studio behind the Time Shifters films had stretched the nine original novels into as many movies as possible—without the author's blessing after the first few—and now that was finished as well. Evan Hall still lived on his mountain above Looking Glass Gap, where, according to his business manager, he did not accept business proposals or business calls related to publishing.

Even Jamie thought I was nuts for continuing to pursue it. *Have you lost your mind?* she'd demanded after four days of hearing me complain about dead ends. *You're brand new at Vida House, and this thing is a total long shot.*

I knew she was right, but the story was haunting me. It was wrecking me in some strange way. At Monday's pub board meeting, I couldn't focus. All I could do was look around the room and think, *Who knows about* The Story Keeper *besides me? Which one of them put it on my desk?*

Hadn't anyone else figured out the secret?

Hadn't anyone else wondered about the rest?

*Let it go, grasshopper,* Jamie had warned as we walked together to the subway at the end of a long Tuesday. *This is me, giving you some good advice. I'm counting on you and all that profit sharing at Vida House so you can float me a loan if the magazine crashes and burns.*

*Yeah, whatever.* Not that I wouldn't have done anything for Jamie, but I was struggling to scrape up the rent right now, myself. On top of that, tucked in Tuesday's mail, I'd found a dog-eared envelope with a Towash, North Carolina, address, a cheery note, and first-day-of-school pictures. I knew what that meant. A request for money wouldn't be far behind.

I was trying hard not to think about it. If I did, I'd want to climb into bed and stay there.

Given my present bank balance, one more unexpected financial hit would be the breaking straw. I should've been playing it safe at work, but I'd already decided to bring the manuscript back to Vida House, and not with the intention of returning it quietly to Slush Mountain. The beauty of my obsession with it was that it was almost enough to drive my sister's note and the back-to-school photos from my mind. Almost.

Wednesday morning, I dressed and left for work early. Mitch had been coming in at the crack of dawn, poring over her war bride project. I needed to catch her while the office was quiet.

By the time I walked past the war room and Slush Mountain

and turned into her office, I was focused completely on *The Story Keeper* and how much I wanted it.

Mitch was busy at her desk as I entered her domain. Her quarters looked like an episode of *Hoarders Gone Wild*. Every blank space was filled with ad proofs, cover comps, finished books, stacks of galley pages, proposals, and manuscripts of all shapes and forms—edge taped, spiral-bound, held together by plastic strips, bulldog clips, and rubber bands—pretty much everything but duct tape, and there was probably some of that under there too. The only clear space was a path from the door to the desk chair and from the desk chair to a credenza that was also hopelessly piled with manuscripts.

There was nowhere to sit, so I didn't.

Sweat broke over my palms, making the folder in my hands feel like it had been left out in a morning fog.

Mitch didn't look up at first. "Yes?" Polite, yet impatient.

"I need to ask your advice on a project."

"Yes?" She was still scanning her computer screen. I waited until she stopped and looked at me.

"Something showed up on my desk. . . ." Blood drained from my face as I prepared to reveal the contraband, leaving me vaguely light-headed. I heard Jamie's warnings. *Those people in the pages aren't going to rescue you when you lose your job, either. And you're never going to find another place like Vida House. . . .* How in the world would I explain all this? How could I even bring it up without sounding like I was mentally off?

Yet the obsession had begun to consume me, and it was only getting stronger.

Mitch's eyes narrowed, drifted lower, until she was focused on the emerging envelope. Was it my imagination, or was there a spark of recognition?

"Mitch, I don't know how this came to be in my office, I promise. I just found it on my desk one morning, but the postmark is twenty years old. I think it came off—"

She lifted a hand, palm out, stopping me. "Hold it. Don't say another word. When did you *find* that thing, exactly?"

"I've had it . . . a few days. Long enough to do a little research on it."

"Why?" A change in posture distanced her as she squinted over the top of her reading glasses. "We haven't given you enough to do here?"

"I want it."

She blinked, then blinked again, dropping her chin and rolling a surprised look. "You . . . *what*? You know where that came from, right? There's *nothing* twenty years old around here, still sitting in an envelope, unless it's off . . ."

"Yes, Slush Mountain. I know."

Mitch checked the doorway behind me, taking in the office still blanketed with morning stillness. Her hand twitched nervously, then whipped off the eyeglasses, tapped them on the chair arm. *Tap, tap, tap-tap-tap-tap-tap.* "I don't know what's happening here, but I'm going to give you a piece of good advice. Put it back. Don't let this happen again."

"I can't," I blurted, and my boss's head jerked backward like I'd landed a blind left hook. I babbled on. "Put it back, I mean. I have a feeling about this thing. I've figured out who wrote it, I think. If you could just look . . ."

"Nope. Cease. Desist. *Alto.* I don't need or want to hear any more about whatever that is." Pausing, she let me dangle on a thread while she gathered her thoughts. "Listen, Jen, I'm not going to tell you what to do. There are no dictators here at Vida. What I *am* going to tell you is that, whatever choice you make from here, you make at your own risk. I know *nothing* about this, you did *not* ask me about it, and no, I do *not* want to see that thing you have in the folder." She softened then, seeming slightly more sympathetic. "I understand falling in love with a project—blindly, even. But my advice is to think long and hard about whether this is worth it."

She waited for the tip of that reality to break the surface before she drove the point home. "It's a huge gamble, Jen, and I'm not exactly sure what it is you're shooting for. But if anyone here would know anything more about that manuscript, it is probably George Vida. And if anyone has the ability to get answers about it, it is probably him as well. But like I said, think about it. Hard. I expect great things from you here, as you get up to speed with projects of your own. I appreciate your input on the war bride proposal. You helped to give it just the right touch at pub board. George Vida likes you, and trust me, he doesn't warm up to every new recruit in that way. But you know the rules about Slush Mountain. Whether George Vida will buy the idea that this thing just *showed up* on your desk, I have no idea. I'm having a hard time with that one right now myself, but . . . I can't quite imagine why, having just joined our team, you'd decide to flout the rules. You seem smarter than that. Much smarter."

I let the envelope fall back into the file folder, feeling the burn of Mitch's comments as she returned to her computer, indicating that I should withdraw from her office and take my secrets with me.

"Thanks for hearing me out, Mitch." Part of me was saying, *She's right. You know she's right.* But part of me was rejoicing in the fact that she hadn't slammed the door on my idea—she'd just told me I had to walk through at my own risk. "I'll give it some more thought."

"I would if I were you. I've seen people here one minute and gone the next. Doesn't happen often, but it does happen. *Loyalty, honesty, teamwork*—it's right there on the Vida House logo. But George Vida also values hunches. Question is, which side will he come down on in this case? Not that I know anything about this whole matter . . . because I don't. Understood?"

"Yes, I understand."

"*If* you're going to pursue it, I'd catch George Vida when the gatekeeper's not around." By *the gatekeeper*, she meant Hollis, of course.

"Thanks, Mitch."

"Don't thank me," she muttered. "Keep in mind, it could just as easily be the rope you hang yourself with."

# Chapter 9

The airplane bounced and rattled over patches of turbulent air, the motion rousing me as the pilot announced the remaining flight time. Blinking against the sleep haze, I swore I heard Friday growling and snuffling, but the report over the PA system reminded me I was far from home by now. I couldn't quite remember why I was traveling, but it didn't seem to matter. I just wanted to catch a little more sleep. . . .

Letting my eyes fall closed, I reached for a memory that was circling, foggy yet. Something about the plane's sound and motion reminded me of riding in a squeaky Radio Flyer wagon downhill over a bumpy road. My mind traveled back and back and back. Back to a rust-eaten red wagon with four of us piled inside, bone-thin limbs and bare feet poking out everywhere.

Laughter and squeals. Marah Diane's high-pitched voice screeching above everything, her brown hair whipping Joey's round-cheeked baby face. And then a rock, a sudden jerk on the steering, a wild tumbling off, and bodies flying everywhere. Cuts, scrapes, blood, tears. Mama running from the trailer house, her skirt gathered up high over long, shapely legs that never saw the light of day otherwise. It wasn't permitted.

The plane bumped over opposing air currents, throwing my head forward, bringing me to awareness. I pressed into the seat, into the memory again.

Marah Diane stood up, pointing a finger, her hand clutched over her knee. Joey lay rag-doll floppy in the ditch water, squalling like a scalded cat, but there wasn't a scratch on his chubby toddler body.

"It was *yer* fault! It was *yer* idea!" Marah Diane's voice was stark and sharp, like the persistent ovenbird calls that split the quiet of the mountain air. *Tattletale birds*, we called them because they cried out *teacher, teacher, teacher, teacher*. I hated the sound—the ovenbird's and Marah Diane's—more often than not. Everything between Marah Diane and me lay bound up in the not-so-silent battle of sisters. With the four of us kids stair-stepped, each two years apart, we were always squeezing each other, fighting for space, but Marah Diane and I were the worst.

When the wagon crashed, I was mostly concerned about Joey. He was special, being a boy, and for as long as I could remember, I'd been given the care of whoever was youngest. My mother was just now starting to pay attention again.

Mama ran to Joey first, passing by Marah Diane and her split knee. Coral Rebecca lay facedown in the road, hidden in the thick white-blonde frizz of hair that had given her the unusual name. She didn't even bother to whimper. At three and a half years old, she just rolled over, sat up, and started looking at the damage. She didn't like to call attention to herself. That was problematic, as she got attention everywhere she went because of her hair.

"It was yer fault!" Marah Diane shouted again, anxious to figure out who would take the blame for this.

"It's nobody's fault." Mama rescued Joseph John from the ditch, checked him over, then turned to the rest of us, looking relieved. There wasn't any evidence on Joey. He'd flown clear of the road before he hit, being lighter and more aerodynamic than the rest of us.

*Aerodynamic.* I'd just learned that word the week before in the third grade over in Towash. We'd been studying the Apollo missions to the moon. It seemed impossible that men had set foot there long before I was even born. The moon looked very small from the mountains of North Carolina.

"C'mon, we'll clean it all right on up. Wasn't no harm done." Mama stood with Joey in her arms and reached for Marah Diane's hand, her eyes soft and comforting. I'd forgotten that about her over the years—how gentle she was, how she kept quiet about things that went wrong when Daddy was gone to the hay fields, in the woods working coonhounds, or away doing day work . . . if there were jobs fit for a man to take. The son of a deacon among the Lane's Hill Brethren Saints couldn't be seen doing just anything. I was proud of that, somehow, the fact that my grandfather held a special position.

I was proud of the fact that my mother was beautiful, too, with her dark hair and bright eyes. Her beauty was whispered about, even though such talk was discouraged, beauty being only a woman's way of tempting a man toward sin. Just as my mama had tempted my daddy. He'd taken a wife from outside the Brethren Saints, a thing that was frowned upon and would assure that deaconry was probably out of his reach. The union was tolerated because my mama joined the church, but it was always made clear enough that the marriage was impure and so was she.

The landing gear touched down, tearing loose the memory, sending it spinning in the plane's wake before I could linger and search for more. So few recollections of my mother remained that looking at those years was like studying a portrait with chunks randomly cut from it. Just frustrating. Slightly disturbing.

Why does a woman bring six children into the world and then leave without a word, never to be heard from again? It was always a question too hard to answer. I'd given up searching for my mother or trying to understand her years ago.

My eyes were dry and grainy, slow to focus. I heard Friday's growl again as the plane rolled to the gate. Something wiggled near my feet, and a yip sat me bolt upright. I looked down, and there was Friday, crammed under the seat in the soft-sided pet carrier I'd borrowed from Jamie's mother in a fit of last-minute desperation when my dog-sitting arrangements fell through.

Everything came back in a rush then—my conversation with George Vida during which my theory about Evan Hall had been met with skepticism, but also with interest. The big boss took the manuscript off my hands so that he could look the situation over himself. By the next morning, Hollis was making trip arrangements for me, and later that day I was being sent on a time-travel mission of sorts—back to the one place I never wanted to go again. Into the Blue Ridge, with its achingly beautiful hills and folds, its familiar sounds and scents, and its hidden spaces of undeniable pain.

In the last twenty-four hours, I had learned two things: One, when George Vida wanted something, he'd go to any lengths to get it. He wanted to know if that manuscript was by Evan Hall, and if it was, he wanted it. Two, small dogs can ride on many flights in a pet carrier, as long as it fits under the seat. *It's no big deal. My mother does it all the time,* Jamie had insisted. *Just take*

*him along. I'll even go pick up Mom's doggy travel bag for you.*
That was her way of alleviating her guilt over refusing to step in
when the kids down the hall couldn't take care of Friday. Jamie's
sister had just set a wedding date and they were planning a dress-
shopping weekend.

So, for better or worse, Friday and I were on this journey of a
thousand miles together. Unlikely partners, of a sort. Friday was
beyond thrilled. Not.

I heard a noise and it was quickly evident that Friday had just
committed an indiscretion of the sort that's fairly inexcusable in
close quarters.

"Eeewww!" the little girl in front of me squealed. "Mama, he
did it again!"

The mom cast a dirty look between the seats as she stood and
made ready to run from the plane as soon as the doors were open.

A hot flush crept up my neck and burned my ears.

"What do you feed that thing?" The thirtysomething guy in
the aisle seat grimaced playfully. We'd talked a bit before I'd fallen
asleep. He was headed to Kitty Hawk to marry his high school
sweetheart in a beach wedding. Wonderful story.

"Sorry. Friday doesn't get out of the house much."

"I can see why," he joked, then held up the aisle traffic while
I tugged Friday's carrier loose.

Friday growled, a whiff of noxious air floated up, and the kid
in the next seat groaned, "Get me out of here!"

Wait until I gave Jamie the blow-by-blow of this. She'd made
*take the dog on the plane* sound so simple, almost like a fun adventure for both pet and owner. With Friday, nothing was simple.

My seatmate touched my arm. "Hey, don't forget your briefcase."

I glanced at it, shocked, then grabbed it and slung it over

my shoulder. So far today, my nerves were a wreck. Two of the reasons were in that briefcase. One being *The Story Keeper* partial, the other being a second envelope from Coral Rebecca. This one wouldn't be filled with school photos and a greeting. I hadn't even worked up the courage to open it yet, just shoved it in my briefcase and brought it along instead.

I felt the weight of it as I hurried from the plane. My sister had no idea I'd just touched down on soil only hours from the old hometown. I still wasn't sure if I intended to tell her. It'd be so much easier to come and go and never say a word.

I contemplated the possibility while dragging Friday and my luggage down the Jetway and into the corridor.

The terminal in Charlotte hadn't changed all that much in ten years. Although it felt smaller now. It'd seemed huge when I'd left for New York City, just one day after Clemson graduation. My first time on a plane or even in an airport.

Wilda had rushed through instructions before letting her son, Richard, take my duffel bag—all I owned—and hand it to me on the curb. I'd been scared to death on the inside, still as a winter dawn on the outside. Clemson was one thing, but New York seemed like the other side of the universe. I'd wanted to run home to Wilda's big house on Honey Creek. My hiding place. My refuge.

But I knew she wouldn't let me. During my three years at Clemson, she'd only offered to bring me home once—just long enough for my little brother's funeral, which was all the time I could stand, anyway. Joey shouldn't have been driving the truck at thirteen, but he was, and then he was gone. My grandmother had made the point that, if I'd been there to watch him, it wouldn't have happened.

After that, Wilda thought it was better if I stayed away, and it undoubtedly was. My family had shown no interest in my college graduation or my plans for grad school and a publishing internship program in New York. No one from Lane's Hill cared enough to tell me good-bye, but Wilda had stood on the airport curb, her chin trembling as I walked away.

Even now, I could still picture her there, Richard by her side, awkwardly waving his good arm until I vanished through the doors. Suddenly it seemed as if they should be outside waiting to greet my return.

They wouldn't be, of course.

*Richard is probably gone by now.* The realization sifted through my mind as Friday and I wound toward the rental car area. Richard had been fighting health issues, even back then. With Wilda's passing not six months after I left for New York, there was no telling what had become of her house and the gardens and the orchard. Someone else probably owned it by now.

The reality settled in as I reached the rental car counter and handed the clerk the paperwork from Hollis.

"Oh, you're headed to Looking Glass *Gap*." He drew out the last word, arching an eyebrow. "Going to the big camp? You haven't got enough luggage. Where's your costume?"

"I'm wearing it, I think." The clueless expression won a laugh.

"Just covering Warrior Week for the press then?" He nodded along with his own conclusion.

"Warrior . . . huh?"

He rested his hands on the counter dramatically. "I didn't think you looked like the type, although you can't always tell. Whole families come through this place—dads, moms, little kids. Sometimes they've got their garb on right here in the airport. Sometimes they're incognito until they get to Looking Glass Lake. But usually I can pick out the Time Shifters folks.

It's Warrior Week. Camp week. They do it in the spring and the fall—the fan bash. But a few of them really believe they're not going to *need* a return flight home, if you know what I mean. So . . . listen . . . if you're just in the area for a quiet vacation, you might want to rethink and book someplace else—maybe Pisgah or Highlands. By the way, have you considered an upgrade to four-wheel drive? Never know about the weather and the roads this time of year." A hand swished vaguely through the air, indicating some nameless mountain road far, far away.

I felt my smile slowly melting. I'd stumbled onto a big fan camp week? Hollis had made all the travel arrangements. She'd mentioned something about the hotels being full and booking what was the last cabin in town, out on Looking Glass Lake. No wonder she'd had such a hard time—Looking Glass Gap was probably in chaos, swelled beyond capacity with Time Shifters enthusiasts.

This was exactly the wrong time to approach Evan Hall. He'd be locked up on the family estate outside town, avoiding the masses while tour buses stopped by his front gate, die-hard readers hoping to catch glimpses of the man who'd started it all. I'd seen a few photos on Internet fan blogs.

"Ohhhh, man. This is not good." My chances of getting anything done here were probably nil. I should've kept a clearer head when George Vida wanted to send me. I should've asked for a week or two to fully study the situation, come up with the best plan of approach. But I'd been afraid he'd change his mind, or I would. Given time, one of us was bound to see reason.

"I thought the big gathering was in the spring." Panic stirred and stretched its wings. So much was riding on this trip. How could I possibly go back to George Vida and tell him I'd accomplished zilch?

"Wild Week in the spring. Warrior Week in the fall. Starts third Thursday in October. Always," the clerk offered.

The manuscript was beginning to feel like a dancing hippo chained to my shoulder.

"Ohhh . . . kay. Okay . . . okay . . ." *Think, think, think.* I looked up and down the airport corridor, noticed an eighteenth-century buccaneer extracting a cape and over-the-knee boots from his Travelite and putting them on. Somewhere farther along, I thought I saw Abraham Lincoln and Mary Todd, arms linked, walking out the door.

"Sure you don't want information on our partner hotels? Somewhere else?" The clerk nose-wrinkled, sniffing the air. "What's that *smell*?"

Friday, tucked in beside the luggage, was once again making his presence known.

"No telling." Where was the fairy godmother with the pumpkin coach and the glass slippers when I needed her? She could've turned Friday into something with couth . . . a footman, maybe. "I'll just take the car as booked. I'd better get going so I can make it there before dark."

The agent handed over my paperwork. "Good luck, then. Enjoy your time in Looking Glass Gap."

# Chapter 10

*A* gush of air rushed into my lungs as I woke, blinked the hand-hewn cabin rafters into view, remembered where I was and why I had come.

I hadn't been plagued by the suffocation dream in years. Now it lay clear in my mind, like a movie left playing after the theater lights come on.

This time in the dream, the six of us had been standing along the shore of Looking Glass Lake. The air smelled of pine and black locust blooms, wild witch hazel and woodsmoke. Marah Diane, Coral Rebecca, Evie Christine, and I had our skirts wrapped up between our legs and tucked in at the waist in a way we never would've dared at home. Joey had rolled his pants up high, and Lily Clarette, born after the two miscarried babies buried in the orchard, wore one of Daddy's old T-shirts, as long on her as a dress.

We were learning to swim, and even in the dream I was aware that this was only a conjuring of my imagination, not a memory.

I'd always known how to swim. Down on Honey Creek, there were quiet, clear-water swimming holes and waterfalls that rushed into churning pools. Marah Diane and I had been skittering away to those places since we were big enough to slip from the house while Mama and the youngest were sleeping.

But in the dream, it was Looking Glass Lake, not a hole on Honey Creek. The cold, spring-fed expanse of water lay so clear and still that its surface was a mirror, solid and flawless, a second sky inside it, a hawk artfully circling.

Looking Glass Gap lay on the other side, far away. Forbidden. I'd already decided to swim across to it, to see the place I'd read about. The place where a magical portal could whisk you away from all the troubles of this world and into the arms of a protector. Nathaniel, a guardian, a Time Shifter, was nothing like the hard men I'd known. His unbreakable, gentle, desperate love for Anna, a mere mortal, was the sort of thing I wanted to believe in.

"Daddy'll git the rod after ye-ew," Marah Diane drawled, a mild speech impediment making the words slow and thick as molasses. "Ye'll git it good. 'He that committeth sin is of the devil, for the devil sinneth from the beginnin'.'"

"It's only water." The fringes glided cool and sweet around my feet as I stepped in.

"Yew can make yer own trouble. I don' care," Marah Diane shouted. "Sinner!"

I swam out until I was far enough away that my sister's words couldn't reach me. Daddy couldn't reach me. No one could. Rolling onto my back, I looked at the sky and watched the hawk and felt free. Finally.

And then something was pulling me down, dragging me beneath the surface. I could see the air but not breathe it, scream but make no sound, reach but touch nothing solid.

Staring at the log beams overhead, I waited for my heartbeat to settle, my mind tossing through the basket of past and present, sorting scraps.

At thirteen, I'd become the one responsible for laundry and supervision and helping to put meals on the table. We'd moved from the little trailer down the road and settled into my grandparents' house so Momaw Leena could help watch us. With my grandfather gone on to glory only months after my mother disappeared, there was space in the house, but no space in my grandmother's heart. We were still tainted goods. Our mother's children. Burdensome things.

Always, in the dream, my siblings were with me, and always Marah Diane scolded against taking those first steps away. And always I finally did it . . . I left them behind, all five of them. Always just when I tasted the first honeysuckle drops of freedom, something grabbed me and pulled me down. Down from the sky, beneath the water, through the ground, where the soil closed over my head like the quicksand in the movies I'd seen only occasionally at school, because we didn't have TV at home.

Always the dreams ended in terrifying, painful, certain death. Exactly what we had all been promised, should we turn away from the ways of Lane's Hill.

It bothered me that the dream was back this morning, that it could propel me from my bed, gasping, even now.

Tossing off the quilt, I stood, then looked around the cabin in the dim morning light. There wasn't much to the place. No doubt it had been built as a fisherman's shack at some time in the past. The main footprint was no more than thirty by thirty. A peaked roof and a small sleeping loft perched over one end, reachable only by a pine-post ladder.

After arriving last night and finding the key in the mailbox at the end of the dirt-trail driveway, I'd slept downstairs on the pull-out sofa without even bothering to open it. I was a little afraid of what the mattress underneath might look like. The sofa was ancient, a harvest-gold-and-brown-plaid Early American style that appeared to have hosted many a fisherman.

The place did have an incredible view, though. Through the pines, the water glistened, as alluring now as it had been last night with the moonlight reflecting against its surface. Looking Glass Lake was as beautiful as Evan Hall had described it in his books, as magical as he'd made it seem. Even though this place was less than an hour's drive from the farm where I'd grown up, I'd never seen it, other than through the words in his books. As a teenager, I'd imagined it many times, but to ask to come here would've been to admit that I'd been reading Time Shifters, and that would have brought swift and certain retribution. Even Wilda Culp wouldn't have approved of my new fascination. Not when I had her vast library of classics at my fingertips.

Outside the cabin, my loaner car looked bedraggled. The washed-out driveway was an adventure in itself. Judging by the condition of the route in, no one had been here in a while. The furniture seemed too well-worn for a rental, and the bulbs in the overhead fixture, high in the eaves near the loft, were burned out. I'd found my way around last night by the dim glow of a floor lamp built from deer antlers stacked around a metal pipe.

This morning, the natural sun was more than adequate, its rays pink and amber as it crept over the mountains on the opposite side of the lake. Down in the gap like this, the hours of direct light would be few, the towns having a cloak of shadow and mist that lent itself to stories of ghosts and haints, and Spearfinger, the Cherokee witch who tempted precocious children away and then ate their livers. The lake felt like a place where Evan Hall's famed race of alien Time Shifters might hide the secret portals through which they warped the fabric of time and space, ever waging war with the Dark Ones. Whatever lay beneath the water would be perfectly concealed by the reflection of trees, sky, and rock bluffs laced with silver ribbons of falling water.

The paintings on the cabin walls recorded the lake in different seasons—the shore and trees sprinkled with snow in the winter, dogwoods and redbuds blooming in the spring, leaves ablaze with color in the autumn. I leaned close to one, glanced out the window, then looked at the canvas again. The view was the same. The painting had been done from here. And done very well. It was nice artwork.

The artist's name lay tucked in the bottom corner amid umber and crimson leaves piled next to an abandoned garden rake. *H. Hall.*

A relative of Evan Hall's, perhaps? Could I possibly be so lucky?

Hard to say. *Hall* wasn't exactly uncommon. Still, there could be a connection. . . .

Friday awakened, yawned, and stretched, watching me from his new favorite chair as I rummaged through the cabin, looking for contact information for the owner, hoping for clues. Hollis hadn't given me any details.

"'Lo-o-o the house." The echo of a voice wound through the window sashes, both surprising me and transporting me in time. In the backwoods, you never approached someone's place without first calling out to make sure you were welcome. A breach of protocol might result in a rifle fired your way, or worse yet, directly *at* you. Where marijuana patches lay hidden among corn crops, meth labs proliferated, and distilling moonshine and strawberry brandy remained a matter of both pride and commerce, people lived in seclusion for a reason. They had secrets to keep.

Friday went on high alert as I crossed to the door and stepped out, still in my sweats with a twisty ball of hair stuck atop my head. A man was walking up from the lake. His face, other than the point of a long, shaggy salt-and-pepper beard, lay hidden in the shadow of his worn brown hat. Coming out of the mist with the dampened light behind him, he seemed to rise from the water itself.

Standing on the porch, shivering in my stocking feet and the single layer of clothing, I waited for him to approach. He didn't meet my eyes as he ascended the steps but instead seemed to watch me from the corners of his vision. Not an uncommon habit around here, but one Miss Wilda Culp had been determined I would leave behind.

*Backward,* she'd called it. *Do not apologize for yourself, Jennia Beth Gibbs. A woman must walk into the world with confidence, and if she can never do it, she is never more than a girl. Look people in the eye when you speak.*

The man on the porch stood several feet away, uncertain of me. Friday moved into position between us, his back arched, a low growl jiggling his fat rolls.

"Friday, hush." He ignored me, of course.

"Everythin' ar'ty the cabin? Anythin' you be a-needin'?"

My mind took a moment to translate. The old-timer-speak here in the Blue Ridge was its own music, a pidgin of crammed-together and alternative words recognizable only if you knew the place.

"It's all good. I found the key in the mailbox, no problem. Thanks for checking." I heard it, then, the slight twang at the end of the sentence, the stretching of the words, a small step toward homecoming.

He glanced upward, just a flash of gray-blue eyes against swarthy skin and dark eyebrows. I thought of all that I'd read about

Melungeons. Could he be one? Had I ever *known* a Melungeon? According to my reading, most had eventually been pushed farther west toward Tennessee, but some had stayed, hidden their ancestry among the dust of family secrets, claimed to be Creole French or Spanish. No doubt Melungeon blood ran deep in these mountains of western North Carolina, the place where the first European explorers discovered strange blue-eyed people already living in log-house villages in 1654.

"Been a-told t' see after ya." The tone conveyed more than words. He wasn't happy to be visiting with me. "Miz Hall gott'er a busy day up to the shop, what wit' all the crazies come round town." Another glance came my way, a little longer this time, an obvious assessment. He was trying to decide if I was one of the crazies.

"I didn't know I was hitting such a busy week. Did you say she has a shop in town? I'd like to thank her for the use of the cabin. I get the impression it isn't normally rented out."

The artist's signature was still in the back of my mind, *H. Hall.* This was as good a place to start as any.

"She don't norm'ly lend it. Nope."

"So you look after the place for her, then?"

"Do thangs she needs did. Gardenin', most-time. Tend the root places."

I nodded, understanding about the root places. My grandmother had them—locations in the woods shown to her by her mother and grandmother. Hidden spaces where ginseng root, wintergreen, black cohosh, and other medicinals grew. Things that could be eaten, traded, sold, or used to treat ailments. Even today, ginseng root was as good as mountain money, and good ginseng slopes were painstakingly guarded from poachers—protected with guns, mantraps, and dogs.

My grandmother never told anyone where her treasure troves

were. As the oldest girl, the secrets would have been mine when I married and started a family of my own. Perhaps now the root places belonged to Marah Diane. Perhaps she gathered wild goods, carried them to town on trade days, and bartered for things her family needed. Barter was more common than cold, hard cash around Lane's Hill and Towash.

I was struck again by how far this place was from New York City. The other side of the world. Or a different world altogether. In the city, you'd never walk into someone's place of business and offer up a handful of dirt-covered roots to pay your bill. In Towash, you'd do it without thinking twice.

"Can you tell me which shop is Ms. Hall's?"

He seemed reluctant to say but finally offered, "Be the med'cine shop. Mountain Leaf."

"Thanks, I'll go by there."

He turned to leave the porch, and Friday advanced a step, nipping the air behind the man's pant leg. I reached down and scooped up the dog as the caretaker paused on the steps, turning back to me. "Anythin' more you be a-needin' here?"

"Lightbulbs, whenever you get a chance. It's not an emergency or anything, though. Just . . . if you think about it."

"Git by here again, on up'n the mornin', if I can. See after it."

"I probably won't be around. Should I leave the key in the box? I have business to take care of in town."

"Miz Hall tol' me." He held up a key to show me he had his own.

"She did?" I hadn't anticipated this at all. What exactly had Hollis said to persuade the cabin's owner to rent it to me? How much had she revealed?

"Said you's one a them writin' people. He don' talk at none a ya. Been crossed thataway oncet too many times."

My pulse sped up. The cat was out of the bag—not only out of the bag, but roaming freely around Evan Hall's hometown, apparently.

There was no choice but to go forward now. "My being here has nothing to do with Time Shifters or Warrior Week or anything like that, I promise you. I just need to meet with him for ten minutes. I have something very important to discuss, and when he knows what it is, I think he'll want to talk with me. Do you have any idea how I can get in touch with him? He's welcome to call me on my cell . . ."

"He don' talk to folks." The man was off my porch and headed toward his boat before I could stop him. "Leave it lay, be best."

"Can you at least tell him I'm here and all I want to do is speak with him for a few minutes?" My voice echoed toward the water, too loud for early morning. "He can reach me here at the cabin. That is, if the phone in there works. Does the phone work?"

The caretaker didn't answer, only climbed into his boat and cast off, the lower part of his form disappearing first, then his head and shoulders fading incrementally into the haze until he was gone altogether.

I set Friday down, and he ran yapping and snarling across the yard all the way to the shore, vanishing into the fog.

The caretaker's unceremonious exit wasn't a confidence builder, but I had, at least, gained a bit of information. Clearly the man was acquainted with Evan Hall, and clearly Ms. Hall knew why I was here, more or less, and she'd chosen to rent this cabin to me anyway. That was a good sign.

"Friday?" I whispered into the damp morning air, but no response came. "Friday, where are you?"

Again, no reply, and a vague uneasiness niggled. The woods could be dangerous for small pets. Bobcats and black bears wandered into yards looking for easy meals, even just a few miles from town like this. On occasion in Towash, black bear sightings had shut down recess when I was a kid. There was no telling what kind of trouble a city dog could get into around here. Friday's idea of wild space was a fenced half-acre dog park.

"Frida-a-a-y!" I called more loudly, conscious of the fact that, even though I couldn't see them through the trees, there were other cabins within earshot. I'd noticed lights and driveways, coming in last night.

Friday didn't reappear, so I grabbed my tennis shoes and started to the lake, the fog seeming to part and close around my knees as I moved closer to the rushes along the shore. The image of a weathered dock and an old red canoe melted into view.

"Friday . . ." I felt like an actress in a horror movie, inching toward certain disaster. "Friday, are you out here?"

Maybe he'd circled back to the cabin. . . .

"Friday?"

Suddenly there he was, bolting my way with his ears and tail tucked, his eyes white-rimmed with terror. Behind him, the reeds swirled and bent, forming a miniature tornado. Something black and gray and angry was hot on his heels. Bear? Bobcat? Dog? Deer?

. . . or a full-grown Canada goose. It burst from cover, wings outstretched, and it was fighting mad.

Friday veered around me at the last minute, and so did the goose, the two of them brushing by on either side before I could scramble after them. We played a strange game of tag, in and out of the trees, around and around the car, me trying to shoo the goose away, the goose nipping and pecking at Friday, Friday yipping and growling, and me zigzagging in and out of the fray, waving my arms and yelling, "Hey, stop! Shoo!

Shoo! Friday, come here! No . . . wait! Just . . . Shoo . . . Fri
. . . Stop! Ouch!"

Finally Friday and I grazed past each other, going opposite
directions. I scooped him up like a fumbled football and dashed
for the cabin with the goose flapping its wings and nipping at
my sweats. Taking the porch steps in one giant leap, I left our
pursuer behind long enough to get in the door and slam it shut,
saving life and limb, if not dignity.

Friday wiggled free, attacking the door with gusto while the
goose pecked the other side, and I threw my head back, letting laughter come. I hadn't been chased by a goose in years.
Grabbing my phone, I snapped a photo of Friday on the inside,
then ran to the front window, took a picture of the goose on
the outside, and sent both to Jamie with one line of text. **Goose
attack. Survived.**

Jamie's response was a smiley face followed by a complaint
that I hadn't let her know I'd safely arrived last night. We texted
back and forth while Friday guarded the door and I made ready
for the day, hurrying through cleaning up and dressing in a pair
of black jeans and a loose-fitting yellow blouse that was simple
enough for casual wear, but dressy enough for business . . . just
in case I happened to have the chance to do any today. I finished
it off with my tall black boots, then stood in front of the mirror.
Basic, understated. Nothing flashy.

The outfit would probably blend in well enough around
town.

"All right, Friday, now the question is . . . what do I do about
you?" I stood looking at him, debating. Back in New York, he
stayed alone in the apartment for hours on end. Other than an
occasional walk, he didn't need, want, or relish company.

But here? He'd already tried to claw his way through the door.

What if he destroyed the place while I was gone? Aside from that, I didn't have anything to feed him for breakfast.

"Okay, listen." I grabbed the leash and shook it at him. "I'm taking you with me, but I want no shenanigans. None. Do you hear me?"

Friday lifted his chin, exposing the collar among his chub bundles, surprisingly cooperative. Maybe he was worried about the goose coming back. Maybe he was just looking forward to an adventure. Hard to say.

"No letting stinkers in the rental car, no threatening strangers, no attacking other dogs. We're trying to blend in around here. Just a couple tourists. Got it?"

Friday didn't answer, but no sooner had we made it to our vehicle, bumped and scratched our way up the driveway, and started toward town than I realized that our chances of fitting in around Looking Glass Gap this week were nil. We hadn't even made it to the outskirts before we passed a Confederate soldier driving a golf cart, waved at a mountain man on a horse, and spied a guy up ahead who looked for all the world like Mel Gibson in *Braveheart*. He was directing traffic. In a kilt. Cars were waiting to pass by him and descend into what looked like a makeshift campground in a patch of bottomland on the way to Looking Glass Gap.

This was the famous Warrior Week encampment. The festivities below seemed to be a cross between a grown-up costume party, a Renaissance festival, a flea market, and a county fair. Tents, horse trailers, cars, motor homes, and campers of all vintages dotted the entire meadow and faded into the woods. In the center of camp near what looked like a jousting ring, open-air vendors offered everything from movie memorabilia and psychic readings to fried crawfish baskets and fresh-squeezed lemonade.

I was tempted to pull in. After all, it was still early. The stores in town might not even be open yet. Aside from that, a parking lot manned by a guy in a kilt was the sort of thing a person shouldn't miss. It would be worth the small delay, in story value if nothing else. I had a feeling this adventure might rival the Tom Brandon tale in the end.

The idea grew more tempting as I inched closer to the front of the line. When I reached the decision point, I couldn't help veering off the highway, offering up the three-dollar parking fee, getting my hand stamped, and asking Braveheart if I could take his picture. He was kind enough to strike a pose.

I sent the photo off to Jamie along with a caption: **We have arrived!**

It was a shame she couldn't see the camp for herself. The place was oddly alluring . . . fascinating, even. Friday seemed to think so too. He stood perched with his paws on the window, watching the goings-on and salivating at the scent of corn dogs, roast turkey legs, and fried onions. I'd never seen him so openly enthusiastic about anything. He passed a cheery look my way when I chuckled at what looked like a *Hunger Games* enthusiast strolling alongside a woman in a Victorian day dress.

"I dunno, Friday, I'm pretty sure we're not just visiting Looking Glass, we've fallen through one." Friday growled in agreement, and I was glad I hadn't left him in the cabin. It would've been a shame for him to miss this, and looking out the window into the fray, I had a feeling I was about to need either confirmation or backup. I wasn't sure which.

# Chapter 11

"Those are for LARPing. We got other ones down there that are the real thing, like if you're gonna actual *go* through a portal." The girl in the woodland elf costume was filled with information. She couldn't have been more than thirteen, a kid clinging to the last vestiges of childhood, seemingly playing dress-up while working behind a vendor table. Her gray-green eyes took me in from beneath flyaway shocks of brown hair that looked like it hadn't been combed in a week.

"Excuse me?" I staggered sideways as Friday body-slammed my leg, then hooked his little claws on my boots and did a surprisingly good imitation of a spider monkey. His eyes were on the foot-long smoked-sausage-and-pancake-batter corn dog that flouted every cardinal rule of the *Eat Healthy for Life* books I'd edited last year. "Friday, stop it!" I shook him off, then pinched another piece of the corn dog and dropped it on the ground to settle him down.

"What's . . . LARPing?"

The girl sighed, discerning that she had a newbie on her hands—someone perhaps not very likely to buy the merchandise. "LARP, like, *live-action role-play?*"

*Live. Action. Role. Play.* I turned the words over in my mind, tried to mesh them with the fascinating yet weirdly bemusing things I'd seen since paying at the front gate. For the most part, the goings-on looked like family fun, and it was sweet, really—mothers, grandmothers, and granddaughters dressed in costumes they'd created together, a twentysomething couple with plans to marry in the camp, confused fathers in street clothes tailing wide-eyed teenage daughters, here for the first time. A dream trip with Dad. I couldn't help envying that bonding experience.

I'd made it to the vendor area, where items of all sorts were being offered in front of RVs and travel trailers like the one manned by the elf child. Several smaller kids scampered about behind her table—a princess girl, a boy in some sort of tunic and tights, and a tiny fairy barely old enough to toddle, her soiled wings made from clothes hangers and colored panty hose. Wings of all types hung on a sale rack nearby.

"I can give you a discount on them wings if you get two pair. Like, one for you and one for the dog? We got dog wings too." The girl braced a hand on her hip. "It's all about findin' you a role . . . like, *becomin'* somebody else, while you're here at the camp. LARP, I mean."

A massive bluetick hound tackled the baby. Friday barked and tried to crawl under the table, taking the leash, my arm, and the corn dog with him. The elf girl paused to rescue her tiny sister, and Friday started a scrap-scarfing contest with the hound. They met over the sausage, which Friday wasn't about to relinquish.

"I gotta give him a A-plus for attitude. He don't know he's a

Chi-weenie dog, does he?" the little salesgirl observed. "He looks like that ain't his first corn dog, neither."

"He has a slow metabolism . . . and he's big-boned." I let go of the leash. Friday wouldn't run off with food around. "Well . . . so . . . what determines whether something will . . . go through the portal or not?" Now I regretted that I hadn't taken time to brush up on Time Shifters details, other than just comparing bits of the writing and watching movie scenes on the Internet.

The girl sighed, now seeming more tweenager and less role-play aficionado. "Okay, so, here's how it is. Stuff don't go through a portal unless it's right for the time period. That's why guns're a problem, sometimes even antique guns, if they been refurbed with modern parts. That was in Time Shifters #3—*The Curse of the Black Drake*? So my dad takes all of ours apart and checks for them things. The LARPing stuff is different. It's just for show, so it don't matter, long's it looks right. It won't go through a portal, but not everybody's into actual travelin'. Lotta people are just here to live it for a few days, you know?"

"That makes sense." Not really. "So have you ever *been* through a portal?" Was this poor kid being raised by people who really believed there were time-travel devices hidden in the Blue Ridge?

She rolled a look, indicating that one of us was woefully misguided. "No, but if you wanna give it a try, I can get you a twenty . . . five . . . twenty-*five* percent discount on anythin' on the costume tables. Early-bird special. This mornin' only. Once my daddy gets up, I can't give this kinda deals." The baby wandered by with a dirt clod in her mouth, and her big sister paused to slap it away. "Stop it, Arlie. Don't put stuff in your mouth. Becca, you're supposed to be watchin' her!"

My emotions ricocheted unexpectedly. I could remember *being* this girl. I'd started minding my father's table at swap meets before I was ten years old. No fairy costumes were involved, but like this family, we sold whatever we could make, grow, or come up with. Knives handcrafted from scrap steel were a specialty.

"Really, I'm just window-shopping." I felt guilty saying it—as if I should buy LARPing equipment or some princess hats, just to be nice. My sisters' kids would probably like the dress-up goods. But in reality, I still hadn't even opened Coral Rebecca's letter, much less decided whether to admit I was nearby.

Now, watching this twelve-year-old manage her parents' brood, I didn't think I could stand to make contact with my sisters. I felt bad for this little girl already, and she wasn't even kin to me. If I saw my sisters' eyes looking up from that face, it'd be unbearable.

A family, obviously suburbanites from up north someplace, approached the display of fairy wings, and I took advantage of the opportunity to exit the scene. I'd dallied around the encampment long enough. The stores in town would be open by now, and with any luck, I'd find Ms. Hall. Fingers crossed that this produced something, but I had a feeling that, after all the non-responses so far, getting through to Evan Hall wouldn't be so easy.

Finding the Mountain Leaf store turned out to be simple enough, though. It lay a short drive from the encampment, in an old two-story corner building downtown, under a massive carved marble header that read *E. B. Hall 1860.*

Edward Bartholomew Hall. I'd learned enough Time Shifters trivia to know that name. After constructing this building for his young bride, then leaving to fight in the War between the States, the real E. B. Hall had disappeared. But there was, among the most die-hard fans, a rumor that Evan Hall was, in reality, two hundred years old and his own ancestor—E. B. Hall himself. A time traveler who had come through a portal and become hung up in time in Looking Glass Gap.

Studying the name on the granite corner plate now, I felt fiction and reality colliding. This place looked like something from Evan Hall's books. The building was solid stone, the relief ornately fashioned. A pair of massive gargoyles guarded the carved marble corners overhead. Clearly there had been money in the Hall family for many generations, yet only a small, fifties-vintage lit sign marked the structure's purpose now. *Mountain Leaf Pharmacy*, it read, and below that in smaller letters, *Prescription Service, Herbs, Natural Medicines, Cards, and Gifts*.

On the window, the words *Local Handicrafts, Handmade Soaps, Candles* had been chalked in using curvy letters with little circles on the end points, the way a teenager might sign a sweetheart note.

I parked in the shade around the block and left Friday sleeping off his breakfast corn dog.

A number of people were in the shop when I entered. About half wore historical costumes and half were in bystander clothes, like me. The same mixture moved past the picture window in front, giving the sun-drenched street the look of a somewhat off-kilter Dickens Christmas village.

I wandered around the shop, collecting soaps and other things that would fit into my suitcase—all apparently formulated right here in the store. By the pharmacy counter, there was also a small case of natural remedies that local people would have used. Ginseng, sassafras root, spicebush, sweet birch, catnip, mint, witch hazel, wild cherry bark, yellow root. No doubt the locals avoided town like the plague during Warrior Week, unless they had to work. The teenager running the counter up front was obviously from "the Gap," as she referred to it while sharing information with tourists. The woman working behind the pharmacy cash register was in her seventies at least, her speech beautifully laced with a faint English brogue.

The pharmacist dangled a prescription bottle out the window and said, "Here's that Amoxil prescription, Miz Hall."

"I got it, Aunt Helen," a little girl at a table behind the pharmacy counter volunteered. Perhaps ten or eleven years old, she looked like the photos of Evan Hall. Dark hair, blue eyes, olive skin. His daughter? Did he have children? His movie-star wife had left him years ago, after only a short marriage. She was persona non grata with the Time Shifters fans, even now.

I made my way to the counter and waited until Mrs. Hall was done with her customer, then introduced myself and finished with, "I'm the one staying in the rental cottage."

"Oh, the reporter," she answered. "Well, I'm Helen Hall. Good to meet you." Her smile widened, creases forming along the rounded lines of her cheeks. She had the earthy look of a woman who spent a great deal of time outdoors—as if she might have personally tried each of the colorful gardening hats hanging on the front rack. Unlike the girl, she was fair skinned and freckled.

"Editor," I corrected. "From Vida House Publishing in New York."

Gray brows knotted behind her thick rainbow-rimmed glasses. Angling her face upward slightly, she gave me a confused look. "Oh . . . I thought the woman who booked the cabin told my sister-in-law you were here working on a story, something about the lake . . . But to tell you the truth, the rental agents aren't supposed to have people call Violet anymore. She's not doing well lately." Shrugging, she snatched a stray pen from the counter and dropped it into the cup nearby. "Maybe Violet did say *editor*. These silly wireless phones. I can't hear worth a flip on them, anyway. That's what happens when you get old. Can't hear, can't see, and your boobs sag. It's not for the faint of heart."

"Aunt Helen!" the little girl squealed, wide-eyed. "Sheesh!"

A spit of laughter escaped me, and I decided immediately that I liked Helen Hall. "The cabin is in a wonderful spot. I enjoyed the view this morning."

"You can swim there in the summertime." The girl moved closer, intent on joining the conversation. "And the canoe's fun too. It leaks once you get in it, but Uncle Clive and me took it out the other day and we didn't sink. The goose there, that's Horatio. He lives under the shed. He likes bread if you got any. He keeps the snakes away, but he's kind of a little sh—"

"That's enough, Hannah." Helen cast a warning look her way. "Finish your science homework before your dad comes for you."

"Oh-kay," Hannah sighed and rolled her eyes, then returned to her schoolbooks.

Helen cast a concerned, slightly sad look her way before turning back to me. "Violet's cousin, Clive, looks after the place. Did he stop by this morning to see if you needed anything? The cabin hasn't been rented in a while. We only offer it up when the real estate people have someone reliable. It's been in the family for years. Don't want any of these party animals booking it and parking twenty campers in the yard."

"No parties, I promise. Just me and my dog, Friday. I hope that's not a problem. He's housebroken and he doesn't chew on things. He wasn't supposed to be coming . . . Well, long story. Anyway, he's harmless, although he did have a little altercation with Horatio, the goose. And yes, a man did stop by and check on me this morning." *He didn't exactly seem thrilled that I was there.* "Everything's fine at the cabin, other than a few lightbulbs. He said he'd replace those."

"Good. You have four-wheel drive, I guess? The trip down the hill can be a challenge."

"Actually, no, but I made it."

A concerned look came my way. "If a rain rolls in, be sure to park up at the mailbox and walk down, just to be safe."

"Thanks, I'll remember that. Maybe it won't rain while I'm here."

Her reply came with a sly smile. "You must not plan to be here very long." I understood the inside joke. Water practically seeped from the air around here. "It's a shame you're not a writer. The cottage is a wonderful place for writers. My nephew used to work there on occasion."

Suddenly the door seemed to be swinging open wide.

"So this is a vacation for you?" Mrs. Hall was still trying to figure me out. Clearly her sister-in-law hadn't gotten all the details from Hollis.

"Working trip," I answered.

She drew back, her chin folding into her neck. "You picked a strange week to come."

I fumbled for the best way to get around to my reason for being here. Could this woman secure five minutes in a room with Evan Hall? Would she even be willing to try? "To tell you the truth, the timing sort of picked me. Something ended up on my desk a week ago, a manuscript. Just a partial—the first three chapters. I flew here to find out more about it."

"Oh? Does the author live here, then?" Now she was watching me through the wary eyes of a deer deciding whether to enter an open field or bolt for the woods.

"I hope so. According to the postmark, the package came from here."

"What's the author's name? Maybe I can help you with directions or a phone number. I know just about everyone in the county. Been here since I fell in love with a sailor and moved inland in '53."

I paused a minute, measuring my next words. This was it, the great reveal. My one chance. "The truth is, I don't know. There was no identifying information with the submission, or if there was information, it had been lost."

"And you flew cross-country to find the author? That isn't normal procedure, I suspect. . . ." The front windows reflected against her glasses, partially obscuring the further narrowing of her eyes, but not the shift in posture, the drawing away.

"The story was special," I admitted. "And . . . well . . . the fact is . . . I wonder if it may have been written by . . . Evan Hall." Was it my imagination, or had the mention of that name turned heads all over the pharmacy, even though I was trying to keep it quiet?

The little girl at the table shifted her focus to me. Helen took the time to redirect her to her homework. I suspected that was a stall tactic.

Helen's face was a mask of sympathy when she returned. "I'm afraid you're on a wild-goose chase. It couldn't be from him. It's a shame, what with all the talent he has, but my nephew hasn't written a thing since he got out from under that legal mess with Time Shifters, and truly, I doubt he ever will again."

It was now or never. At least she hadn't thrown me out yet. "This manuscript is twenty years old."

She increased the distance between us even farther. "Well, now *that's* quite the story." An incredulous frown came my way, and she focused on my hand, curled around my purse strap. I realized she was looking at the stamp that'd been put there when I'd entered the Warrior Weekend campground.

"I'm not one of *them*," I rushed. "I mean, I read some of the books when I was a teenager, but this doesn't have anything to do with Time Shifters. This manuscript was written before that." I was losing her, and fast. I'd made enough deals to know when one was going south. Crossed arms had replaced the welcoming look. She'd decided I was some kind of a stalker . . . or a nut. "I just . . . Look, I stuck my neck way out to come here, but sometimes I run across a story, and I know it needs to be told. I really . . ." Another customer had moved into line behind me. My time was up. "*The Story Keeper*. It's about two young people trapped in the mountains around 1890. Rand and Sarra?" I blurted. "Does any of that ring a bell at all?"

Her lips parted slightly, then pursed, a flash of some emotion quickly vanishing. Had she recognized something?

"Not that I can say." Her arms knotted more tightly over her chest, forming an impenetrable barricade. "And please don't go trying to sneak onto Evan's place to find him like the rest of these yahoos, either. My sister-in-law, his grandmother, isn't well. The sheriff was out there again yesterday, dragging away people who'd shinnied the fence, thinking to find time portals. Evan just wants to be left alone. He has a right to his privacy."

My desperation flared. This was falling apart faster than I could rake it back together. "I'm not here to cause trouble for him. I promise . . . Please just listen to—"

"I have customers." She looked past me to the person next in line. "Yes, Elmira. I have your prescription right here."

I had a vision of my whole future tumbling off a cliff. What would happen if I went back to Vida House empty-handed, a blind-swing strikeout on a bad pitch? Would I even have a job, and if I did, how would I ever reestablish credibility? By now, word of this far-fetched trip was undoubtedly circulating. My new coworkers probably thought George Vida and I had gone round the bend together.

But beyond that, there was a deeper sense of loss. Until now, I hadn't really allowed myself to believe that I might fail to pull this one off, that I might never know the rest of Rand and Sarra's story. Grief struck with sudden power—as if someone were dying right in front of me, and I couldn't do anything to stop it.

"Thank you for talking with me." I sidestepped to take my purchases up front. The homework girl watched intently, startled by the reversal of the conversational mood. I doubted that Helen Hall gave visitors the bum's rush very often.

"Oh, I'm not in any hurry," the woman next in line offered. "You can ring her up back here, Helen."

"We're finished, Elmira," Helen said flatly.

I glanced up, and Elmira eyed me quizzically. Before I knew what was happening, I was in sixth-grade English class watching those stern lips form a thin line as she looked over her shoulder, the chalk still dangling next to her name on the board.

"Mrs. *Penberthy*?" She hadn't changed a bit. Perhaps she'd aged a little, but she was a memory come to life. When I was twelve, she'd figured out that I hated reading because I couldn't *see*. She was the one who'd arranged an eye exam and secured glasses from the Lions Club after no one at home took care of it.

Her mental catalog was still as sharp as ever. "Why . . . Jennia Beth Gibbs. Good heavens, child! Look at you. I haven't heard a thing of you in years. How are you, sweet one?" She opened her arms, and within moments I went from abject rejection to the embrace of the eternally beloved. I would never forget everything Mrs. Penberthy had done for me, and how she'd stood up to my father and threatened to report to child services if *anything* happened to the eyeglasses he thought I didn't need.

"I'm good." The same scent still wafted from her—dressing powder, old lace, and cats. I closed my eyes and took it in.

"You're *well*," she corrected.

"Yes, very well, thank you." That was what she'd taught us to say. Etiquette lessons came with sixth-grade English in Towash. Heaven knows, some of us needed them.

"That's my girl." The praise fell over me like fairy dust, just as it always had. Before Wilda Culp, there'd been Mrs. Penberthy. The first person I'd ever seen brave enough to give my father what for.

She shuffled me to one side of the pharmacy counter, still sandwiching my chin between her cool, bone-thin hands. "Oh, sweetness, tell me where you've been. You do know that Wilda Culp passed some years ago? She was so proud of you. Her son passed as well, but only recently. He survived with all the medical troubles much longer than anyone thought he would."

"Yes, I knew . . . about Wilda, I mean, not about Richard." Shame crept over me. I hadn't come home for Wilda's funeral. I didn't have the money or any way of getting here at the time, but that wasn't really the reason. I wanted to keep pretending she was still living in that big house on Honey Creek, and as long as I never saw her body in the coffin, I could. I didn't have to be alone in the world again.

"And what are you doing now? What's brought you back home?"

"I'm an editor at Vida House Publishing in New York." I was conscious of both Helen Hall and Hannah tracking our conversation from behind the pharmacy counter. "I came here to see about a manuscript, actually."

Mrs. Penberthy caught a breath. "Oh. Oh, my, how interesting that must be! And how wonderful. I'm so very proud of you. You always were a smart little thing. Such a hard worker. I knew you'd go far."

"Thank you, Mrs. Penberthy. I don't think I ever told you this, but . . ." Tears prickled and I swallowed hard to keep them down. "But you made such a difference to me. To a lot of us."

A wink and a secret smile answered. "Oh, I knew, sweet. A good teacher can see it. No one has to tell her."

She hugged me again, then held me away, her expression growing more somber. "I thought you might have come home because of your father." Her concern was obvious, and I knew, because I knew Mrs. Penberthy, that it wasn't concern for my father as much as concern for how the family connections might drag me under. She understood the difficult scenarios of kinship and poverty all too well. "That accident seems to have caused him quite a bit of trouble."

"Accident?" The question was hanging in the air before I thought about how much it revealed in terms of our current family dynamics. I had no idea my father had been in an accident, much less a serious one.

Mrs. Penberthy began to speak, stopped, began again. "His arm . . . the one he almost lost in the hay mower?" She was trying to be polite now. Undoubtedly, she could tell I was completely confused. "My daughter teaches at Towash Elementary. She has one of your sister's little girls in her class. Sounds as if the man's lucky he didn't die of the infection in the hospital. It's been hard on the family and a long time getting the arm to heal. He won't listen to the doctors or cooperate with any therapy, of course." Her opinion of my father peppered the tone.

An awkward conversational pause descended, neither of us knowing what to say next. Guilt struck quickly, a skillful and ravenous hunter. No doubt this was why Coral Rebecca had sent the second letter. When an entire family is surviving on the ragged edge—this one borrowing from that one, then asking from the next one—the circle of dependence forms a lopsided card castle just waiting to be toppled by an unexpected wind.

"But enough of that." Mrs. Penberthy sought a graceful exit, gripping my upper arms as if to prop me like a scarecrow. "It is so very lovely to see you, Jennia Beth, and congratulations on all of your success. It does an old teacher's heart good. It certainly does. We always hold hope, but so much of the time we never know."

I realized suddenly that, all those years ago while Mrs. Penberthy was facing down my father, she was committing more effort to me than I could've possibly guessed. For no specific reason, other than her own beautiful spirit, she'd decided I was worth saving.

The tears pressed again. "Thank you, Mrs. Penberthy. That means a lot."

"It's Elmira. You're all grown up now. You've earned the privilege."

"It wouldn't seem right." I hugged her again, and both of us laughed before she stepped up to the pharmacy counter.

I was once again aware of Helen Hall and Hannah nearby. No telling what they'd made of the whole dialogue. Hannah and I exchanged glances as I started toward the front counter. I smiled, trying to reassure her.

Helen Hall caught me just before I turned the corner to the greeting card aisle. "I'll do what I can. If there's any possibility, I'll call you. We have your cell phone number on the rental paperwork, I'm sure." Still holding Mrs. Penberthy's prescription, she slid her fingers contemplatively along the edge. "But I can't make promises."

# Chapter 12

## The Story Keeper

### CHAPTER FOUR

Sarra waited for him to head toward camp so she could follow along behind. She'd trailed the younger one down to the water in the dark on purpose, keepin' close to him, but just shy of his reach. Seemed he was the most likely one to be different from Jep and the men they'd left trussed up like hogs back at the night camp. They'd used the slave irons on the boy, Revi, and left a bowie knife there aside of him. Whenever he did finally wake, he'd be some time sawin' through that saplin' tree to get hisself loose so's he could untie the others. Few days, mayhap.

She was free of that bunch for now, but could be she'd just swapped one boilin' pot for another. Somethin' about the old muleteer warned her agin trustin' him. She'd caught him watching her with eyes that burned, now that the moon'd sunk behind the hills and the full dark had made them stop till morn.

But this man—*Rand*, the muleteer'd called him as they fled with the wagon neath the moon glow—it was harder to say what sort was he. These last weeks, she'd come to wonder if any men were good. She didn't want one aback of her in the dark no matter who he was. It's the things aback of you, you had to fret over. You learnt that, fetchin' up in the mountains, or you didn't live long enough to learn nary a thing at all.

He stopped to let her by, waiting like she was a addled thing, a rabbit froze in the grass.

"Don't be afraid," he said. The words were meant for a comfort, but she knew better than to let them be that.

She didn't answer. She'd spoke not a word to neither man yet. Better they think she was a wild creature, a whiff of smoke, or a haint.

Straightening her back, she pulled her blanket closer to keep off the chill. Her body ached in every part, her ankles raw and swolt up from the leg irons, but she made herself move ahead of him on long strides, puttin' distance betwixt them as he lugged the water bucket for the mules and the saddle horse. There was no fire to show the way to camp. Only the dim lantern light. Enough to carry them through this night's last, long hours.

Enough for her to gather what she needed before sneakin' off— food from the wagon, a knife, a pistol if she could get it. One lay in the saddle poke on Rand's horse. She'd fare better if she took the horse, too, but a small bit of thievin' was bothersome enough, and a wrong thing. She wouldn't make it more by stealing the man's mount.

Still, home was far off. Even if she could find her way along the roads and the rivers, no tellin' if she'd ever reach it afoot. And Jep and his men would be loose soon enough. They'd come for her, mayhap with Brown Drigger's dogs, too.

Her hope went soft as she sat down by the lamp and tented the blanket round herself. Across the flame, the old man had tossed a gunnysack on the ground, laid hisself back agin it. He eyeballed her through half-closed lids. "You can talk, girl," he said. "I know you ain't gone mute."

She said nothing.

"You try'a put a hex on me, I'll cut yer eyeballs out." He took his knife from the scabbard and laid it on his chest. "I don't cotton to yer kind, y'hear? You be a looksome thang, but you ain't worth dyin' over. The tenderbelly there's got too much nobleness. Shoulda kilt 'em all and buried 'em where nobody'd find the bones. Now we got us trouble. And that daddy a yourn's out there someplace too."

She stared into the single flame, not looking his way nor toward the sound of Rand seein' after the horse. A chill sliced under the blanket, testing Aginisi's careful weave. Sarra tucked it over and under best she could, pretended it was Aginisi's broad, leather-thick hands sheltering her. She bent her head forward to rest on her knees, warming the hollow space with her own breath. Snow was building somewhere over the mountains. She could feel it.

She hoped not tonight nor in the morn, but it was comin'. Snow could change everything. It hid scents but kept tracks for all to find. Heavy snow would get you away, but a scattering like was apt to come this time of year, it'd lead the devil right to you.

The wagon tarp rustled. Metal clanked on metal, each sound pricking her mind, showing her how close by Rand was, how far off. Even through her cocoon, she heard him come to the lamp. The dull brush of his clothes and the near-silent scrape of his boots tugged her mind. He stopped aside her a minute. She didn't move, didn't breathe. He touched her shoulder. The muscle and sinew in her pulled tight, but she stopped short of flinching. She wouldn't let herself.

"Do you need anything?" he asked. "I can salve those wounds if you like. It'll ease the pain."

She didn't answer.

Somethin' fell soft over her then, somethin' heavy and frost-crisp from the night. Another blanket. She didn't grip it but just let it lie there, felt it cut the wind.

It'd been a long time since a kindness had come her way from a man's hand. Not since Gran-dey, with his white hair and round belly and the big voice that filled up the cabin. He was a Scotsman, so she knew it that all Scotsmen were good folk. Mayhap Rand was a Scotsman too, but there wasn't no way to know without askin'.

It'd been years since the time Gran-dey shed this world without warnin', his body death-still and so big and heavy it'd took Sarra and Aginisi and the mule, all three, to get him buried. Now she could see him again—mayhap her mind had gone trickish, but he was there with his thick white beard, takin' her to his knee to read from the Book— somethin' even Aginisi couldn't do. They'd all sit together, Aginisi and Mama and Sarra, and listen while Gran-dey told them words of places far off and people long gone, their deeds still remembered.

Those was fine times, when she was bitty, but they hurt too. Fine times do when they're gone away. Aginisi had told her that after Sarra's own mama was no more for this world.

*All things pass, suga' pea. All the things a this worl' got a time for bornin' and time for dyin', and a time for troublin' and a time for restin'.*

*Ssshhh . . . ,* Aginisi's voice whispered in her mind. *It's time for restin' now, child.*

❖

I stopped reading, looked up, and was almost surprised to find myself alone on the screened side porch of Helen Hall's cabin rather than in a makeshift mountain camp, hidden beneath a blanket as the moon fell behind the peaks and the inky-thick darkness of the early-morning hours set in. On Looking Glass Lake, evening had come as well. A bobcat screamed somewhere in the woods, lending to the illusion that I was living the story, in the body of that frightened, confused girl whose only hope lay with an out-of-place young man she wondered if she could trust.

I had absolutely no idea how this new piece of the manuscript—two complete chapters—had come to be waiting for me at the cabin when I'd returned after supper.

After leaving the pharmacy, I'd spent the day in town with my laptop, getting some work done at a coffee shop while Friday slept under the table and crowds of Time Shifters enthusiasts came and went. I'd hoped Helen Hall would call, and I'd be right down the street . . . just in case she had managed to set up a meeting. But the call never came. When the restaurant started filling up with evening diners, I'd eaten supper and then given up waiting.

The cabin seemed to be just as I had left it, dead lightbulbs and all. There were no tire tracks except the ones from my rental car, no clues as to who had been here. I'd thought at first that the manila envelope tucked between the screen and front door probably contained the rental bill.

*Well, not only does he not want to talk to me, but he's told her to kick me out. Great.* That's what had gone through my mind. It never entered my thought process that the very thing I'd come here for could be inside that envelope. More of *The Story Keeper,* the paper yellowed, the print a nonstandard font choice like the originals.

Wilda would've complained that the author did not know his business. She detested slapdash work and lack of preparation in writing and in life.

*A wise woman is always properly prepared. She understands the value of a job done to perfection. She knows that she must be fully capable of making her way independently in a man's world, Jennia Beth,* she'd said while tapping out the newspaper column she'd created to supplement her teaching income after finding herself alone with a son to raise. *It isn't what girls of my generation were reared to believe, but our reality is often a far stretch from the things we have dreamed. It is our ability to adapt that determines our survival.*

I turned back to the manuscript, wondering . . . If I found myself in the situation of the young girl in the story, would I have what it took to survive?

And did *she*?

# Chapter 13

## The Story Keeper

### CHAPTER FIVE

Rand rolled over slowly, his head throbbing as he struggled to part his eyelids and take in the day. The pain was intense. He pushed upright and tried to bring his mind to full reason. It was later than he'd anticipated, the sun pressing past the rock dome overhead and reaching toward their camp.

How odd that Ira hadn't roused him yet. Typically they departed at dawn each morning, eating only leftover corn pone or hardtack beef as their early meal.

He was cold . . . and sore . . .

A sweet scent cloyed him as a bit of loose cloth tumbled away from his face. He picked it up, smelled it, identified the odor immediately. Ether frolics were all the rage among the young set in Charleston. The scent of the substance was like nothing else. There was no mistaking it.

Memories rushed upon him, the previous day dashing through his mind, breakneck—Brown Drigger's cabin, the sudden and hasty departure, the pistol aimed his way on Ira's lap. Jep, Revi the boy, the other men, the girl in chains, her strange blue eyes, Grandfather's cross, the altercation, the flight from that place while there was moonlight enough . . .

Ira carried ether for sale, as did many merchants.

Rand staggered to his feet, stumbled in a circle, taking in what had been their encampment. The wagon space lay empty.

"No!" His voice was guttural, rage-filled. Furious, he kicked his sleeping pallet, swept it into the air. "You . . . you worthless old goat!"

He thought of the girl then, and fear struck him. Whirling unsteadily, he found her place empty, her woven blanket gone, along with the covering he'd given her. Only an imprint in the pine straw testified to the fact that she'd existed at all. Scanning the trees, he discovered her atop a boulder nearby, her skirt tucked up to allow her to bolt, her lean, narrow legs tightly coiled like a cat's.

She did not move but watched him carefully, her eyes seeming to glow against her olive skin. The swollen cheek had abated somewhat, so she studied him through both eyes now.

His first impulse on seeing her was anger. In less than a day since crossing his path, she'd caused his world to collapse, left him in ruin. Now here he stood in foreign country, dangerous country, on foot, alone, with pursuers perhaps trailing him already.

"The scurvy old lout has gone off!" Rand's head spun, still ether-laden, prompting him to trip over the blankets and fall. Scrambling forward on feet and palms, he labored toward the ridge. If he could just gain a glimpse of the wagon, he could run cross-country and chase it down. "Bristle-faced, foul-mouthed old . . . When I get my hands on you, I'll break your worthless neck. I'll yank off your ears and feed them to the vermin. I'll . . ."

Sarra couldn't hear the rest . . . only his voice rumblin' off the mountain's face and shakin' loose the winter birds from their hidin' places. She didn't follow as he staggered off up the hill, but she didn't leave, neither. Hard to say why she hadn't run earlier on, when she'd woke and saw the muleteer makin' ready to light off.

Her mind was slow to ken it all at first—why the muleteer was up movin' about by hisself in the early morn. She'd spied him through a gap in her blanket, watched him wet the rag from a brown bottle, then lay the rag over Rand's face and sprinkle a fair bit on the bedroll before he corked the bottle again.

The old man looked her way then. "Jus' stay where you is, gal. Don't be movin' nary a twitch. Gimme trouble, and you'll be left here, dead."

She didn't stir. Just waited. She'd got everything she needed while both men slept, and she'd a'ready hid it in the brush. She was just waitin' for first light, herself. She hadn't meant to sink off to sleep again, but sleep had come and got her anyhow. Now the muleteer had beat her to it and he meant to take ever'thing. He'd even throwed the saddle up in the wagon and tied the horse on. The only thing he hadn't got was the saddle pokes Rand had kept tucked up next to him while he slept. Sarra had got those herself.

Soon enough, the wagon and the mules rattled over the hill and down the holler, the horse tuggin' the bridle rein. She was free to go then. But somethin' wouldn't let her just scat off and leave Rand there laid out on the ground not knowin' nary a thing. Instead, she'd waited, guardin' over him with the pistol she'd stole and tucked up in her skirt pocket.

*Go*, a voice inside her was whisperin' now that he'd come full awake. *Run*. But instead, of all the strange and wondersome things, it was a smile tickled her lips as he stopped on the ridge, lifted a boot, slammed it to the ground, then hopped round in a circle fisting the air.

He was more boy than man. Never in her life had she seen somethin' so powerful act such a fool. Never in her life had she seen a Jasper come to the mountain understandin' so little of it, or with so little knowin' of how a body could survive agin it.

This part-man-part-boy with his beardless face and his gold hair was like none she'd ever come across before.

Rand felt his spirits fall into his boots as he gazed over the endless patchwork of tree-clad peaks and naked rock faces. No sign of Ira, the mule wagon, or the horse anywhere—just layer upon layer of folded earth, clothed in mist and stone and trees. The old man was long gone. Undoubtedly he'd been plotting this since last night.

"You ignoramus!" he cursed himself, punching one hand into the other, then shaking both because, in the cold, it hurt. He should've known better than to assume that Ira would aid that piteous creature in escaping her pursuers.

A man who took things for granted here was a fool, and fools died young.

And he was far too young to die.

It was a hard lesson, but one he would not again forget. *"Be not hasty in thy spirit to be angry: for anger resteth in the bosom of fools."* The verse from Ecclesiastes, uttered to him so many times by his grandfather, came again. Closing his eyes, he took the crisp, morning air in long drafts, turned his face toward heaven, felt fragile pinpoints of ice as they fell cool against his rage. An autumn snow had begun to sprinkle the peak. He was only now noticing it.

Could God hear him in this place, far from any proper house of worship, far from any ordained member of the clergy? Never before had he suffered trial in the wilderness without his grandfather or father nearby, without their faith to carry his own. But now he was separated from all of this. Even his Bible was gone, apparently. When he had stirred the blankets with his foot, neither the pack nor his pistol had been unearthed.

Ira had left him with nothing. As good as dead. And the girl along with him.

Slowly, he turned and walked back to camp. He expected the girl to have fled but instead found her standing in the space where the pine straw had been swept away for the lantern. Her hand was folded, the knuckles pressed to her lips, the wrist scabbed and swollen this morning. The expression in her eyes perplexed him. He could not read it. What must she think of him?

Wordlessly, he turned away from her, tasting a sour stew of anger and humiliation spiced with fear. What he needed to do was calmly assess the situation and draft a plan of action. What he wanted to do was grab something, anything, and tear it to ribbons.

He settled for an intermediate course. He was not calm, but he did not destroy what little they had, which amounted to a few blankets and the clothing they wore. Bracing his fingers on his belt and drumming the tips, he considered the way forward. So this was the sum total of the assets in their favor—this, and a morning that sprinkled snow.

*Buck up, sonny boy,* Father whispered in his mind. *The Lord has afforded breath for another day. The situation could be worse.*

They'd only come a certain distance from Brown Drigger's store. There would be a solid chance of making the trek back to that place, but to what ends? With his saddle pack gone, he had no money to purchase supplies there, and no certainty that Brown Drigger wouldn't attempt to imprison the girl again. Aside from that, there remained the danger that Jep and his men would regain their freedom and travel in that direction.

There were supplies to be had at Jep's camp, and perhaps horses to be found somewhere nearby. Rand and Ira had scattered their mounts into the night before leaving the camp. But the plan was not without great risk. A trip into the lion's den might well reveal that the lion was now loosed and on the prowl. Rand would need to circle around carefully . . .

"Can you bring us back to the camp where we left Jep and his men last night?" He cleared his throat and stood a bit taller to brace his wounded pride. He loathed the idea of her knowing how completely taken by surprise he was. Perhaps, if he seemed calm, he could win her cooperation rather than inciting her to panic.

Her chin lifted and her eyes widened. She shook her head quite vehemently.

He'd frightened her further, and the last thing he needed was a hysterical woman in his charge.

"No." The word, her first spoken, caught him aback. "Be a town two days yander, mayhap three. I can find us the way. Ain't safe round here. Brown Drigger gits them dogs after us, won't be no hidin'."

"A settlement so close? Are you certain?" He had doubt of it. During the trip in, Ira had complained vehemently of the remoteness of the Drigger outpost.

"Two days . . . if'n you ain't real slow." Sidestepping toward the woods, she indicated that he should momentarily remain where he was.

Waiting for her to return, he thanked God for his good fortune. The girl was not mute in terms of English language, she knew the way to a settlement, and she seemed to be possessed of normal mental faculties. Last night's talk of witches and spells had unsettled him to a greater degree than he cared to admit. She was just a woman. Flesh and blood. Little more than a child, really, fallen into the hands of dangerous men. Helpless.

He heard her rustling in the underbrush, first to one side of the small clearing, then another. When she returned, her slim, brown fingers held a cache of wild persimmons and hickory nuts. The vividness of the colors struck him momentarily, a still life somehow mesmerizing. She'd drawn near to him before he noticed something familiar slung over her shoulder. His saddle pack.

"My things." He reached more quickly than he should have, and she drew away, startled, the persimmons and hickories spilling to the ground, the bags landing between them. He took up the packs, looked first in one and then in the other, found hardtack and bread that had not been there the day before. A bit of jerked meat, as well, and his pistol. There was also spare ammunition, something that had been carried in his valise in the wagon bed, not in the saddlebags, and a new hunting knife of the sort Ira kept in a crate for sale.

He glanced at her in confusion, looked into the packs again, then down at her as she regathered the bright-crimson fruit and basketed it in her skirt. A dawning understanding came upon him.

"You stole my pack," he blurted. "And my pistol." She'd pillaged the camp while they slept. She'd been prepared to . . . to leave alone?

She paused to look his way. "The muleteer would'a looked after you."

He searched through to the bottom of the satchel, found his grandfather's Bible there, as well as his field-study glass, which could be useful later for starting fires, assuming enough sun presented itself. The leather-wrapped bundle that contained his journals had been removed, along with his nib pens and ink. She must have hidden them somewhere near camp as she resupplied with goods from the wagon. "My books are gone. Where are my books and my pens?"

She stood up, examined a persimmon as though she intended to make a meal of it, then and there. "Can't eat no book full'a leaves. Most'a them you got ain't even good for doctorin.'" Shrugging, she bit into the persimmon, wincing as the juice touched her split lip. "Oughta be shuckin' off now. More snow comin', and Jep and them men too. They go to Brown Drigger over it, he'll git them dogs after us."

"I'll *have* my books back." He stretched out a palm expectantly, towering a foot over her, at least.

"Was the dogs found me out, first time I run off."

"I *said*, I'll have my books returned. . . ."

The phone sounded inside the cabin. It was on its third ring by the time I realized what it was. On the opposite side of the porch, Friday turned an ear back and forth, bewildered by the sound. He'd never heard a landline let out its warbling, mechanical ring.

Setting the last of the pages down unread, I ran inside with Friday battling to beat me through the door.

I caught the phone on the fifth ring, answered it breathless.

"Your cell phone number wasn't handy, so I just called this one." Helen Hall didn't bother to introduce herself, but her voice was hard to mistake, and aside from that, I'd been hoping against hope all afternoon and evening that she would call. "Hello? Are you there?" she asked.

"Yes, yes, I am. Sorry. The dog and I just tripped over each other." I scooched Friday aside with my foot, and he attacked my shoe with vigor. *I'll let Horatio make a meal out of you,* I wanted to tell him, but of course I couldn't. "I'm sorry, Helen. What did you say?" Pressing the receiver close and plugging my other ear, I sifted her voice from the static and Friday's racket.

The trailing end of the sentence came through: ". . . meet me at the pharmacy tomorrow after lunch? I have an idea for you."

# Chapter 14

I left Friday in the cabin with food, water, and a stern talking-to, then departed for the pharmacy early. A mixture of curiosity and anticipation had every nerve in my body vibrating like a live electrical wire. The possibility that, this very afternoon, I might have my questions answered about Evan Hall and *The Story Keeper* was as intoxicating as the ether that had overtaken Rand as Ira ran away. Helen Hall's idea, the one she'd called about yesterday, was that I accompany her up the mountain to see her sister-in-law. Up the mountain to Evan Hall's well-protected compound on the ancestral family land, where his grandmother, Violet Hall, still lived.

I'd spent the evening and most of the morning reading and rereading what I had of *The Story Keeper*. After two days' travel on foot, Rand and Sarra were still nowhere near civilization. They'd seen no sign of Jep and his men but had, on occasion, heard the far-off baying of hounds. By now they were undoubtedly being followed. To say I was obsessed at this point would've been a massive understatement.

Still, niggling at the back of my mind was Coral Rebecca's second letter. I'd finally opened it last night as I lay in the loft bed listening to Friday snore on the sofa downstairs. Inside was an explanation of my father's accident and a plea for money, with Coral Rebecca acting as the family emissary, as usual. The roof on the old farmhouse was disintegrating and the ancient wiring, not replaced since long before our time, was outdated. It had sparked a small fire in the bedroom where my youngest sister, Lily Clarette, still lived.

There was no money for repairs, so they'd cut the electricity to Lily Clarette's room. For now, she was getting by without lights. Marah Diane and her husband, living down the hill in a trailer with their kids, were behind on their payments because they'd helped Daddy out with his medical bills. The church had gathered clothes for Marah Diane's twins to start the new school year, but even the church was struggling these days. The congregation of Lane's Hill Brethren Saints had dwindled after the closing of the moldings mill and then the garment factory in Towash. Brethren members had moved away looking for work like everyone else. My second-to-youngest sister, Evie Christine, was expecting another baby. She and Marah Diane were excited that the baby would be within two years of Marah Diane's littlest. Playmates . . .

The endlessness of my family's situation, the weight of it, was staggering. What could I do that would make any difference? What had I done so far? Nothing. Nothing but throw temporary patches on a dam that was crumbling. Behind it, the water kept building, swirling, swelling. All I'd managed to do, while digging myself into a credit card nightmare, was prolong a situation in which young marriages were encouraged and pregnancies were heralded as accomplishments, whether there was money to provide for the babies or not.

My stomach churned as I wound along the mountain road toward town, passing the brightly colored melee of the Warrior Week encampment. Did those people have any idea? I wondered. Did the tourists have any understanding of the real lives being scratched from these mountains? There was no need for time portals here. There were still places in Appalachia where people lived in them. Lost in time, captives of the beauty and the ugliness that entailed. The majesty of the mountains. The ugliness of poverty, lack of education, hunger, kids with teeth rotted out because they were raised on baby bottles filled with soda pop and sugar water.

*I can't stand this. I can't.* I didn't know who I was talking to. God, I supposed, though we didn't really speak these days. God, and the ragged white church on Lane's Hill, and fear, and pain, and punishment, and shame, and guilt were so inexorably linked within me. It was too hard to sort out what was true, to figure out who God might be apart from the doctrines designed to keep the people of Lane's Hill *on* Lane's Hill. It had always been easier to sweep the whole bundle aside and leave it in a tangle, forgotten.

But this trip was already tugging at the strings, its strange chain of connections suggesting that my coming here couldn't be the result of random coincidences. Events like these hinted, sometimes even shouted, that the God of my childhood and Lane's Hill, the threatening figure who scorned and despised me because of my mother's sinful nature, might instead be a God of both purpose and provision. That he might have been looking after me all these years, laying down a path while I worked to convince myself that I was going my own way.

There was a part of me that knew I'd been brought back here for a purpose.

A reckoning was coming, and in some sense I'd always known that freedom lay on the other side of it. Freedom lay in unraveling lies from truth—about myself, about my family, and about God.

There was no way to walk through that reckoning without returning to the place where all the things I'd been hiding from were now screaming for attention. I wasn't sure of the timing yet, but before this trip was over, I'd go back to Lane's Hill. I'd known it since reading Coral Rebecca's letter.

Ahead, the town of Looking Glass Gap was so different from the places I'd grown up. Perched on a hillside like a postcard image, it was peaceful and serene, a beautiful distraction. The buildings had been nicely restored and the streets bustled with vibrant activity. Evan Hall's money and fame had elevated this town, turned it into a tourist destination similar to Highlands and Asheville.

I parked near the pharmacy, even though it was still too early to meet Helen. Midmorning had barely passed, and she'd told me to come after lunch, so I strolled down the street, taking in the bizarre combinations of Time Shifters memorabilia, reproduction clothing and weaponry, movie posters, local handicrafts, and antique treasures.

In the corner of the ice cream store, I watched customers posing with a life-size cutout of Evan Hall. The cardboard image sported a black peasant-style shirt, black breeches, and over-the-knee boots like pirates wore. The bit part Evan Hall had played in the first Time Shifters movie was a YouTube favorite that had gathered several million fan hits. Enthusiasts knew exactly where to spot him among the crew of a storm-damaged Portuguese galleon, where a rebel group of Time Shifters aided the sailors in reaching North Carolina's Outer Banks. There, the survivors would limp into the village of Sir Walter Raleigh's mysterious Lost Colonists, who had long since given up their original settlement on Roanoke Island and intermingled with native populations farther south on Hatteras.

In Evan Hall's version of history, the *Melingee*, an isolative and mysterious race, lived in the Blue Ridge of North Carolina and Tennessee. They were descendants of the Time Shifters whose portal had malfunctioned, leaving them unable to reenter the intergalactic byways. Instead, they were trapped on Earth, in the New World with the Lost Colonists and the native tribes, twenty years before the arrival of the Pilgrims. After intermarrying and producing halfling children, many wanted to stay. By the third book, they'd managed to travel through time on Earth as a means of escaping pursuit, but without being able to predict where the portals would deposit them each time.

I didn't know why I hadn't connected the dots before now. Evan Hall's Melingee represented the Melungeons. Dark hair, olive skin, startlingly bright blue or silver eyes. Just as with the Melungeons, his Melingee predated other European settlers. The rumors and legends later historically attributed to Melungeons—that they were a strange race of blue-eyed devils and tricksters who practiced magic—were, in the fictional version, really the result of the supernatural abilities of the alien Time Shifters.

Could Evan Hall's interest in the hidden people of the mountains have begun with the story of Rand and Sarra? Could they have been the basis for Nathaniel and Anna, whose time-spanning, forbidden love captivated the imaginations of readers from eleven to eighty-one and sold millions of books, not to mention the movie tickets and attractively packaged DVD sets?

Hard to say. Hard to know where to place the dividing line

between fantasy and history in Evan Hall's work. There was just enough truth to create the illusion that all of it was real. The Time Shifters books made use of Blue Ridge legends, ghost stories, and oddities like the Stumphouse Tunnel—a railroad passageway abandoned mid-construction during the Civil War. In the Time Shifters version, this eerie tunnel to nowhere was actually the location of a portal that had been taken over by the Dark Ones, then fused into rock during a great battle.

Those who seemed bent on making a lifestyle out of Time Shifters took regular pilgrimages to Stumphouse and to Issaqueena Falls, where Anna and Nathaniel used a secret portal to evade pursuit.

At a corner table in the ice cream shop, a couple of guys in hooded capes were having a technical discussion about the physics of Stumphouse and time travel.

I was so caught up in eavesdropping, I didn't realize I was late until the appointment calendar on my phone beeped.

Leaving the scientists to battle it out, I hurried down to the pharmacy and met Helen Hall, then offered to drive us up the mountain.

"That would be lovely." She slipped into a canvas jacket as she followed me out. "We'll be a bit rushed, I'm afraid. My sister-in-law has a doctor's appointment over in Charlotte late this afternoon."

"I really appreciate your help in this." While a quick trip might not be the ideal circumstance, I couldn't risk the opportunity evaporating altogether. I still wasn't exactly certain what Helen had in mind today, but at this point I was game for anything that brought me closer to Evan Hall.

"Well, if there's anyone who'll know whether my nephew had something to do with the manuscript you're wondering about, it would be Violet. She raised him and his little brother after their parents passed."

"I'd love to meet her." I knew about Evan Hall's tragic history. The entire family had been trapped in a fire at a vacation cabin. Only Evan and his younger brother, Jake, had managed to escape. His parents and older sister had perished in the fire.

"Thank you for driving," Helen said as we started out of town. "My son doesn't like it when I drive myself up the mountain these days. It's an odd thing when your children start telling you what to do."

"I guess it would be." I flashed over the news of my father and thought about my sisters. It was impossible to imagine that they would be taking charge. Daddy's word had always been law. "This is a beautiful drive. I can see why you wouldn't want to give it up. I think that's why I admired the art in the cabin so much. It captures all the seasons here."

The comment drew a soulful sigh. "Those were some of my favorite works. They're years old now, of course. I taught community college for quite a while. But when my husband had his stroke, I was faced with either keeping the pharmacy open or teaching. The town needs a pharmacy, so instructing the art classes had to go by the way. The store, and taking care of my husband, the grandkids, and now Violet, gives me about all I can handle." The struggle showed in her expression, the quiet festering of a dream given up in exchange for difficult realities. "But I enjoyed the teaching years. It was a chance to encourage some talented young people. Not many around here manage to escape all the way to Clemson, but community college is a start, at least."

"It's a good start." I'd so wanted Coral Rebecca to go to college. I'd tried to talk her into it, but after I left, Daddy had been even more determined that no one else would break away.

"I knew Wilda Culp," Helen offered, and I glanced her direction, but her face was hidden in shadow as the road slipped under an outcropping of rock. "Not well, but we worked together on a few fund-raisers for an aid society. She wanted to start something to serve the women of the area, especially the young ones. Oh . . . I guess that's thirteen or fourteen years ago now."

*Thirteen or fourteen years . . .* I was just leaving for Clemson. Wilda had big plans for the future, apparently. "She never told me about that."

"Well, I don't think she got very far with it before they diagnosed the lung cancer. And I'm sure nothing much happened on the project after that. She was the one to do it. The one with connections outside the community."

"It sounds like her." I had always hoped that after I left, my sisters might find the same shelter at Wilda's house that I'd found, but everything about Wilda was disapproved of at home. My father only allowed me to go there because the more I came to look like my mother, the less he and Momaw Leena wanted me around. Once Marah Diane was old enough to look after the littler kids, the family seemed just as happy to have me out earning a paycheck, and Wilda paid well.

"I would've enjoyed knowing her better, I think," Helen said.

We talked about the scenery then, chatting aimlessly about the dwindling of small-town economies and the areas where vacation cabins were taking over what had once been farmland.

"Won't be long until the snow comes and things go quiet for the winter," Helen commented finally. "Just the skiers and waterfowl hunters passing through."

"I noticed the chill this morning." I thought of Sarra, my mind hopscotching and landing squarely in the story. She'd felt winter coming too. There was something in the air when the seasons shifted, and if you knew this place, your bones told you weather was coming. Bodies quickened, woodpiles were stocked, local folks ran to grocery stores and laid in supplies. The roads could be impassable and the power could go out for weeks on some of the rural routes, but not this early in the season.

We rounded a curve, and the smattering of rusty roadside barbed wire and pine-rail fences gave way to an expanse of seemingly endless twelve-foot chain link, the kind intended to keep deer in or people out, or both. Every twenty feet or so, No Trespassing signs made the intent clear.

I had a feeling we'd reached the fringes of Evan Hall's domain. The fences stretched for miles, stark, imposing, out of place with the landscape. For generations, these forests had been separated by little more than geography and aging livestock wire or split-rail fences on the valley land. There was nothing that couldn't be shinnied through or hopped over. Other than the occasional mantrap set near some moonshiner's still or marijuana patch—and you learned to avoid those—the land and the fading remnants of old homesteads and graveyards were open to whoever wanted to pass by.

We slipped across a small, covered bridge, and darkness shrouded the car until we came out the other side. Ahead, a gateway emerged, a dozen or so cars parked randomly in the ditch around it. The scene looked like it had come straight from some of the fan blogs I'd read. People were snapping pictures by the brass insignia on the rock wall beside the guard shack and taking videos through the ornate iron gate.

They moved aside as we passed, peering into the vehicle to see if we might be anyone important. A security man in a cowboy hat and a brown T-shirt that read *Hall Ranch* came to check us in.

"It's just us," Helen said.

He waved us through as the envious onlookers watched.

"Is it always this way?" I hadn't quite imagined the horde. The man was literally a prisoner on his own mountain.

Helen sighed. "More so when they're having one of their gatherings in town. In a way, I suppose it's evidence of Evan's talent, but in another way, it's such foolishness. The poor boy should be able to have his own life. He isn't the sort for all this hullabaloo, but it seems as though the more he retreats from these people, the more they chase after him."

"Maybe that's part of the reason. It keeps the mystery alive, creates the illusion that there's something to hide." I was probably overstepping my bounds, but it had occurred to me that Evan Hall and I might actually be useful to each other. When an author came out with something in a completely different genre, it tended to quell the fires of prior works. And because *The Story Keeper* was an older manuscript, it might be free of any contractual ties to the publishing house that had produced his Time Shifters books. "If I can just have a few minutes to speak with your nephew, I think I can explain why this could be a mutually beneficial arrangement."

My palms started to sweat. I gripped and ungripped the steering wheel, my pulse suddenly ramping up. Quite possibly, this was it. Either the beginning or the end.

"My nephew can be a very stubborn man," Helen warned.

"Yes, I've heard."

A chuckle puffed from her, the sound releasing tension like a pop-up valve. "But you are a very pretty girl. It isn't easy for a man to say no to a pretty young woman face-to-face . . . particularly when he's lonely. And the two of you do have the publishing business in common."

I drew back, casting a glance at her as the road narrowed and crawled along the edge of the mountain like tinsel clinging to a giant Christmas tree. What was she suggesting? Was this a business meeting or . . . some sort of a matchmaking scheme?

I groped for something to say but came up empty.

"Both Violet and I would like to see Evan return to his writing, and not more of the Time Shifters books either. Before those came along, Evan wrote beautiful tales about the people and the mountains and the heart of this place. Writing was therapy for him after Violet brought him back here to live, I think. He was only twelve, but he could spin a yarn even then."

She pointed ahead to where the road split, one fork fading to dirt and traveling level around the mountain, and the paved road winding toward the peak. "Right at the Y here. The other one goes to the back side of the ranch."

We continued upward, past an old stone farmhouse and barn hidden in the trees against a bluff, past two horses nibbling moss off a rock, and then through a stand of wild rhododendron, where a doe calmly lifted her head and watched us drive by. Finally we emerged in a hilltop compound complete with a large paved parking area, a six-bay garage, a swimming pool and cabana, a guesthouse, and a palatial home.

I made an effort not to react by sucking in a breath. Evan Hall lived well. Regardless of how he felt about the Time Shifters books, he'd clearly reaped the benefits.

We parked beneath the two-story portico in front and entered the house without knocking, Helen calling out as we moved through a cavernous vestibule that had a woman's touch . . . or an interior decorator's.

"Violet? Vi-i-i-olet . . . where are you, hon?"

Violet beckoned us from the living room, where we found her settled atop a well-worn quilt in an oversize leather recliner. The arrangement of pillows and the gathering of books, magazines, and needlework around her evidenced the fact that she spent a great deal of time there. Her wan figure seemed almost a part of the chair, but her smile was bright and welcoming.

Helen swept a kiss across her cheek before she introduced me and we sat.

The two women spoke briefly about business at the pharmacy, the Warrior Week incomers, and Violet's afternoon doctor's appointment in Charlotte. Oncologist. The body language during that part of the conversation wasn't good.

Violet turned her attention to me. "Helen says you're not a stranger to these parts." It was the proper way to begin a Southern conversation—*Where are you from? Who are your people? Where do you attend church?* Living in the city, I'd grown out of practice at this sort of thing. There, a business conversation began with business.

"I grew up near Towash." It struck me then, the irony. Thirteen years of trying to erase this place from my speech, my mind, my history, and now those connections were an asset. I felt like an opportunist at a high school reunion, mining old relationships to sell used cars or vinyl siding. "I think that's why the *Story Keeper* manuscript grabbed me to this degree. There is such a sense of place . . . of life as it would've been here at the turn of the century." I watched for any spark of recognition, any sign that they might be responsible for the manuscript showing up at my door.

Violet shifted away a bit, frowning. I'd moved the conversation toward business too quickly. "And who are your people over in Towash? I don't recall any Gibbses."

"My family lives west of, about twelve miles. Off Honey Creek." I purposely didn't say Lane's Hill. No doubt she'd heard of it. The Brethren Saints had roughly the same reputation that Melungeons carried in Rand and Sarra's day—secretive, strange, given to odd ways of dressing and cultish practices. Suspicious of outsiders.

Violet let her head fall against the cushion, a smile playing briefly where suspicion had been. "Oh, my, when we were girls, we'd take our little canoe down Honey Creek and paddle for miles! It was a grand life, growing up here . . . before all the fences." A frown lent emotion to the last sentence.

So Violet didn't approve of cordoning off the mountain either. She understood that it wasn't considered very neighborly. *The Story Keeper* was so tenderly written, it was hard to equate that with guard shacks and the starkness of twelve-foot chain link.

A door opened somewhere in the house, and an electronic alarm system beeped, the sound quickly fading into the echo of a child's footsteps clomping up the entry hall at a rapid pace. Hannah burst into the room a moment later, skidding to a stop when she saw that it was occupied.

"Hannah." Violet withheld the smile teasing her lips. "What have you been told about running in the house?"

"Tooo . . . not to?" Hannah surveyed the room, spotted me there on the sofa, and headed my way, running again, her cowboy boots sliding on the tile. "Hey!" She threw her arms out, and the next thing I knew, I was being chair-tackled in an exuberant hug. I was momentarily struck by how good it felt.

She lingered in front of me as she pushed to her feet again. "Nobody told me you were coming." A suspicious look and a cocked eyebrow went toward the older ladies.

Violet extended an arm and cupped her fingers in the air. "Come sit here with Granny for a minute. I thought you and your daddy were going fishing together today, sugar pie."

Hannah perched on Violet's chair arm, slumping forward. "He has to do some work, so we can't."

A critical look and a bit of eye dialogue passed behind the little girl's back. I felt like an intruder, eavesdropping on an ongoing family *situation*.

"It was supposed to be his day off." Helen clipped the words.

In the foyer, out of sight, the door opened and closed. The electronic chime beeped again. A man's boot steps echoed this time.

I prepared myself to meet Evan Hall, perhaps not under the best of circumstances, but the guy who entered didn't quite fit the image I'd formed. There was a resemblance—dark hair, blue eyes, brooding lips—but he was shorter than I'd thought he would be. Not *short*, necessarily, but I'd had the image of Evan Hall as well over six feet.

He didn't look our way as he rounded the corner, though he hitched a step as if surprised to find people there in the formal living room. "Just gotta grab my wallet. I'm headed to town. Those Time Shifters morons tore up some more fence."

"I thought you were taking your daughter fishing." Helen tracked him like a chicken on a grasshopper as he continued to a door off the foyer.

"She's been waiting for a week," Violet added.

He ducked into a small room, an office by the look of it. "Tell Evan's idiotic fans to stop tearing things up."

So this wasn't Evan Hall, and Hannah wasn't Evan's daughter. . . .

"I can't stand those people sometimes." Hannah sided with her father, her hands flipping through the air, then landing with a slap. "They ruined our whole stupid day."

Helen's nostrils flared and more silent words were exchanged. Her opinion was obvious. *Your daddy ruined your day.*

I sat trying to act as if I were weirdly oblivious to the undercurrents mole-tunneling below the surface.

Exiting the office, Hannah's father glanced our way and stopped midstride. "Didn't know we had company." He took me in more carefully, smiled a little.

"This is Jennia Beth," Hannah volunteered. Apparently she'd picked up my name from Mrs. Penberthy in the pharmacy. I hadn't been Jennia Beth in years.

I stood as he crossed the floor, and Helen rose to make introductions. She, too, used Jennia Beth as she acquainted me with her nephew Jake Hall, Evan Hall's younger brother. Like Evan, he was striking in his appearance, nice-looking. Cowboy hat, deep-blue eyes, good tan. But there was something weathered and hard-lived about Jake Hall, though I guessed him to be not that much older than me, maybe in his midthirties or so.

"Jen," I corrected.

"Nice of you to come brighten up this place a bit." He flashed a smile and then an unabashedly flirty look that pushed toward embarrassing, given the company.

"I'm enjoying the visit."

"You live around here?" Why did I have the feeling that Jake Hall said that to women often? I wondered if Evan would be this . . . overt. Somehow I didn't picture him as the type. I hoped he wasn't. That would complicate things.

"Jennia Beth's stayin' in the cabin on the lake," Hannah offered.

Her father never even glanced her way. "Oh. Nice. Great view there. Secluded, even though it's actually not that far from the neighbors. You meet Uncle Clive yet? Don't let him scare you.

He didn't quite come *all* the way back from combat duty, if you know what I mean, but he's harmless."

"Jake, that's unkind," Violet complained. "That's my cousin you're speaking of."

Jake answered with a shrug and a wry smirk.

"Horatio attacked her dog," Hannah piped up. Once again, her father didn't look her way.

"Maybe Hannah would just as soon ride to town with you instead of staying here," Helen suggested, and a gush of sympathy hit me. Everyone seemed to be trying to elbow Hannah off right now. I understood why Helen and Violet didn't want extra ears around, but the poor kid . . .

"Might take some time for me to find what I'm after." Jake disengaged and backed away a step. "Hannah'd just be bored, wouldn't you, pine knot? Uncle Clive oughta be by here later with the mower blades he honed up for me. Maybe y'all two can hit that honey hole on the lake y'all went to yesterday, finish stockin' Clive's old freezer with fish fillets." He flashed a smile at his daughter then, turning the charm her way as he ruffled her hair.

"Yeah, maybe. I guess so." Hannah's look of adoration was heart melting. "I s'pose I'll just go ride awhile."

"Not so far this time," Violet warned. "You worried us yesterday. You were gone too long. And not on the gray gelding. That's too much horse for you. If you're going out by yourself again, take Blackberry."

Hannah opened her mouth to protest, and Violet lifted a finger, silencing her with one quick look.

"Sheesh . . . oh-kay already." An eye roll offered adolescent attitude. Where was this kid's mother? I wondered. And how did Evan Hall fit into this human drama?

158

In short order, Hannah and her father were gone. We resumed our conversation, but time was running out, and both women were ready to get around to the dialogue about Evan and the manuscript.

Violet turned my way with a very pointed look. "I won't do anything that could cause my grandson trouble. He has enough on his shoulders, with an ailing old woman to take care of, and now his brother and Hannah having moved in. Evan was only a boy when he sold those Time Shifters books. Barely eighteen years old. He didn't make all the right decisions, and it's cost him dearly in terms of legal brouhaha. Aside from that, always there are hangers-on trying to fill their pockets from him any way they can. People take advantage."

"Yes," Helen echoed. "We don't want to do anything to cause Evan further unhappiness. If it weren't for the fact that you are local . . . well, and that I had one of my *feelings* about you when you came in, I wouldn't have contacted Violet about this at all. Or brought you here."

"Of course. And I appreciate it more than I can say." Time to get down to brass tacks. I might've been out of practice at the roundabout paths of *Who are your people?* and *Where do you hail from?* but negotiations I could do. "I promise you, I'm not here to take advantage of anyone. Vida House is extremely reputable. That's one of the reasons I went to work there. It's a place I can feel good about. I genuinely believe this could be a beneficial thing for all involved." I went on, explaining how Evan's moving into a new publishing channel might help to subdue the lingering Time Shifters mania.

When I was finished, Violet steepled her thin fingers and tapped the ends together. She checked the old-fashioned clock ticking on the mantel. "You'll have to be careful in how you approach my nephew. He can be very . . . intractable sometimes. Too independent for his own good."

*"Pppffff!"* Helen punctuated.

"Who, Uncle Evan?" Suddenly Hannah was passing through the room again. The women clammed up immediately.

"Nothing, sweet. I thought you were gone riding." Violet glanced at the clock a second time, pushing herself upright in her chair. Helen leaned out and looked toward the front door. My pulse sped up as I clued into the fact that Evan Hall's arrival might be imminent.

Hannah snatched a pink camouflage baseball cap off the coatrack by the doors overlooking the pool, then wandered our way. "Forgot to get my hat."

"Have a good ride. Molly's coming to clean, so if you need anything while we're gone to the doctor, she'll be here."

"I don't gotta have a babysitter. I can watch after myself."

Violet frowned. "Don't be snippy, Hannah. It isn't nice. Did you need something else?" She worked herself farther upward in her chair, struggling to swivel so she could see her great-granddaughter. Even that small bit of effort seemed too much. This poor woman didn't need to be left with the care of an eleven-year-old. She wasn't up to it.

Scuffing a foot across the tile, Hannah tipped her head, long dark hair falling over the shoulder of her sweatshirt. "I thought Jennia Beth might wanna see Blackberry." A hopeful look came my way. "You like horses, don't you?"

I opened my mouth to answer, but Violet beat me to it. "She came to talk about business, sweet. You go on and ride."

"Business about Uncle Evan?"

"Hannah . . ."

"I just asked a question."

"Straighten up or you'll be in your room, rather than out having a nice time with Blackberry."

"Are you gonna ask him about his book, like you said at Aunt Helen's store?" Hannah ignored her grandmother and focused in my direction.

"Hannah!" The rebukes of both women rose toward the ceiling.

"It's okay." I felt things spinning toward some embarrassing confrontation. How often did this sort of thing happen around here?

"Never mind." Hannah gave up and wandered away, looking glum. The three of us watched her disappear through the glass doors and climb the stone steps to the yard, her shoulders slumped and her arms hanging.

"I apologize." Violet sagged in her seat. "She's a darling child, but she warts people, I'm afraid. She's very lonesome here."

"She misses her mama." Helen's disgust was obvious. "Divorce. Her mother doesn't want custody. She's moved to Nashville to chase her dreams, or so she says."

A vapor trail of feelings swept through me, sudden and powerful, overwhelming. I remembered waking up one morning to find my grandmother in my mother's place. *Your mama run off and she ain't gonna be back.* That was all I was ever told.

"You look a bit like Hannah's mother." Helen's observation came unexpectedly. "That could be why she's acting out so."

I was temporarily mute. What was the right response for something like that?

Violet once again checked the clock. "I don't know *where* Evan is."

I slid to the front of my chair. "You know what, I don't mind going to look at Hannah's horse. I'd like to, actually, if it's all right. I loved to ride when I was her age. We had mostly coon-hunting mules, though. My family raised and sold them." Coon dogs and mules were our family industry, if we had one.

"Oh, go ahead." Violet shooshed me toward the door. "When Evan comes in, we'll warm him up for you. Work on him a bit."

I took advantage of the chance to excuse myself, then followed Hannah's path through the glass doors, around the pool, and up the neatly manicured stone steps. Nearby, a water feature flowed down the slope, an occasional autumn leaf tumbling along the surface. The gardens on all sides were immaculately kept, the seasonal debris having been carefully cleared. Obviously this place had a groundskeeper along with a maid.

I was struck again by the fact that, for all appearances, this was a beautiful life. A perfect life. It's so easy to make assumptions, passing by other people's homes at a distance. To be so certain that the goings-on inside mirror the exteriors—that glittering facades and squeaky-clean windows equate to perfect families, yet the reality is that containers often tell nothing of the contents.

Hardship finds its way into every life. It's just much easier to see our own than other people's.

Hannah had finished cinching her saddle and was preparing to mount when I stepped into the barn.

"Hey!" she said, unbuckling the halter and leading her gelding by the reins. "This is Blackberry. He was Uncle Evan's horse, like, way back when. He knows tricks like take a bow and count with one foot and lay down. I can bring him outside and show you, if you want."

Graying around the eyes and the muzzle, Blackberry had clearly seen a few turns around the pasture in his time. He made my acquaintance by nuzzling my shirt, then letting out a big horse sigh, peppering me with snot. Just like the good old days. The mules were famous for that. "He looks a fine fellow."

"You talk kinda funny. Like . . . you're on TV or somethin'."

"I live in New York City. Maybe that's why it sounds different to you."

"Yeah, I guess so. What's it like there?"

I thought about that for a minute. For the first time in years, the city seemed a world away, like a place I'd seen in a movie but never really lived. "It's nice. Exciting. There's always something happening. I like it there."

Hannah finger-combed a bit of Blackberry's mane. "Do you like it *here*?"

"The mountains are beautiful too—in a different way, though. I'll bet you have a lot of fun, with the horses and the pool and everything." The change in her expression told me immediately that I shouldn't have brought it up. Hannah wasn't happy to be here.

"It's boring."

"Well, Blackberry is probably glad you're around. I'm sure he likes getting out and having some adventures again." Blackberry rolled a look my way, as in, *Lady, are you nuts?*

Hannah threw the reins over the horse's neck. "He's a pooh. He'd stand around and just get fatter and fatter if he could. He's lucky I came to get him back in shape." Reaching up and covering his ear, she added, "The gray horse is more fun. He's faster. He's got some long name, but I call him Silverbear."

"Nice." I chuckled.

A vehicle rumbled into the parking area outside, and Hannah stopped with her foot halfway to the stirrup. "That's Uncle Evan, I bet. Hold Blackberry. I'll go get him." Before I could stop her, she'd tossed the reins at me and bolted for the door. I caught the horse, then looped the reins through a tie ring, hoping to catch Evan in front and maybe walk back to the house together before my reasons for being here came up. A stable wasn't the place to discuss business. This would undoubtedly go better with the help of Helen and Violet. I needed backup, and Blackberry probably wasn't the right one for that.

When I exited the barn, Hannah was climbing the rails of an open-topped livestock trailer to peer inside. She waved me over excitedly. "Look! Uncle Evan's got goats. Awwww . . . look at the baby one. It's so cute!" In the trailer, a goat stuck its nose through the slats and belched out a long, loud complaint.

The truck doors opened. A stocky cowboy emerged from the driver's side, and Evan Hall exited from the other. I recognized him immediately. He rounded the vehicle on long, agile strides that brought to mind the film scene on the deck of the Portuguese galleon. In reality, the tiny image on the Internet didn't do him justice.

A breath stuttered in my chest, and a wave of intimidation hit. This was such a weird situation. I considered just pretending I hadn't heard Hannah and catching the path back to the house, hoping he had failed to notice me there.

"Jennia Beth, come look!" Hannah blew my cover, and both Evan Hall and the other man looked my way.

I reluctantly emerged from the shadow of the stable, and the stocky cowboy and I crossed paths as he proceeded in. "Ma'am," he said, tipping his hat in passing.

At the trailer, Evan was explaining to Hannah that the goats weren't staying. They'd wandered onto the place through one of the broken fences.

"Oh, but the baby one is so cute! Can we just keep *it*, Uncle

Ev?" Hannah hooked herself over the top rail and leaned far into the trailer to touch the nose of the curious baby.

"Don't fall over," her uncle teased. "They're man-eaters." He grabbed her dangling legs and pretended to upend her, raising a squeal.

He seemed like an okay kind of guy. He actually gave off an easygoing vibe. Not what I'd anticipated. Based on the interviews and press photos, I'd imagined him to be intense, contemplative, reserved.

"This is Jennia Beth." Hannah delivered an upside-down introduction through the trailer slats. "She's stayin' in the lake cabin."

Evan Hall turned to me and offered his hand. "Good to meet you, Jennia Beth."

He smiled as I returned the greeting, and I had to admit, it was dazzling. Those loony women in the ice cream shop could have picked worse guys to hang their fantasies on.

"She came up here with Aunt Helen," Hannah reported.

A dark eyebrow straightened in confusion. "Did Aunt Helen realize that Granny Vi has a doctor's appointment today? We're leaving here in a minute." He caught my gaze for an instant, then added, "Sorry."

"That's okay."

The baby goat stood on its hind legs, stretching upward to nibble Hannah's fingers. "Look! Look, Uncle Ev. He likes me *so* much. Look how cute he is, Jennia Beth."

"We're not keeping him, Hannah," Evan reminded gently.

I peeked through the slats and slipped a hand in to stroke the baby's soft, fuzzy ears. Velvet. Just like I remembered. There was nothing sweeter in the world than a baby goat's ears. "He's only a day or two old. He's lucky something didn't eat him before you found him." I peered across at the frightened nanny. "She's probably a young mother. Doesn't know any better than to wander off on her own." At the farm, we'd always had an old donkey who lived with the goats to chase off predators. Donkeys were surprisingly adept at guard duty.

"See, he *needs* us, Uncle Ev." Hannah twisted upright to continue the negotiations. The little goat bleated at her, and she leaned in again. "He's just a *baby* baby."

Evan caught her boot to prevent an accidental nosedive. A wry twist played on his lips as he turned my way. "Thanks a lot."

"Sorry." Then I was smiling at him, and he was smiling back. I wasn't even sure how that happened, but I was momentarily caught up in it. Whether it was the man or the Time Shifters mystique or the sensitivity of the writing in *The Story Keeper*, I couldn't say, but I was fascinated by him. So far, he wasn't anything like I'd thought he would be.

"Awww . . . ," Hannah whined softly. "The mama doesn't even wanna take care of her. Poor baby."

Evan's smile fell, a veiled look crossing his face. He turned away, keeping the emotion to himself. "Come on down from there, Hannah, before you fall. Mike went inside to call around and see if he can figure out who the goats belong to."

The little girl climbed off the trailer. "Maybe Mike won't find anybody." Her expression turned glum.

"They most likely belong to Mrs. Masterson."

That caused Hannah's long face to drop another notch. "Great. She'll probably sue us again."

"Hannah . . ." Evan's reproachful look reminded me of his grandmother's. "That's enough of that."

"Okay." Apparently she didn't disregard Uncle Evan the way she did Granny Vi.

"But we'll make sure he doesn't starve. We'll milk the mama and figure out a bottle if we need to." His cloudy expression had lifted when he turned back to me. "Any experience milking goats?"

"More than I'd care to admit." Goat-milk soaps and creams were one of my grandmother's swap meet industries. She used the herbs harvested from her secret gathering places to create medicinal mixtures for arthritis, chest colds, colic, fever, and other ailments. One of my regrets about the years after my mother left was that I'd spent so much time avoiding my grandmother, I hadn't learned the old ways or how to gather and process the mountain plants.

"That may come in handy." Evan winked, and a strange glitter sprinkled through me.

Hannah toyed with the goat's soft nose through the slats. "Jennia Beth's from New York City."

A warning note sounded in my brain. Suddenly we were plowing a little too close to the corn. The last thing I needed was for Hannah to clue him in as to why I was here. Helen's warning was still in the back of my mind. *My nephew can be a very stubborn man.*

Evan gave me an interested look. Not suspicious or standoffish, but pleasantly interested. "So, a New York City girl who knows goats?" He slipped his hands into his jeans pockets, stood waiting to see what I would say.

"I grew up over by Towash. With goats. I'm just back for a few days." I was probably flattering myself, but he seemed a little disappointed by the last part. I wondered how often visitors came to the compound—how often he had anyone new to talk to.

"Oh . . . well, it's a nice time of year to be on the lake." He scanned me with more than idle curiosity. His mind was turning it over now. The man was trying to figure me out, trying to add up the numbers. "Not so peaceful during Warrior Week, though."

"Oh, she's not here for Warrior Week." Hannah turned her attention from the goat to us. "Jennia Beth's here for *business*."

A cold, hard fist slammed dead center in the pit of my stomach. Fortunately, Evan seemed preoccupied. The stocky cowboy, Mike, had just come out of the barn. "Why's Blackberry wandering down the pasture with the saddle on and the bridle reins draggin'?" he called across the driveway.

"Oh, shoot!" Hannah started toward the barn, and Mike joined her in hot pursuit of Blackberry.

"That's my fault," I admitted. "I was afraid if I tied him fast, he might pull away and break the reins, so I just looped them."

But when I turned back, Evan wasn't watching Mike and Hannah dash into the pasture; instead, he'd leveled an intense look at me. "What kind of business?"

My thoughts scattered and adrenaline surged through my body. This wasn't at all how things were supposed to happen. I liked to control my negotiations. That was how I made them successful. But now that he'd asked, I couldn't exactly lie. "I came here about a manuscript."

"You're in *publishing*?" He spit it out like it was a dirty word, his hands leaving his pockets and bracing on his hips, the muscles in his jaw tight and angry.

"Yes, I am. I'd just like five minutes of your time. I'm an editor at Vida—"

"And you lured my aunt into bringing you up here?" He leaned toward me so that I was forced to crane upward to meet his gaze.

"No. It wasn't like that. She and your grandmother were hoping we could—"

"So in order to get what you wanted, you took advantage of my aunt, my grandmother who's dying of cancer, and a little girl whose mother just ditched her six months ago? Nice. Do you people have any conscience? At all?"

Guilt stabbed. Hard. Had I taken advantage? Was he right? "If you'll just *listen* for a minute. Just let me get a whole sentence out."

He leaned even closer, so close that I saw the flecks of silver in the centers of his eyes. Molten, just now. "Lady, I don't *need* a whole sentence. Whatever you've got to say, I am *not* interested, and you are leaving."

"I drove your aunt up here," I protested. This was a disaster. What was I supposed to do now, strand the woman and bolt like a stray dog caught in the yard?

"I'll see that she gets home." He pointed the way to the front gate before he turned and started toward the barn on clipped, angry strides, leaving me dumbfounded. "Get in your car and get off my place. Now."

# Chapter 15

## The Story Keeper

### CHAPTER SIX

It troubled Rand no small bit, this habit of hers. It had been troubling him for three days now. Each morning when he woke, he found Sarra sitting on her handwoven blanket, knees folded beneath her, the necklace lying before her on the ground. Her ritual was identical, day by day. Always, the object of her worship—the necklace bearing the six beads and the carved-bone locket box—was removed with great ceremony. Then the sliding lid of the box was unfastened, and the parts of it were lifted to the sky with reverence before being placed upon the ground. When possible, a salvaged ember lay between the lid and base, its smoke carving a thin trail in the early light, the stream broken exactly three times by her hands as she waved the smoke over herself, anointing in some strange way, breathing in the essence of her deity as she performed her morning sacramental.

It was not so much the pagan nature of the ceremony that disturbed him—he'd seen such things in his travels with his father. It was the strange and seemingly blasphemous intermingling of native words and symbols with those that were holy and sacred to his own faith.

Along the leather cord that held her box, the various beads were adorned with carved animal totems—fish, birds, and what appeared to be a sea turtle. He might have doubted it this far from the ocean, but the necklace also contained slips of purple wampum shell of the variety often traded among native tribes as items of value. He had also come to recognize the narrow etching on the exterior of the box as the Maltese cross, similar to those he had viewed in the ancient churches of southern Europe.

Inside the box, on the reverse of the lid and the interior base itself, were carvings. He had come close enough during her worship to discern them as that of a man and a woman. The images had clearly been painted at one time, perhaps gilded even, but the colors had largely worn through, leading him to believe that the box was quite old.

He had gathered, both by looking and by listening to her ceremonials, that the images were perhaps those of the Virgin Mary and Jesus the Christ, and that the girl knew, in some rudimentary form, whom the reliefs were intended to represent. Interspersed in her prayers were the names of the Holy Mother and the Son of God, uttered along with portions of a guttural language unfamiliar to him—Cherokee, perhaps. As she prayed, she touched the turtle, the fish, the birds, and each bead along the necklace strand lying before her.

The juxtaposition of sacred images with earth totems disturbed Rand more each day. These were the sort of affronts that his grandfather had quite often preached against. As bishop, it had always been his responsibility to correct in mission churches the inevitable entry of local superstitions. It was, of course, important that the missions emphasize strict adherence to the approved teachings of the church.

This morning, he took the journal and gold-nibbed pen from his saddle pack and began a sketch as he watched her. With three days passed on the trail and no recent signs of pursuit, he'd begun to take note of her means of gathering foodstuffs and other supplies from what the forest provided. As he had cataloged these things in his book, it was only prudent to catalog her as well.

Or so he told himself. In truth, he was fascinated by her in some way he could not fully comprehend nor cared to consciously examine. Though she was not one to speak unless spoken to in this uneasy partnership of theirs, he understood that her intent was to return to the place from whence she'd come, that place being far away. She had traveled the distance with her father, and Rand had come to understand that her father was of no higher estate than Jep and his cohorts.

At whatever point they did finally reach this town she knew of, Rand hoped to arrange some sort of safe care for her, purchase a horse for himself, and then decide how to proceed from that point. These last rigorous days had gone some distance toward quelling his wanderlust, and another light snow had begun this morning. They'd camped on a ridge, and from here he could see the dark and ominous clouds billowing in. Snow clouds, though Sarra appeared strangely oblivious to the flakes settling over her skin and resting like gems on her long, dark lashes as she continued her morning chant.

> "O-gi-do-da ga-lv-la-di céus
> ga-lv-quo-di-yu ge-se-s-di santificado
> tsa-gv-wi-yu-hi . . ."

For a moment, Rand became lost in her song, and he too forgot the snow. Instead, he found himself approximating her words on the page opposite the rendering of her. He let go his fear that brimstone might soon enough rain from the very heavens to which she had raised her face, and he found himself studying her—an opportunity he'd seldom been allowed these past three days of flight, lest she be given to the assumption that he was no different from the men who had deprived her of her liberty and sought to savagely violate her person. The one time Rand had touched her, intending only to steady her as they crossed a frigid stream, she had pulled away so quickly that it set both of them off-balance, dooming them to sodden clothing below the knee for several hours. The drying out of those things had necessitated their larger fire last eve.

He'd reminded himself to take care in his manner toward her in the future. He could only imagine what horrors the hand of a man might conjure in her thoughts, what this poor, bruised and battered creature had endured.

"De cada dia de-s-gi-du-gv-i na-s-gi-ya tsi-di-ga-yo-tsi-

ne-ho tso-tsi-du-gi

perdoai-nos as nossas ofensas,

assim como nós perdoamos a quem nos tem ofendido.

E não nos deixeis cair em tentação, mas u-yo ge-sv-i

e men."

He transcribed the last of the chant and labeled the sketch of her, though he was not certain why. It was unlikely he would ever forget the details of this woman with whom he had endured the most tenuous and uncomfortable hours of his life.

*Sarra, a Melungeon girl*, he wrote, and then, realizing that if he should yet perish here, his wish was for his family to know what had become of him, he added the date and a note pleading that anyone who might find his journal would return it to his family.

The silence struck him suddenly, and he looked at Sarra, found that she had focused on him and was now peering curiously toward his sketch. He turned away, embarrassed, and closed his book. When a time presented itself, he would make further notations about her rituals.

The idea possessed him with a certain guilt, a conviction that rather than observing, perhaps he should have been instructing her against these practices. Instead he found himself, day upon day, with breathless curiosity, watching this wretched but strangely alluring creature....

Sarra couldn't ken why he was lookin' at her that way, though it didn't figure to matter much. She could get shed of him if she'd a need to, but they had a better chance together, and truth be told, he wouldn't last out a day on his own. If Jep and the others didn't get him, the mountains would.

When he sat watchin' her that way, though, seemin' to try to cipher her from the inside out, she thought mayhap it'd be sooner 'stead of later that she'd pull foot and disappear off in the trees or fade away down some holler, and leave him to hisself. Then she'd trek back home to Aginisi's mountain in Tennessee country. But each time she thought of that place, she wondered whether she could find the way there on her own.

So many times on the trail with her daddy, she'd crawled inside herself, took her mind back home to Aginisi's cabin, and she knew she was losin' track of things as they traveled, lettin' the rivers and the hollers and the strange-shaped rock faces slip by unmarked in her mind. But there was a grievin' pain inside her, and it shot clean to the bone in this body, and all she could do was leave her eyes and her ears and the body behind and sail across her mind to the known places—the ones where Gran-dey kept her safe with the Good Book and Aginisi taught her the Lord's Prayer how *she* knew it, some in Cherokee and some in the old talk that'd come across the sea with the story keepers, long time ago.

Sarra'd said the Lord's Prayer each day before leavin' out from camp with Rand in tow. It was a mattersome thing to start the day with openin' the little prayer box and offering up these mornin' words, just as Aginisi had taught her. The words were a comfort, remindin' her that even though she's so far from home, she wasn't but a whisper from Father God. He lived down all the deepest hollers and up all the highest mountains, just as the Good Book promised. Always, he was within hearin' distance.

Many's the time they'd prayed together, her and Aginisi, after Gran-dey was gone. Things was harder then, but the prayers said had scared off wolves scratchin' round the cabin in the winter and brought food when the corn pone ran short, when they'd used all the good things that'd been put up from last summer's garden and the crocks waited, washed and empty in the root house. It was prayers that kept them through the hungry days and cold nights when the wild things ran near, hungry theirselves. Was prayers that put the foot of a little snowshoe hare in a snare or brought a possum out routin' close to the cabin for no reason at all. Close enough for a clear shot at him. It was prayers that made the shot go true and gave meat when meat was needed.

All them things, Gran-dey taught her first and Aginisi taught too. All them things, Sarra learnt in that little cabin tucked along the crick. When she said the prayer, she heard Aginisi's voice and knew that Aginisi had spoke true in the last moments before Sarra was took away by her daddy, leavin' Aginisi to wait out the end hours of dyin' by herself.

*There's none can move us too far a piece for love to find us, child. It's love what ties us to heaven. A-le e-tsa-lv-quo-di-yu ge-sv ni-go-hi-lv-i.*

The glory is forever. Those were Aginisi's last words to her in Cherokee. Her death words. It was a done thing now.

From the corner of her eye, Sarra saw Rand watchin' her as she tied Aginisi's prayer box round her neck, where the breath of them prayers would be close to her heart while she walked. Long's Rand didn't touch her, she'd let him walk along again. She owed him that for savin' her life, at least. It was a right thing she was doin'.

She did wonder about him some, though. Why he'd took the risk for her. And why he'd come to this place at all, with the cold season settin' in. Why he scratched in that book of his and made pictures in it and tucked leaves tween the pages now and again. Why he watched her the troublesome way he did. Why he wanted to know about the roots and the leaves and the things the forest give to eat.

Why he was so different from anybody she'd ever come across before.

She'd thought to ask after him some, to understand his strange ways, but it was safer to keep shy of him, having nothin' more to do with him than just walkin' alongside and sharin' a night camp.

"Ain't a good sky," she said, tucking her skirt twixt her legs as she squatted down nearby him, but out of reach, to bind up her blankets. "More snow's a-comin'." Sooner or later, it'd be heavier than just a dustin', she knew. She'd kept them to the slopes so far, even though the goin' was hard. Less chance they'd be seen. Down on the cricks and rivers, the snow'd be less, but the people'd be more. Brown Drigger and his dogs would use the old trails along the bottoms, and so would Jep and his men. No need of them venturin' up the higher country. They knew, soon enough, the weather'd bring her right to their hands.

"Well, surely we're near the settlement you mentioned. You said two days, perhaps three."

She didn't hear him right off. Instead, she was watchin' his book. He'd scratched a picture in it today. She couldn't gander what it was, but she wanted to. Might be she'd sneak a look later, while he was off to hisself someplace without his possibles bag.

Her mind was slow to turn to what he'd said—*the settlement*. By then, his eyes were narrowin' at her. She'd given somethin' away without meanin' to.

"There is no settlement, and you've no idea where we're going. That's the truth of it!" He stood, a hand flyin' airborne like he meant to throw it from his body.

She shied away, scrambled back to her feet, and lifted an arm to block the blow. In the time with her daddy, Brown Drigger, and Pegleg Molly, her reflexes had got good.

"Stop that!" His look was fire now. Hot. Angered. And somethin' else that caught her unawares. He looked like she'd hurt him in some way, like the lie had broke somethin' between them. "Stop looking at me as though you're expecting a beating."

She was, of course, but she mustered up a couple words. "I ain't."

"I'm *not*," he spat, his chin jutting out to give meaning.

"*You* ain't?" He was likely the strangest man she'd ever knew. Wasn't much chance she'd be givin' *him* a beatin'. He outweighed her by twicet.

"No. You're *not*. I'm *not*." Both hands fluttered through the air this time, his voice rising. A bird skittered from the tree above. "*Ain't* is a foul word. Nothing for a young woman's mouth. Good heavens, were you reared in a den of blackguards as well as liars?"

There were words she didn't ken, but she knew enough, and she thought of Aginisi and Gran-dey, who'd raised her up and kept her safe and taught her all there was to know of survivin' from what the forest give. Aginisi and Gran-dey, who were gone now. Who'd been spoke ill of . . . by this helpless buckwheater who knew nothin' of how to keep hisself alive on the mountain.

Her hackles rose up as she scooped her blanket and the tiny bundle of tinder she'd tucked close to her skin to keep it warm and dry for tonight's fire. Hitchin' up her pack, she went to walkin' without givin' him much as another word.

~

Rand had doubled in on himself and begun to bolt before he comprehended that the sound was natural rather than man-made. They had reached the river's edge, but the snow had begun to fall in earnest, dimming the afternoon light and casting the mountains into shadow. Laden with autumn leaves and the new cache of snow, the trees moaned like lost souls, the occasional splitting of wood and falling of branches creating a sound not unlike the crack of a rifle shot and the reverberation of exploding powder.

No one would pursue them in this weather. There was no small hazard to traveling beneath the trees now, but in truth it was the bone-shattering cold that stole his attention from all else. Inside his boots, his feet were wet, numb, raw, burning and tingling with each step. He imagined what Sarra must be suffering in her homemade ankle-high moccasins. But she remained stark and stiff ahead. She'd not spoken to him since morning. Eventually, he cared little one way or the other. He'd wrapped his head and shoulders in his bedroll, unable to do anything but bend to the icy wind and follow the tracks she left behind.

It was he who first heard a lamb's prattle during a break in the wind—he who first looked up and saw the squat roof of a lean-to cabin on the opposite river shore, the curls of smoke from its chimney sifting away in the driving wind, so that neither he nor Sarra had smelled it.

*Thank God,* he thought. *Thank God!* He'd begun to wonder, only to himself, if in spite of all they'd survived, this was how they would go—frozen solid in the storm. Nothing to do with Jep and his men after all.

He forced his heavy legs to step up, to catch her, and he tugged the makeshift pack she'd created from one of her blankets. Her hair fell ice-tipped over his fingers as he pointed to the cabin on the far bank, then hurried to the shore to seek a means of crossing the water without further soaking his feet. A fallen log, lying top bank to top bank, offered a rickety bridge, and he shinnied over with his legs dangling on either side, rather than trust himself to balance on numb feet.

Sarra met him on the other shore, having clearly been there some time. He occasioned a quick remembrance of Revi's talk about Melungeons and the witching of forest spirits, which he quickly brushed away. Of course she'd not flown over the water but traversed it by some other means.

She hung back in the brush, he noticed as he stumbled up a small knoll, made more miserable, weary, and uncomfortable by the prospect of shelter and a warm fire not far away. He was quite certain he caught the scent of something cooking.

The bleating lamb was being dragged by a young girl in a dark wool cloak. She spied him before he could speak and ran to the house. Soon, a haggard-looking woman hurried from the door pointing a rifle in Rand's direction, her gray hair flying loose in the wind.

"Keep ye right 'ere." Her sharp drawl was barely recognizable as English. "Why ye come up'n here?"

He lifted his hands carefully, opening the blanket, allowing the wind to slice mercilessly in. "Seeking food and a place to shelter for the night. I've lost my mount and saddle several days ago, up the mountain. I can pay you." The last statement gained her attention. He had expected that it would. Offers of actual coin were rare in these parts.

She lowered the rifle a bit but didn't speak. From the porch, two half-grown red-haired girls watched him, now sharing the cloak.

"We need your help," he said in hopes of convincing the woman. "We mean no harm to anyone."

She peered suspiciously past him toward the brush. "Who ye got back 'ere? What'cha be hidin'?"

Too late, he realized his mistake. She suspected ambush. "No one but my traveling companion. A girl. We are only seeking shelter." He called for Sarra to show herself, and she did slowly, timidly leaving a snow-sugared growth of sapling pine.

The woman studied her, narrow-eyed. "Ye come nearish, gal. Up'n here a'side yer man."

Sarra did as she was asked, and the woman's chin rose as if she'd scented something foul. She returned her attention to Rand, circled the rifle barrel in his direction. "I'll sup ye, if'n ye pay fer it, but not her. Ain't havin' her kind round 'ere."

"For the love of God, woman. We're half-frozen to death."

"Said I ain't a-havin' her devil kind." The unmistakable cock of the rifle returned his attention to the woman. "Town a Three Forks be ten mile downwater. Take 'er there."

"We'll never survive ten more miles in this storm. Night will catch us before then." He'd been avoiding thinking of that grim reality—of how they'd fare, wet and bedraggled as they were—when the temperatures dropped and darkness came.

"Town be ten mile downwater. Bes' git a-walkin', ain't ye?"

"Have you at least a mount I might purchase? And food?"

"Not fer her. Her witchin' hand not be touched to nothin' a' our'n. Be off with ye now." She advanced a step, her finger twitching on the trigger, leaving him no option but to retreat, and Sarra with him. Not until they'd cleared the brush and stumbled some distance downriver did he catch his breath and cease expecting a bullet in the back.

"Sarra," he said finally. "Sarra, stop. I need a moment to think." His mind had turned back to the cabin, entertaining an idea that would have seemed unconscionable scant days before. There was the pistol in his pack. Perhaps he should circle back and take what they needed by force. Their very lives depended on it. Were there others in the cabin? A man? What might they be facing if they attempted this course?

What if he were forced to fire in defense? There were the little girls to consider. Mere innocents. He couldn't risk injuring them. . . .

What now? What next? How could he preserve both Sarra's life and his own?

She turned to him, her lips wind-chapped, cracked and bloodied, pressed tightly together to hide trembling, her eyes silver-pooled at the corners, her body quaking.

"Sarra," he said softly, reaching for her.

She pulled away, turning her shoulder and curling into herself, into the shelter of the brush rather than what protection his body could offer.

"Don't despair." He reached for her again, but a sound from the hill overhead stopped him. A soft, human sound. From behind an ancient, gnarled hickory, the girl in the wool cloak beckoned, a shaft of light catching the escaped curls of her red hair, causing her to appear almost otherworldly, so that he wondered if hypothermic hallucinations had descended upon him and death might be nearer than he'd thought.

He checked Sarra, noted that she was watching as well. The girl motioned them to come to her. *Perhaps*, he thought, *the woman in the house has seen reason after all.* He climbed the hill, following the girl, who did not speak but remained always some distance ahead, checking now and again to be certain they followed. Her face, circled by the hood, held the sweetness of an angel. She led them not toward the cabin, but farther up the slope, where she vanished among a nest of boulders, then reappeared atop one.

Turning to Sarra, Rand grabbed her before she could move away. "Stay here."

She shook her head and for the first time touched him willingly. "No." Her eyes were wide, fearful.

"Wait for me," he ordered more firmly.

She didn't, of course. He'd not moved far before he heard her behind him. They climbed the rocks in tandem and emerged along a ledge where an outcropping provided a providence he'd almost lost hope of. Shelter. Deep, dry, protected from both snow and wind. Standing in the center, the child smiled at him, then produced from beneath her cloak both a bundle of dry tinder and a poke fashioned of tow sack fabric. It fell open as she dropped it, revealing foodstuffs.

"Thank you," he breathed and wondered again if perhaps he were collapsed along the trail, his blood slowly running thick and ceasing, his mind only conjuring. "Your name. What is your name?" Until his dying day, he would commit this forest child, this tiny savior, to his prayers.

She uttered a guttural sound, made a motion that gave him to know she was mute, yet acute of mind.

Her lips formed an impish twist, and then she turned and was gone.

Together, he and Sarra descended upon the poke, ravenous for the potatoes, leeks, and goat cheese that had undoubtedly been spirited from root cellar stores somewhere near the house.

When he'd dropped the final bit in his mouth—he'd saved a bite of the goat cheese to enjoy last—he sat back on his heels and found Sarra licking her frost-cracked lips.

"Guess'n we'd best get us a fire," she said cheerfully, and for the first time since their acquaintance, she smiled. The shy, uncertain gesture surprised Rand, and he found himself smiling in return. Though his own face was wind-blistered and it should have been uncomfortable, he felt nothing but a sudden rush of warmth through his body, a draining of desperation and an inpouring of blessing.

"Guess we'd better."

I paused at the end of the chapter, letting my mind rise from the frigid mountain. On the lake outside the cabin, a loon called, the sound thin and threadlike in the cool, smoky air, lending to the illusion that story and reality were one.

Friday had parked himself in a chair by the window. Lifting his head, he turned slowly toward the glass and growled. Uneasiness brushed over my skin, though I couldn't say why.

My cell phone vibrated as I was contemplating heating the chai tea I'd brought from town. When I answered, Jamie was breathless on the other end. "I've been going crazy! You should never text me something like that when I'm tied up and can't answer. You *know* I've been stuck in the bridal bizarre all day, and if I'm on my phone, my sister will have a fit. She wants my *full* attention. Ish! So you found more of it again this evening? More of the mysterious, marvelous manuscript? Did you find the *man* to go with the *man*uscript, by any chance?"

Jamie's rapid-fire questions were a strangely abrupt transition back to the real world. "Okay, wait, take a breath over there and I'll give you the details." I checked the clock. Only nine, though it seemed like it should've been later. I filled Jamie in on the latest installment of *The Story Keeper*. "I still have more of it to read."

"Well . . . but who's bringing it? And why this way? Why all the cloak-and-dagger drama?"

"I have no idea. To tell you the truth, it's starting to spook me a little, but I *love* the story. It's fascinating."

"Maybe Evan Hall himself is behind all this. Have you thought of that angle? Maybe it's some sort of ploy to . . . drive up the price? No . . . I guess that doesn't make much sense. The man does have gold fingers, after all. He can pretty much get whatever he wants for anything he'd dump on the market. All he'd have to do is put the manuscript up for auction. He'd have every house in New York jumping on it. . . ." Jamie paused to search for further alternatives.

"Yes, I know."

"Maybe he's just . . . like . . . enjoying the chase. Yanking your chain a little. Based on some of the press, I get the impression he's not the most . . . normal kind of guy."

"He seemed normal enough. Hostile. But normal."

"Wait. Hold the phone. You *talked* to him? When? Where? How?"

"Yes, I did." Just thinking back to this afternoon made my blood simmer and then boil. The simmer came from the moments by the goat trailer, when everything had been pleasant and friendly. The boil came from the cold-eyed accusation that I would use two old women and a little girl to get what I wanted.

While filling Jamie in on the details, I grabbed yesterday's leftover nachos and heated them up. Friday came along to the kitchen to let me know he had no problem with leftovers, especially nachos. He whimper-growled and shot accusing looks my way until I shared.

"Needless to say—" I reached into the freezer for the half gallon of Moose Tracks ice cream I'd broken down and purchased after hanging around town, unsuccessfully trying to catch Helen Hall and explain why I'd abandoned her on the mountain— "negotiations broke down in the most gruesome of ways. So here I am now with another new chunk of the manuscript, but once again, no answers. Oh . . . and I've permanently alienated the guy I was supposed to be warming up. This just keeps getting more and more bizarre. I'm worried that I've made the biggest mistake of my life by pursuing this thing."

Jamie's end of the phone buzzed with uncharacteristically dead air. "I should've nixed my sister's shopping weekend and come with you. Listen, I could still grab a flight tomorrow, take some time off work, and—"

I didn't wait for the rest. "No, Jamie, this may take a few days, and you don't need to be away from work, especially with the situation at the magazine right now."

As much as company—or confirmation for all the strange things that had happened so far—would've been nice, I couldn't have Jamie along for any number of reasons, not the least of those being the letter from my sister. With my mission here seemingly falling apart, I couldn't put off the visit to Lane's Hill any longer. Tomorrow I'd have to confront Coral Rebecca, face to face. "Besides, I'm starting to feel like I'm off down a goat trail, anyway. No reason for both of us to waste our time."

"Off down a goat trail," Jamie repeated, laughing. "Listen to you—you sound all country already."

She was only joking, of course, but as we said good-bye, the comment continued to nibble at my mind. I felt the past coming for me, the memories surfacing like waterlogged debris overgrown with moss and impossibly tangled. The silt of conflicting emotions covered everything having to do with family. It had been that way for as long as I could remember. By the age of eight, I'd already started to see that life on Lane's Hill and the clockwork additions to our family weren't—couldn't be—normal. Joey was barely a year and a half old, and Mama was pregnant with another one. Daddy had come forward at the end of Sunday service to announce it to the Brethren Saints.

There'd been congratulations and pats on the back, but all I felt was a wave of despair coming my way, threatening to pull me under. Every time Mama got over nursing one baby and came back to normal, she was expecting another. When this new one showed up, we'd go through it all again.

*Breed like rabbits over there in Lane's Hill, the whole bunch of them,* I'd heard one of the mothers at the second-grade Christmas party say. I was sitting in the corner, forbidden from participating. *Can't feed them or keep them clothed, clean, and properly immunized half the time, but they can sure make 'em. It's primeval. That's what it is.*

I didn't know that big word, *primeval,* but I sorted out a piece of it—*evil.* My mind struggled to make sense of it.

*How could she say that? How could she say that about my mama?*

What did these women, these party moms, know? They lived lives of disobedience, of deadness, of eventual doom. They didn't follow the ways of the Brethren Saints, and all who fell outside the Brethren circle were destined to burn in the fires, sooner or later.

One of the moms set a cupcake on the desk where I waited

in the corner. *Here, sweetie. Surely you can at least have a snack and some punch. I scraped off the Christmas decoration and put the punch in a plain Dixie cup, okay?*

The sugary liquid swilled over my tongue, cool and tantalizing—the sort of treat that came and went around our home, depending on how fortunes were, on whether Daddy had sold a coon mule or a hunting dog recently, on whether the hay had come in thick or sparse.

I watched the other kids enjoying the Christmas party, tasted the cupcake, and began to wonder again why our lives were so different—how we could be right and everyone else could be wrong.

When Daddy'd announced the new baby in church, I'd looked around and thought, *Where we gonna put it?* Our trailer was bursting at the seams already, and so was the church. Pew after pew held families like our own. *Blessed are the faithful, for the Lord shall multiply their number.* Sunday after Sunday the girls of Lane's Hill were told that godliness was in obeying the decrees of the elders, *keeping pleasant*, being meek and cooperative, and above all, growing the number of the Brethren Saints.

How that could have ever made sense to me was now beyond my comprehension, as was the fact that it still made sense to my sisters.

Pushing away the thought, I rubbed my eyes, turned back to the manuscript, and reentered Rand and Sarra's world, opting for it rather than my own.

# Chapter 16

## The Story Keeper

### CHAPTER SEVEN

A sound caught Rand's ear, just audible over the noise of his own movement through the brush. He'd found a woodpile washed up along the river. Overnight, they'd burned much of what was close to the cave and scavenged the rest this morning. In their shelter, Sarra worked to protect their fire from drifting snow and driving winds that allowed them no chance of making the trip ten miles downriver until such time as the storm broke.

The rustle heightened his nerves but excited him. They'd not been resourceful enough in their use of the food the girl had given them, and she'd not come again thus far today. Save for the last few hickory nuts, they'd had nothing. He slid the pistol from his belt, listened. Something was moving quietly along the deer trail. A faint grunt traveled his way, the sound unfamiliar.

Hooves clattered against rock. A deer perhaps, but he'd mistaken the location. It was farther down the bank. He advanced several hurried steps, cocked the pistol, ran three paces more, and slid around a bush just in time to see his quarry, a scrawny-looking doe, bolting toward the water. Startled by his appearance, the doe twisted in midair and skittered down the bank.

He rushed after it, his breath coming fast now. Fresh venison for their next meal. An end to the gnawing hunger that had hounded them. The doe would give them all the meat they needed. He could fairly smell venison on a spit, roast—

Something small, black, and round stopped him short at the edge of the cover. He caught a scent—heavy, musky, familiar. His blood thickened, froze. Bear scat. The grunt he'd heard. He should've known . . .

The deer hadn't bolted idly into the open.

His stomach leapt and sank and leapt. Blood rushed to his limbs, but he forced himself to remain within his faculties. *Carefully, silently,* he thought. The creature in the brush paused and stretched upward, its nose protruding from the snow-laden leaves, scenting the air.

A black bear. Fully grown.

Rand didn't dare attempt to run. He'd been warned by Ira and by his own father. He froze in place, the stench choking his lungs, snowflakes touching his skin, then melting. Seconds fled, options rushing breakneck through his mind, scattering before he could focus on any one of them.

If he could reach the tumble of boulders nearby, scramble atop, perhaps the animal would decide he wasn't worth the trouble. At the very least, he'd be in a position to shoot more than once. It was unlikely he'd drop such a beast with one pistol shot. . . .

The bear broke the stalemate before Rand had decided on a course of action. Stumbling in its bulky balance, the creature crashed downward through brush, emitting a thunderous roar that echoed against the mountainside. The noise exploded past Rand and catapulted him to action. He did the very thing he'd been told not to do. He ran for all he was worth and didn't look back. There was no need. He could feel his attacker breathing down his neck, hear branches splintering and pebbles tumbling. He prayed for swift feet and aimed for the leeward side of the boulders, the area not coated by ice and snow.

He might have sprouted wings just then and grown the feet of a mountain goat as well. He couldn't have said. He was atop the boulders before his mind could register the process. Luckily, the bear did itself the misfortune of attempting to climb over a glaze of ice. It slid downward, landed, rolled, then regained its feet, roared furiously, and attempted the climb again, this time circling and batting the rock, testing its surface not three feet from Rand's boot bottoms.

Rand sighted the pistol, steadied his hand, waited until the shot was ideal. The explosion knocked him slightly off-balance on his icy perch, so for a moment he feared he'd be joining the bear. Only when it staggered backward, wobbled like a drunken sailor, then fell, did Rand finally allow himself to sink to his haunches and double forward, letting the blood rush to his head again. Some time passed before he had regained his faculties.

"Whew." He mopped icy moisture from his forehead, then glanced down at himself to be certain that he had, indeed, just survived his first confrontation with a black bear, without suffering so much as a scratch. Everything seemed in one piece.

"Whew!"

A bit more enthusiasm came over him then, prompted him to leave his perch and inch toward the fallen mass of fur.

He found a rock, tossed it. The bear lay motionless.

The thrill of the hunt rushed in, replacing the basic joy of survival with the ecstasy of triumph. "One shot! What a mountain man! What courage! What gumption!" He imagined the words in some eastern tabloid alongside an image of the bear. "What magnificent cunning and—"

Sarra's frantic call stopped him midsentence. He heard her running through the brush along the deer trail now.

Quickly he moved behind the kill, hid the pistol in his belt, and drew his knife from its scabbard. Bracing a boot on the bear's belly, he struck a commanding pose.

He was waiting thusly when she burst from cover, wielding a tree branch as a club. Her breathless state and white-rimmed eyes made it clear enough that she'd assumed the worst.

He arched his chest, jutted his chin, and wiped his knife on the bear's hide, though it was clean as a hound's tooth, not having been used in the kill. "No need for concern. Had to wrestle down a bear, but all's well."

Her eyes further widened, two silver coins against her hickory skin. Her hair blew loose in the wind, bits of snow feathering it. She'd not even grabbed up a blanket before charging to his aid. One careful step and then two, she narrowed the gap between them. "Wh-what come a yer pistol?"

"No need. He wasn't really worth wasting a bullet. Killed him with my bare hands instead." He thought of his sisters and how susceptible they always were to his teasing. Never was the time they didn't fall headlong into his traps.

Sarra stopped opposite him, the carcass between them. She prodded it with the stick, frowned, a furrow carving itself in her brow. "A shot come off close enough for hearin.'" A wary glance over her shoulder showed her concern that perhaps the shot had originated from somewhere nearby, and they were not alone.

Shrugging, Rand lifted a foot down from his kill. This was the first time he'd seen her appear genuinely impressed with something he'd done. He rather liked it. His mind spun another line along the web. "Oh, that was *after* I killed this big fella. I shot the pistol to warn off the *other* bear."

"There was two?" She wheeled now, a quick, nervous movement.

He bit back a chuckle. "There were two, just strolling together. I suppose they meant to have me for lunch. Why, the pair of them stood up on their hind legs and as much as told me so. 'Rand Champlain,' they said, 'you haven't got much meat on you, but we're two hungry bears on this snowy day.'"

She swiveled slowly in his direction, her nostrils flaring, her lips drifting apart, hovering between a smile and a frown. Recoiling, she eyed him from beneath dark lashes. "And what'd you clabber-mouth back at 'em?"

Sheathing the knife, he acted out the drama with his hands. "I said, 'Fellas, I'm one hungry man and you two had best be on your way before I decide to have *you* for lunch.' When they didn't leave, I knew I'd have to fight them, of course."

"A'course." Her hands found resting places on her hips. "And what happen't then, I'm wonderin.'" Her eyes glittered bright and acute, her lips glistening with the moisture of a salve she'd created of crushed yarrow root. Poised along the snowy riverbank, she was an image of something wild, mysterious.

He suddenly left off all thoughts of former pranks and his sisters.

"It was two against one, and they were bigger than me, but I wasn't scared. I have to give due credit to the bears. They were quite gentle-manlike, and they came at me only one at a time—the big one first. When I killed him, the little one turned tail and ran off. I sent a shot after him, just to make sure he'd cleared the area."

She bent forward over the bear and looked more closely. "Truth be tolt?" A smile attempted to take her mouth then, but she held it from him. "Good them bears was mannersome, ain't it?"

Rand met her gaze and grinned. She was, he realized now, the first thing that had crossed his mind when he'd faced the bear. He'd feared leaving her here. He'd wondered who would protect her if he could not.

Strangely, he'd seen the reflection of that concern when she'd burst onto the riverbank, brandishing her weapon. Perhaps she feared losing him as much as he feared losing her.

Something inside him struggled to find shape, and he had no reference points for it. Indeed, it fell upon him like a fruit collected from some heretofore unknown tree. It was unlike other things. He owned no label that would categorize it. He knew only that he could not leave this wild and dangerous country until he'd found a suitable place for Sarra. A safe place.

She met his gaze momentarily, seemed perhaps as bewildered as he. Then she stretched her hand toward the knife, her fingers brushing his along the handle. He did not resist but let her take charge of it.

"What . . . ?" No intelligible grouping of words came to his mind. The stories, spinning within him only moments ago, had flown.

Sliding the knife from the scabbard, Sarra moved over the kill, grabbing the bear's thick hide. "The meat," she said.

Somewhere in the distance, Rand heard what might have been the far-off baying of a hound, and at once he was reminded that his shot had undoubtedly echoed along mile upon mile of river and mountain.

## CHAPTER EIGHT

Sarra rose early for the wood gatherin', letting Rand stay there asleep. Outside, the snow fluttered down yet and the cold painted smoke on her breath. There'd be no travelin' on today. A body could freeze in such weather, and with the killin' of the bear, they had want of nothin' else but more tinder to keep the fire. They'd let it burn low overnight, but they'd heard no more sign of hound nor men. Nothin' but the wind stirrin' the high trees and groans of the heavy-burdened branches.

The mornin' was quiet neath the tall timber, too, but some critter had come out to scratch round. 'Twasn't big enough to worry over—a rabbit or a bushy-tailed squirrel hunting nuts—but somethin' was nearby. She listened after it as she tended to herself and gathered wood. A branch of oak had come down overnight, dead enough, and she reckoned she could break it some smaller and drag it upslope to stoke the mornin' fire.

The critter wandered into the open then. A rabbit. Wasn't any need in killing it, so she only watched as it spotted her and hunkered low. She thought of its heart beatin' fast, its muscles drawed up, fear skitterin' through.

"Sssshhhh," she whispered, moving toward it. "Git on home, little friend." This was the thing Aginisi said to the critters that wasn't to be took for food nor skins.

*All breath in ever'thing been give by Father God, Granddaughter,* she'd say. *Not a one he ain't mindful a. All lives be mattersome to him. Not a one oughtn't to be mattersome to us, same way.*

The rabbit held still in its place, so close now, she could've touched it if she'd a mind to. "Too cold for bein' out this mornin'." She leaned toward it, taking pleasure in the nearness, in the gentleness of the wild thing. Just a young'un. Not yet full growed. If it lived the winter, it'd mate and raise litters, come spring.

If it lived.

Its dark eye mirrored the trees and sky, a tiny world all its own. She stared into it, took in the quiet of it, the beauty.

Somethin' moved in the tree shadow, the reflection shifting in the rabbit's eye. Sarra heard it then—hooves strikin', breath laborin', the sound almost gone in the snow.

Her heart caught like the rabbit's, and *she* was the wild thing, afraid of drawin' breath or movin'.

She squatted lower, turned just enough to see. Horse and rider were climbin' up the slope. He would've spotted her, if he'd looked her way, but instead he was watchin' something else—the track her and Rand had padded down while carrying the meat uphill to string in a tree not far off from their camp.

She knew the horse, a skewbald bay. She'd rode many a mile tossed over its withers, the saddle and the slave chain cuttin' her in halves.

Cupping her breath, afraid even the curl of cold-smoke might pull Revi's eye her way, she stayed where she was. Beside her, the rabbit tensed, ready for flight. If it was to bolt now, the boy would hear it and look.

*Steady, little friend.* The thought was no more than a whisper in her mind.

Moments crept off as she waited, her thoughts runnin' ahead. Up above, Rand was asleep yet, the pistol at his side. He'd have no chance against Revi. Where'd Jep and the others gone? Mayhap they'd found the cave a'ready?

She prayed it wasn't so, closed her eyes and asked Father God to lead them off someplace else.

Revi was near past before she crept back toward cover. One step. Two. Three. She made herself quiet, small, melted in without a sound, then took a twig and shooed the rabbit off the other way. It scampered toward the horse before wheelin' itself round and skitterin' toward the river.

Revi stopped his mount, spun it end for end so's it slid and staggered in rock and snow, its mouth gapin' and belchin' out steam.

"You hear somethin'?" Revi's voice echoed through the trees.

No answer come. How far away was Jep? Where were the others? Had Rand heard the voice? Had he woke?

Revi scanned the slope toward the river, then circled. Sarra closed her eyes as he passed close, castin' off the smell of wood fire and mash whiskey and the horse's salt lather. They'd rode hard, even in the snow.

Blood thumped in her ears as she peered through the brush, saw the horse's white feet, smelled its breath, caught sight of its ear twitchin' her way. The animal sidestepped, lost its footin' over a log, and staggered a pace or two.

"Har now! Har now, ya sorry snake!" Revi scolded the animal, slashing the loose rein against its flank.

A gunshot rang out someplace back toward the cabin where they'd met the woman and little girls. A second shot answered. Revi wheeled his mount and clattered off down the trail bent low to his saddle, lookin' here and yon over his shoulders, wonderin' after the sound.

Sarra couldn't make herself move. Her body quaked and air burned her lungs as she dragged in breath. Her stomach boiled up her throat and tears stung, sourish and hot.

"Sarra." She heard his whisper before his hand caught her arm and pulled her from the brush. "Are you hurt?"

She couldn't answer but to shake her head.

"We must move," Rand whispered. "Sarra, we must leave. Do you hear me? We can't stay here."

He led her like a child, took her a short ways to where he'd dropped a blanket and his poke. Slingin' them on his back, he grabbed up her hand again, and they ran blind and careless, fear nippin' at their legs.

Tears stung her eyes, streamin' warm, then cold, over her skin. She couldn't keep them back, and she couldn't let them take holt, neither. Her and Rand made the river and crossed over and stayed 'long its shore where the shelter of the bank had held off the snow and their feet wouldn't leave tracks. There was no thought in her mind but to run far and fast as her body'd take her. Only when legs and lungs give out did they stop for breath.

His cheeks were red and hot as he faced her, the tails of his hair stringed with ice. "Have you gone daft, leaving while I was asleep yet? When I looked and you weren't there . . ." His hand caught her arm again. "It's only luck that I woke. That I came searching for you. That I spotted Revi before he found me out."

"I w-went wood gatherin'." Her voice shook with the tears.

"With no gun? For the love of heaven, I was beset by a bear here yesterday. And we heard the hounds." His mouth hung slack, then snapped together. "We knew they could have homed in on the shot yesterday."

Her mind run like a mouse huntin' a hole to scramble in. She couldn't fess up to what was true—that she'd sat long and watched him sleep, takin' the chance to look without him looking back. She'd studied the line of his chin, the thin sprouts of pale beard, the hay-colored curls that fell over his forehead, the curve of his mouth, the way his lips twitched like he was talkin' to someone in his dream. She remembered the smile there as he'd boasted of the bear, and then she was smilin' herself while she watched him sleep.

Then come a yearning, a strange feel she couldn't place, and it troubled her some and drove her to the wood fetchin' alone. She'd hoped to clear her mind in the early-morning cold.

"I was listenin' out for hounds and watchin' for bear scat." She stopped her chin tremblin' and lifted it instead. Truth told, she should've been listenin' better, but her mind was pondering that thing she'd felt while watchin' him asleep beside the fire. "Been livin' with bear all my born days."

She didn't wait for his answer but turned off and started into the woods. The storm was closing again, the wind cuttin' straight to her bones and the snow fallin' thick. It'd cover their tracks and their scent, but they'd never make it ten mile downwater before they froze solid. She'd have to hunt them a place to den up and cover theirselves over good with pine straw and leaves to keep warm.

With only two blankets tween them now, it'd be a long, bitter wait for the snow to stop and the sun to poke through. She prayed it'd happen before another night passed, and then she believed it would. Father God was one for listenin' and answerin' them who asked of him and believed on him.

He was close by, even in the storm.

~

A smile parted the man's thick gray beard, and he waved a hand toward Rand. "Relax, friend, I ain't gonna bite'cha. Fella don't git many chances to visit with his own kinda folk round here. We got to help each other where we can. I been watchin' you since you come stumbling into Three Forks yesterdey. Mind if'n I sit?"

Rand motioned the man in. He couldn't see the harm in it, though he leaned back in his chair and slipped a hand into his pack, touching both the pistol and his grandfather's Bible. He and Sarra had attracted no small bit of attention, dragging in on foot yesterday as they had, weather-beaten and nearing exhaustion after walking downriver to Three Forks when the storm finally broke. It was a measure of good fortune that the day had warmed considerably, the sun quickly beginning to melt the snow. They'd made their way along the water's edge, skirting occasional habitations to avoid witnesses to their passing wherever possible.

Rand had managed to secure accommodations in Three Forks, but the reception had been an uneasy one, and it had left him with the conclusion that he could not arrange a safe place for Sarra here and travel on alone, as he had planned.

In fact, the sooner they were away from this place, the better. He was eager to purchase mounts from the string of stock due in town within a day or two, and then leave the Trask Rooming House behind. They'd been relegated to a space off the stable, Sarra being unwelcome in the rudely appointed addition that offered dining and several boarding rooms. The lean-to where she slept yet this morning seemed more fit for sheltering animals than humankind, but in truth they were both greatly relieved to have come through their ordeal in the wilderness and finally found shelter, as well as a warm fire.

The stranger set his coffee on the slab-wood table between them, then leaned forward and rubbed his weather-raw hands together. "Snowmelt's gonna make the road wet 'n' slow."

"Yes, I imagine it will."

"Headin' out soon, are ya?"

Rand's back stiffened. He'd been unprepared, he supposed, for the reception here thus far. He had always been accustomed to receiving the respect given the Champlain name, and if the name did not speak, his money typically did.

"Yes, we'll be leaving as soon as I'm able to purchase mounts. I'm told there's not one to be had in the village until a new stock string arrives in a day or two."

He caught something in the man's expression, a slight narrowing behind the smudged spectacles, a twitch of the cheek. "That stock string'd be mine, and it's due here this mornin'—mules and draft animals to take up the valley to Soldier's Rock. Got me the contract to put in a timber and sash mill there."

In another circumstance, Rand would have questioned the man about his work, and taken in the details with great interest. Instead, he said, "I've been promised that another string is to be delivered any day now. Saddle stock."

The man removed his eyeglasses then, introduced himself as Hudson Johns, to which Rand replied with his own name.

Hudson twisted the glasses between his fingers, leaning close. "Son, supposin' you tell me how you and yer Melungeon woman come to walk in here without a pot 'n' spoon between ya?"

Rand stalled for time by taking a sip of his coffee. Did he dare be honest with this man? Who could say what sort of reward might have been placed on Sarra's return by now? Or on his own head?

"Y'ain't been up here long, have ya? I ain't seen ya round ner heard of ya."

A hint of relief caused Rand to loosen his fingers on the pistol. If Hudson had not heard of him, then most likely the story, as well as Jep and Brown Drigger, had not traveled here. Three Forks would be a safe enough place to wait for available saddle horses. "No. I haven't been in the area long. I came just weeks ago from Charleston to winter in the mountains. I'm afraid I fell into some difficulty before the storm and lost my mount along with the bulk of my provisions."

"Get youself robbed, did ya?"

"In a manner of speaking."

"You get your little Melungeon woman somewhere in that fracas?" Hudson chuckled. Coffee sloshed over his sleeve and he seemed untroubled by the stain. Indeed, the garment appeared to have seen similar treatment since its last washing.

His assumption disturbed Rand, as did the laughter and the odd regard from the widow Trask behind the cookstove. "She isn't my . . . woman." He was uncomfortable even speaking the word, as it suggested an unholy arrangement of a sort he would never have considered.

Hudson stroked the thick, frost-colored beard that hung low

over his woolen vest. "Can't recall when I ever seen a Melungeon gal fetchin' as that one. I'm figurin' it could be the losin' of the horse had somethin' to do with the takin' of the gal." Raising a palm, he added, "Now don't go spitish on me, young feller. I understand it. Got me a little Cherokee wife, myself. Bonnie. She's a good sort. Fine a woman as ever there was. Some folk don't understand it, but a man can't do his decidin' by what other folks thinks."

Rand drew himself taller, angling away from the idea and all that it implied. "I'm only up for the winter. I plan to travel west from here, and when the year is up, I'll return to Charleston. I have commitments there."

"Not wantin' to leave no tangles behind here when ya go?" Hudson interpreted.

"Yes . . . I suppose you could put it that way."

Hudson tossed back his head and gave a belly laugh that again attracted the widow Trask's attention. "Might be you ain't realized it yet, but you're tangled up a'ready. Any man comes here and survives for more'n a month is tangled, and 'sides that, I seen how you's lookin' at that girl yesterdey."

Rand shrugged off the assertion, though those selfsame thoughts had perturbed him before. Only this morning, he'd risen from his pallet and thought first of Sarra, asleep just on the other side of the curtain. "I'll be returning home at summer's end."

"Could be ya will." There was a knowing twinkle in Hudson's eye as he brought himself close again to restrict their conversation from the widow Trask's ears. "I ain't tryin' to rile ya, son. Just tryin' to get an understandin' of how much trouble you're like to be. I'm leavin' out this mornin', and I still got need for good, strong men. The girl could help my Bonnie tend after the food and the washin'. If you can cipher numbers, read, and write, I'll pay a third-again more'n my hired men get. Back-east investors want this mill sawin' lumber by spring. Ain't gonna be an easy job in this weather, but old Hudson's built up many a mill, and I ain't never missed deliverin' on time yet. Won't be lettin' it happen this time, neither. Been some diphtheria goin' round this winter. I've had me a hard time puttin' on a full crew."

Rand considered the idea warily. He had no way of knowing whether the offer could be trusted. On the other hand, if Hudson were a decent sort of fellow, perhaps he and his Cherokee wife could be persuaded to keep Sarra in their employ and look after her beyond the building of the mill. "I haven't been in search of a position, however . . ."

The intensity of Hudson's gaze bisected Rand's sentence, leaving him gaping at the man, mute.

"Son, before you say no, you better listen at me a minute. The only stock string comin' into Three Forks anytime soon's the one that'll be goin' up the mountain to my mill site. There ain't any more arrivin', and if somebody told ya there was, that'd be because somebody's tryin' to *keep* you in Three Forks for a *reason*. If you're wise, you'll say, 'Yes sir, Mr. Johns,' real nice-like, and then you'll git your gal and scamper off to my mule wagon out back and wait up under the canvas till I leave out. Somethin' bad's afoot here, and I been feelin' it ever since you two come stumblin' up that trail."

# Chapter 17

The sound was barely audible over the rush of water in the old wall sink. Turning off the tap, I listened. Someone was knocking, the noise insistent, demanding.

I looked in the mirror, had the moment of panic that comes from uncertainty combined with lack of makeup and wet hair.

The knock outside grew louder and more rapid.

"Just a minute." Scuttling into shoes and finger-combing my hair, I hurried to the door.

When I opened it, standing on the other side was none other than Evan Hall. Not. Looking. Happy.

His arms were crossed over his chest, his chin set, his lips clenched in a thin line. They parted only enough to admit three gruff words. "You're still here." His languid Southern drawl stretched the sentence, made it sound almost polite in a strange sort of way.

"Yes, I am." This was the last, last, last thing I needed this morning. After the showdown at Evan Hall's estate yesterday, and then finding more *Story Keeper* chapters, I'd almost put Coral Rebecca and the family problems out of my mind, but today there wasn't much choice. I had to drive over to Lane's Hill and confront the latest crisis in person, while I still could. I was a basket case already, and I hadn't even left the cabin yet.

"And why is that?" He scratched an index finger alongside his lip, let it hang there a moment. His gaze took me in—dark, icy, but probing also, as if he were trying to figure out whether I believed him, whether I felt sufficiently threatened.

"'Stay on the trail until you get answers.' They taught us that in journalism class at Clemson." Nobody, but *nobody*, had treated me with this much disdain since I'd left Lane's Hill behind. Suddenly my hackles were standing at full attention.

Friday must have sensed the escalating hostilities. He circumvented my feet, nudged past the screen door, and moved onto the porch, taking up a position between the intruder and me.

"Clemson," Evan Hall repeated, his lips forming a rueful twist. "Clever of your publisher to send someone with local ties. Sort of a stealth attack. I have to give them credit. No one has tried exactly that before."

"Purely an accident. The manuscript that brought me here just *happened* to end up on my desk. I didn't ask for it." Somewhere beyond the irritation, a tiny caution flag struggled for attention. *Be careful what you reveal,* it warned. If the manuscript was his, and someone was delivering pieces of it to the cabin without his knowledge, he could stop further chapters from showing up.

A harsh, sardonic laugh answered. "I haven't sent a manuscript out on a cold call in twenty years."

I met his gaze, the pent-up tension of the morning spurring

me forward when I probably should have been pulling on the reins. "This thing is twenty years old. It came from some ancient slush, but there was no cover letter and no return address."

That set him back a moment, brought a slight pause, a split-second regrouping. Just as quickly, the surprised look was gone. "It isn't mine."

"Then we have nothing to talk about, do we?" What was wrong with me? I was supposed to be negotiating with this man, not widening the gulf. I never let my emotions get in the way of business. Growing up, I'd learned to keep anger, outrage, pain, and all other reactions locked inside. Girls who didn't keep pleasant were sharply reminded why they should.

But right now, I wanted to strike back, and Evan Hall was within reach.

His eyes flared. "You expect me to believe that malarkey about some manuscript from a twenty-year-old slush pile? My aunt and my grandmother may have swallowed that line, but—"

"Look it up. Vida House Publishing. George Vida. Yes, we still shuffle paper, and we still have an actual slush pile. There's been more than one article written about it."

His fingers twitched, rattling the car keys. I'd stumped him temporarily. It felt good. "Do we have an understanding?"

"About what?"

"About your *leaving*. I'd rather not have to take out yet another restraining order."

In retrospect, it seemed impossible that this lout could have so tenderly encapsulated the mind of a sixteen-year-old girl trapped by prejudice and dangerous men, or the gentle stirrings of an impossible love between young people from two different worlds.

What if Evan Hall wasn't the one I was chasing at all? What if I really was completely off base?

"Stay away from my aunt . . . and my grandmother . . . and my house."

"I was invited there."

"They're old. They're vulnerable. It's bad enough that my family has to live with the crazies sneaking onto the property, the lurkers at the gate, and all the rest of it. I'm not having some rabid opportunist take advantage of them. Or Hannah. I'd rather not take legal action."

Flames wicked off my skin and singed the hairs standing on the back of my neck. "You know what, I've been editing nonfiction for *ten years*, including enough true crime to choke a horse. I've read so much legal mumbo jumbo I could practically *be* a lawyer by now. Your aunt owns a store, and the store is open to the public. I've rented a cabin that belongs to her and your grandmother. I was asked to come along on the trip up the mountain yesterday. That is so far from stalking that you can't even throw a rock and *hit* stalking from there." My voice echoed through the trees and onto the lake, startling a flock of mallards along the shore. Friday turned to watch their flight, while Evan Hall and I stood locked in a combat of wills and secondhand legal knowledge.

He trained the key-jangling finger my way and took a step closer. Friday, God bless him, bristled the hair on his pudgy little back and went into attack mode, trying to take down the great Time Shifters mastermind boot toe first. It was the only time Friday had ever been good for something other than wet-mopping floors and consuming unwanted leftovers.

Evan Hall's chin jutted out as he nudged the dog away. "There! Your mutt bit me. You know what the number one civil lawsuit is? Dog bites."

The rage in me shattered like glass, and a laugh punched

through. I swallowed it. "Oh, *puh*-lease. I'll go to the press and tell them you went *legal* because you were attacked by a *Chihuahua*." The screen door slammed behind me as I stepped out to capture Friday. "If you really didn't have anything to do with the *Story Keeper* manuscript, then just leave me alone before . . . before I . . . sic my dog on you again."

His lips actually twitched at one corner, even though he was trying to fight it.

I remembered, in an inconvenient way, what a nice smile he had before the brooding celebrity persona came out.

"Well now, *there's* a threat."

"It's not a threat. It's a promise. Go ahead, make my day." I shook Friday at him, and Friday bit air in a wild semicircle, effectively turning himself into a canine buzz saw.

Evan coughed in his throat, but the hint of mirth quickly faded into a weary smirk.

I football-tucked Friday against my hip. "Listen, I'm not trying to hurt anybody. I'm just trying to do my job."

His eyes narrowed slightly, held mine. Something electric and dangerous crackled between us, the jolt momentarily stunning me. "Keep away from my mountain, Ms. Gibbs. Whether you're invited or not. And stay away from Hannah. She's got enough issues in her life. She misses her mother, and she doesn't need someone pretending to be her friend."

I grabbed the screen door, opened it, said, "I have the cabin rented for a week. I intend to stay." Actually, the cabin only rented by the week. Hollis hadn't expected me to need that many days when she'd booked the place.

I'd led George Vida to believe I'd have this mystery sorted out quickly. The thought made me ill. I was like a gambler pushing all my chips toward the pot and slowly drawing one losing card after another. These mountains, with their legacy of painful ties and jagged memories, were the worst place for me to be risking everything. The dangers here weren't just professional, they were personal.

Evan Hall's footsteps faded as I slammed the door behind me. Leaning against it, I let my eyes fall closed and sank to the welcome mat as the tears pressed through. I didn't even know all the places they came from. Now, yesterday, years ago.

A hundred torn places left ragged for want of a mending thread.

Friday, pinned against my legs, wiggled around and licked the salt from my skin.

I gave in and let the tears happen. *A good rain smooths out the soil,* Wilda Culp used to say. I needed a good rain.

When I rose from the floor, I felt logy and numb, more in tune with a nap than a confrontation with my family. I finished dressing, then readied Friday to go along on the journey because, in reality, I didn't want to do it alone. Friday, at least, was glad to be getting out of the cabin after being left behind yesterday. He stretched his chin upward again, lifting his neck folds off the collar so I could clip the leash.

When we stepped off the porch, Horatio was waiting near the corner of the yard, ready to stage an ambush. He raised his head and lifted his wings, and Friday tried to climb me like a tree.

"Stop!" I yelled, pointing a murderous finger at the goose. "I am *not* in the mood."

Horatio, either offended or surprised, froze where he was and just stood displaying his wingspan as Friday and I got in the car, then circled the yard and began to crawl up the driveway, the wheels spinning and grinding on washouts and loose rocks.

Friday threatened Horatio through the rear window, then

moved enthusiastically from seat to seat, taking in the view as we hit the open road. He barked at the Warrior Week encampment, yipped at yard dogs, and slathered up the glass while taking on a pair of pit bulls in a passing pickup truck.

Finally the passenger seat and a nap called him home, and I took advantage of the quiet, rolling down the window and letting the cool autumn air swirl over me as I drove through Looking Glass Gap. The streets were unusually quiet, and it was only after I passed a tall, white-clapboard church that I realized why.

No wonder I hadn't heard from Helen this morning. This was Sunday.

I wasn't even certain why I kept driving. My entire family would be in church for a couple hours yet. It was the perfect excuse to turn around and go back to the cabin, but if I did, it was entirely possible that I'd never have the courage to make this trip again.

Something heavy began to settle on me—an inconvenient realization. At home, Sunday was usually just another workday. One in which I didn't have to get up and go into the office, but I still devoted my hours to my job. Somehow I'd always told myself that was fine, but now I felt guilty. Maybe it was the stark beauty of the mountain autumn, the flash of maples and sweet gums clad in incredible color, the deep-green steeple of pines stretching toward the sky, but my thoughts turned upward. I imagined Sarra and her prayers, her belief that God was vibrant and ever present.

I imagined Rand and his fear that, in the wilderness, God could not hear him at all.

The truth was, I yearned, in a soul-deep way, to be Sarra. To *feel* that God was so very close, so very concerned with my particular life, so very ready to protect and to love. Always nearby. Always listening. Always leading.

But I simply didn't know how to get from here to there—how to finally disconnect the ties of the Brethren Saints and step into a faith that exchanged bondage for freedom. The old threads were still there, hidden beneath the surface.

Turning off the highway, I wandered along a winding country road, contemplating, killing time, letting the passing miles settle my thoughts. The pavement ended as the road wound farther down the hollow. Overhead, the trees closed in and the land grew more hardscrabble. Ragtag homes patched with tar paper and decaying trailer houses leaned against the wind and squatted in the shelter of trees. Mailboxes yawned on crooked posts, their domes bashed by teenagers enjoying midnight drive-by sprees with baseball bats. Dogs barked, straining against chains. Skinny, weary-looking horses, mules, and milk cows ignored my passing, intent on the search for food among bare dirt and rocks.

On the porch of a trailer house, a toddler in saggy, dirt-gray underwear wandered with a baby bottle dangling in one hand, seemingly mindless of the cooler weather this morning. In the ditch out front, a pair of boys in grungy jeans squatted beside a puddle, a rusted coffee can waiting between them. Not far down the road, a teenage girl in black cowboy boots twisted around and around on a tire swing, her head tipped back, blonde hair flying. Sixteen, maybe seventeen. There was a dirty playpen in the yard with a baby trying to climb from it.

The girl stopped swinging and looked hopefully past the fence as my car rattled by.

I wondered if the baby was hers.

She yelled something, pointed at the road. I just kept driving until she finally faded out of sight.

Near a slant-sided log house that looked like it could've been there since the days of Brown Drigger, a woman was digging with a small hand hoe alongside a creek. Harvesting leeks, I realized. This was the season for it. Time to string them together and hang them in the root cellar for later use.

*"We remember the fish, which we did eat in Egypt freely; the cucumbers, and the melons, and the leeks, and the onions, and the garlick,"* Wilda Culp said in my mind. *Numbers 11:5.*

*See, I am not the heathen they tell you I am, Jennia Beth Gibbs. But there are many who quote the Bible yet understand not a word. God is the great mystery, and we must each delve into mystery. No one else can know him for you. That, my girl, is truth.*

*Yes, ma'am,* I'd responded blandly. When she said things like that, it scared me. It was so far from what I'd been taught. I already had my mama's impure blood to make up for, and I didn't want to end up in the fiery pit. For the most part I tried not to listen when Wilda Culp strayed into the realms of religion.

The leek-digging woman straightened, bracing a hand on the small of her back. She watched me with consternation from beneath her sunbonnet.

A half mile farther along, I crossed a small bridge, rounded a corner, and discovered the reason. The road ended abruptly at a twelve-foot chain-link fence that was incongruously modern and decidedly familiar.

I should've known, from the direction the road was going, that it would eventually conflict with the domain of Evan Hall. No telling how many of these old logging trails he'd managed to remove from public use when he'd sectioned off his mountaintop.

Apparently my sightseeing trip was over, but it didn't matter, I supposed. By the time I wandered all the way back to the highway and drove to Towash, then twelve miles beyond to Lane's Hill, Coral Rebecca might be home. I wanted to talk to her first. The letter had come from her. Of all my sisters, Coral Rebecca, the quiet one, was the most *together*. Her husband was still work-ing for the timber company, last I'd heard, which meant they had regular income other than welfare, disability, and whatever they could make at swap meets.

A bird flitted past as I slowed to cross the bridge again. Its perch caught my eye—a rusted sign, the letters and numbers almost faded beyond reading.

1947

Sarra Bend Bridge

I blinked, hit the brakes, and looked again. *Sarra Bend Bridge.* It wasn't my imagination.

The bird flitted off as I exited the car, blocking Friday's hasty attempt to follow. Somewhere upstream, a waterfall rushed and gurgled. Its music enveloped me, giving the moment a dreamlike quality as I moved toward the sign, touched the surface, ran my fingers along the clinging scraps of paint, marveled that it could be there.

Had someone—Evan Hall or whoever the story's author really was—named a character after this place, or had this place been named for a woman who *really existed*? Could the story be true?

Grabbing my phone, I snapped a photo, intent on preserv-ing the proof. Proof of *what*, I had no idea. The mystery teased my senses as I returned to the car and rolled slowly onward, the bridge fading in the rearview.

I stopped where the woman was digging, got out again, and walked to the edge of the grass, Friday watching from the window.

"Ya lost?" She shook the dirt off a clump of roots before look-ing up. In the shadow of the bonnet, her face was weathered and leathery, her mouth puckered inward, indicating the absence of teeth.

"I didn't realize the road was closed off down there."

"Been while now, thataway. No town down there n'more." She returned to digging, offering neither an opinion nor interest in more conversation.

"I was wondering about the bridge. There's a sign on it that says *Sarra Bend Bridge*. Do you know where that name came from?"

Bracing a hand on her back, she mopped her forehead with an arm and observed me. "Be Sarra Crick there, and Sagua Falls up a piece." The trowel traced the line of tall trees at the end of a cleared field. "Been such long's I knowed it. My pap brung the mule teams fer takin' out the old mill bridge so's this'un could go up, back in Depression days. Them letters was a-scratched in a bur oak tree up the way yander-piece. *S-A-R-R-A*.

"Mama never did cotton it much. Said the Cherokee done it, and it were a heathen word. But she's a nervish type, my mama. Growed up over'ta Asheville. Never did like it too good down t'holler. Back when there wadn't no highway, folk went on this-away to Towash. Was a mill 'n' a mill town down the crick. Ain't there n'more."

Nodding toward the road, she dusted her hands. "Used'a have us a stand, front a the house. Sold vegdables and rootstocks. Not many folk wander down here n'more . . . less they're a-stayin'." A practiced eye turned skyward, and the light caught her time-weathered face. "Rain's a-comin. You bes' git out while ya can."

# Chapter 18

Clouds stretched over the mountains, muting the afternoon light in Coral Rebecca's yard. Beneath a thick growth of pines, the blue modular house nuzzled a rock ridge. A pretty location. The place was clean and well kept, but small for a family of four. In a winter-barren garden spot nearby, the last of the fall onions waited to be harvested. White bedsheets snapped on a clothesline, the breeze breathing life into them.

I recognized the front porch from some of Coral Rebecca's Christmas pictures, I thought.

Across the yard, two pairs of small feet cavorted behind the clothesline. Little-girl giggles danced over the grass, then halted at the noise of my car door closing. An imp who looked startlingly like Coral Rebecca peeked around the edge of a sheet, and then another girl, slightly older, trotted out a few steps and stood with her head tipped, looking at me. She resembled Coral

Rebecca too. White-blonde hair, luminous blue eyes, thin limbs draped in pale skin that didn't take to the sun, except to burn.

"Deedee?" I guessed, based on the last set of photos. The ones that had arrived just before the request for money. This was Diane Lenelle, named after my sister and my grandmother, but they called her Deedee.

Her younger sister wandered out, and Deedee extended an arm to stop her from coming closer. The motion was so familiar, I almost felt it in my bones—that quick, protective instinct between siblings who never felt fully safe. Who weren't quite certain of anything. I hadn't been prepared for the girls to remind me so much of us. It almost hurt to look at them, garbed in long, old-fashioned dresses that fell below the calves. Burgundy cotton. Homemade. Sunday clothes, no doubt. Their curly hair was French braided in double plaits behind their heads.

"I'm your aunt Jennia Beth." Even after hearing it a few times over the recent days, it still felt strange to say it. I had been *Jen* for so many years now. The only time I saw *Jennia Beth* was on insurance forms and legal paperwork, and I hated it even then. "Is your mama around?"

Deedee flicked a glance toward the house, gauging whether she should attempt to run past me, calculating the risk of abandoning her little sister with a stranger in the yard. The thought process was evident, just from watching.

"It's okay. You two go on in and tell her Jennia Beth is here. I'll wait." I retreated a few steps to let them know I wasn't planning to nab anyone on the way by. Kids among the Brethren Saints were taught to be careful of outsiders. Deedee bolted with her sister in hand, trying to move the three-year-old at a six-year-old's pace.

After they were gone, I stood looking at the trees, trying to wrap my mind around all of this, to prepare myself to appear in my sister's yard after so many years. She would wonder why I was here. She'd expected a check, not a surprise visit. What if she felt that she was being hijacked? What if, by showing up without letting her know first, I was starting things off on the wrong foot?

But then, this discussion wouldn't be ending in a good place, no matter how it began. I couldn't tell Coral Rebecca what she wanted to hear.

A chill slid under my bomber jacket, and I hugged my arms, shivering against the wind from the gathering storm. The woman at Sarra Creek was right. A cold rain wouldn't be more than a few hours behind. The clouds churning over the far peaks mirrored my thoughts as I waited.

I hoped Coral Rebecca came out of the house alone. I had the impression of her husband as a pretty decent guy, but in truth we'd never met. Levi had grown up in Towash. He'd joined the church in order to marry Coral Rebecca during her senior year of high school. I'd always wondered how deeply those who married in could accept the way of life on Lane's Hill. My mother seemed to have tried. It was hard to believe that, to her, my father, his family, and the Brethren Saints had represented stability, and that false sense of continuity was the lure that brought her in. She'd grown up being passed around between relatives and drug-addicted parents, enduring worse situations than the one she found herself in when my father moved her to the little trailer down the road from his parents' house.

Even though I resented my mother for leaving, for not being strong enough to take us with her, I had always hoped that the world she found after ours was better to her. I pictured her living in a house with flowers like the ones now frost-browned in Coral Rebecca's gardens, but I'd never know for sure.

My sister emerged from the front door with a hand shading her eyes, despite the dim afternoon. At the edge of the porch, she hesitated, then took a step, hesitated, then took another.

"Jennia Beth?" She stopped when she reached the front walkway, which was just a dirt path etched out by foot traffic. "Oh, my word! Jennia Beth! It *is* you!"

Coral Rebecca ran through the brown grass, her skirt swirling around her ankles, her feet bare, her open arms answering the question of whether she would be glad to see me here.

She wrapped me in an embrace, and the first thing that struck me was that my sister still smelled the same, still *felt* the same. Her hugs were gentle, like everything else about her—as if she feared she might do damage if she hung on too hard. She smelled of the goat-milk soap we sold at swap meets. The scent of it had always seemed to cling in her hair. The skin of her cheek was as soft as it had been when she was a child. Tiny curls, escaped from her plait, tickled my cheek, just as they had when she was a toddler and Mama moved her into my bed to ready the crib for Joey.

Marah Diane had thrown such a fit that day. She didn't want to be shifted to the mattress on the floor to sleep alone. . . .

"Why're you here?" Coral Rebecca released me but threaded her fingers through mine and held on as if she were afraid I might skate away on the puffs of wind buffeting the clothesline.

I explained the working trip while the linens popped and whiplashed in the breeze. Coral Rebecca cast a concerned look in that direction. "You can get those," I said. "I'll help you."

The girls had wandered onto the porch by then, the littlest watching us with a thumb in her mouth. Coral Rebecca sent Deedee in for a laundry basket and shoes, and we went after the sheets together, the girls surreptitiously trying to get a look at me as we completed the task and went inside.

For a while, the conversation was pleasant, touching on innocuous topics. The house was quiet, empty except for Coral Rebecca and the girls. The men—Levi, my father, and Marah Diane's husband—had gone over to the next county to talk with a guy who wanted to trade a four-wheeler for one of my father's coonhounds.

"'Course they won't do no business on the Sabbath," Coral Rebecca was quick to assure me as she poured sweet tea for the two of us in mismatched plastic tumblers. "But they needed Levi to drive 'em in our truck, and today's the only day he's got off from the timber comp'ny. He's workin' all the others."

I glanced at the little girls standing near the bedraggled sofa, shyly watching Coral Rebecca and me. I wondered if they saw much of their dad. The logging life was one of long hours and dangerous realities. *Six-day workweek and ya hope ya come home*— that was always my father's reason for not getting involved with timbering.

"It'll sure help a whole lot if Daddy can trade off the dog. He's already got a neighbor who wants to buy the four-wheeler off a him for cash." My sister was leading around to money now. Her big, deepwater-blue eyes glided toward the girls. Nervousness, worry, concern etched her birdlike features. I knew the source. Despite the fact that her husband worked long hours, six days a week, there was nothing extra in this tiny house. The furniture was threadbare, secondhand and thirdhand. Coral Rebecca's dress was faded, well-worn, and the tennis shoes she'd put on to gather the wash looked like they'd been glued back together a dozen times.

My family was leaning on her and Levi, sucking the life out of this tiny house. Coral Rebecca would never be able to admit that, even to herself. She was too tender. Too unfailingly kind.

Even as we sat drinking tea, she was probably wondering how she and Levi would foot the bill for the extra gas consumed in driving my father and my brother-in-law to attempt the trade of the dog today. Assuming the deal went through, no one would offer reimbursement.

Guilt settled heavy and cold. I felt it sitting on my chest like snow mass from an avalanche, choking the breath from me. These people were stealing my sister's life. She wouldn't have written to me if she weren't desperate for some kind of relief.

How could I tell her no? And then . . . how could I say yes? I couldn't keep digging myself further and further into a credit card hole in order to send money here.

"How are Evie Christine and Lily Clarette?" I barely knew my two youngest sisters. They were just girls when I'd seen them at Joey's funeral, only a few years older than Coral Rebecca's little ones.

"They're fine . . . just fine." My sister drawled the words, the sound strangely musical. Coral Rebecca always had such a pretty voice, but she was too timid to sing if she knew anyone was listening. "Evie Christine and Marah Diane are *both* expectin'— Marah Diane just found out the other day. They're so excited. We all are. It's a blessin'. I'm gonna wash up all the baby clothes and the high chair and everythin'."

But Coral Rebecca's expression didn't speak of blessing. It spoke of anxiety. Two more mouths to feed. More shoes, more diapers, more space. More needs, where needs were already going unsatisfied.

"I might'a told you that already in my letter." A glance fluttered up again, then she focused on her tea glass, poked the ice cubes down with a fingertip. "I'm sorry if I'm repeatin' myself. I'm nervous, I guess."

226

"Nervous? Why?"

She was too polite to tell the truth. "I just am, I guess. You know I'm not too good at talkin' to people. . . ."

"Mama, the dogs're gettin' after that car out yander," Deedee observed, and both girls pressed close to the window.

"Oh no! Friday!" I stood and hurried the few steps to the front door. Friday had been sound asleep when I'd arrived. I'd forgotten all about him. He and the yard dogs were probably scrapping the rental car right now.

The girls scampered through the door behind me, Deedee lifting her skirt and passing me in a barefooted mad dash, her thin legs as agile as a doe's. The girl could fly, just like her mother. The coaches had begged Coral Rebecca to run track at school, thought she might earn a scholarship even, but my father had forbidden it.

By the time I reached the car, Deedee was dragging a lanky bluetick hound off the car, kicking at a mutt, and yelling at a third dog. Her younger sister arrived a few steps behind me and rescued a puppy from underneath the vehicle, while I opened the door and extricated Friday.

"You ga a puppy!" the younger girl giggled.

"Oh, he's not a puppy. He's a grown-up. He won't get any bigger." Friday displayed a full mouth of teeth, either trying to prove his age or get his bluff in on the hound as it dragged Deedee closer.

"What kinda dog is tha-ut?" Deedee drawled, giving Friday a cross-eyed look.

"He's a Chihuahua. A fat one."

"He don't look too friendly-like."

"He isn't." Other than the girls across the hall, who were older, Friday had never been around children as far as I knew. "He's grouchy."

"Where'd ya git 'im?"

"I found him."

"We got a couple'a *them* kind." Deedee indicated the mutts now sniffing around our legs. "Papaw said he'd come shoot 'em for us, but Daddy said just let 'em be. They ain't hurtin' nothin'. That'un had pups, too. But just this pup lived. Sissy likes it."

Sissy offered up the puppy, and surprisingly Friday didn't try to eat it.

"He's cute," I said, but I had a feeling the last thing Coral Rebecca needed around here was another mouth to feed.

I returned to the house in a gaggle of dogs and kids, Friday wiggling in my arms, trying to alternately threaten and sniff noses with everyone. One of the mutts stepped on Friday's leash as I reached for the door, and the girls and I paused a moment outside the screen, untangling everyone.

Coral Rebecca was on the phone in the kitchen, the olive-green cord wrapped around her finger, her back turned to the door. Her voice drifted through the screen. "I don' know. She said she's here for work. . . . I don' know, Marah Diane. I think you jus' need a come down here, and the two a you oughta visit. . . . Yes, she got my letter. She said so. We didn' talk on it much but . . . Okay. . . . Okay. . . . Well, jus' bring the kids. They can play with Deedee and Sissy."

The screen door slammed behind me as I went in.

Coral Rebecca's shoulders jerked beneath a heavy white sweater she must've pulled on while I was outside. She turned toward me, pressed a smile, and said into the phone, "Jus' come on down soon's you're ready, then, Marah Diane. We'll be here."

Depositing the receiver, she crossed back to the table, frowning at Friday as I set him down on the little patch of chipped-up linoleum in the entryway.

"What in the world's that?"

"It's a *She-wow-ya*." Deedee's approximation was adorable. She dropped to her knees beside Friday, then squinted up at me. "'Cept'n, this is a *boy* dog. Did you know tha-ut? It's gotta be a *He*-wow-ya."

Coral Rebecca slapped her hand over her mouth, and a snicker broke through. A giggle tickled my throat, and in an instant, my sister and I were laughing together for the first time since childhood. I stood next to Friday for a minute, just to make sure everything was all right as the girls investigated his ears and admired his tiny toenails. He seemed to be enjoying it, actually. Maybe he'd been a little girl's dog before ending up abandoned in a Dumpster.

"Well . . . I hate to . . . tell ya this but . . . he ain't real pretty," Coral Rebecca chugged out, her laugh high and sweet.

"Ma-*ma*!" Deedee protested. "I think he's purdy."

"Him lotta purdy, Mama," Sissy added earnestly.

"You're a-hurtin' his feelin's." Deedee gave Friday a hug to bolster his flagging self-image. Friday wagged his tail. Actually moved it rapidly from left to right in direct response to human contact. I didn't know he had it in him.

"I hope it's all right to bring him in here." I returned to the table. "I was afraid the coon dog would eat him."

"He might." Coral Rebecca looked toward the bluetick, now hovering beyond the screen with a bitter expression on his face.

"Friday doesn't have fleas or anything," I assured my sister.

"Oh, we got fleas in the house all-time anyhow," Coral Rebecca said casually as we reclaimed our chairs. Culture shock struck me again. Back home, if your dog even sat down to *scratch* in the dog park, people gave you dirty looks.

Coral Rebecca and I each sipped from our tea glass, an

awkward lull threatening as the laughter faded. My sister broke the stalemate, mustering a cheerful look. "Marah Diane'll be on up here'n a minute. I knew she'd wanna see you."

I closed my eyes, swallowed, felt myself being backed up against a cold, hard moment of truth. "I can't send money, Coral Rebecca. I changed jobs, and so there's a gap between paychecks and . . . I just don't have it to send."

She blinked rapidly, the first hint of tears moistening the soft, pink rims of her eyes. She turned her face away so I wouldn't see. "But you make all that money, Jennia Beth. You got a big-deal job and everythin'."

I felt sick. How was I going to do this? How could I go through with it?

Yet how could I not? "Listen, the truth is that I'm already so far in debt, it's ridiculous. I have to stop. It costs a lot to live in New York City, even in a tiny apartment like mine. That's just the way things are. My expenses eat up most of what I make, and then . . ." How could I be saying this? How could I be saying this to my sister? She was in the same position I was in. Worse, because she had children to worry about.

I rubbed my forehead, trying to smooth out the thoughts with my fingertips, searching for a nice frame for them, but there wasn't one. Finally I just let it spill. "Every time I start to get caught up on my own bills, a letter comes, and somebody's on the brink of disaster." *In fact, I never even hear from anyone unless there's a money request on the way.* I didn't say it. I wouldn't. But we both knew.

Her hands left the tea glass, then rested on the Formica tabletop, one kneading the other. "I understand." Unspoken words trailed those two: *But Marah Diane won't and neither will Daddy.*

"I'm sorry."

"I know." A long, slow breath deflated her until her thin shoulders protruded like a clothes hanger inside the sweater. "I know you love us, Jennia Beth. I do." A tear slipped from beneath her pale lashes and traced the long marionette line trembling at the edge of her mouth. At just twenty-seven, my sister looked like she was in her late thirties. This place, this life, was slowly breaking her down. Draining everything from her.

There was so much I wanted to say before Marah Diane showed up. "And I think you and Levi need to do the same. I know it sounds harsh, but you can't keep letting them bleed you dry. You have your own family to take care of. Your own kids to worry about."

She grabbed a napkin to dab her nose. "Kin looks after kin. You know that's how it is."

"I know that your *kin* should care as much about your well-being as they do their own," I snapped, even though I shouldn't have. This wasn't Coral Rebecca's fault. As always, she was the quiet victim here. The nice one. The sweet one. The one who went along. The one who tried to make peace. "I *know* that, if people love you, they support you. They don't sit around making excuses about why they can't work while you're working yourself to death to support *them*. Your husband has one day a week off, Coral Rebecca. One. How many days does Daddy or Marah Diane's husband get up and pack a lunch pail and head off to work . . . anywhere? And the last I heard, Evie Christine's husband had quit his job too."

"His truck broke down and he couldn't get there n'more."

"It's always something." I sounded like an ogre. I felt like one. But I was just so tired of all this, so sick of being trapped in the same cycle, even though I'd moved hundreds of miles from here.

Leaning away from me, my sister pulled her hands off the

table as if the angst were a toxic spill and she feared she might be contaminated. Sin was leaking into the room. Anyone who criticized the way of life on Lane's Hill was sinful. "Roy and Waylon are workin' the farm for Daddy . . . and they help him with the dogs and the mules. Daddy can't do as much since the accident."

"The farm isn't a *living*, Coral Rebecca. Particularly not for three families." It never had been, really. Growing up, we'd barely managed to scrape by on farming, trading, money won at coon hunts, and the sale of the dogs and mules. Never once had I seen my father look for regular work of any kind.

"And Daddy's busy with the church a lot, bein' a deacon now," Coral Rebecca added, in full defense mode.

"Don't get me started on the Brethren Saints."

Coral Rebecca pulled a breath, her eyes wide, her chair scooting back a few inches. "Jennia Beth!"

I was conscious of my nieces now frozen by the door.

"Girls, go on outside and wait for Marah Diane and the kids. Jus' play in the yard whenever they git here. Leave the little dog inside. He'll be all right."

"But, Mama, I can lock up our dogs in the pen—"

"Go *now!*" Coral Rebecca shrieked, and the girls hurried out the door. My sister turned to me with the fire of righteous indignation in her eye. "I will *not* have you speakin' that way in front a my kids. How dare you!"

I swallowed the venom, but it burned going down. There was so much I wanted to say to her about the things I learned after leaving Lane's Hill behind and the things I was only now beginning to learn. Rand's journey and Sarra's had started to weave itself inside me, creating a tapestry of thought and understanding.

"I'm not trying to offend you, Coral Rebecca. I just . . . see things differently now. I don't agree with what the Brethren Saints tell people."

"And I pray for you about that. I do." Her mouth was set, her body rigid in the chair. "I wish all the time that you never did go away, Jennia Beth."

"I'm glad I left." Tears welled up and spilled. My sisters and I would always be yelling to one another from opposite sides of a mountain, our voices little more than echoes in the trees. We'd never understand each other. "It was the best thing I ever did."

"You don't mean that."

"Yes, I do." I couldn't even look at her. Her voice was so sad, so steeped in misery. Was she realizing what I was realizing—that we'd never be the way sisters were supposed to be?

She reached across the table, laid her hand over mine, one trembling circle encompassing another. "You can come back, Jennia Beth. If you repent and turn from your ways, Daddy and the elders might—"

"These people made Mama's life miserable. Don't you remember any of that? No matter how hard she tried, she wasn't good enough. They didn't show her any mercy. Any kindness. She wasn't *holy* and *pure* enough for them."

"Jennia Beth!" A hand flew toward her mouth, stopped in midair, and smoothed escaped wisps into her plait instead.

"Besides, if I came home, we'd all starve to death apparently and—" I clamped my teeth over the rest, reminded myself again that Coral Rebecca was just as trapped here as I had been. But there was a small, very human part of me that struggled with the fact that the same family that criticized and condemned me was perfectly happy to take my money.

"That's not fair. Daddy just wants you to be right with God."

"Have you ever wondered *why* Daddy and the Brethren Saints are in charge of God? Doesn't God get to decide for himself?"

"It's not for a woman to know what's in the mind a the Almighty."

"But it is for Daddy? He and the elders are right, and the whole rest of the world is wrong?"

"I didn't say that."

"Yes, you did." We'd been told that a thousand times. Approval from the Brethren Saints *was* approval from God. The rest of the world was condemned, doomed to eventually burn in the fiery pit. "You just said that it was up to Daddy and the church to decide whether God would have me back or not."

"I don't wanna talk about this."

An old, rust-colored truck rattled up in the yard and saved us from having to go any farther, not that there seemed to be anywhere to go from here.

I recognized Marah Diane crossing the yard as four kids squeezed out of the front seat and conferenced with Deedee, Sissy, and the stray puppy.

"You shouldn't say them things to Marah Diane," Coral Rebecca warned nervously.

But it was evident from Marah Diane's stiff arms and determined stride that she'd come ready to do battle.

"There's no point in my saying those things to her." If I said *black*, Marah Diane would say *white*. "She won't listen."

"She can't." Coral Rebecca cast a sad look my way, and for just a minute, I thought, *She knows. She knows how twisted all of this is.*

Marah Diane was in the doorway a moment later, slightly off-balance as she fought the wind to close the crooked storm door. Friday moved off the linoleum and positioned himself under an end table as if he sensed the presence of an incoming missile and felt the need of a fallout shelter.

Seeing her face was a shock at first. When Coral Rebecca sent photos, the adults were almost never in them. Just the children, all lined up on a fallen tree limb or the front steps or back porch or a picnic quilt at a coon hunt or at the holiday dinner table in the old farmhouse. The scenes were all serene, the background information carefully controlled.

Marah Diane had aged to the degree that I almost wouldn't have known her, but for the honey-colored hazel eyes. Her once-brown hair, now darkened almost to black, was pulled tightly back in a plait, the look as severe as the downturned curve of her mouth. Her face seemed puffy, deep circles framing her eyes. Mostly, she just looked . . . tired. She had always taken after my grandmother, but now the resemblance was startling. That was my grandmother's ever-present facial expression—angry, weary, impatient.

Heavy pants of breath escaped her as she moved through the door. After four babies, and with another on the way, she'd put on a lot of weight.

"It really *is* you." She blinked, blinked again, either to indicate that she barely recognized me too or that she hadn't fully believed Coral Rebecca's phone call.

Or perhaps she was just waiting to see what kind of greeting I would offer—letting me make the first move.

"It's really me."

Coral Rebecca stood, so I did too. Marah Diane moved in only far enough to close the door behind herself. She glanced at Coral Rebecca, and from the corner of my eye I saw our younger sister shake her head. "Jennia Beth just changed to a new job, and she can't afford to help out right now." Her voice was barely a whisper in the room. A peace plea with a white flag so threadbare you could see right through it.

Marah Diane's lips clamped, wrinkles forming around the edges. My mind flew back to a thousand little-girl arguments. We'd so seldom had kind words for one another, Marah Diane and me.

"You told her *no*," she wheeled toward me. "You came here and let her *ask* you so you could have yourself the fun of tellin' her *no* to her face. And there, Coral Rebecca's always been nothin' but sweet to you. She always made sure and kep' you up on every-thin', even if it's not like you cared one little *bit* 'bout this fam'ly. She probably hugged your neck when you got here. You shoulda saved your trouble, Coral Rebecca. She don't care nothin' about her kin. She didn't come here to help. She just come here to have a good laugh at us."

I felt my teeth grinding so hard they were loosening at the roots. "I came here for *work*. I came to Looking Glass Gap about a manuscript that crossed my desk."

Her head jerked and her face tightened like I'd slapped her. "Well, listen at *you*, Miss High-and-Mighty. It figures you'd be over there with the rest'a them crazy people in the Gap. You oughta be ashamed. Momaw Leena would turn a loop in her grave. You always were just like Mama. You got a dose a her sinful nature before she went away."

I gripped the back of the chair, felt my eyes bugging out of my head. In a way, Marah Diane was doing me a favor, I guessed. Every word from her mouth was like a stepping stone, making it easier to walk away.

"You're selfish, just like her."

"Marah Diane, that's not fair!" Coral Rebecca's voice rose to a shriek, rattling the rusty ceiling fans. It stilled both of us momentarily. Long enough for me to gather my wits. I hadn't been prepared for Marah Diane's full frontal attack. I suppose I hadn't thought she'd really do it after all these years of not seeing one another.

"Well, at least I guess I know what all of you think of me." The words came out measured and clear. Calm. Surprising, since my chest felt like an emotional cyclone was at work, churning up layers of debris I thought had decomposed years ago.

Something warm touched my shoulder. I realized it was Coral Rebecca's hand. "We don't feel like that, Jennia Beth. We're grateful for all you done to help. We are."

"*Ffff!*" Marah Diane spat. "Stop tryin' to make her feel better. She's just afraid she'll have to give up some Botox or another fancy coat like that one she's got there. She oughta feel bad. Kin looks after kin. That's how it is."

"For how *long*?" I took a step toward her, the movement so sudden that it startled Friday into action. He bolted to the center of the room, positioning like a referee in a prizefighting match. "How long am I supposed to keep paying your way? And Daddy's? And now Evie Christine and her husband are on the farm too? Why doesn't somebody go to *work*?"

"We *farm*!"

"The farm has never been a living. You know that. All of you know that. It's an excuse."

Marah Diane's nostrils flared, her skin red and moist. "Our family's been on that land for a hundred and fifty years. We make honest money. Not like what *you* do. Follow your sinful nature, just like Mama. Well, walk out on us, same's she did, then. There's the door. Go on and don't come back." She stepped aside to allow a clear exit path.

Friday stood his ground, his growl menacing the room.

"Stop!" Coral Rebecca wailed, her voice thick with tears. "This is *my* house. And there will *not* be fightin' in my house! You two are my sisters, and I love you both, and I don't want us fightin'!"

I took a breath then. Marah Diane and I both did. For an instant, the blaze seemed to be under Coral Rebecca's control. Then Marah Diane stirred the embers again. "Well, before you go waltzin' off back to your *big-deal* job in your *big-deal* city, you oughta come down the road, since nobody's home right now, and see how your own daddy is really livin'."

# Chapter 19

*I* wonder if it's ever possible to fully cast off twisted family bonds and move through the world without them slowly digging into the skin . . . like a puppy collar left in place too long by a neglectful owner who doesn't care about the damage being done. The binding slowly gets tighter until it becomes inseparable from the skin.

My family's situation was like one of those sad stories on the news. The kind you can't fully imagine until the pictures flash on the screen. Things were worse than I'd ever thought they could be.

The old farmhouse that had belonged to my grandparents was a wreck, thick with the smell of mold and mildew and rife with evidence of leaks in the roof. The ceiling tiles had fallen through in several places. In the kitchen, the cabinets were largely bare, yet the countertops were littered with to-go food containers that no one had bothered to throw away. Bugs, rat droppings, and spilled potato chips dotted the filthy corners behind furniture. I was glad I'd left Friday to wait in the car. I didn't want him eating that stuff. No one should be living like this.

A window broken during the electrical fire in my youngest sister's bedroom had been repaired with plastic and duct tape. Now with the power to that part of the house shut off, Lily Clarette was trying to finish high school by the light of an oil lamp, while taking care of my father and essentially helping to raise Marah Diane's four kids.

Lily Clarette was already talking about getting married. At seventeen. And everyone seemed to be celebrating that. Coral Rebecca hoped she would complete her last year of high school first. Marah Diane couldn't see the point. *She* hadn't graduated from high school, after all. Lily Clarette's intended had recently turned twenty-one and gotten a job driving a propane delivery truck for his uncle. In Marah Diane's view, the couple was all set to start a life. One of my sisters had even spotted a wedding dress in a resale shop.

"Might be they'll let her put it on hold till we can get the money," Marah Diane groused as she told me about the dress. "Don't guess you'll wanna kick in for it."

I just stood with my mouth agape, surveying Lily Clarette's chemistry book and oil lamp on the desk beneath a duct-taped window. Atop the bed crammed next to it, a lopsided teddy bear lay tangled in the sheets. Lily Clarette was still a child, for heaven's sake.

"I think she should finish high school first," I managed to croak out. The smell of charred wood burned my throat and made my eyes water. How could Lily Clarette be expected to form any dreams in this place? Any at all?

"'Course you do," Marah Diane grumbled. "She's found her

a good man with a good job. A man of the church. Not like he's gonna just wait forever, bein' twenty-one."

I didn't even answer. I just stared at her.

What was *wrong* with these people?

I'd forgotten. I'd forgotten how horrible, how hopeless, how incredibly sad this place, this life, was. It started to seem unreal after you were away from it for a while. And then, all at once, it was uncomfortably real again. Staring me down from all directions.

I glanced at the chemistry equations written in Lily Clarette's notebook. The top of a quiz peeked from between the pages. A ninety-three. Lily Clarette had always been smart, but she had to be beyond exceptional if she was surviving all of this and doing well in chemistry.

Thunder rumbled in the distance, drew my attention through the duct-tape-and-plastic kaleidoscope to Marah Diane's children playing in the yard with the hounds.

*All these little kids. All these little kids, growing up this way . . .*

What hope was there?

*A gift isn't anything more than magnificent litter if you leave it unopened.* Wilda Culp again. She'd told me that as she pushed me to struggle through high school with the needs of five young siblings always pressing in. I'd come so close to ending up like Lily Clarette. There was Jason, who'd graduated a year before me, had a job with a heavy-equipment company, whispered all the things I needed to hear.

*I can take care a you, Jennia Beth, and I can help your family out, like a son's supposed to do.* He'd been just a boy himself, poor thing, trying to take on my problems.

All of it played in my head again as I climbed into my car to leave my father's house behind. Down the road, Marah Diane and Roy's trailer house didn't look much better than the rest of the place. The roof was covered with plastic sheeting held down by old tires. I was still paying off the three thousand dollars I'd sent to Marah Diane for a new roof on the trailer last year. There was no new roof on the trailer.

I watched her rattle home with two kids in the pickup bed, two kids in the front, and one on the way. So far, the only interaction I'd seen her have with them was to yell in frustration. Four children under the age of twelve were more than a handful. My sister was obviously overwhelmed.

*And don't look at me like that,* she'd snapped when she'd caught me surreptitiously checking for a baby bump. *Every little child is a blessin'. If you ever had one, you'd understand.*

Five minutes before, she'd yanked one of her girls up by the arm, smacked her on the backside, and said, *Hush up, you hear me? You are not even worth havin' sometimes.*

Her voice rang in my ears as I left the farm, the conversations traveling with me, replaying in my head over and over and over while Friday rolled concerned looks my way. Perhaps he sensed that I was on the brink of some sort of emotional collapse. Finally free from the stench of mildew, old carpet, and charred wallboard, I felt myself coming completely unstrung.

My visit here hadn't solved anything. We'd just decided we should leave, in case the men's dog trade didn't work out and they came home early, in foul moods.

Meanwhile, the money the traded-for ATV might bring in was already being spent. Marah Diane had begun formulating plans to have a combined birthday party for her girls and Coral Rebecca's.

Rolling down the window, I tried to let the crisp late-afternoon air soothe the heat of my frustration. Without even meaning to, I slowed the car as I passed the familiar turnoff to Wilda Culp's house.

For a moment, I was tempted to veer off, but I didn't. The place wouldn't be the same anymore, with Wilda and Richard gone. It was easier to imagine that Wilda's haven lay frozen in time, a glass-globe centerpiece with the seasons passing inside it. Falling leaves in autumn, snow in the winter, wildflowers in spring, multicolored sprays of climbing roses in midsummer. As beautiful as always.

I turned off, instead, fifteen minutes later, taking a cutoff onto the winding back road that followed Honey Creek through a long, slim hollow where a Cherokee trade road had traveled in ancient times. The road would circle back to the highway eventually. We'd often used this thirty-mile stretch to either circumvent Towash, avoid law enforcement officers who might stop us for out-of-date tags or poached game, or bypass slow-moving trucks on the mountain highway.

For now, this was peace. A chance to temporarily leave behind the burden.

The road narrowed and roughened as the miles passed, the creek peeking through here and there, its surface a soft, shimmering gray, reflecting the cloudy sky. The rustling waters of Honey Creek were the welcome face of an old friend.

How many difficult teenage hours had I spent along these banks, seeking refuge with one of Wilda's Readers Digest Condensed volumes or a smuggled library book or my school-work? Around my grandparents' house after my mother left, there was no room for books other than the Bible, and that was only quoted and wielded, never read. There were portions that didn't fit with the things taught on Lane's Hill. The worst whipping I could ever remember came just after I brought up that issue and pointed to a page in the family Bible as evidence.

After that, I learned to leave such things alone.

The car rattled over a chuckhole, toppling my purse onto the floorboard. Friday cracked an eye open, then slid from the seat to look for edibles. Before I could stop him, he was helping himself to a roll of Life Savers, paper and all. He looked up with his lips wrapped around one end of the tube, his minty-fresh breath whistling through the hole.

"Friday, quit. You'll end up constipated . . . or worse," Leaning over, I grabbed the other end, and we played an awkward game of tug-of-war. "Friday, leave it alone, that's—"

The sudden drop-off in the road caught me completely by surprise, and we took a redneck roller-coaster ride, going just short of airborne. The car landed with a thump, and mud spewed wildly as we clattered across a washboard of potholes, then bumped upward onto a stretch of pavement. It was smooth and new, and something metal glinted through the trees ahead, out of place with the back-roads scenery.

"What in the world . . . ?"

Friday hopped onto the seat to check it out for himself.

We passed under the branches of an overhanging oak, came out the other side, and all of a sudden, the unidentified foreign object on Honey Creek Road looked very familiar.

"I can*not* believe it." Letting the car drift to a stop, I craned toward the window and took in an endless span of twelve-foot chain-link fence. No guard shack, but the gate and *E. H.* script atop were unmistakable. *Evan Hall.* Again. Not only did the man own an entire mountain and the old road just past Sarra Bend Bridge, but he'd taken possession of Honey Creek Road as well. Thanks to him, we'd have to turn around and travel the twenty or so miles back the way we'd come to get to the highway. Because Evan Hall *owned* the road. He literally must've landgrabbed half the county.

"You have *got* to be *kidding*. Friday, can you believe this?"

Friday didn't have an answer, but he seemed stumped as well.

A growl started low in my throat and gradually grew louder, and Friday squeezed himself toward the passenger door, suddenly worried.

I was tempted to ram the gate, or at least leave a really nasty note on it, but there was a camera perched atop. It'd be just my luck that the video would end up being used as evidence in my stalking trial. The only good thing was that the roadblock gave me a new focus for my anger. I'd temporarily forgotten all about the family problems, or maybe they were just fuel to the fire, but I was livid. Insanely so.

Gunning the engine, I peeled out and whipped around, purposely making a wide loop, intent on slinging as much mud and gravel as I could. Given the front-wheel-drive nature of the car, it was an idiotic plan—I was largely showering my own ride—but it felt good. A protest against the day. Against family bonds. Against people owning roads and locking other people out and . . .

The mud was flying and the wheels were spinning, but I realized that Friday and I were moving sideways down the ditch.

Not. Good.

I knew better. I should have known better. I'd grown up on dirt roads.

Gunning the engine sent the car lurching forward, pinning Friday upright against his seat so that he looked like he was begging, which seemed appropriate, because that made two of us.

*Please. Please, please, please, please, please . . .*

We crawled toward the pavement, slinging mud, digging deeper, slinging mud, digging deeper . . .

"Come on, baby. Come on, baby. If you get me out of this one, I'll take you to the car wash, I promise."

The pavement drew closer, inch by inch. The engine roared. The transmission squealed long and loud. I prayed it wouldn't drop out right then and there.

Another forward lurch. Hope crept up. And then . . . we weren't going anywhere but *down*. I didn't stop until I'd mired it up to the axles, a foot shy of the pavement.

The breath I'd been holding seeped out of me as my forehead sank to the steering wheel. A long, low moan slowly filled the space inside the car, and I realized it was coming from me, not Friday. On the passenger seat, he joined in with a howl.

Hoping against hope, I tried the cell phone. No reception, of course. My available options had just narrowed considerably. I could either walk back the way I'd come—and I hadn't passed any sort of house for at least ten miles—or I could take my chances with Evan Hall.

He would never believe I hadn't gotten the car stuck here on purpose. Did I care what he thought? Not really, but another altercation wouldn't help in building trust, and after having found Sarra Bridge only a stone's throw from his property, I was more convinced than ever that I needed to somehow win his trust. He knew more about that manuscript than he was admitting.

Sadly, all roads seemed to lead to Evan Hall at this point.

The memory of his annoying, haughty smirk taunted me as I walked to the gate with Friday in tow, positioned myself in front of the camera, and gave the international distress signal for *I'm stuck in the mud and I can't get out*. Then I stood there wondering if anyone would come. What was I going to do, exactly, if no one did? It'd be dark before I could walk to the nearest house, and who could say, this far off the beaten path, whether that place belonged to anyone who could be trusted?

There wasn't even a flashlight in the car, other than the one on my cell phone. And all I had for food was a half roll of slobbered-up Life Savers.

*Now what?*

Fifteen minutes ticked by. I waved, stood, waved. No one came.

Thunder rumbled over the mountains. The storm was taking longer to top the crest than I'd thought it would, but it *was* coming. A chilly, wet wind swept through the valley as proof. I wrapped my arms, shivering. I wasn't dressed for the kind of weather that could hit after dark when the first hints of winter blew in. How cold would it get tonight?

"Hey!" I hollered at the camera. "Hey! My car's stuck in the mud! I need help! Hey!"

I pictured Evan Hall in his mountaintop fortress, casually turning off the switch, saying to the security men, "Just leave her there. Then we won't have to worry about her anymore." He wanted to be rid of me after all.

It was hard to believe that only a couple weeks ago, I'd been on top of the world, at the height of my career, walking the peaceful morning streets of New York City, on my way to the first pub board meeting at my dream job. Everything was almost perfect . . . until *The Story Keeper* showed up on my desk. Until I opened it and discovered that sixteen-year-old girl hiding under the cabin.

Friday looked up to see if I had any new ideas. He was already starting to shiver, not being a cold-weather dog. In fall and winter, he required a sweater even for short trips to the dog park.

"Come on, come on. Think." *Think, think, think.* But a lump was forming in my throat. What I really wanted to do was cry. *Cry, cry, cry.*

Instead I surveyed the fence, trying to decide whether I could climb over the top. I was in pretty decent shape. I could probably make it, but what about Friday? There was only an inch or two between the bottom of the gate and the driveway. Not nearly enough space to stuff him through. And if I did go over, it had to be several miles to Evan Hall's house from here. Straight up the mountain. Of course someone might . . .

The rumble of an ATV came like a whisper from heaven. Salvation, of a sort. Relief melted through me, warming the chill. The noise was headed this way. Growing louder.

I'd been discovered.

Minutes later, a camouflage four-wheeler raced from the draw and careened across the pasture, going airborne over small bumps.

I recognized Jake Hall even before he skidded a 180 in the driveway and came to a dramatic stop on the other side of the gate. "They told me someone was stuck down here," he offered, kicking one leg over the four-wheeler and sitting sidesaddle like he hadn't quite decided what to do with me yet. "Didn't know it was you."

"Would you have come if you did?"

An easy smile parted his lips and crinkled the corners of his eyes. He and Evan had the same smile. The charming kind. "I'm not like my brother." He said it with some relish, and whatever the meaning behind that was, I found it comforting. *Not like my brother* sounded good right now.

I thumbed over my shoulder toward the car. "I'm stuck. I had no idea Honey Creek Road had been blocked off." The bitterness surfaced. I couldn't help it.

"Well, let's see what we can do." He slid from the four-wheeler, entered a code on the keypad, and the gate magically opened. "We'll figure it out."

I was shocked for a moment. Was this the brother I'd formed a somewhat-negative opinion of yesterday? He actually seemed . . . nice. Really nice. A willing rescuer of chicks and Chihuahuas hopelessly stuck in the mud.

Unfortunately, after looking at the car, he quickly determined that we wouldn't be extricating it without equipment. "I'll take you on up to the house, then Mike and I'll bring one of the tractors down. Too cold to be standin' out here, and you're not dressed for it." A flirty look came my way as we walked to the four-wheeler. I couldn't help myself—I smiled back. Right now I felt pretty kindly toward Mr. Jake Hall. Maybe I'd just caught him in a bad moment yesterday and jumped to too many conclusions.

"Hop on," he said, letting me straddle the seat before he kicked a leg over, then scooped up Friday's shivering body with one hand. "Hold tight. I don't wanna lose ya."

I couldn't help flashing back to the way the four-wheeler had barreled across the pasture a few minutes ago. "Just hang on to Friday, okay?"

"Darlin', I *live* for Friday." It was a pretty lame line, but it made me laugh as we started up the driveway at a much-calmer pace than the one that had brought him to my rescue.

I was right about how far we were from Evan Hall's compound. By the time we made it to the top of the mountain, a chilly drizzle was falling, and Friday and I had achieved Popsicle status. My teeth chattered and Friday trembled like a leaf in a gale as we pulled under the portico in front of the stable.

"You two go on inside." Jake handed Friday to me. "I'll find Mike and we'll get the car taken care of. Just use the back door by the pool. Shorter that way."

"Are you sure it's okay?"

"Evan's not here, if that's what you mean. Heard he was a jerk yesterday. Not surprised. It's his world. We're all just livin' in it."

"I can go back with you, and as soon as the car's out of the ditch, I'll drive home the way I came." If I could get out of here without Evan Hall knowing I'd breached his compound again, it would be so much better.

Friday shuddered and gave me a pleading look, as in, *Hello, Chihuahua in grave danger of frostbite here.*

Jake eyeballed the sky. "Nah, look, that rain's gonna hit anytime. You don't wanna be out in it. Head on in and talk to Granny Vi. Hannah'll be happy you're here. She likes you. You shouldn't drive back out Honey Creek Road anyhow, trust me. Turns to a mudhole when it's wet. We'll be doing good to get your car out before the rain slams us."

"I'm so sorry for the trouble." I felt like such an idiot.

He winked and cast a slow, easy smile, leaning my way as if he were sharing a secret. "I don't mind it. I'd be doin' something anyway. Might as well be this." The cell phone on his belt rang, and he ignored it. "The boss man don't tolerate no slackers."

That backed me up a little. Whatever the issues were here, I wanted no part of them. I had my own warped family dynamics to worry about.

But somehow, I did wonder . . . what was the history? Whose fault was it? Was this just leftover sibling rivalry, or did it run deeper?

"Okay, well, if there's anything I can do to help . . ."

"There's not. Go on in and warm up."

He strode off toward the little room I'd seen the cowboy disappear into the other day, and I carried Friday to the house. It felt strange, letting myself through the door. A chime announced my entrance.

"Hannah?" Violet's voice came from somewhere beyond the cavernous living room where we'd chatted on my last visit.

"No, ma'am, it's Jen Gibbs. I came by yesterday with Helen?" I wiped my feet on the rug, then dusted Friday's paws back and forth to clean them. Better if he didn't leave tracks behind. Evidence.

With any luck Evan Hall would never know we'd set foot in his house again.

I found Violet in a small parlor just past the office. She was sitting by a fireplace, her hands clasped around a cup of hot tea. She sighed when she saw me. "I was hoping you were Hannah."

"I'm sorry."

"She's been out on that horse for hours again, and now it's cold and the rain's coming." Her lips trembled, and it was clear enough from looking at her that she'd been sitting there worrying awhile. "I've been calling Jake for an hour. He hasn't picked up."

"I'm sure Hannah's fine." Clearly Hannah's father had no clue where she was. That seemed wrong, considering that Violet was agonizing over it. "I could go look . . . or see if I can catch Jake . . . or anyone. My car's stuck in the mud on Honey Creek Road. Jake was heading down there to pull it out." Outside, the tractor rumbled past in high gear.

Violet shook her head and tucked a lap quilt closer despite the fact that a fire crackled in the massive marble hearth and the room was warm. "I called down to the barn a bit ago and the boy there hadn't seen her. I can't even think of his name just now. Isn't that terrible? I've gotten myself in a dither. The boy said he'd go and look for her."

"Oh . . . okay. Well, is there anything I can do? Can I get anything for you?"

"Add a log to the fire. It's cold in here. These nor'easters.

I hate these nor'easters. I think I'll move to Florida with all the other retirees." She attempted a laugh—for my benefit, I thought—as I stoked the fire with one hand while clutching Friday with the other.

"And don't tell Evan about Hannah," Violet added. "Land's sake, don't tell Evan. There's enough trouble between the two boys already. Brothers oughtn't fight." She stared absently into the flames, and I sat down in the chair across from her, Friday in my lap, even though he wanted to get down. He'd had at least a year's worth of physical contact in less than eight hours.

Violet sighed. "I'm sorry you caught them both in a mood yesterday. Did you discuss the manuscript with Evan? Did he know anything about it?"

"We didn't really get very far. I don't think it was the best timing," I said vaguely, gathering that she had no idea he'd chased me off or that he'd paid me a visit this morning.

"He was concerned over my appointment, I think," Violet offered, and I instantly felt like an ogre. Evan Hall did have plenty to worry about, other than books. "And then our news wasn't so good."

"I'm really sorry."

"I wish all of them wouldn't fuss over me so."

"When you love someone, you can't help it." My voice caught.

"Did you come back to talk with Evan again today? He isn't here just now."

"No. My car is stuck in the mud on Honey Creek Road. Jake was kind enough to rescue me and go back to pull the car out."

Her face brightened as if this were new information. "He'll surely manage it, don't you worry. Jake has always been so handy with tools and tractors and such. As a boy, he was always taking things apart. We gave him his grandfather's train set once, and he had it in pieces, next we knew." Her hands fluttered, indicating the mess. "Evan had such a fit at him for dismantling it. He never liked things out of order. But Jake put it all back together again. That child could fix anything if he wanted to."

The picture slowly began painting itself in my mind. Evan, the artistic, studious type. Jake, the hands-on type. Brothers, yet completely different. "It's funny how we each get our own set of skills. My sisters and I are as opposite as night and day."

Violet's hands lowered slowly to the chair, pulled the quilt higher again. "It's been hard for Jake, falling in Evan's shadow. Evan was always the older one, the bigger one, the faster one, the better student. The one who did everything right." Her fingers worried a seam in the quilt, absently twisting a loose thread. "He's a tough act to follow."

"I guess he would be." The words tasted sour, coming out.

Her gaze returned to the fire. "It isn't Evan's fault that Hannah's mother left and Jake ended up in such a spot, though Jake seems to blame him for it. It's just a bad situation. Sometimes a woman isn't fit for mothering. She doesn't take to it. The boys had such a good mother. Sophie loved them so. I never thought they'd choose women who weren't like their mama. Sophie was so beautiful and talented, but kind, too. I remember the first time Robby brought her home from university for a visit. I loved her right off, and I could see that he did too. Robby would've gone to the ends of the earth for Sophie. When you love someone, you find a way. I suppose Jake thought he was getting something like Sophie when he married Hannah's mother, but . . ." She stopped midsentence, stretched toward the door. "Was that the chime?"

"I didn't hear anything."

Her body folded in on itself again. "Where *is* that girl?"

Outside the window, the drizzle had turned to a scattering of droplets.

"Let me go out to the barn and look for her." If Hannah was outside, there was no sense in Violet worrying while we sat here rehashing the past.

"I'd like it if you would. She shouldn't be wandering in this weather. There are umbrellas in the hall tree by the door. You can leave your little dog here. He looks to be enjoying the fire." She motioned to a rug by the hearth.

Friday was more than happy to remain behind while I located an umbrella and walked outside, the damp wind pressing through my jacket and jeans.

I found Hannah in the barn, squeezing the water off Blackberry's coat with a metal sweat scraper.

"Hey!" she said and trotted down the aisle to give me an exuberant hug laced with the familiar smells of rain, saddle leather, hay, and horse hair. She looked as happy as a lark. Apparently she had no inkling that she might be in trouble. I hated to be the purveyor of bad news, but poor Violet had been worrying herself silly.

"You'd better go check in at the house. They've been concerned about you." *They* seemed a kinder way to say it, rather than indicating only her great-grandmother realized she was gone.

But Hannah knew. "Granny Vi?"

"Yes."

"She was sleepin' when I left. I put a note for her." She seemed completely comfortable with that, as if she in no way found it odd for an eleven-year-old to be out rambling for hours in a gathering storm.

"The weather made her nervous, I think."

"Granny Vi worries a lot. I know what I'm doin'. I been goin' in the woods since I was little. Back at our old place, it was right up against the parkland, and I could cross over the fence and go everywhere. My mama never cared, long's I put the horse up when I got back. My mama rodeos and she sings. She's good at it. She's gonna be a big star. I miss my old horse. He's more fun than Blackberry. They sold him in the divorce."

*My mama never cared.* That spoke volumes. "Well, Blackberry here looks like a keeper to me, but it's not very nice to scare your granny Vi. If you *know* she's worried, maybe you should check in more often."

"Then I couldn't go as far." She cocked her head as if I were communicating in Martian. Had this kid never been forced to answer to anybody? "I'm okay. Anyway, I wasn't far off. I was down in my special place and I didn't hear the rain start, that's all. We got a little wet on the way back. I didn't want Blackberry to catch a cold. My mama'd skin me alive for puttin' the horses away wet."

I held out my hand for the sweat scraper. "Tell you what, I'll take care of Blackberry and you go on and let your granny Vi know that you're back and you're okay."

"You could tell her." Dark brows rose into hopeful arches.

"No, I think you'd better."

"Okay." With a dramatic sigh, she handed over the grooming tool, and then she was gone.

I took my time with Blackberry, hoping to hear the tractor return with my car. It felt good to be in a barn again, hearing the rustling of animals and hay, the fluttering of birds in the rafters, the soft drumming of rain on the tin roof. Blackberry's bushy hide slid wet and slick beneath my fingers as I worked, and I let myself sink into the feel of it, relaxing as the horse's muscles softened. Back home, my favorite hours of the day had been the ones when I was up early, out in the barn with time to slip a bridle on one of the mules. I'd ride bareback through the woods as the rocks and the trees awoke, the forest floor coming to life with flowers opening and tiny creatures stirring.

I'd always told myself that when I grew up, I'd have a horse of my very own. A good saddle horse, and I'd keep him right in back of my house, ready at all times for an adventure or an escape.

I hadn't been on a horse in years.

I was almost tempted to sink my fingers into Blackberry's mane and swing on board. Silly, of course, but as I finished grooming him, I imagined how it would feel.

He was almost dry before Hannah returned. She brought Friday with her and settled him on a bale of hay in the aisle. "Sorry it took so long. I had to help Granny Vi with some stuff, *and* she made me put on dry clothes. Sheesh! Then she fell asleep again finally. We can go inside and make some cocoa. It's cold out here, kinda. You wanna see my room?"

I thought of what Helen and Violet had said about my resemblance to Hannah's mom, and Evan's warning not to lead her on. "I think I'd better wait out here for your dad to come back with my car, but thanks."

Her nose crinkled, freckles scrunching together. "My dad's got your car?"

"It was stuck in the mud down on Honey Creek Road."

"Ohhh . . . that road's got some real bad spots. I ride there sometimes and go along the creek. I got the key code for all the gates."

"I used to play on that creek when I was growing up. I loved it there."

"That's cool." Hannah was enthusiastic. "Maybe we could go

sometime. You could ride the gray horse. Or else you could have Blackberry, and I can ride the gray horse. Daddy doesn't believe I can handle him, but I totally can. He's fun."

"I don't think I'll be in town long enough, but that would be a blast. Thanks for inviting me."

Her lips twisted to one side, and she scratched Friday's head as I untied Blackberry. "Are you and Uncle Evan gonna make a book together? The one you talked about to Granny Vi and Aunt Helen?"

"I'm not sure all of that's going to work out. Your uncle Evan said the manuscript isn't his."

"Oh." That little mind was working so quickly, there was smoke coming from her ears. "Well, are you gonna stick around until you figure out who *did* write it, then?"

*Are you gonna stick around . . . ?* Sadly, I'd had a feeling that was where the whole conversation was headed. "I think I've just about done all I can. I have to get back to New York. There are lots of other books waiting."

"I might write a book."

"I believe you might."

"You could have *my* book." There was such hope in those wide blue eyes. *Why me?* I wanted to say. Didn't she know I was the last person she should be asking to fill the void here in this big house? Just the thought made me uncomfortable. I didn't want any more ties to these mountains.

Looping the lead rope in my hand, I guided Blackberry toward his stall. "You'll have to send it to me in New York when you get it finished. I'd love to read anything you write." A thought teased the corners of my mind, noticeable in that it was so out of place. What if I could encourage my nieces and nephews from afar, or even other kids who were growing up around here? What if something could be done with their writing, their stories?

Some sort of an anthology . . . or a compilation . . . a fundraiser for scholarships . . .

I shoved the inspiration to the back burner, where it could simmer a while. One boiling pot at a time was enough.

"Yeah, I guess so." Her disappointment was clear. I felt bad for being the one causing it, but the ebbing of our conversation was a relief in a way. We went about putting Blackberry in his stall and bedding him down, while Friday looked on from his hay-bale perch. I peeked around for signs of the baby goat but didn't see him. I knew better than to scratch another sore spot by asking. This little girl had suffered too many disappointments already. If I thought she could keep it, I would've called my relatives and tried to track down a bottle-baby goat to give her, although this wasn't the normal time of year for birthing.

The tractor rumbled up the drive just as we were finishing. My rental car, looking muddy and bedraggled, came along with it.

Jake met us under the portico. "You did 'er up good." He pointed to the mud spewed on the side of the car and the long grass still clinging to the undercarriage.

"I'm an overachiever," I joked, and he laughed.

"I better follow behind you on back to town, just to make sure everything's okay. Lemme grab my wallet."

"Can I go, Daddy?" Hannah chimed in, stopping him before he could angle toward the house. Her hands clung around the sleeve of his wet jacket.

"You oughta hang here." The answer was quick and annoyingly dismissive. He wrestled his arm away and patted her on the head. "Somebody's gotta look after Granny Vi."

I blinked, blinked again. *Seriously?* The eleven-year-old was supposed to stay here and look after the ailing grandmother, and who was looking after the eleven-year-old all this time? "You know what? No . . . I'm fine. I'll be fine. I'm sure the car's in good shape. It's just mud. I don't want to take up any more of your time. I'm sorry to have interrupted your day with my stupidity."

"Take ya to dinner." Jake turned the flirt on, and not in any surreptitious way. Mike, who'd been driving the tractor, cast an eye in our direction as he walked to the barn office. No doubt he saw my face turning ten shades of red.

"Oh no . . . honestly, I'm fine. I . . . have to get back and . . ." I grabbed Friday's leash and prepared to bolt. "And . . . get some work done yet tonight."

Jake slapped a hand to his chest, wincing as if he'd been struck by a bullet. "Rejected." He grinned and then swayed on his feet just a bit. I caught a whiff of something and got a clue. Jake had tipped a beer or two while pulling my car out of the ditch. He was smack-dab in his happy place right now.

He definitely didn't need to be driving anyone to town.

"Thanks so much for helping me. It's a terrible night to get out. And look, you're all muddy and wet. You guys just go on with your evening. Thanks so much!"

I was out of there like a rocket, dragging Friday behind me.

# Chapter 20

Nudging the fried pie away, I pushed the phone closer to my ear and focused on the conversation. On the picnic bench beside me, Friday perked up, sensing a potential snack. He wasn't bothered by the fact that the thing tasted like it'd been sitting in the Gordo's Pie Palace concession trailer since yesterday.

My boss was determined, and it didn't take a genius to figure out that Mitch was just the messenger. The real pressure was coming from George Vida. The fiction team had been to a book expo over the weekend, and not only had they seen a newly repackaged offering of the Time Shifters series on display to accompany the release of the final movie, but there was, as Mitch put it, a pervasive rumor that a contract for a new Evan Hall series was all but signed.

"That's not . . . possible," I stammered, caught completely unprepared for Mitch's call and the blindside revelation. "Mitch, I just don't see any indication of that. I've had a couple of conversations with the man already, and unless he's one whale of an actor, the unending fan mania from this thing is his nemesis. I don't think there's any chance he plans to go back to the Time Shifters series."

I sounded so sure of myself, but the truth was that I'd been hanging around for two days since the infamous stuck-in-the-mud incident, and I'd seen no further signs of manuscript pages or Evan Hall. It looked like I had reached the end of the trail, yet somehow I couldn't quite face it. I kept leaving the cabin for periods of time and coming back, hoping more of the manuscript would appear. I'd had a couple of conversations with Helen, and according to her, Evan was being stubborn. He refused to even consider meeting with me again.

Prior to Mitch's call, I'd been killing time away from the cabin, again—nibbling the fried food and watching a group of medieval elves and warriors LARPing in the open area known to insiders (such as myself) as the Field of Honor. Sadly, I'd spent so much time hanging around the Warrior Week grounds these last couple days, I now knew the lingo.

"The rumor about the new Time Shifters contract came from a solid source," Mitch insisted.

"He hasn't touched the Time Shifters stories in, what, more than ten years? I know they split the last few books into multiple releases and milked it with a hardcover, then softcover, rollout, but I *talked* to the man. He's off the project. Way off. There's just no way he's writing another Time Shifters novel."

The adolescent elf girl who'd originally introduced me to the concept of LARPing turned my way. She was standing alongside the Field of Honor, watching the morning's combat with other bystanders. Suddenly it was clear that she'd also been listening in on my call.

Leaning away, I shielded the phone with my shoulder. "Listen, Mitch—"

"You're already out on a limb, Jen. I really can't even believe George Vida let you go down there." She didn't wait for me to finish. "I know you've got a history of taking risks and coming up with big wins. I think that's why he encouraged you to strike off on this one, but I'm going to give you some advice . . . because you *are* new here and there are things you probably don't understand. The big guy can seem all easygoing and grandfatherly when he wants to, but he does *not* like to lose. He tests people, especially when they're new."

"I understand." My stomach sloshed like a water balloon rolling down a steep hill.

"Find out what's going on there and get a bead on whether that manuscript you're after *is* by Evan Hall, and whether we have *any* chance at it, and if the answer is anything but a resounding *yes*, get out of there."

"Okay . . . okay, I will."

Mitch was playing hardball now. As we ended the call, I sat gazing across the Field of Honor, taking in a raised dais that featured a guillotine and three sets of wooden stocks. I had a ghostly vision of myself bound in shackles there with Friday at my feet, his hair bristling and sharp little teeth bared as he tried to defend my life.

Rubbing my forehead, I looked down at the phone.

The elf girl was beside me before I really noticed her. "I remember you." She twizzled an index finger my way. "You were the one who didn't know what LARP was."

"That's me." *Just as clueless as I look, apparently.* Evan Hall had agreed to write a new Time Shifters series? How could that possibly be?

The girl slid onto the bench across from me. Her hunched-over-the-table posture indicated that the two of us were going to talk turkey now. Seemingly as an afterthought, she stuck out a hand and introduced herself. "Hey, I'm Robin, by the way."

"Jen . . . Gibbs."

"I heard you on the phone. Have you *seen* Evan Hall, like, in person?"

"Yes. No. I haven't. No." This was the last thing I needed—a rabid mini fan on my case.

Her eyes brightened, her face grew intense, and for a moment, she reminded me of Jamie at a fashion-sample warehouse sale. "Could you get him to autograph some things?"

*You're not hearing me.* "No, really. I'm serious. He's not a friend of mine or anything. I bumped into him once. That's all. I can't help you out. I'm sorry."

"Because . . . the thing is . . . the camp is *way* crowded this year, and we got here late because my daddy had to finish bringin' the hay in for our neighbor." She thumbed vaguely over her shoulder. "And Mama sews, like, *all year* for the two Time Shifters weeks, and we usually sell out 'cause our stuff's good, but this year we're just not sellin' that much, and propane's got so high, I don't know how we're gonna fill the tank at home without us makin' more money here. And with the baby crawlin' around on the floor a lot still . . . well, she gets cold."

"Robin, I can't help you. I'm sorry." This kid had serious sales skills, but at least some of this was true. And those eyes. Those great big eyes filled with hope and surrounded by ratty hair that looked like no one had bothered to brush it or make her wash it in a week. There was a flash of fear when she talked about the propane bill. I could see it, and I recognized it. A girl barely into her teenage years shouldn't know how much a tank of propane costs, but some do.

264

She wasn't giving up easily. "Hardly *anybody's* got signed stuff of his to sell anymore, and if we had some, it'd be worth a *bunch*." She looked away, then added, "Else, I wouldn't ask. I don't wanna be a bother."

I heard a faint, distant noise. I think it was the sound of my resolve crumbling in the face of a superior force. "Okay, listen. If I get a chance, I'll ask. But don't get your hopes up." Maybe I could put in a bid with Helen and see if she could accomplish the request. "So you live nearby?" I couldn't help asking, even though in truth, I didn't want to get involved.

"Next county over. In Sarroh Valley, about ten miles out of Culver. Ever been there?"

The word caught me off guard. "How is that spelled? Sarroh Valley?" It had about eight syllables the way Robin said it, but I wondered . . .

A sardonic gaze rolled my way. "I *know* how to spell it, if that's what you're wonderin'. I go to school. Got me all A's, too. It's me that looks up all the hist'ry books at the library and figures out what the clothes oughta look like that Mama makes. I'm not *stupid.*"

"Oh, I think I figured out that much already."

"*S-A-R-R-A.* It's just down a piece from the old La Belle Mission School. You know that place?"

*La Belle*—the name of Rand's family home in Charleston?

"Maybe . . . but I'm not sure." The name was like a single note out of place, but it held my attention. La Belle Mission School in Sarra Valley. Perhaps Sarra Creek traveled there eventually.

"Did you say you like to go to the library around here some-where? Do they have much on local history, genealogy, that kind of thing?" It was worth a shot. If I couldn't follow the manuscript anymore, maybe I could follow the history. And a good librarian would be just the one to ask. Maybe Rand and Sarra really were more than fiction.

"Oh, sure. They got a great library here in Looking Glass Gap, thanks to all that money from the Hall family. Got a big ol' room full a stuff about local hist'ry." She stretched across the table again. "Hey, I got some necklaces that'd go so good with that shirt. Just right over there at the booth. Wanna see?"

I agreed because I had a feeling that making a buy was about all I'd be able to do for Robin. I wished I could offer more. The mountains were filled with smart little girls like her who deserved better than they got.

I gathered up Friday and followed her back to the booth. Before we'd finished there, I was the proud new owner of a necklace, earrings, and a bracelet, all hand-strung by Robin. The necklace had a pendant made from a bit of Carolina beach glass that Robin had wire-wrapped herself. It made me think of Sarra's necklace in the story.

Robin looked pleased as I clipped my new jewelry into place. She made sure to remind me again about the autographs, and I made sure to remind her again that the chances weren't very good.

Leaving the festival grounds behind, I couldn't help thinking about her and wondering what her life was like. At the same time, I didn't want to know. Not really. I was still in avoidance mode over my own family. I had no idea what I was going to do about that situation.

Maybe the best thing really was to take Mitch's advice and retreat to New York, focus on issues I could handle, projects I could control. Things that weren't so complicated. So seemingly impossible. Maybe I'd have a clearer head there . . . about the problems on Lane's Hill and *The Story Keeper*.

Indecision struck with paralyzing intensity in the Warrior Week parking lot, and I just sat there staring out the window, unsure of what to do next. I finally settled for composing an e-mail to the big boss, explaining my situation. I asked for a few more days to try to work things out here. I lied again and said I was hopeful.

My tangled web of excuses zipped through the ether to Vida House as I left the encampment behind, turned onto the highway, and headed toward the cabin to gather what I had of the manuscript and take it to the library. Maybe I could turn up something there. Perhaps, by some miracle, when I came home this evening, another envelope would be tucked inside the door.

A quote from the manuscript came to mind: *Where there is life, there is hope.* Rand, Sarra, and their story were still alive inside me. I was hanging on by my fingernails, but I was hanging on.

My phone chimed, and I reached for it to see if it was my answer from the office, but it was a voice mail from Jamie, just now showing up on my phone but apparently left earlier that morning. "Hey, thinking about you as I head into work. Hadn't heard from you in a couple days. Everything okay? Anyway, let me know. I was a little worried."

*Me too,* I thought as I glanced down to slip the phone back into my purse. *Just a little.*

An unexpected blur of movement caught the corner of my eye, jerking my attention back to the windshield. Breath hitched in my chest, and I dropped the phone, stomping on the brake. The pickup in front of me fishtailed, the back tires locking up and laying down rubber. Ahead, a chain reaction progressed, the seconds seeming to slow and stretch. At the start of the line, a cattle truck skidded sideways. Its wheels belched out smoke. A swirling cloud of dust and dead leaves overtook my car, blocking the view for an instant, then wafting away.

Something large and white skittered through the ditch and vanished behind the cattle hauler, then appeared again—a horse. It was bolting wild and blind, its head pulled sharply to one side as the rider tried to turn it away from an oncoming car.

Minutes seemed to pass before the semi vibrated to a final stop in a curtain of haze, everything still happening at once. My vehicle came to rest just inches from the pickup's bumper. People hit hazard lights. The semi driver exited his vehicle. A guy in steampunk clothes ran up the center stripe to flag oncoming traffic.

I imagined some Time Shifters fan's vacation tragically cut short by an unthinkable accident. What shape were the horse and rider in? Had the truck hit them? Had someone called 911? Should I get out? Move my car to the shoulder? See about the horse and rider? Could I help?

The steampunk guy trotted up the center stripe again, waving for people to get back in their vehicles and yelling that everything was fine.

A long, slow breath passed through me, and I blew out the tension, waiting for traffic to move. *Thank God* was all I could think. Suddenly the phone call from the office and the questions about my mission here seemed very small. Unimportant in the larger scheme of things. Someone had been very lucky today. The incident could have ended so differently.

Traffic inched forward, revealing a glimpse of the rider standing on the opposite side of the horse. Circumventing the cattle truck as it rested cockeyed on the shoulder, I could just make out jeans and boots. Pink ones.

The trailer was empty—probably the reason the driver had been able to stop in such a short distance. In the ditch, he was having words with the horse owner. Ms. Pink Boots was probably getting an education right about now.

Rolling past the cab, I glanced in the rearview at the scene playing out on the roadside, caught a glimpse of a dark head, a ponytail.

*Hannah?*

The gray horse. The one she wasn't supposed to ride? What in the world was she doing all the way down here?

I whipped the car around in a clear space, rushed back, U-turned onto the shoulder, and drove up behind the truck. The man was leading the horse now, gesturing and talking to Hannah as she followed along.

Friday spotted her and tried to jump out the door with me as I slipped through. "Stop it!" I yelled, and for once he did as he was told.

The truck driver jerked at the sound of my voice, his surprise evident. "I was just tryin' to help the girl out," he defended. The reaction seemed strange. Creepy, even. Like I'd caught him at something. "She got herself in a pickle. She don't want her daddy to know she took the horse out. I told her I'll put 'im in the trailer, give her and the horse a ride wherever she needs to go, keep 'er outta trouble with her old man."

I was momentarily dumbfounded. This guy didn't know Hannah, and she didn't know him. She was about to get in a truck with some middle-aged man she'd never met?

My stomach turned over and my mind raced to at least a dozen places I didn't want it to go. What did he have in mind in return for this favor?

Even Hannah looked slightly unsure of the situation, but she was still following him like a lost lamb. He had the horse in one hand and her wrist in the other.

"Hannah, what's going on?"

As soon as I said her name, the truck driver tried to give

her the reins back. In fact, he couldn't get rid of the horse, or Hannah, fast enough. "Sounds like you know who she is."

"It's okay," Hannah pleaded, focusing on me rather than taking the horse's reins. "He's gonna bring me back over by our pasture gate on Sarra Creek, and I can go in that way. He knows where it is."

Heat and disbelief swirled through me in a dizzy dust devil of emotion. There was no way this great big truck would make it down Sarra Creek Road. Where would he even turn around down there?

I snaked out a hand, snatched the reins to the gray. "That's okay. I'll take care of it."

The driver looked at my car, and me, and the horse and Hannah, probably wondering how I intended to single-handedly get everything off the side of the road at once. Backing away, he lifted his palms in a show of innocence that was just . . . odd. "She don't need to be on that horse."

"She's not getting back on the horse."

Hannah's chin lifted. "I can ride him. He's fine in the woods. I just got on the wrong trail down there, and it came out by the road, and he got spooked from the cars and—"

"Hannah, be quiet."

"But the guy said he can take me . . ." She cast a glance toward the truck, still searching for any way out that didn't include her family knowing where she'd been.

"I *said* we're fine."

The driver snorted and shook his head, then hooked his thumbs somewhere under his beer belly. "Y'all have at it." He walked back to his truck. A moment later, the Jake brake released and the rig coughed and wheezed its way onto the road.

"*Now* what're we s'posed to do?" Hannah was snippy in a desperate sort of way.

I leaned over, met her face-to-irritated-face. "I'll *tell* you what we're going to do. You're going to take these reins, and then you're going to *lead* this horse the three-quarters of a mile, or however much farther it is, to the cabin. And I'm going to follow along with the car. Then we're putting this horse in the backyard fence behind the cabin, and I'm driving you home." *And man-oh-man, am I going to have some words for you on the way there.*

# Chapter 21

The big house was empty when we arrived, not a sign of Evan or Hannah's great-grandmother or anyone else. Just a huge, shadowy shell that sat dusty and uncomfortably quiet in the afternoon light. It seemed like such a sad place to drop a little girl. I thought of my sisters' kids and the tiny houses they lived in. Was this home so much better? More rooms, fewer people. More toys, but no one to play with. A stack of what looked like leftover birthday presents sat piled in the corner of the garage. The gifts were still in boxes with bits of tape and paper clinging to them. Hannah had everything, and yet *things* didn't solve the problem.

I wondered how often Hannah left the property and took trail rides along the roads. She'd mentioned Honey Creek before, and that she had the key code to the ranch gates, but I hadn't really thought about what that could mean. Did she usually talk to people she ran across as she was out riding? What if, sooner or later, she met the wrong person when she was alone in a deserted area?

I wanted to tell someone what I'd seen, but there was no one here.

"Can you and Friday stay awhile? We could watch a movie or somethin'." Her eyes rolled my way, far too trusting, far too invested, considering that she barely knew me. This child was so overwhelmingly lonesome, so fundamentally lost. She missed her mother. I understood that in the most visceral way. When you're suddenly forced to navigate the world without the person who's supposed to teach you how to take the spirit of a little girl and fill the body of a woman, it's so incredibly hard to find your feet.

She needed someone, and I realized more than ever that a long-distance friend wasn't going to fill the bill. She needed someone to be here and stand in that empty place. Her great-grandmother and Helen were wonderful, but they didn't have the time and energy a girl like Hannah required.

Hugging one arm around herself, she rubbed away a rash of goose bumps. "I hate being in this place by myself."

"Hannah, I probably shouldn't—"

"Oh, hey, I love your necklace. That's so cool. Is that beach glass?" She changed the subject, examining the hand-strung shell–and–sea glass creation I'd purchased earlier.

"Yes, it is. A girl named Robin at the Warrior Week camp made it. She's not much older than you, actually."

"That's cool. So . . . we've got *The Matrix 3*." Hannah slyly angled toward the *Can you stay?* question again, taking a hopeful sidestep toward the cavernous living room where a giant-screen TV hung above the fireplace.

"I can stay awhile, I guess." With any luck, the housekeeper or Helen or Violet or Jake or one of the hired hands would show up before Evan did. I could relate the story of Hannah's incident today and leave it in their hands.

"Or *Oblivion*. My dad just brought that one home," she chattered on, her tone artificially bright now.

"Have you got anything happy? Like . . . Disney or something? Friday doesn't like violent movies. They give him nightmares."

A playful smirk answered. "We've got *The Little Mermaid* somewhere. Does Friday like beach movies?"

"Beach movies are Friday's favorite." I so needed to be working, not watching Disney movies, but what was I supposed to do? I couldn't just leave her here.

Hannah began searching the cabinet beside the towering rock mantel. "I guess it's downstairs in the theater room. Wanna go down there? I could turn on the popcorn maker and make us some popcorn."

"Friday loves theater rooms and popcorn."

Friday recognized one of his favorite words, *popcorn*, and growl-whined in curmudgeonly agreement.

Hannah giggled, and I realized something. It was the first time I'd seen a smile that traveled all the way to her eyes and wasn't weighed down with twenty pounds of worry. The kind of smile an eleven-year-old kid should have. "'Kay."

I followed her through Evan Hall's massive house, past bedrooms that looked as though they'd never been used and artwork that I guessed was Helen's. At the end of the corridor, we traveled down a staircase lined with press photos, framed newspaper articles, movie posters, and writing awards.

A fully equipped theater room waited below, a semicircle of leather recliner couches giving the area a designer look. On one end, an antique concession counter featured a full-size popcorn

popper, a soda machine, minibar, refrigerator, and all the com-
forts of home. Along the far wall, a row of glass doors led to a
stone patio and a walk-out deck with an outdoor fireplace and an
incredible view of the valley below. The area was made for entertaining. Oddly, there were no tables or chairs on the patio—only
twigs, pine straw, and fresh fall leaves. The place looked deserted.

Hannah moved to the popcorn popper and grabbed supplies
from the cabinet.

"Are you sure it's okay for you to be turning that thing on by
yourself?" The machine was taller than she was.

She measured the oil and corn and stood on her toes to dump
them in. "No problem. I do it all the time. The soda machine has
tokens up top. Just get what you want outta there, 'kay?"

"Okay." I set Friday down and he wandered to the popcorn
area, sniffing for freebies.

"You can have some in a minute," Hannah giggled.

"He doesn't need more than a bite or two. He's trying to
watch his girlish figure."

"Ummm . . . I'm thinkin' it's too late already." She laughed
harder, and it was so good to see her happy that for a minute I
was tempted to forget the whole roadside incident. I couldn't, of
course. Her family needed to know, and aside from that, there
was a horse in my backyard at the cabin.

Right now, that seemed as far from Hannah's mind as it could
possibly be. Maybe she was trying to distract me, or perhaps she
was in denial. I couldn't tell, but suddenly we were like girlfriends
at a sleepover.

"Hey, you wanna watch one of the Time Shifters movies?
Uncle Evan *hates* those things, but we've got the DVDs upstairs.
I only turn them on if he's not here."

Temptation nibbled, but I could just imagine the stink if

Evan Hall came home and caught me—the woman he already didn't like—in his house watching the Time Shifters videos, which he hated. I'd end up on the other end of a lawsuit for sure . . . or in jail.

Hannah clued in to my hesitation. "It's okay. The alarm dinger goes off if anyone comes in, and I can switch it over to *Little Mermaid*, like, super quick. This thing loads four DVDs at once. You can watch movies till your eyes pop out."

"Well, that sounds appealing."

"*Ffff!* You're funny." Her brows skewed, one up and one down, like she still couldn't quite decide what to think of me. "I like it in here. Nobody *ever* comes downstairs. It's *all* mine. I'll go get the movies." She bolted for the door and disappeared up the stairs.

"Nice digs," I muttered, but the truth was that there was something vaguely sad about this room. It had the feeling of a place that was built with great excitement and hope, a place expecting a crowd that never showed.

I wondered about Evan's actress ex-wife. Was this area her domain? Was that why Evan never used it? For some crazy reason, I wanted to understand the man. Even though I knew I should leave it alone, the questions about him wouldn't stop nagging me. Who was he really?

The cell rang in my purse as the popcorn popper poofed fluffy white kernels into the glass case. I grabbed the phone and answered, still focused on the view.

Coral Rebecca was on the other end. Before I'd even tuned in, she'd rushed out several sentences of an invitation to a family birthday party for her girls and Marah Diane's twins. Tomorrow. On the grounds behind the church. "Daddy says it'll be okay if you come, but . . . not wearin' pants, okay?"

I let myself out onto the patio and shut the door behind me, allowing a cold blast of air to chill the heat in my cheeks. *Daddy says it'll be okay* . . . The man I hadn't seen in twelve years, since my little brother's funeral . . . that was all he could say? All he cared about was how I dressed? Whether or not I met his parameters and those of the Brethren Saints?

"I don't know if I can be there." I closed my eyes to the view of miles and miles of the Blue Ridge, folded in ribbons of autumn yellows and ambers, laced with the green of pines. My heart burned and so did my eyes.

"Don't be that way, Jennia Beth," my sister pleaded. "You hadn't even seen Evie Christine and her kids or Lily Clarette yet. We all want you to be there with us."

I lumbered through a lame excuse about this being a working trip for me but finally ended with "I'll try."

"Please come," Coral Rebecca added. "My girls been askin' about you ever since you were here the other day . . . and . . . well . . . I just . . . I been prayin' for a long time that you'd come back and we'd all be fam'ly again."

My guts twisted like someone was wringing them dry. "I'll have to see what tomorrow brings, okay?" I was the answer to my sister's prayers? How could that be?

"I love you, Jennia Beth. I know you don't believe that."

"I do believe it." But it was so much more convenient for me not to acknowledge the ties—to tear loose the bonds of a shared childhood and move on. Yet the strings were still there, sewn into my skin. They pulled and tugged in a way I couldn't describe. "I love you too."

I walked back into the theater room feeling numb, sat down in a recliner as the movie queued up, and tried to zone out as Evan Hall's fantasy world lit up the big screen. Time Shifters, if nothing else, was a perfect escape, just as it had been when I'd crouched behind my grandmother's springhouse to read the books.

Watching the story now, I was conscious of deeper themes I couldn't have put into words as a teenager—themes that had resonated with me even back then. The Time Shifters, for all their superpowers, were prisoners in a way, just as I was. The small group of elite soldiers who'd arrived here were trapped within Earth's limited centuries, never able to find peace, ever under threat of the Dark Ones. They had an inconvenient habit of falling in love with mere humans and risking interrupting the proper flow of human events. It was forbidden to transport human love interests through time. Humans were to be stripped of their memories and left behind when a Time Shifter was discovered by the Dark Ones and forced to flee through a portal. Yet Nathaniel found himself inexorably compelled by his love for Anna. He couldn't strip her of her memories, yet he couldn't share his immortality with her. All he could do was escape through time with her, breaking the First Law, running from both the Dark Ones and the Guardians in his own troop, joining those who had become mutineers for the sake of love.

Now I found myself, like the people in the Warrior Week camp, vaguely wishing I could step through a rabbit hole and leave everything behind. I wanted to live in a magical world where love mattered above all else. Was such a thing even possible in the real world? My experience with love had always been that it grew like kudzu vine, slowly overtaking the host and choking the life out of it.

It was such a cynical perspective. That wasn't who I wanted to be. I wanted to be someone who could forgive and trust and reach out, despite the past.

Could accepting Coral Rebecca's invitation be a first step? Did I have it in me to do that? The gathering was being held on the church grounds, of all places. Brethren Saints and family members I hadn't seen in years would be there. The men would most likely ignore me. The women would exchange reproachful looks while minding the table and chatting back and forth in their artificially singsong voices, keeping pleasant, as always, each of them aware that failure to do so would bring swift and certain rebuke, first from the family, and potentially from the elders' council as well.

Could I watch all of that again? Could I stand it? The three hours of Joey's funeral had been almost more than I could endure without exploding and sending shrapnel in all directions.

The sensor over the movie room door chimed and a notification popped up on the screen: *Garage Entry*.

Hannah switched the movie, then jumped out of her seat and rushed across the room to put the Time Shifters DVD back in its case. She tucked it behind a stack of clutter and plopped down in her seat again, seeming unconcerned. "I can stick it back in the office when he's outside sometime."

Reality hit with the quick snap of a rubber band striking skin. "You *stole* that from your uncle's office?"

"It's okay." She wagged her chin, suddenly more teenager than little girl. "No big deal."

"If you're not supposed to do that, it is. You said your uncle didn't *like* the movies. You didn't say you weren't allowed to mess with the DVDs."

Her dark hair fanned over the cushion as she rolled onto her back, lying sideways in the recliner to look at me. "There aren't really any rules. My daddy doesn't care."

"It's your uncle Evan's house." I stood up, paced to the door, then back, not sure what to do. Was it better to be caught casually watching movies with Hannah or on my way toward the nearest exit?

Hannah drummed her dangling feet against the recliner arm. "Ummm . . . you know what happened today? Uncle Evan doesn't . . . ummm . . . he doesn't need anything else to worry about, so we can just not tell him, and I'll tell my dad when he gets back, and he can go get the horse." I could almost see her hardening beneath a layer of attitude. This wasn't the vulnerable, frightened girl who'd asked me not to leave her alone in the house a couple hours ago.

"That's your *uncle* coming in?" I checked the stairway. Empty so far. How did she know who was here?

"Yeah, my dad never parks in the garage. That's Uncle Evan and Granny Vi. They're back from her treatment, I bet."

*Okay, be calm. Calm. Calm. You do have a reason for being here and something you need to tell the man.* "Hannah, I'm not lying to your uncle."

"You don't have to *lie*. Just don't *tell* him. My dad'll come get the horse. It's fine."

"Your uncle's going to wonder why I'm *here*."

"I'll just say I called you." Her gaze rolled toward the screen with casual disinterest.

There were footsteps in the hallway overhead now. I couldn't help myself—I grabbed my purse, slipped into my jacket, and moved out of the direct line of sight.

Hannah frowned at me. "What're you doin'? Seriously, it's no big deal."

"What's no big deal?" Evan's voice. He came halfway down the steps and stopped.

"Hey, Uncle Evan." Hannah craned to see him through the

doorway. "If we watch another movie. I told Jennia Beth it's no big deal."

Another half-dozen rapid, angry-sounding footfalls, and he was in the room, staring at me, clearly stupefied by my presence there. Even his skilled and creative mind could not conjure a reason why I would be in his theater room watching *The Little Mermaid* with his niece. His mouth dropped open slightly and an eye flash came my way. That expression spoke volumes. It said, *I cannot believe the nerve of you, woman.*

I quickly began working toward a graceful exit. "I really do need to go. Now that there's someone home with you." The last part was an attempt at explaining myself. A little. At least.

Hannah pivoted her feet to the floor, crossed the room, and wrapped her arms around my waist. "Thanks for coming to watch movies with me. Do you *have* to go?" She gave me a con-spiratorial look, and the meaning was clear enough. *Don't tell.*

"Yes, I really do." I peeled her off, held her face in my hands, and saw the sad, vulnerable little girl again. "I meant what I said in the car on the way up here, okay? Never again. Anything like that. You hear me?"

She sighed, then slipped from my grasp and returned to flop across the recliner.

Evan jerked his chin toward the doorway, and I followed him from the room, hoping to leave without running into Granny Vi. She didn't need to be party to a spit-and-scratch match between her grandson and me, or to know about today's incident on the side of the highway.

Neither Evan nor I spoke until we had made it down the hall and out a door that led to a sunken stairway area.

"The driveway's that direction." He motioned toward the stone steps—telling, not asking—and I complied by starting up the stairs.

"I'm assuming you must've hidden your car around back because I didn't see it on the way in," he spat.

I could feel my temper moving into simmer mode. I didn't deserve this. I was only trying to help, and really, after Coral Rebecca's call, I was still smarting, off-balance, and not in the mood to take another punch. "I parked where Hannah said to park."

"I told you to stay away from Hannah. What were you doing, casing my house for more of your mystery manuscript?"

Cresting the stairs, I wheeled at him. "Believe it or not, Evan Hall, everything isn't about *you*. Today didn't have anything to do with the manuscript. But it has *everything* to do with that little girl in there. And if you cared about her as much as you care about who's infiltrating your precious mountain, maybe you'd be asking how I ended up here with her today."

"You have no *idea* what's going on in this family."

"I know what it's like to be a kid with no mother around. She needs someone, and not her great-grandmother, who's too ill to keep up with her, or a dad who seems to think it is *okay* for his daughter to ride all over the county by herself on a horse she has no business taking out of the barnyard. She almost got *run over* today. On the highway. And when I pulled up, some creepy trucker was offering her a ride, and she was going to take him up on it so that she could get the horse back home without anyone knowing."

The emotional current hit tsunami strength and picked up debris, the stress of the day, the week, this *place* rising up and spilling over, rushing down the stairs like a flood. He could drown in it for all I cared. Maybe when he finally thought about his niece climbing into some stranger's truck, he'd wake up and realize I was just doing what any decent person would've done.

But right now he was as stone-faced as usual. In fact, he looked like he wasn't about to accept any explanation if it came from me.

"You know what . . . ? Whatever," I bit out, tossing my hands. "You believe what you want to believe about me, but *talk* to Hannah. Someone needs to be watching her."

His eyes narrowed, his chin rising defensively. I'd hit a sensitive spot. "Her dad was supposed to be here with—"

"It's not about who's *supposed* to be doing what!" The breath-stealing weight of pent-up frustration pressed down hard. I was slowly, slowly being submerged in my own life here, and there seemed to be no good way out. Every time I bailed a bucketful of water, three more fell in my face. "It is about *her*. About what *she* needs. I don't know what's going on around here and I don't even care. I have enough family issues of my own to worry about, believe me, and . . ."

The dam burst, tears rushed in, and I did the only thing I could. I turned and ran for my car.

The car door handle rebelled when I yanked it, my grip slipped, and three fingernails bent backward. Snatching the remote from my pocket, I clicked, pulled the handle again, and the same three fingernails ripped to the quick when it didn't give. "This stupid thing!" The next thing I knew, I was pounding the window, completely losing it.

I heard Evan behind me before I felt his hand on my arm, stopping me from taking another swing. The key chain clattered to the concrete and he picked it up. "Hold on a minute."

"Give me my keys!" Pulling away blindly, I stumbled against the car and hit the side mirror.

He kept the keys out of reach. "I said, just hold on a minute." Beneath the air of command, his voice was gentle, no longer rage-hardened. "I apologize, all right? It's been a rough day with Granny Vi, and then some idiots at the gate wouldn't get out of the way, and then I get home and something's going on with Hannah . . . again. I'm sorry. I shouldn't have jumped to conclusions. Tell me what happened today, exactly."

I sniffed, burbled, looked for something to wipe my nose with. On top of the emotional overload, it was cold out here. Evan reached into his pocket, pulled out a roll of gauze that had come from either the hospital or the horse barn, and handed it to me.

I mopped my face. The rest of the roll slipped from my hand and unwound across the driveway, drawing a ribbon toward the house. "I'm . . . I'm sorry too." I let the tail of the gauze loose in the wind, and it sailed away, swirling like tissue at a naughty kid's midnight toilet paper raid. "Wait. No, I'm not. You're a jerk."

"Sometimes," he admitted, a rueful twist teasing his lips. "I have been known to aim at the wrong target. Jake was supposed to be here with Hannah today while we went to Charlotte. And from what you're saying, he wasn't."

I repeated the story, more calmly and in detail this time— where I'd found Hannah, where the gray horse was now, and what had happened on the side of the road. "And the thing is, she was ten steps away from the guy's truck, and when I think about that, it scares me to death. I wouldn't even have let that guy drive *me* someplace."

Evan paced away and then back, his hands braced stiffly on his belt. "When I find Jake, I'm going to kill him. You know, I don't ask much from him for being here. Stop drinking and take care of his kid, that's all. She needs her daddy."

The overload of debris-laden issues swelled in me again. I thought of the phone call from Coral Rebecca, my father saying it would be okay if I came to the family birthday party. *Okay.* "She needs *someone*. It doesn't have to be her daddy."

He seemed surprised at first that I would say it. Sadness quickly replaced the shock. "It should be her dad." He lifted his hands, let them fall and hang helplessly at his sides. "I do everything for him. I'm still trying to get him out of a DUI from before he moved here. And he had Hannah in the car with him when he did it. What's it going to take for him to wake up?"

I thought of my own father again, of all the times I'd wanted him to stop and look at me, to see *me* instead of a reminder of my mama. Of all the times I'd wanted to be able to tell him my ideas or troubles or fears. Of all the times I'd needed him to simply say those three little words that every girl yearns to hear from her dad. All these years later, I was still waiting.

"Some people don't wake up. Ever." I was talking to myself as much as to Evan. "I grew up with my father off in the woods half the time and preaching and taking a rod to us the other half, and it still hasn't changed. What mattered most was that someone else stepped in for me, filled the gap. Wilda Culp wasn't my mom and she wasn't my dad, but she was someone I could count on. Someone steady and consistent. It wasn't perfect, but it was enough—just knowing I had one person who was reliable every time."

He turned his back to the car, leaned against it, and crossed his arms, letting his head fall forward. I stood beside him, soaking the last of the warmth from the metal. It'd be cold again tonight.

"I can't stop wanting Jake to be better than he is. I've tried, but I can't."

This was a side of Evan I hadn't seen before. The battered, broken side dealing with painful family realities. Just like me.

"Maybe it'll happen at some point, but Hannah needs someone now, not later. She really is a great kid."

"I know she is." He looked my way, his eyes catching the light and taking on a silver hue. Suddenly I was aware of our nearness, of his shoulder touching mine. I couldn't feel his warmth through my jacket, yet I could. "She likes you a lot. It's possible that she was headed to Uncle Clive's place on the lake today, but I have a feeling she might've been on her way down there to the cabin when you found her with the horse. She's asked me over and over if you were coming back."

A wall started upward brick by brick. I could hear it building between us. *Clink, clink, clink.* Evan couldn't see the barrier, but I could. "I'd love to keep in touch with Hannah, but I'm only here for a couple more days at most. They're ready for me to get back to the office."

"Leaving empty-handed?" He seemed surprised and maybe even a little disappointed that I was giving up.

"Not leaving with what I came for, I guess."

He softened, his gaze meeting mine, pulling me in momentarily. "There's no manuscript to find, you know. *The Story Keeper.* All I ever wrote of that thing was seven, eight chapters . . . maybe. What you read in the partial was most of it. I based it on a story I'd heard growing up—one of those mountain tales that've been handed down. The partial did a good job of gathering rejection letters, but that's about it. I haven't thought about that thing in years."

I searched his face. Was this the truth finally? "I'm guessing that nobody got beyond the hand-drawn title page."

Groaning, he booted an acorn, watching as it rolled away. "That's how green I was. I thought it was sheer brilliance, coming up with my own cover and putting it on that bright-blue paper. I thought that would really make it stand out, grab attention at all those big publishing houses in New York, and I'd take the place by storm. I didn't have a clue that you were supposed to write the *whole* book first. I was pretty much fresh off the boat when I sent out those first submissions. It was shocking when the rejection letters started coming. Shocking, I tell you."

"Well, the artwork on the title page actually wasn't that bad."

"I can't believe after all these years you found that thing."

"Evan, I didn't *find* it. It found me. I wasn't embellishing the other day. *The Story Keeper* ended up on my desk one morning with no explanation. That's the truth. People aren't even supposed to take things off Slush Mountain."

"It's forbidden territory, yes, I know." His gaze wandered my way again, soft wrinkles of amusement fanning over his cheeks. "I checked on you. I do still have a few friends around New York. You landed the Tom Brandon memoir a couple years ago. Quite a coup."

A strange giddy feeling twinkled through me before I knew what was happening. I didn't want it to be there. But it was. He'd taken the time to ask about me, to find out some things.

"Yes, I did. I was proud of that Tom Brandon deal." It was a relief to have moved the conversation back to business. Safer territory. Beyond *The Story Keeper*, anything happening between Evan Hall and me was a non-possibility. My life was in New York. I wanted no more ties to these mountains than I already had. Besides, I'd vowed never again to mix business with pleasure after the disastrous relationship that had left me minus a job and plus a dog.

*Dog* . . . Gee whiz, I'd completely forgotten about Friday. He was still downstairs in Evan's theater room, sound asleep in a popcorn coma.

"I'll bet." Evan was sizing me up now. "The snowmobile thing and the night in the mountains was quite a story. You'll go pretty far to get what you want."

I leaned away a bit, trying to gain a clearer perspective on his meaning. "It was good business, but getting stuck on the mountain overnight wasn't part of the plan. The thing is, *The Story Keeper* is different. I went after the Tom Brandon memoir because it had Tom Brandon's name attached to it. When I opened the envelope with that partial in it a couple weeks ago— your partial—I didn't know who wrote it, but from the first page I felt a connection to that girl under the cabin. It's really good."

"It's long gone. Who knows where by now. Probably down at the bottom of the county landfill. I had some of my writing stuff stored in the cabin at one time—I used to work there occasionally—but we cleaned it out years ago when Aunt Helen and Granny Vi started offering the place for rent. I bagged the old junk up myself and tossed it on the dump trailer. The partial you have is all that's left of the original eight or so chapters."

He seemed to be on the level, and yet what he was telling me didn't fit. "Evan, someone's been bringing chapters of that manuscript and leaving them wedged in the cabin door. I've read eight chapters now. From what you're saying, I guess that's all of it. Maybe that's why nothing new has shown up in the last couple days."

"Chapters?" His disbelief was obvious. I couldn't blame him. But I could also see the wheels turning. He was trying to figure out how it could be true. One thing was for certain—he had nothing to do with those mysterious deliveries to the cabin.

# Chapter 22

The phone conversation replayed in my head as I drove—my youngest sister, Lily Clarette, calling to ask whether I was coming to this afternoon's birthday party. "I just wanna see you before you go, okay?" She had Coral Rebecca's sweet, musical voice. I wondered if she also possessed the same singing talent. I realized I'd never talked to her on the phone. Not once. She'd written to me about school projects a couple times over the years, but that was it.

I didn't even know her voice. There was something so wrong in that.

"Maybe I can try to get by there. We'll see."

I'd secured a few more days here on Looking Glass Lake—how could I not, after talking to Evan? He was as baffled by the appearance of the manuscript pages at the cabin as I was. He had come by to see them when he'd picked up the horse and confirmed that they were his. He was trying to get to the bottom of the whole thing. Granny Vi and Helen wouldn't admit to having anything to do with it.

According to Evan, I'd now read all that had ever existed of *The Story Keeper*. We'd sat on the cabin porch and chatted about it as Hannah soothed the nervous gray horse through the stock trailer window.

Suddenly Evan Hall and I were no longer enemies. The mystery had, in some way, turned us into uneasy allies. Both of us wanted to know where those chapters had come from.

Neither of us knew who else to ask.

The mystery was both fascinating and frustrating, but the memory of Lily Clarette's call edged out the questions about *The Story Keeper* as I drove. "Come on, Jennia Beth. Just for a little while. Coral Rebecca says Levi's takin' a half day off work and goin' over to the Walmart in Sylva to pick up this big ol' cake, and we dug round the old barn and found the pitchin' horseshoes. It's gonna be fun. Daddy and Roy got the dog all traded for the four-wheeler, and the four-wheeler's already sold, so everybody's happy. Coral Rebecca wants you to come so bad. She's gonna be heartbroke if you don't. We've never, ever all been together."

We had, but of course, Lily Clarette couldn't remember it. Other than those few e-mails back and forth to her account at school and her *Flat Stanley* project in the fourth grade, we were complete strangers. "I'll try. I will. I'm in the middle of something work-related here, though. It's a little unpredictable."

My sister sighed. "In Isaiah it says, 'Remember ye not the former things, neither consider the things of old. Behold, I will do a new thing.' It's time for a new thing, Jennia Beth."

The Scripture came out of nowhere, blindsided me. Something

crippled and battered inside me rose toward the words. I recognized it as hope. "Okay. I'll be there."

Now here I was, snaking through the mountains with window herb gardens and kid-size sandpile sets neatly gift-wrapped in the backseat. Friday and I had stopped by the Mountain Leaf store on the way to find presents, so as not to show up empty-handed. Given the family's financial state and the condition of Daddy's house, the kids' birthdays might be pretty slim.

Apparently, though, someone had managed enough money to order a customized birthday cake at the Walmart bakery, or else they'd leaned on Coral Rebecca and Levi to pay for it.

*Don't think about it, don't think about it . . .*

My jaw was already stiffening up, bones and teeth clenching, stress taking over.

I tried to focus, instead, on the research materials I'd picked up from the library in Looking Glass Gap. The librarian had been unbelievably helpful. She hadn't been able to find anything about the origins of Sarra Creek, other than that the name predated the establishment of the La Belle Mission. She'd given me a book about La Belle, a mission school founded around 1904, as well as copies of census documents and tax rolls from the turn of the century, but I hadn't found Rand Champlain's name or Sarra's mentioned anywhere.

Driving the winding road, slipping through sunlight and shade, I lost myself in time, gazing over mountain slopes and into settlements tucked in lush valleys. My imagination ran along deer trails and and old Cherokee trade routes, painting images of Rand and Sarra here and there as they fought to survive. Beyond that, there was the deeper question: Could they overcome the barriers that separated them? Could there be any kind of life for the two of them together?

It was entirely possible that I might never find the answers. The librarian knew her stuff, but in terms of historical proof, she hadn't been able to turn up anything beyond the folktales Evan had been told about a young white man and a part-Cherokee girl who'd jumped over the falls rather than allow themselves to be separated. According to legend, the spirits of the star-crossed lovers still wandered the hollows along Sarra Creek, their love creating rainbows over the Sagua Falls on sunlit days.

It struck me again that, unless something magically turned up in these library materials, I was quite possibly at the end of the line. What if Rand and Sarra really were no more than an old mountain tale? What if there was no more history to discover or the history had been lost forever? While Evan was interested in digging up the facts if we could, he wasn't interested in inventing an ending for Rand and Sarra's story. He said he couldn't see the point.

I had to face the fact that in the long run, the only solution might be to let it go.

Perhaps this entire trip wasn't even about my discovering a long-lost story or about my dusting it off and bringing it to print. Maybe this trip was about *my* story, about writing a new chapter rather than discovering what had been written long ago.

Maybe here, where peace had always eluded me, I could finally make peace with the past.

What if I wasn't strong enough to face the reckoning—the one I'd sensed when I'd started on this trip?

*Turn around, make excuses, go back to the cabin.* The voice of doubt was almost too strong to resist.

I tried to silence it as I circled through Towash, but sitting at the crossroads, I debated again, fought angel and devil until a car with a dragging tailpipe rumbled up behind me and honked, forcing a decision. The turn toward Lane's Hill was almost more than I could muster. Doubt and ghosts haunted the slowly narrowing road that led to the remnants of a turn-of-the-century post office and store, marking what had once been a tiny community at a water crossing. I felt the whispers closing in, the ghosts peering through the car windows, pounding on the glass, threatening to overtake me.

A quarter mile farther along, the dirt road to Lane's Hill Church seemed almost abandoned. Tree limbs clawed the car like fingernails, the long, high moans drilling into my brain. The tires slid in muddy ruts, and a rising sense of doom gathered, growing stronger with each revolution of the wheels, becoming almost unbearable when I passed the place where Joey had liked to catch salamanders while the adults lingered uphill at the church. Friday woke and positioned himself with paws on the dashboard, seeming to sense the change inside the car, the taking on of greater and greater weight, the increasing lack of oxygen.

I felt like I was suffocating.

Ahead, the tiny, squat building peeked through the trees, then came into view. The short steeple and faded clapboard were strangely unremarkable, considering how large this place had loomed in my memory. I had both dreaded and feared it, and now, gazing at it as I pulled in among the hodgepodge of vehicles, I realized how insignificant it was. Just a building, created by men, filled with bits of God's Word torn from context and recombined like the pieces of a ransom note.

There had never been, I realized now, anything but hate and fear and punishment here. Brutal control. This building was not the gateway to heaven or hell. There was no love or grace here— none of the things that had confused me when I tried reading the family Bible myself. Men had wrested this place from God, turned it into a golden calf, an idol. If I continued to give power to it, I was as lost as the people who still gathered at the foot of this ragged tar paper–and–tin god of their own making.

It was time to take away from Lane's Hill what should never have belonged to Lane's Hill in the first place.

With a fortifying breath, I squared myself and stepped from the car, then retrieved the gifts from the backseat, determined to take this next step toward freedom.

A hum of voices stirred the air as I rounded the building. Beneath the trees, tables had been set among the aging teeter-totters and swing sets that marked the remains of an old school, long since closed down by busing and consolidation. Girls with hair in frayed plaits and boys in oversize hand-me-down jeans ran among the rotted swings and lopsided merry-go-rounds, playing games of tag, their high-pitched voices conjuring the past.

So many times after prayer meetings we'd slipped away to the old schoolyard, where the laughter and boisterous games of childhood were permitted. In church, even the youngest were made to sit statue still, in the proper position for worship. Fidgeting earned a quick, sharp strike of the short rod—a small, thin length of dowel wood carried in the pocket or tucked in the Bible of a parent. Longer, more powerful rods waited at home, for use when needed.

I wondered if that was still the practice here. It was hard to imagine Coral Rebecca hitting her girls or allowing anyone else to. Other members of the flock, observing behavior deemed improper among any of the children, were authorized to strike the offender. Here on Lane's Hill, you learned that judgment was a perpetual shadow . . . or else you constantly took a beating.

Deedee, Coral Rebecca's eldest, spotted Friday on his leash and the stack of gifts balanced in my hands as I approached.

The little redhead with her, one of Marah Diane's girls, gave the presents a wide-eyed look, which narrowed and grew wary when she saw who was carrying them. I'd barely met Marah Diane's kids on my visit to the farm, she was so busy scolding her brood and chasing them away. I could only imagine what they'd heard about me. I had, at least, worn a dress today, as per my father's wishes—a midcalf wool shift with a peasant-style top. I'd picked it up at Robin's booth in the Time Shifters camp and belted it with a scarf from my suitcase. Combined with a blazer and dress boots, the ensemble wasn't bad.

One of the boys tagged the redhead, and she and Deedee broke into a run, skimming past me so closely that I felt a breeze. Marah Diane glanced my way, her eyes widening. Coming toward me, she scolded the kids and told them to keep clear of the fish fryer.

"I can't stay for prayer meeting after the party," I preempted as we met. I hadn't missed the fact that this was Wednesday, which meant that a gathering of the Brethren Saints would commence about the time this party wrapped up.

Right now, however, the grounds looked deceptively festive. Birthday tables waited, complete with colorful plates, napkins, and plastic silverware. A huge pan of beans and a giant hunk of cheese—commodity food probably contributed by someone who was on the Cherokee tribal rolls and eligible for staples—sat ready to feed the crowd of family and church friends. Fried fish and what looked like venison tenderloin or backstrap waited on a platter, and there was a propane burner blazing under a pot of grease nearby.

"I didn't think *you'd* come inside," Marah Diane bit out, surveying my clothes again. "I guess Coral Rebecca told you to dress proper."

*Don't react. Don't react.* "I brought something for the kids. Where should I put these?"

"Over there, with the rest a the presents." She motioned to a table near the building. A quick glance at the contents left me openmouthed. There were four new bicycles next to the full-sheet bakery cake and other wrapped gifts.

"Daddy and Roy got the money for that four-wheeler already." Marah Diane lifted her chin, looked down her nose at me. "Cash. Twenty-five *hundred* dollars."

Heat boiled under my collar, pressing toward my face. *What about the roof, the bills, the floor that's falling through, the broken window in Lily Clarette's bedroom—the bedroom that doesn't even have electricity right now?*

As always, it was feast into famine around here.

"The girls get to have them a good birthday for once." She licked her lips, relishing the conflict I was struggling to keep from spilling all over the party. The windfall generated by the dog trade would be gone in a month, spent on shopping sprees and loaned off to relatives who were desperate at the moment . . . until all were equally desperate again. That was how it worked.

"Oh" was all I could come up with.

"You can put your presents back there on the table. It was nice of you to carry them somethin'." She gave the gift bags a dismissive look that said, *You could've afforded bigger stuff, but you're too selfish.*

Her attention turned to the fryer, where Coral Rebecca and Levi were breading bags of home-caught fish fillets. Around the table, several of my aunts worked, while the men sat nearby in lawn chairs, my father among them, his back turned my way. Either the group hadn't noticed me yet, or none of them cared that I'd shown up. Hard to say which.

"I better see about the fish." Marah Diane walked away and left me standing at the gift table, awkwardly trying to decide what to do next. Finally I set the presents with the rest and tried to tell myself there were worse things they could have spent the money on than bicycles. The kids would enjoy them at least.

"I'm real glad you came." Coral Rebecca surprised me from behind, but she stood a distance away rather than embracing me as she had when I'd visited her home. Her arms remained crossed self-consciously. We were both aware of the curious looks now coming our way, the hushed whispers circling the group. The air around us was so tight with expectation, you could've strummed "Pretty Polly" on it. "That was awful sweet of you to bring somethin' for all the kids."

"Well, after our talk the other day, I was afraid there might not be much." I bit back the rest. Now wasn't the time.

"Don't get mad." Coral Rebecca knew what I was thinking. It was probably written all over my face. "It wasn't *that* much money. Marah Diane and Roy wanted to give the girls a special birthday. And with both of us goin' in halves, Levi and I only had to borrow a little bit to get Sissy a bike and pay our part a the food."

"You and Levi had to borrow to do this?"

"It's okay. Levi's got some knives for sale with one of his buddies up at Warrior Week. They already sold one, so when somebody buys the others, we'll come out all right."

"What if the knives don't sell? What if you and Levi end up in a bind?"

"It'll be all right. It's always all right."

*Then why do you send me letters whenever a kid needs a tooth fixed or a vehicle breaks down or somebody's three months behind on their payments?* I couldn't say it, and even that frustrated me.

My sister looked like an animal pinned in the corner of a cage. Trapped between me and the net wire. "Come on and say hi to Daddy and see everybody. Join the party, Jennia Beth. My kids have been so excited ever since Marah Diane told them there was gonna be a birthday get-together after all. The girls are about to have a fit to hop on those bikes. They never get anythin' new. It's always some ol' junk somebody had before them."

I followed her to the picnic tables and tried my best to pretend I didn't notice the tension in the air, the looks trailing my every move, the disapproving women surveying my clothes and my hair, which was hanging in a loose ponytail rather than a proper plait.

My father didn't budge as I passed the circle of lawn chairs. "Jennia Beth," he said flatly. The words were meant as an acknowledgment, I guessed, but they sounded more like a rebuke.

"Hi, Daddy."

He returned to his conversation with the man across from him, either a church member or a distant cousin.

That was it, after twelve years away. I sank down on one of the picnic benches near the food, just . . . numb. In some remote corner of my soul, the little girl in me had imagined this moment so differently. I hadn't been ready for the truth.

When would I get used to the fact that my father didn't *care*? He didn't want to know where I lived or what I did or who I was. He was just indifferent to me.

One of my nephews—Marah Diane's youngest—toddled by, stumbled over a twig, and bumped his head on the table leg. I rescued him from underneath and bounced him in my lap, glad for the distraction. Relaxing against me, he fingered my keys, then pressed the button on the remote, laughing when the car horn beeped in the parking lot.

"Twain! Twain!" He giggled. "Is a choo-choo!"

"Push it again." I guided his chubby thumb. "Oh! There it goes. There's the train!" The soft tickle of his foamy baby curls and the smell of soil and little boy reminded me of Joey. He'd been such a fussy baby, colicky and sickly. Countless nights I'd sat out on the porch with him, watching the full moon and letting him take in the cool, moist air to stop the coughing and crying. No one had ever loved me like my little brother loved me.

Resting my chin on the baby's head, I closed my eyes and let the memory wash over me. There were times in the quiet of midnight, our small home filled with breath and stirrings, that the blanket of family covered and surrounded me and made me feel warm and safe. There were times when I'd thought my life would be here on this mountain—find a man, raise kids, scratch out a living somehow. It'd seemed like something to look forward to, occasionally. A right kind of life.

And then there were times when I looked at my mother, when she shrank into corners as my father belittled, berated, yelled and threatened, grabbed and twisted, and deposited my beautiful mother crying in a heap on the floor, the red slashes of the rod across her skin. Properly subjugated. There were times when out-of-control anger took things even further than that. During those times, our home was pure terror.

Those were the nights I knew I'd rather be dead than spend the rest of my life here. Like this.

There had to be something else in the world. Some other way.

But now, smelling the scent of Marah Diane's little one, I felt the surprising pull of my sisters' lives, of the future I'd left behind here. There was a part of me that wanted a baby like this one, a home, a family, and all the things that didn't fit inside the busy, demanding routine I had created.

That yearning seeped in while I was still reeling from the blow of my father's greeting, and the effect was surprisingly powerful here, among the familiar sights and smells of family.

"He likes you."

I looked up, and Lily Clarette was standing over the bench, watching me.

"That baby never goes to nobody he don't know. Not without cryin'. He's a lil' pill worm." She made a face at the baby, and he giggled, reaching for her. "No, no, I don't want ya. You just stay right where you're at."

I wouldn't even have known Lily Clarette, but for Coral Rebecca's occasional photos of family events. My youngest sister was practically a woman now, her body tall and slim, her hair a darker brown than when she was little, her skin a smooth, slightly olive tone, her eyes a clear, golden hazel like mine and Marah Diane's. I hadn't realized from the photos how much she looked like Mama . . . and like me.

I wondered how my father felt about the resemblance that had grown as Lily Clarette did.

She stood a few feet away as if she were uncertain whether she should get too close, but she was curious nonetheless.

I wanted to open my arms and enfold my little sister in a greeting, but I was afraid I might frighten her off or cause her trouble with the Brethren Saints later on. "Can you sit a minute?" I said instead. "I haven't heard from you in forever. I think the last time you sent me an e-mail was . . . what . . . maybe a couple years ago? You had some kind of big project in the science fair, and you asked me to proofread your research paper." It was wrong that I hadn't kept up since then. I wasn't even sure how the thread of communication had died—whether it was on my end or Lily Clarette's. It was easy for me to become so caught up in work that weeks and even months went by, and I never made it to the bottom of my personal e-mail box. Maybe she just got tired of waiting.

"Oh yeah, that." She rolled her eyes and the reaction was so delightfully teenage that I found myself smiling at it. Lily Clarette had a surprisingly spunky personality. "I just ended up makin' it to the state science fair, but I didn't win there or get the scholarship money, so it wasn't no big deal." Her shoulders rose and lowered, and her gaze darted toward the lawn chair circle in a way that made me wonder what my father's opinion of Lily Clarette's achievement had been.

"Are you *kidding*? That's awesome. You're probably the first Gibbs to ever make the state finals in anything." I was joking, sort of, although it was true. Kids who are fighting issues at home aren't prone to being standouts at school.

"It's not good to be boastful."

The muscles along my spine stiffened. Those words could've come straight from my father's mouth. *Just who d'you think you are, girl? The queen a Paris? That Culp woman been puttin' big ideas in your head again?*

"It's okay to be proud of yourself when you've achieved something."

"Pride's a sinful thing."

"Abilities come from God, Lily Clarette."

"Not always." She studied her hands, picked at a frayed fingernail uncomfortably.

The baby relaxed against my chest, his breaths lengthening. I shifted to keep his head from slipping. The movement was natural, old, familiar. Like a nursery school song you realize you can still sing by heart. "If they don't come from God, where do they come from?"

I imagined what must've happened during Lily Clarette's run at the state science fair. No doubt there was a Wilda Culp or a Mrs. Penberthy out there who wanted something better for my youngest sister and knew she could achieve it. I pictured the conflict between my father and the teacher. My father pulling one way, the teacher pushing the other. My father trying to keep Lily Clarette in her place, to make her feel guilty for having a brain and wanting to actually use it.

Now I realized there was a reason Lily Clarette had written to me from school that year and shared the news of her success. She was looking for support, and I was so busy chasing my next big project, I hadn't plugged in like I should've. And it was almost too late. She was in her senior year of high school and thinking about dropping out to marry a twenty-one-year-old . . . with the family's blessing.

"Anythin' comes from the devil if it tempts us from the righteous way," Lily Clarette answered by rote.

I paused to think. As with most of the things I'd been told in my childhood, there was just enough truth to wind around the subject and hold it prisoner, slowly strangling the life out of it. "Who's to say it *isn't* God's plan for you to use your talent for science? Maybe become a doctor and do something in environmental research? There are so many issues with the timber companies and old mining slag heaps and contamination of the groundwater through runoff. Isn't that what your project was related to?"

Another noncommittal shrug. "A little."

"Have you thought about going on to study *anything*?"

Marah Diane was looking our way now, her jaw clenched, her chin jutting forward. Whispers drifted from the lawn chair circle, but I couldn't make out the words. A young guy with long sideburns had stopped talking to watch us from beneath the brim of his Ford cap. I wondered if he was Lily Clarette's intended.

"College or anything? Maybe WCU over in Cullowhee?" I pressed because I sensed that my time was running out. "There are so many scholarships out there, Lily Clarette. Not just the ones from the state science fair."

Her eyes, a deep golden hue in the sunlight, rose and searched mine. Was she considering it?

"I'll help you every way I can. Whatever you need, really. Materials to study for the SATs, help finding scholarships. If you need me to cosign on college loans, I'll do it. I could make some contacts at Clemson for you. I don't have clout there like Wilda Culp did . . ." *But Evan Hall undoubtedly does.* Would he help my sister? "But I'll try."

Lily Clarette's lips pressed together. She swallowed hard. Blinked rapidly as if the picture stung her eyes. "Clemson's so far away. . . ."

"Well, then maybe the community college to start off?" I was rushing now. Lily Clarette couldn't see it because her back was turned, but something was brewing in the men's circle. My father had called Marah Diane over, and it wasn't hard to tell that the conversation was about me.

Judging by Coral Rebecca's body language, she'd noticed as well and was concerned. Her eyes darted about as she whispered to Levi, who had forgone the men's gathering to help his wife at the fryers. That frightened, agonized look was the one she always wore when she knew the fighting was about to start.

"I could help you find an apartment. Something close to campus so that you could walk." None of my sisters even had actual driver's licenses, as far as I knew. Navigating city streets would be a terrifying obstacle for Lily Clarette, just as it had been for me.

Her eyes were the size of the pale-green eggs from the exotic hen my father brought home when I was ten. When we went out to gather after that, it had been a game—seeing who could find the green egg the gray hen had laid.

The look on Lily Clarette's face was half terror and half fascination. "I don't know. . . . I'd have to talk to Daddy." She smoothed wisps of hair nervously into her plait. "And Craig."

I laid my hand on hers almost desperately. "You don't *have* to talk to anybody, Lily Clarette. It's *your* life. You're almost eighteen years old." I did remember her birthday, even though I knew so little else about her. She was born the year a heavy snow came the first week in November. My mother had wanted to name her *Winter*, but my father refused. He'd never heard of anyone with that name. In reality, after two lost pregnancies, he was hoping for at least one more boy to go with Joey, and Lily Clarette was a disappointment. My father didn't care what my mother named her, as long as it wasn't something that would turn heads in the church.

"I'll see what Daddy says," she repeated, which was as good as giving up. "He's been needin' me more since the accident. He was in a real bad way for a while . . ." I could tell she wanted to add more, but the excuses weren't coming fast enough. "Just because you turn eighteen don't mean you're not bound to honor your daddy. I got Mama's nature in me . . . more'n most. I fight it, but it's there. I don't wanna stray down the wrong path like Mama and . . ."

"And me?" No doubt I'd been held up as an example of the path that shouldn't be taken.

"I didn't say that. Don't be puttin' words in my mouth." Color stole into her cheeks, peppering the skin with a watercolor wash of pink pinpoints. "I'm not like Marah Diane and Evie Christine.

I understand why you went off to Clemson, Jennia Beth. I'm not sayin' I agree with all of it, but I understand. And I know that Coral Rebecca wrote you for money lots of times, and you always sent it. Sometimes we wouldn't've made it without that. I'm not dumb." She slid her hand from mine, rested it in her lap, clutched it with the other one.

"I know you're not. That's why I want you to at least give this some thought. Your future is wide open, Lily Clarette. Get out in the world and *see* what you want to do. You can always come back here if that's what you decide is right for you, but at least you'll know what's beyond Lane's Hill."

"I know what's out there." Her nose wrinkled in obvious distaste. "Big cities where people get mugged and murdered and they're living stacked on top of everybody. I'd lose my mind in a place like that."

A chuckle forced itself past my lips. I'd said almost the same thing to Wilda Culp when she'd started this discussion my junior year of high school. "It's not like what they tell you, Lily Clarette. The city is . . . interesting. It's busy. It's always active and there's so much to see and do. There are opportunities beyond what you've been exposed to here. Come visit me this winter. Check it out and see for yourself what you think." I wasn't sure how I'd pay for the plane ticket or how I'd even get her to the Charlotte airport—or how I'd wrestle her away from Daddy—but I was determined. I'd find a way.

There was a light in her for a moment, the yearning of a curious, capable mind. "Oh . . . I don't know. . . ." She glanced over her shoulder toward the men, noticed for the first time the conference happening there. "I mean, I'll just have to wait 'n' see." The dreamy-eyed look faded as quickly as it had come. "You don't have to worry yourself about me, Jennia Beth. I know what I'm doin'. Craig's got a good job, and if he gets some money ahead, he might even be able to buy the propane company off'a his uncle someday. I'm gonna live a different kind of life from Marah Diane and Evie Christine, I promise."

I glanced up, saw Marah Diane headed our way. "Just think about coming for a visit, at least. At Christmas. How about that? We'll do Christmas in the city. There's still plenty of time after that for you to decide where you want to be once you graduate." I opened my purse, slid out one of my business cards, tucked it into her hand, and folded her fingers over the edge. "Don't decide right now, okay? E-mail me or call me and we can talk some more."

The card seemed to tug at her attention, though she turned her hand over quickly, hiding it in the folds of her skirt. "Craig's not gonna wait while I go flittin' off all over the world. He's twenty-one. He's ready to have a life. A family."

"If he loves you, he'll wait until *you're* ready." I was almost whispering now, trying to keep the conversation between the two of us. The minute the family got wind of this, they'd jump in on the opposite side, and Lily Clarette would be a pawn in a twisted power play.

"Lily Clarette." Marah Diane's voice was shrill. "Go help Coral Rebecca get the food on." She spoke in a way that allowed no argument, clearly indicating that she was the one in charge.

"We were talking," I protested.

"Seems like you might be helpin' get the food on too. Or did you forget how?" She snatched the toddler from my lap, stood him on his feet half-awake, and gave him a little push on the rear. "You go on and play with the other kids. If you'd'a gone on and took a nap when I told'ja, you wouldn't be fallin' out when there's a birthday party happenin'."

The little boy caught his balance and waddled away, his chubby legs bowed outward like a mini linebacker's, his bare feet moving over the stony ground with not a hint of tenderness.

Lily Clarette abandoned the bench almost as quickly.

"You leave her be," Marah Diane hissed, wagging a finger in my face in a way that gave the lawn chair crowd a good view.

I drew back, shocked. "Excuse me?"

"You *know* what I'm talkin' about."

"I don't think I do."

"You let her make up her own mind. Don't you be fillin' her with none of your poison. She's a good girl, and she's got a good life ahead a her. In the church, with a man of the Brethren Saints, and you can't *stand* that because you hadn't got nothin'." Her voice rose over the gathering, attracted attention, and I knew she wanted it to. Some part of this was for show. Female-on-female rebuke was always encouraged first, then the men came in if necessary.

My temper flared as heads turned our way. "You don't want me to answer that. Trust me." I looked around for Friday so I could gather him up and leave. No way was I doing this now. If Marah Diane really started in on our issues, the fallout would be cataclysmic.

"Well, why *not*? You know every little thang there is to know, don't ya? You with your big job and your New York money. You're so much *smarter* than all a us."

"Marah Diane, stop it. This is your kids' birthday party, for heaven's sake." I stood up to gain an equal footing. "What in the world is wrong with you?"

By the swings and teeter-totters, the kids stopped playing and watched us with grim expectation. I recognized those looks. Those faces were waiting for the bomb to drop. Expecting a perfectly normal day to be upended by conflict and chaos. They knew the pattern, just as we always had. Contentment was the enemy in this family—something to wage war against.

Marah Diane leaned closer. "Don't you go tellin' *me* how to raise *my* kids when you hadn't even *got* any."

"Food's on!" Coral Rebecca called out as if she hadn't noticed the apocalypse brewing nearby.

"Let's eat before it gets cold," Levi added. God bless Levi. I didn't even know him and I liked him. He and Coral Rebecca seemed almost as frustrated by our family dynamic as I was.

There was a rustling and a shift in the action as people rose from lawn chairs and moved to the table, where my father, the eldest male host, would speak over the food to make it clean to eat.

Marah Diane gave me one last warning look as we parted ways. I skirted the table and found a spot on the women's end near Coral Rebecca and her children. Friday sneaked in under my feet, ready to patrol for snacks.

After my father cleaned the food, the meal ensued with all the normal rhythms, a strange mixture of past and present. Our happiest times had always been when everyone was sated by the presence of food. What there was and how much we had depended on the season. We ate largely what the farm and forest proved, living the organic life before organic was cool.

I chatted with Coral Rebecca and watched her with her girls. She and Levi smiled down the table at each other, and I realized they would've been sitting together if not for the fact that Brethren Saints rules designated separate sections of the table for men and women. I wondered if Craig, the man Lily Clarette had picked out, was anything like Levi. As much as I wanted to prevent her from marrying so young, I hoped he was.

When the meal ended, Marah Diane brought in the cake,

making a fuss about the candles and swatting playfully at little hands reaching toward the icing. The kids giggled, the sound high and sweet. A birthday cake like this was such an unusual treat, it was hard not to enjoy watching them wait for pieces and then savor the bounty. Even my father seemed to be pleased by it. He laughed and conversed with the young man I had guessed to be Lily Clarette's intended.

When the kids' plates were empty again, the birthday girls began clamoring for their gifts.

"You'll get 'em when your daddy says its time," Marah Diane scolded, giving her husband a pleading look.

"It's *my* table," my father corrected. "And I got somethin' to say."

A lump of icing turned solid in my throat. I wasn't even sure why at first, and then I realized the end of the meal had always been when the need for correction was attended to. At that point, if my father felt that someone had transgressed, wrongdoings were announced in front of the family, and punishments were handed out. If you'd done something bad enough to have earned the long rod, you were expected to walk calmly outside and prepare for a whipping.

Now I noticed the unsteadiness in him, how much weight he'd lost, how deep the hollows around his eyes had grown, how his hands shook as he braced his palms on the table, one arm twisted and scarred from his accident, three fingers missing.

His gaze swept the listeners, moving past me without stopping. Even the smallest of the children fell silent, slid back in their chairs. I fought to keep myself from shrinking along with them as he spoke.

"Craig Johns made his bid for Lily Clarette's hand just now, and I find him to be a good 'n' righteous man a the church. And so I've give him my permission. It'll be fine for them to marry soon as they pick them a time. You'uns make sure and do your congratulatin'."

My father lowered himself slowly to his seat. In the instant before chatter picked up, I leaned in and turned Lily Clarette's way. Her gaze was trained on her plate, her skin as pale as milk. When she looked up, she'd pasted on a smile, but it didn't reach her eyes. She hadn't anticipated today's announcement at all.

An excited round of conversation swept the women's end of the table, the birthday party temporarily forgotten in favor of the making of plans, talking about the used wedding dress in the resale shop, which could now be purchased with some of the money from the dog trade, and discussing who had fabric that could be used in a wedding quilt or furniture that could be passed along to help the couple piece together a home.

On the men's end of the table, back-patting and congratulations ensued, intermingled with talk of the fact that, if the dog business could be expanded, Craig could perhaps quit his job driving trucks and go to work for my father.

Everything I'd eaten was suddenly churning in my stomach. I leaned over to Coral Rebecca and said quietly, "I need to go, okay? Tell everyone good-bye for me when things settle down."

I'd call her tomorrow, see what she thought about the situation with Lily Clarette. Surely there was something we could do to make her think twice about quitting school and slipping into the used wedding dress, just because it was my father's plan.

I abandoned my seat and started walking, calmly at first, then faster, Friday jogging along behind. My mind was spinning like a tornado whipping across a freshly plowed field, gathering debris and chaff as it went.

I didn't even realize where I was headed until I'd gotten in my car, raced down the driveway, and wound a few miles up the dirt road. Suddenly everything was familiar. I'd traveled this back way via all means of transportation known to man—horse, mule, rusty farm truck, on foot, even on an old bicycle we'd fixed up after we found it in a dump.

Wilda's house lay hidden just past the T in the road, to the left and up the rise. Holding my breath, I waited for the first sight of it, and then there it was—still nestled among the valley pines, still painted a dusty shade of blue, even though the color was fading.

The farm's presence slipped over me, strong and steadfast like Wilda herself. Comfort fell like a blanket, and there in the driveway, I closed my eyes to the darkened windows, the time-ravaged exterior, the overgrown gardens. Resting my head on the steering wheel, I let the tears come and pretended Wilda was still here to wipe them away.

# Chapter 23

A front blew over the mountains as I drove back from Wilda's house, and a chilly rain had started to fall before I reached the cabin. I didn't dare try the driveway in the car. The trek downhill on foot, in the dark, slogging along under my umbrella, mud oozing through the seams of my boots, was pretty much the last straw. With only my cell phone as a flashlight, I stumbled over rocks and slipped in tiny rivulets of runoff, Friday clinging near my feet.

*I am out of here. I am so out.* I could not wait to leave this place, and if it weren't for the fact that it was too late to make the trip all the way to the airport tonight, I would've been gone already.

In my mind, I was back in New York, my familiar routines a pair of comfortable old shoes as I slipped back into them.

A streak of lightning lit the yard and the sky broke open,

wind rushing off the lake and folding my umbrella inside out. By the time I stumbled onto the porch, I was drenched, blinded by a curtain of wet hair, and in an ugly mood. Friday scratched frantically at the door, anxious to be inside.

"Hold on a minute!" Fumbling with the keys, I hit the porch light switch. The flickering bulb illuminated something that hadn't been there when I left—something rectangular and brown . . . and familiar. An envelope, but wedged behind the metal Welcome sign this time. I pinched it between two wet fingers and took it inside, dropping it carefully on the coffee table before hurrying to the bathroom to shiver my way into sweats and dry socks.

Why, all of a sudden, another delivery after three days with none? Who'd brought it here? What could possibly be inside? Assuming that Evan was telling the truth, the eight chapters I'd already read were all that existed.

Friday seemed to be wondering as well. When I returned to the living room, he was standing with his paws on the table, sniffing the envelope as if he'd detected something of interest.

"What's in there, Friday?" This one was thin, lightweight. Maybe it really was the cabin bill this time.

I opened the flap, peered in, and thumbed the pages apart, making out rows and rows of print. Definitely not the cabin bill. This was . . . more of the manuscript. But how . . . and who?

An eerie sensation crept over me, a feeling of being watched. I checked the corners and hidden spaces of the cabin, then climbed the loft ladder and peeked upstairs. Except for the unexpected delivery on the porch, everything was just as I'd left it.

Why was someone still playing this game of cat and mouse? What did this person hope to gain?

The weariness of the day evaporated, and curiosity wound

through the air like a fragrance—irresistible, tantalizing. I drank
it in as the pages slid free.

"Chapter 15?"

Friday perked an ear and tilted his head. Perhaps even he realized that the next chapter should have been chapter 9. Perhaps
even he knew that, according to Evan, the chapter in my hand
right now didn't exist.

Could this be part of another manuscript? Even something
unrelated to *The Story Keeper*?

These pages were different. Narrower margins, a change of
font. The paper had aged to a deep shade of ecru, grown stiff.
The first few sheets were moth-eaten around the edges. They'd
been typed on an old manual typewriter. Just like the machine on
which Wilda Culp had hammered out her newspaper columns,
year after year after year. I ran my finger along the underside,
felt the indentations, imagined that I could hear keys striking
paper with varying amounts of force. *Pinkie, index finger, middle,
pinkie, ring finger . . .*

*Plink, plink, plink, plink, plink . . .*

The author had given this installment a chapter title as well
as a number.

*Chapter 15*
*Deep Winter*

# Chapter 24

### Chapter 15
### Deep Winter

'Twas well past the ides of December that Sarra began to find herself dispatched about the mill camp without supervision from time to time, sent scurrying for this reason or that upon the orders of Hudson's Cherokee wife, Bonnie. Since their arrival at Sagua Falls in Hudson's wagon, Bonnie had generally detained Sarra close at hand, seeming to protect her in a motherly fashion. Yet as the disagreeable nature of the highland winter added to the complexity of their daily responsibilities, the Cherokee woman found it necessary, if not prudent, to more often send Sarra off to accomplish short tasks alone.

On one such task, having been emboldened by several successful endeavors, Sarra found herself within the chink-log structure that comprised the mill store. Discovering the store to be devoid of occupants, save for the kindly old shopkeep, she

dallied over a supply of bobbles obtained by the keeper in anticipation of the arrival of millworker wives and families to greet
the commencement of spring operations. The men being bent to
their building of the mill structures at this particular time of day,
Sarra supposed it safe to momentarily peruse this wondrous collection of merchandise, prior to continuing upon her given task.

"Believe you forgot these." The interruption of a voice startled
her, quite unaware.

Sarra briskly pivoted to find a man referred to as Hoffsteader
a scant foot or two away. He extended a hand, loosely dangling
a string of silvered glass beads. These were of the sort often
employed for trading purposes and not an item of great expense,
but to her eyes they were delightful. Having never before
become acquainted with jewels of any sort, beyond the hand-
hewn bone beads and carved prayer box given her by her Cherokee grandmother, she had, on several occasions, cast yearning
sidelong glances in the particular direction of the silvered beads.

Her hand ascended to them of its own volition now, but
quickly she drew back her fingers. "No. Those ain't mine. I ain't
after nothin' but the salt and the flour for the fryin'." She presented the basket of foodstuffs for which Bonnie had dispatched
her. Using these things, they would fry the meat of a fat doe that
had been harvested the evening prior by Hoffsteader himself.
He was, doubtless, aware of this, as it was his work to see to
the acquisition of wild game, to extend the meager winter stores
through to spring.

A sudden intake of breath was her reaction as Hoffsteader

captured her hand in his own and placed the bead threads there. "But you oughta have 'em. They's the color a your eyes, but a mite less fetchin'."

Sarra gaped mutely at the strings that now rested along her palm. Never had someone spoken words of such nature to her! Never had a stranger presented a gift, and in a way that fairly insisted she must accept!

"Those were sure enough made for a fetchin' neck, I'd say." Hoffsteader's fingers traversed the air as if it were his intention to shift aside her hair and examine the skin where the beads might eventually rest.

Sarra recoiled without deliberate thought of the motion. The precious beads skated from her fingers and clattered upon the floor. Her balance faltered fleetingly before she found her feet again, if not her voice.

Removing his hat most gallantly, Hoffsteader bowed forward, recovering the beads and bundling them within his robust fingers as if they were tiny toys. "Didn't mean to scare you none."

Bonnie's innumerable warnings eclipsed the unruly thrum of Sarra's own heart, drawing her a step farther distant. *Don't keep no comp'ny with the men. They's too many of 'em lonesome and coldsome here.*

She withdrew yet another step but found herself hemmed against the rough-hewn shelving along the wall. 'Twas no small bit distressing, day upon day, to live among so many men and belong to none of them. Most certainly, she could have managed such an arrangement, had she desired it. On occasion these weeks gone by, she had considered that perhaps she should. Were she to wed one of these men, Jep and Brown Drigger would be compelled to surrender their quest after her. The stealing of a man's wife was a killing offense, and in the highlands where life remained subject to mountain law, that sort of killing was oft accomplished in the most brutal fashion. Hoffsteader being a strong specimen, a crack shot, and of mountain and Cherokee blood himself, he could doubtless protect her quite well.

Hoffsteader's voice was tender and alluring as if he were calling a pup to his side. "It was writ all in your face. I seen you lookin'. Reckon you could mark them as a gift. Just tween friends."

"I . . ." She hadn't a notion of a proper response. "They's looksome, but I only come for the flour and the salt for Bonnie." Hitching the basket against her hip, she cast eyes toward the door. The small, low-roofed building had gathered the feel of a trap, far too devoid of maneuvering space.

"Well, I was headed thataway myself." He had swept the basket from her hands before she could fully circumvent his person. "Time I took the rest a that doe's carcass and tossed it off the rock bluff, where it won't be bringin' up varmints."

Finding little alternative, Sarra followed along, listening as he nattered on about a bobcat that had boldly marauded near the camp on several nights prior.

She did not reply but nodded politely and with certain fascination, not having imagined Hoffsteader to be the sort for telling tales. In fact, she had spoken with him not at all in the foregone weeks at Sagua Creek. He often vanished for days on end, then reappeared when he possessed stores to deliver. He was expert in the ways of mountain wildlife. Similarly, he was versed in the using of roots and leaves to flavor food and cure ills, and he oft gathered those as well.

Perhaps, Sarra thought now, it would be prudent to attempt to turn her heart toward this man, if a heart could be turned by sheer force of will. Perhaps he might aid her in making the way home to Aginisi's cabin, come spring, to bury the bones and pray over them properly.

She watched the mud squelch beneath her boots and considered these most arduous questions as Hoffsteader told of the bobcat and the means by which it had eluded him the day previous.

"I'm a man to catch what I set my sights fer, sooner 'r later." He halted stride at the doorway leading to Bonnie and Hudson's coarsely made cookhouse. His regard held her firmly again. She was not naive to his desirous look, and a portion of her very being instinctively cowered away. Warranted or not, his lustful expression recalled memories of long nights in Brown Drigger's cabin.

"What mischief do we have here?" Randolph's voice disturbed the stillness of winter afternoon. Sarra took up her basket from Hoffsteader's grasp and twisted about to see Randolph exiting the trees nearby. Oftentimes he ambled in the wood with his book and his pen. Today he carried a small branch from the plant Aginisi titled *shee-show* in Cherokee. It grew close by the water's edge and maintained its leaves in the cold months.

A coal burned in Rand's blue eyes as he regarded Hoffsteader, who in response straightened his own chest and lifted
his chin much like a cur dog resolved to hold its territory. "Mind
if I ask why that'd be a concern a yourn?"

"I mind." Randolph entwined his arms most comfortably and
claimed for himself a leaning place against the cookhouse wood
stack.

"Ain't your woman, is she?" Hoffsteader nodded in Sarra's
direction.

"I brought her here. It is my responsibility to see to her well-
being, certainly."

A bit of injury was done Sarra by the answer. Within her
bloomed a yearning that Randolph might have responded to the
question with a single, spare word: *Yes*.

"I don't aim to do 'er no harm. Just to spend a bit of time in
her comp'ny. Reckon she's up to decidin' on that fer her own
self."

Randolph settled a hand upon Sarra's arm then and brought
her nearer his person. His touch was gentle, albeit firm. "I'd say
it would be best if you sallied along, Hoffsteader."

Sarra's thoughts scattered in the way of nest mouselings
discovered beneath the empty crocks in spring.

Hoffsteader upheld his position momentarily before finally
stepping away, a malicious mirth creasing his lips. "You
oughtn't leave such a fine thing wanderin' alone while you're off
afield, then. 'Nother fella might come 'long and make his intentions knowed."

He left then, and Sarra stood with Randolph, watching the man depart the field.

"What in blazes was the meaning of that?" Randolph demanded, a stern frown lowering his chin. His gaze settled on the foodstuffs basket, and hers did as well. 'Twas then she observed that Hoffsteader had left the silver beads atop the flour.

"Was him that bought those," she muttered, indicating the beads. Some bit of wickedness caused her to quite impulsively add, "Said they's a color a my eyes."

"Oh, Hoffsteader said as much, did he?" He removed the beads from her basket, taking measure of them in his hand. "Well. I'll see they're returned. All sorts of men are here at Sagua Falls, Sarra. With all sorts of intentions, and many not honorable. Do you understand that?"

Her ire stirred and spite reared within her. She thought to grab the bobbles back, to say, *Them's mine now. He give them to me.* Yet she comprehended Randolph's meaning, though she wished she did not. The beads would come at a price. All things offered by men came at a price.

Even the largesse Randolph had extended her—saving her life, bringing her here—had come at a cost. The deeper grew the winter, the more greatly she feared it would be much higher than she could bear to pay. An ache strained inside her and grew by the day. It pierced her through each time she considered his departure in spring. She possessed no words with which to classify the pain. 'Twas not a sensation she had experienced prior, but in some fashion, a feeling not unlike the blinding torment of leaving Aginisi to die alone.

"And Hoffsteader was wrong, most certainly." Randolph's voice moderated, only for her ears and his. "Your eyes are much more lovely than these bits of glass . . . or any."

She regarded him deeply then, and the yearning wrenched her, split her open as surely as one of Brown Drigger's carcass hogs. The pain wrested heart and stomach and soul from her body, leaving her hollow.

Randolph's cold fingers caressed her face and she did not withdraw from him but rather tended nearer. It was a thing she had not thought herself capable of again, trusting the touch of a man's hand.

"We'd best go inside," he whispered.

"Bonnie and the fixin's are waitin'," she agreed. Soon enough the men would be in. They would come hungry for the fresh meat tonight.

Yet a question circled her awareness, its wings outstretched, riding the drafts of air. When Randolph looked deeply into her in such a way, what did he see?

Closing the beads into his fist, he tucked them in his coat pocket. "I'll ensure these are taken care of and Hoffsteader is well aware of it."

Sarra nodded and followed along inside but thought of the beads. Perhaps she should have considered retaining them instead. Perhaps she should have been thinking to know more of a man who would not soon enough depart the mountain.

~

Inclining over his paper, Randolph lifted his pen again and continued the communiqué to his family—the selfsame missive he had attempted on many occasions since his arrival at Sagua Camp. A fortuitous gathering of warm days had provided snowmelt to some degree, and mail would soon be given conveyance to a post via mule train.

At this juncture, his family would doubtless be wondering after him—his mother and his darling sisters fretting that some most dire circumstance had befallen his person. Reading the letter again, he observed the clear, straight lines upon it, the evidence of the steady hand with which he had described the mill camp and managed to create the impression that his reason for lingering here was purely an academic interest in the process of establishing a mill town.

He finished his description by offering comfort.

*In all, you should not fret over me, if indeed you have*
*been tempted to such foolishness. I am well, bolstered*
*by the crispness of the mountain air and the loveliness*
*of its vistas. The Blue Ridge is, indeed, a hint of heaven,*
*if there is such a thing in this world. I continue, of*
*course, my study of its flora and fauna and my efforts to*
*introduce its people to the truths of the church and the*
*one true God. . . .*

Eyelids falling to rest, he braced his forehead within his hand and faltered once again in his effort. *The one true God* . . . against whom all untruths were the bleak markers of sin. He had been less than forthright with his family, as well as with himself.

How often during those cold nights he had imagined his loved ones gathered to the comfortable old hearths as they sipped warm tea, told stories, and recited evening prayers! How frequently he had wished to be among them, enjoying Old Hast's tea cakes and delicacies!

Why now did his mind fail to reach for them? Why did they seem so far distant?

His regard strayed over the room until he spied Sarra nestled near the fire, attending the sewing Bonnie had given her. It had become their custom, Sarra's and his, to linger here after Hudson and Bonnie were off to bed. In time, Sarra would retire to her cot in the kitchen room, and Randolph would lay out his pallet here by the fire, gazing into curling flame and considering the many weeks they had sheltered in this place. December was half past. 'Twas already deep winter.

Spring suddenly seemed too close at hand.

Sarra sobered as she turned from her mending now, as if a thought had discovered her most unexpectedly. "Why d'you scratch in that there book s'much? Many's a time I seen you go off with it."

The question caught Randolph unawares. He cast about, seeking an answer. How could he hope to elucidate to her the sciences of botany and ornithology and the aspiration for academic discovery? In Sarra's world, there existed no locus of reference for such things. She understood the ways in which plants might be employed, and means by which they grew, and at which times they came to flower head, but never would it have occurred to her to study, catalog, and record such occurrences, other than within her mind.

By what means could he explain that this journey, this year in the untamed wilderness, even possessed of ill-fated twists and the struggle for survival, was a holy experience he desired to document? Upon the passing of yet another decade, the Appalachian highlands and foothills would doubtless find themselves crossed by railroad throughways and dotted by mill towns not unlike the settlement Hudson had been retained to create. The world was changing.

"I was writing to my family just now," he replied obtusely. "So that it might seem as if they are not so far away. I know how very much they treasure receiving word and enjoy hearing of the things I've seen and experienced here—particularly my sister Lucinda. I think she will be an adventurer herself, when she is grown." He was again reminded that Sarra, this silver-eyed girl of the highlands, was Lucinda's contemporary in age, if not position. Spare past sixteen.

She was little more than a girl, yet alone in the world and faced with incomprehensible and cruel circumstances. He hoped to secure for her a suitable safekeeping before his departure, the difficulty being that he possessed no concept of the manner in which such a thing might take shape. The possibilities for a girl of Melungeon blood were slim, and the obfuscations were many, particularly as Sarra had no family to see after her.

Then did she avert her eyes from him, giving him to wonder at her emotions. "You're missin' them a passel." 'Twas a statement rather than a question, her voice cracking. The delicate line of her jaw firmed with resolve. In the firelight, she was lovely as a master's work of art, her skin a soft, burnished hue, the long, thick curls of her hair falling black as midnight along her shoulder as she turned to her mending again.

Randolph watched her in consternation. Perhaps she had suspected his thoughts, or perhaps his mention of family had awakened her memories of her Cherokee grandmother in Tennessee.

"Yes. I do miss them. With Christmas drawing near, I cannot help myself, knowing that they will gather together for the holiday—all of them around the table. There will be laughing and telling of fine stories—and my space there will remain empty." He imagined this as he spoke, and a twinge of homesickness pricked him, as sharp and afflicting as a witch's needle in a child's fairy story. "Do you know of Christmas, Sarra?"

"Don't ever'body?" She cast a queer look his way—half smile, half frown. "Many's a time Gran-dey'd read us the tale from the Book. Is it Christmas now?"

"Not now, but soon." He reclined in his chair, sipped Bonnie's wild wintergreen tea, for which he'd advanced an affinity these weeks, and told Sarra of Christmas in Charleston, his words conjuring the ships in harbor, the chimes of St. Michael's and St. Philip's, the floating lanterns released to the tide by children, and the deep, melodious songs of the Gullah women as they worked. "Not a holiday in all the world is the like of Christmas in the Holy City by the sea."

A thought seized him then. He sketched a rough representation of the town skyline, crowned with its beautiful steeples, and displayed this for Sarra's viewing while explaining each of the buildings in its size, shape, and purpose. He imagined that he would one day present the city to her, with its stately old churches and the fine homes of a gentler time standing guard against the sea. He would walk with Sarra along the Battery and bring her to the harbor to view the tall ships there. He envisioned her naive observation of both the magnificent and the ordinary of that place he loved.

What would be her thoughts in those fine, first moments?

As quickly as the pondering arrived, he banished it, feeling shamed by the notion and the flight of fancy it implied. There remained no place in Charleston for a girl of mixed blood like Sarra, nor would such a place exist within his lifetime. Never would tolerance of her be had in polite society. Not abovestairs, and even the women in his mother's kitchen would not permit her company. Some wealthy man would undoubtedly soon take her to mistress, lured by her exotic beauty, yet ashamed of what she was.

Charleston had nothing to offer to this highland girl, nor did he. To allow the dwelling of his mind on this even momentarily presented a disservice to Sarra and to himself, but most especially to his family.

Yet, just today, as he had wandered along the creek, he had sat long beneath an oak, gazed upon ice-glazed waters, and touched the bark-bare space on a tree trunk where he had carved Sarra's name. He had fancied that she might delight in seeing her name preserved in letter form, but he'd not shown the etching to her. He lacked the courage.

Still, there remained this and other myriad wonders he yearned to share with her. So very much of the world, but all was certainly as reckless a dream as the image of their strolling the streets of Charleston in polite company. Though by reason he knew this, some other force within him would not cease its cursed imaginings.

Her eyes widened with the brightness of polished coin. She'd halted her mending to listen. "Aginisi give me tales a the sea folk. Her mama's people come a that place." She slipped the bone necklace from beneath her blouse, held it reverently, allowing him to see. "This come a them, long time back. Come over the water as they come."

"Aginisi? Your grandmother gave you this?" His curiosity piqued now, he leaned closer but did not rise and move to her, so fragile seemed the moment that he wished not to disturb it. He had often wondered after the necklace and the meaning of the odd mixture of totems there. "I had assumed she was of these mountains—a Cherokee."

Sarra considered this. "Our folk come a many places, Aginisi told it. She give me the tale a the sea folk, but the tale a the mountain folk too. Both of them's in her blood, so she give me stories from one and stories from t'other. Said it was fer me to keep them stories safe. 'Sarra,' she says many a time, 'all things a flesh and blood pass, but stories is the one part goes on here'n this world. You ken the stories, and when I'm shed a this place, then it'll be you who's the story keeper.'"

The flesh dimpled on Rand's neck, curiosity pulling him nearer as he sat watching her.

"You hopin' to hear my stories?" She contemplated him then in a way that seemed to pierce him through, riveting him in place.

"Yes, Sarra, I am."

"I'll tell first the tale a the Cherokee and how the mountains was made for them."

"I'd like that very much." He turned the page in his journal, intending to record the folk legend as she spoke.

"It come long time ago, when all the lands was flat. The Great Buzzard, the father of all the buzzards that's livin' now, or ever did draw breath, flew hisself over all the whole, wide land." Her long, slim fingers outstretched and drew a gentle arc in the air, caressing imaginary vistas. "When the Great Buzzard come a Cherokee country, he was powerful tired by then. His wings begun flappin' slow and strikin' the ground as he's sinkin'. In all the places they hit down hard, there come a valley, and where they's swep' up again, up come a mountain."

By the firelight, she drew the mountain for him to see, mirth creasing the corners of her eyes as if she relished his breath-less regard of her. "When all the animals above seen what'd happent, they's afraid the whole world'd come a be mountains, so they called back the Great Buzzard, but the Cherokee country, where he a'ready been, it's full a mountains to this day." Her lips curved upward as she completed the story, and he found himself reclining languidly in his chair, smiling along with her.

"'Tis a fine tale," he told her. "And this is the means by which the world has come to be as it is, on the wings of a buzzard, of all things?"

"'Tis a fine tale," she agreed, mimicking almost exactly the intonation and measure with which he'd said the words. "But in the beginnin', Father God made the heaven and the earth. Folk learnt of it long ago from the ones that come over the sea. They come in a canoe big's a cabin, all the way from a fer-off yander place. Place like that one you done made in yer book, I reckon."

His mind scrambled to comprehend. "Sailors, then? There were seamen who came to these mountains and brought their religion?" He'd heard occasionally of generations-old Creole races descended from shipwrecked sailors, slaves, and native peoples. Perhaps even the progeny of Sir Walter Raleigh's ill-fated lost colony on Roanoke Island had journeyed here. Given what Ira Nelson had told him of Melungeons—neither black nor white nor Indian—her story of the sea people touched upon the fascinating possibility that Sarra herself could be descended of ancient mariners who'd arrived upon these shores long before the famed founding of Jamestown.

He observed again her fingering of the beads around her neck. "Tell me more of the necklace you wear."

"It come from the sea people, long time back."

"And it is an item of worship? I have seen you performing some form of rituals with it."

"It's for prayin'," she corrected.

"Does your box answer the prayers? Does it have special powers?" For some time, he had desired to come to this discussion with her—to give her a correctness of faith and leave her with an unblemished understanding of the teachings of the holy church. If he could offer nothing more to her, he could offer this singular, and most vital, bit of instruction.

She worried her lip between her teeth, laid the necklace against her chest, and returned to her mending. "That there buildin' got itself powers? You pray to it?" A backhanded motion signified his sketch.

He drew away, shocked and most greatly appalled! "Why, no, of course not! A proper Christian does not pray to *things*, Sarra. A proper Christian prays to the One Most High. The church building is a house of God, a place we go to be close to him." How could she possibly understand such a thing, never having seen worship, entered a cathedral, or been schooled in the catechisms?

"Mayhap he's here, too." She traced the box's etched cross with her fingertip, then made the same motion over her heart. "And here. Mayhap he's near in all places." Her regard rose from the mending. "Who was it formed the mountain and made the wind and the dark a mornin'?"

*For, lo, he that formeth the mountains, and createth the*

wind, and declareth unto man what is his thought, that maketh the morning darkness, and treadeth upon the high places of the earth, the Lord, the God of hosts, is his name. The Scripture, among many written in the forward pages of his grandfather's Bible, murmured among his thoughts, quickly eclipsing all others, and found him unprepared, so as to cause him only to stare mutely into her.

*And treadeth upon the high places of the earth . . .*

He knew this Scripture well, yet he himself had fretted greatly in recent weeks that, were he to perish here, far from a proper church, he might not be found fit to enter in the gates of heaven. This quite uncomfortably implied that he feared God had not walked with him into the wilderness.

In an instant of dawning understanding, the truth came upon him quite clearly. Indeed, faith was not a matter of routines and external trappings. Faith was a thing in the way of blood, breath, and sinew—an essential part of the man, and as such it traveled with the man.

This place, this wilderness, was not a place apart from God, for in all the world, there could not be such a place. All existed by God and was God's own. The heavenly Father was neither farther nor closer here, but as near as the thoughts and fears and hopes cast to him. As near as the focus and condition of Randolph's own heart.

It troubled him to imagine what his family would say of this conclusion, this new understanding of his. It troubled him to consider what they would say of Sarra and her prayer necklace, which was in essence no different from the cross he carried in his pocket.

"Our Lord has made all things, Sarra," he said simply, and she returned to her mending and he to his journal to sketch the profile of her alongside the fire and ponder his own thoughts.

With startling clarity as he withdrew to himself, he was given to understand that a great portion of his very being would be left behind when he returned to Charleston. The deepest measures, the corners of the soul he was only beginning to understand, would remain here in the Blue Ridge.

Abandoned would be the portion that thrilled at each sight of this wild country. The part that was slowly coming—though he understood the impossibility of it—to love Sarra.

Yet behind him remained his family, his life by the sea, and that he verily treasured as well. The thought of not watching his sisters grow, of never again wiling away long afternoons on the piazza of La Belle or hearing the songs of the kitchen women drift from belowstairs or feeling his mother's tender kiss brush against his cheek could not be borne by him.

His family and La Belle had been his heart long before he knew of this far country, long before he looked into Sarra's face and found himself captured by her. He had given his word to return to Charleston at the closing of the coming summer. To dishonor that vow would be to shatter the hearts of his mother, his grandmother, his sisters. To disappoint the hopes of his dead father and the esteemed Champlain lineage.

As the lone son, it was for him to carry on the family name.

To be the father of children who would be doted upon in the grand halls of La Belle, and who would someday have the place as their inheritance.

Sarra's children could not fill the halls of La Belle. Indeed, they would not even be welcomed there.

It was not in him to disappoint the understood obligations and long-held hopes that now, as always, rested squarely upon his shoulders.

# Chapter 25

The first ring shattered the silence in the cabin and propelled me from sleep, the break coming too hard and fast, too unexpectedly. A pulse thrummed in my throat against a sudden intake of air.

Outside, the storm had faded into silence. Sometime after I'd finished reading, rereading, and analyzing the new chapter, then surrendered to the pull of heavy eyelids, the thunder had died, a hush replacing it. The air seeping around the loft window smelled frosty and cool. An oddly vulnerable feeling clung to me, seeming to hang like a mist in the cabin. Maybe it was just the tattered remnants of the family discussion at the birthday party or the reality of another mysterious delivery, this one clearly from a different author, but something didn't feel right.

I picked up the phone, checked the time. Only 9:50. I'd been in bed less than an hour, but it seemed like longer. The number on the screen was local—not one I recognized.

My thumb hovered over the button and I moved to the window. A light snow had started to fall. Cotton-soft flakes sifted downward in the porch light, quickly melting on the wet ground.

The phone rang again, demanding attention.

"Hello?"

A hum of static answered, but I couldn't shake the feeling that someone was there. I heard breathing, I thought.

"Hello?"

The faint sound of a sniffle. Someone female. Maybe a misdial? Or could it be Hannah? How would she know my number? I'd left my card with Evan. Maybe it was sitting around his house somewhere.

"Hannah? Is that you?"

"No . . ." The voice was barely audible, thick with tears. "I'm . . ." A stifled sob, and then, "I'm s-sorry. I di—I didn't . . . I shouldn' bother you, Jennia Beth. I . . . I didn't know who else to . . . to . . ."

"Lily Clarette?" My thoughts ran in two completely opposite directions, like a river splitting around a logjam, a whirlpool of indecision forming at the obstruction. Had something terrible happened, or had she just worked up the courage to finish our conversation?

Another stifled sob. "I'm at . . . at the Algers store, b-but they're closin'. I h-hadn't got anyplace . . . to . . . N-n- . . . never mind. I . . ."

"I'm coming. Listen, Lily Clarette, do you hear me? I'm coming. You stay right there." I combed through memories, dredging up roads, locations, directions. "The Algers in Towash, across from the old depot?" What was she doing in a grocery store at nearly ten o'clock at night, calling me? "Are you okay? What happened?" I was already moving around the loft, grabbing jeans and a sweatshirt as Lily Clarette disintegrated into a whimper on the other end of the line.

"Hurry, Jennia Beth. Ohhh, hur-hurry. If Craig comes 'n' finds me . . ."

"Lily Clarette, what's going *on*?" A shiver rattled my body as I struggled to change clothes one-handed. "Tell me what happened."

"Just come . . . okay?"

"It'll take me a while to get there. If Craig shows up, you tell him you're not leaving, do you hear me? If he comes, you call the police if you need to. Lily Clarette? Lily . . . are you there?"

She was gone. I redialed the number, but no one answered.

Friday was on alert as I hurried down the ladder and to the entryway, cramming my arms into my jacket and my feet into wet boots. The latch felt frosty against my fingers.

"You stay here," I told Friday, and he stopped as I opened the door. His forehead furrowed over his bug eyes as if he sensed that something dire had happened.

"It's okay. It'll be okay." I hoped that was true. The weather here varied from mountain to mountain and bald to gap. I had no idea what the conditions might be between Looking Glass Lake and Towash, how long it would take me to make the trip, or what might be waiting when I arrived. Around the cabin, the snowfall was incongruously quiet and peaceful, but as I ran uphill to the road, the wind cut in, its bite pressing through my jacket and jeans.

Ice had formed a glittery sugar crust over the mailbox and the car door. Teeth chattering, I cracked the seal, slid into the seat, and shut the cold outside. Winding along the cabin road, the car wobbled like a ship at sea, caught broadside by gusts that seemed determined to prevent it from traveling onward.

The wind intensified as I turned onto the highway, flakes flying toward the headlights as if the car were a vortex pulling them in, then casting them loose. Heavy-laden branches hung low over the road, narrowing the curves and obscuring the view of cabins and homes, making the three-mile drive to town seem strangely desolate.

Looking Glass Gap lay quiet and peaceful, the stores dark, a few white-tinged cars parked along the main street. No sign of Time Shifters fans or anyone else. Beyond the shelter of the buildings, the storm picked up again, the wind whipping around curves and outcroppings of rock, slapping the car like a child playing fitfully with a toy.

Halfway to Towash, I tried the number Lily Clarette had left on my phone. Again, no answer.

"Just wait for me." Somewhere deep within, I hoped that the unseen bond of sisters could carry the words across miles of cold stone peaks and wind-whispered hollows. "Please wait."

What had happened to Lily Clarette since I'd left the party? Had she decided to run? Would my father or Craig come after her if she did? What would they do to her if they found her?

The questions cycled over and over, keeping time with the wipers, always unanswered.

In Towash, a covering of white had settled over the ditches and framed the tiny rain rivers along the roadsides. Algers grocery store lay shrouded in shadow when I arrived, only the security lights and the old neons burning, the parking lot empty. Cruising past the front windows, I felt my heart clench. No one there. Had Craig already come?

Had Lily Clarette decided to go home with him after all? Had she been forced to?

Cool pinpricks touched my skin as I exited the car, hurried

to the glass, leaned close to block the reflected light. Even from outside the doors, the place held familiar scents. Stillness, dead crickets piled in hidden corners, ceiling tiles slowly turning to dust, salvage groceries, borax powder sprinkled to keep the roaches away.

No sign of my sister.

Where could she have gone? Had she started walking when the store closed? In which direction? It was too cold to be out tonight.

A movement near the corner of the building stopped me. Squinting against the flickering neon, I made out the faintest hint of a face. Gooseflesh raced over my arms, a prickling sense of uncertainty.

"Lily Clarette?"

She emerged slowly, ghostly pale, her arms wrapped around her midsection, her body curled inward. She was shivering, wearing only the dress, shoes, and sweat jacket she'd had on at the party. A fine layer of snow had settled over her dark hair like a veil.

"Oh, honey, you're freezing. What are you doing out here?" I opened my arms, and she came to me one step at a time, uncertain at first, then running, finally hitting me with such force that she knocked me back a step. I wrapped myself around my sister, breathed in the cold, snowy scent of her. "Why didn't you let them know you needed to wait inside?"

"They had to *close*." Her voice was hoarse with tears.

"You should have told them you needed help."

"I couldn't," she whispered, and I understood the unspoken truth. It would never have occurred to her to protest leaving the store when she was told it was closing. The women of Lane's Hill were always silent and obedient.

"I was afraid you wouldn't come." She shivered violently.

"Of course I came." I stroked her hair, the warmth of my hand turning frost into moisture. "I'll always come, Lily Clarette." It was such a strange thing to say, so inaccurate. All these years, I hadn't been here. I hadn't done anything to change her life, to help her.

Now, holding her in my arms, I remembered the day Mama had birthed her at home, only a midwife from the church there to help. I'd looked at that downy-haired baby girl in the cradle, and in some way, I had resented her very presence in the world. There was already so little to go around.

How could I ever have thought of my sister that way?

"Come on, let's get in where it's warm." I guided her toward the car. Right now, we needed to leave Towash behind, to be somewhere sheltered and safe so that I could find out what had happened.

But in the car, she closed her eyes and turned her head toward the window, her body huddled, her thin shoulders shaking. I cranked the heater, restrained myself from asking any questions. She needed time to settle and cut the chill. I needed to focus on the driving. The temperature outside was dropping by the minute, the road turning dangerous, the layer of moisture beginning to freeze.

Before we reached Looking Glass Lake, we'd passed two vehicles in the ditch. I should've stopped to help, but I didn't. A jacked-up four-wheel-drive truck was following closely behind us. Wild scenarios as to who might be in it nipped at my heels, dredging up the night I'd left Lane's Hill without telling anyone, barely eighteen years old, terrified as I stole down Honey Creek under the light of a summer moon, grocery bags full of belongings clutched in my arms.

Every rustle in the woods stole my breath. I was certain I'd been found out—that my father or the Brethren Saints had come after me. Lane's Hill didn't give up its own without a fight. Rather than being proud of me for getting the scholarship to Clemson with Wilda's help, my father had called me to repentance, citing the lies and deceit that had gone into the application process. I had dishonored him and, like my mother, made plans to flee into the sin of the world. I'd been threatened with a caning before the church, and I had meekly complied with the order to repent, all the while tasting the bile of it in my throat, feeling the bitterness grow and harden in me. I knew I was leaving—my plans with Wilda had already been made—and I was counting down the days. My father never would've known about it at all if the high school guidance counselor hadn't sent a scholarship letter home via Marah Diane.

Now, here sat Lily Clarette, seemingly in much the same position. My father and Lane's Hill had her by the throat.

But this time I was an adult, and I was ready for the fight.

The pickup truck passed by as I pulled onto the cabin road. Watching it go, I caught a breath of relief. No one in my family knew where I was staying. They wouldn't find us here. I hoped. If they canvassed the area around Looking Glass Gap, would they see my rental car parked on the patch of gravel by the mailbox? Would they recognize it? I didn't dare pull down to the cabin. We'd never get out in the morning . . . and I was taking Lily Clarette from here in the morning. Straight to Charlotte and then home to New York, where none of these people could touch us.

"We'll have to walk down. The driveway isn't good."

Lily Clarette nodded, still quaking, the dampness clinging to her hair and clothes as she reached for the car door.

"Here, take my coat." I moved to slip it off as a gust swept through the open door.

"No, I'm fine." She climbed from the car, huddled over, and waited, then curled close to my side as we made our way down the driveway. Near the horizon, the moon found a slice of cloudless sky. Its glow silvered the new coating of snow and the surface of the lake, painting a scene that seemed strangely peaceful after we reached the shelter of the trees.

"It's pretty here," Lily Clarette offered as we stepped onto the porch. She seemed embarrassed, uncertain of where our conversation should go now. Perhaps the gravity of it all had hit her. She glanced over her shoulder toward the driveway, seeming to reconsider things while I unlocked the cabin door.

"Don't worry. You're safe now. Nobody knows where I'm staying." Touching her shoulder, I attempted to guide her across the threshold, but she winced away. I realized she wasn't just holding her arm because she was cold; she was protecting it.

"Did Craig do that? Does he hit you?"

She stood shivering, scanning the cabin's interior as I closed and latched the door. On the chair across the room, Friday awakened and stretched, giving our visitor a quick appraisal.

"Lily Clarette, did *Craig* do that to you?"

Her head hung forward as she sank to the sofa, balancing on the edge, hands clasped in her lap.

Shrugging off my coat, I sat beside her, smoothed away the strands of loose hair matted to her cheek. Was the mark there a shadow or a bruise?

"He never has before, really."

"What do you mean, *really*?"

"Nothin' like this." Her body rattled, the quaking traveling from head to toe. She needed some dry clothes and a blanket.

Something warm to drink. But I was afraid to move, afraid that when she really thought about all this, she'd pull away.

"But he's been physical with you before?"

"Not in a bad way. Nothin' that . . ." Her gaze searched the floor as if she were looking for answers there, trying to make sense of it all. But none of this made sense.

"Lily Clarette, it's *not* okay. He shouldn't be hurting you. Not for any reason."

"It's the job of the husband to rule over his wife. It's in Scripture. He's worried about me. Worried about the things I'm thinkin' sometimes."

I felt sick, not only physically, but heartsick somewhere deep in my soul. Was this what my sisters' marriages were like? Was this why Marah Diane was so angry all the time and why Evie Christine seemed afraid to even come near me? "There's nothing in Scripture that says it's okay for a man to beat up someone who's smaller and weaker than he is. And Craig isn't your husband, either."

"He's gonna be."

"Why?" I couldn't stand this. The idea of this bright, beautiful girl, my sister, being forced into this kind of future was wrong in every possible way. How could she be sitting here with bruises, still thinking about it? Still unable to let go?

"Daddy wants it. Daddy says it's a good match. Everybody in the Brethren Saints thinks it's a good match."

"It doesn't matter what they think!" My voice reverberated through the cabin, startling Friday. He stood and crossed the floor, then jumped onto the couch to monitor the goings-on.

"That's easy enough for you to say, Jennia Beth, but I'm nothin' like you. I don't want some big life someplace else. I want a good life here."

"You're seventeen years old, Lily Clarette. It's too soon to really know what you want. Being seventeen is about seeing what's out there in the world so you can decide from all your options. Craig isn't the only option you have. There are so many more."

"I shouldn't've come here. You're just confusin' me. I told Craig I wanna wait till I'm out of high school, maybe even see about community college or somethin'. He didn't like it much. He thinks I don't believe he can make us a good livin'."

"Is *that* what the fight was about?"

"It wasn't a fight . . ." But I could see it in her face even though she was trying to hide it. "He just got his pride hurt, and he took me outta his truck and said if I thought I was too good for him, maybe I oughta walk back home and think on it till I got my mind right."

"With a *storm* coming in?"

"I walked to town instead. I was afraid he'd went to the house to tell Daddy what I said. After givin' his blessin' at the party, Daddy'd be mad as a scalded cat. I was afraid he'd take me to the elder council so they could fix my thinkin'."

"You were close enough to walk to *town* when Craig left you on the side of the road?" I was livid. My father's farm was twelve miles from Towash. Craig had left my sister on the side of the road, alone, that far from home to . . . teach her a lesson?

"Don't get riled, okay? You'll make it worse than it is already. Thanks for comin' and gettin' me, but I've gotta sort it out my own self." Closing her eyes, she rested against the sofa. "I'm just real tired right now. I can't think what to do."

I stood, smoothed a hand over my sister's hair, remembered swaddling her in a quilt as the midwife handed her over and she took her first breaths. "I'll get a blanket and some dry clothes for you."

"Just a blanket," she whispered. "I don't wanna be any trouble."

# Chapter 26

The drumbeat of a startled pulse followed me to the front window. High-beam lights bounced across the yard as a vehicle worked its way down the slushy, snow-covered driveway. I grabbed the fireplace poker I'd set near the door—the only thing in the cabin that could remotely serve as a weapon, other than the knives in the kitchen, and I couldn't make my mind go there. But who could say what a man who would drag a seventeen-year-old girl from his truck, leave bruises on her, and abandon her on the side of the road was capable of? All of this to someone he supposedly loved. What could he be driven to do if he thought he was really losing her?

I prepared myself for confrontation, thinking, *If you touch either one of us, I will make sure you rot in jail, no matter what it takes.*

The words sounded bold in my mind, but amid them were evening-news horror stories of domestic violence incidents with terrible, sad endings. People who thought they could handle it . . . until the situation spun wildly out of control. There were plenty of men who had not changed much since Jep and his cronies put Brown Drigger's hounds on Sarra's trail. Among the Brethren Saints, this sort of thing was a matter of pride, reputation, and survival. When one person left, there was always the threat that others would follow. When one person questioned, there was always the danger that others would question.

The vehicle rambled to a stop, sliding in the muck. Squinting against the headlights, I made out the silhouette of a Jeep. Black, shiny, four-wheel drive with large, knobby tires. Not at all the sort of thing Craig could afford. Or anyone in my family. Maybe they'd enlisted more help?

I glanced toward the loft. No sign that Lily Clarette had been awakened by the noise. If someone was here looking for her, I'd start by insisting that I hadn't seen her and threatening to call the sheriff. Hopefully things wouldn't go beyond that. Slipping into my jacket and shoes, I drew myself up straight, then stepped onto the porch, clutching my cell phone in one hand and hiding the fireplace iron behind my back.

The driver, dressed in a camo coat and hunting coveralls, approached in a rush. I squeezed the iron more tightly, kept my thumb poised on the cell phone panic app. How long would it take the police to get here if I called for help?

"What do you want?" I confronted him first, taking a cue from a long-ago city dwellers' self-defense course. *Don't wait for something to happen. Seize control of the situation and be the aggressor. Confront your attacker before he's ready.*

He stopped at the top of the steps, surprised, and my confidence surged. Above the hills across the lake, the faintest hint of gray had begun to highlight the sky. It would be morning soon, and Lily Clarette and I could escape. I squinted at the man, try-ing to make out the face inside the hood. My fingers tightened, loosened, tightened again.

The visitor pushed back his hood.

Every muscle in my body relaxed, then just as quickly crack-led with new anxiety. "Evan?"

Urgency radiated from him. "Have you seen Hannah? Is she here? I noticed two sets of tracks in the snow by your car. *Is Hannah here?*" A fleeting hope lit in his face, an expression that begged me to say yes. A terrible, painful vulnerability followed it.

"No, of course not." My mind was still struggling to catch up, the events of the night rushing through at random. "Why would Hannah be here?"

He came closer, stretched out his hand as if to grab me, his blue eyes almost wild. I stepped back against the cabin wall, revealing the fireplace poker out of reflex.

He glanced at the weapon, then at me, confused. "Listen, if she's been here, you have to tell me. We think she might've run away."

"Run away?" Surely this wasn't real. Surely this was some strange dream. A nightmare. "Why in the world would she do that?"

"I had to tell her dad to get sober or get out. Jake ran his truck off into a ditch yesterday. Drunk. He had some woman with him from that bar down by the river, and she took a pretty good knock on the head. They're lucky they're not both dead. Hannah might've heard us arguing after I brought him home. I don't know. I went to town to talk to my lawyer, to see what I could do about Hannah, because of course, that was the first thing Jake threatened—that he'd take her if he moved out."

Scrubbing his fingers across his forehead, he closed worry-lined eyes. "When I came home, my foreman said Jake had left by himself in one of the trucks, but I couldn't find Hannah anywhere. The little horse she likes, Blackberry, was missing too. I don't know if she meant to take off, or if she just went out riding and . . . got lost, but Hannah *knows* these mountains and so does that old horse. He's mountain-bred, not the type to do anything stupid. A night like this, with the weather coming in, all she'd have to do is give him his head and he'd find his way home. But we've had people out looking everywhere. Then I thought about the cabin, and how interested Hannah is in you, and when I drove by, I saw the car parked up there and the two sets of tracks. I was sure . . ."

More than anything, I wanted to tell him Hannah was safe and warm inside. "I have my sister here. She had a fight with her boyfriend, and he got rough with her. I drove over to Towash to pick her up. I haven't seen Hannah since we watched movies at your place, the day before yesterday."

I looked toward the lake. "What about your uncle Clive? The day I caught her on the highway, you said she might've been headed to his cabin. Could she have ended up there?"

Evan shook his head. "I already checked. The dog food dishes are gone, which means he headed off to one of his hunting camps. Sometimes he disappears for a week or two at a time."

"Evan . . . he wouldn't . . ." Maybe it was just my suspicious nature, but my one meeting with Uncle Clive hadn't left the best impression, and then there were the things Jake had said—indications that Uncle Clive might not be mentally stable. "He wouldn't take Hannah without telling you . . . would he?"

Evan's reaction was quick and decisive. "No. No, Uncle Clive wouldn't do that. He's crazy about Hannah."

*That's what I'm afraid of,* I thought, but I didn't say it. Evan seemed so sure.

I let the thought die, reached for other suggestions, but I had none.

Evan glanced toward the cabin, then nodded at the iron stick in my hand. "Is everything okay? Does your sister's boyfriend know where to find you?"

"No. We're fine. I'm just a little paranoid. I plan to call the family and let them know where she is after we're out of here in the morning."

"You're leaving?" His gaze captured mine again. I wondered at the meaning behind that look.

"Well, I . . . Not now, no. Let me wake up Lily Clarette and tell her what's happened. I can help look for Hannah." My mind careened down a terrible trail of possibilities. I thought about the mishap with the trucker. Surely Hannah wouldn't get into a car with someone. After our talk about the horse incident, surely she understood the dangers.

Evan shook his head. "You haven't got the gear for it, and we don't need anyone else lost in the storm."

"I grew up here, remember? I know how to find my way around. I can help. I'm not just going to sit here waiting."

He followed me as far as the door, catching my shoulder and turning me around so that the distance between us suddenly felt intimate. "Listen, I'm sorry I didn't get on top of things when you talked to me about Hannah the other day. I really thought I could force Jake to step up the way he needs to, but you were right. If I would've taken it in hand . . ."

"Let's just find her." I slid my hand up and covered his, felt the leather glove cool between us. "Where should Lily Clarette and I go when we're ready? I mean, where have you already looked for her?" I stepped inside to grab a notepad. "Give me your cell number, in case." The typed manuscript pages and envelope lay in a clutter on the coffee table. Evan never even noticed as he stood in the doorway. Instead, he gazed at Helen's painting of the lake in autumn as if he were hoping to spot Hannah coming up the path.

"Start looking from here. Around the lake and along the old timber road up the mountain. Anyone you can find, ask them if they've seen signs of Hannah or the horse." He pulled a business card from his pocket and gave it to me. "Maybe someone saw her pass by here yesterday. The sheriff's department and the forest service are launching a grid search, and they're calling in help. The thing is, we don't even know exactly how long she's been gone or which way she went. The driveway gates at the ranch have surveillance cameras on them, but the pasture gates and water gaps don't. She could've left through any one of those. I was tied up with the lawyer quite a while yesterday, and then when I got home, Granny Vi was in bed. There was a video playing in the theater room, and it was almost dark before I realized Hannah wasn't down there. The sheriff says a lot of the Time Shifters folks made a mass exodus ahead of the snow. There are some weed-smoking wack jobs in that group. I just hope she didn't run into one of them somewhere."

"She'd never abandon Blackberry. Wherever she's at, they're together." It was the only reassuring thing I could come up with.

"Let's hope," he said softly, and then he disappeared through the cabin doorway. A moment later, the Jeep roared off, sloshing through the inch of snow and up the driveway. A shiver slid over me as I closed the door, but it had nothing to do with the weather. I couldn't help thinking about that little girl, alone somewhere in the dark.

I woke Lily Clarette, and we did our best to garb up in what clothes I had. Lily Clarette layered her dress over the top of the sweats, hiding what would have been forbidden garments at home.

"We're not gonna be able to stay out too long without some coveralls and coats and boots," she pointed out. "Not when it's like this."

"I know. But we have to do something. We can at least check around the lake and knock on doors, see if anyone had noticed Hannah passing by yesterday. If they haven't found her soon, we'll go into town and get some better gear."

Wrapping blankets over our heads, we set out along the lakeshore. The wet wind effortlessly cut through the layers of jeans and sweats from my suitcase, proving that it was by far the stronger force.

Beside me, Lily Clarette pulled her blanket tighter. "You want this jacket?" she asked as the walking trail around the lake divided, one branch traveling uphill toward cabins on the slope, and the other leading to older waterside homes. We paused at the fork, looking both ways and checking the ground for anything but the tiny pinpoint tracks of deer. Unfortunately, with so much Warrior Week activity, the indentations of tracks and hoofprints lay everywhere beneath the dusting of snow.

"No, I'm fine. You keep it."

"We'd do best to split up," Lily Clarette suggested. "I can hike on up the timber road, and you head down to the lake. If she was here, no tellin' which way she'd a gone. You know how little girls wander off sometimes."

I looked at my sister, realized she wasn't a little girl anymore. She was a young woman. All the same, I didn't want to let her go. Only a few hours before, I'd been worried about her boyfriend finding us. Now I was sending her to walk a dimly lit path by herself and knock on strangers' doors. I couldn't help thinking about what Evan had said. *There are some weed-smoking wack jobs in that group....* Who might be staying in these cabins right now? Who might be wandering the woods?

"Maybe we should keep together."

"We'll get a bunch more done if we don't." Lily Clarette's breath swirled on the air as she looked up the hill. "If I'm gonna go stay in the big city with you, I've gotta learn to do things for my own self, right?" It was the first indication she'd given of her thinking this morning.

The determined, upward tilt of her chin was a mirror of Mama's on the good days when no one was around to temper her. The spunk that had helped her survive a horrible upbringing showed when my father and my grandparents weren't watching.

I gave in, even though I didn't want to. "Okay, here. Take my cell phone, at least. If you have any problems or you find anything, call 911. I'll keep going along the shore, and I'll be back here in thirty minutes. By then, at least someplace in town will be open, and we can get heavy clothes before we check the other side of the lake . . . if they haven't found Hannah yet." It seemed important to keep saying it, to assume the best.

Lily Clarette gave the phone an uncertain look, then nodded and tucked it into her pocket, and we parted ways. I watched her disappear up the hill before I took the other path, circling the ice-crusted lakeshore as loons and year-round geese dozed in the shelter of frost-covered docks, their heads still tucked beneath their wings. Deer, nibbling in the leeward spaces beside trees, paused to look up from their morning fodder, disturbed by my passing. I knocked on cabin doors, awoke sleepy vacationers, spoke to a photographer who'd braved the early-morning chill. No signs of Hannah.

I had nothing to report when I returned to the fork to meet Lily Clarette again, but somehow I'd managed to fan the hope that a call had already come in on the cell—that Lily Clarette would tell me the whole thing was over, Hannah was safe and warm. My sister and I would pack the car, grab some breakfast in Looking Glass Gap, leave for a hotel in Charlotte where Craig and the family couldn't find us.

Up the hill, Lily Clarette melted from the fog, her dress whipping around her legs as she came my way. The forlorn look told me she'd had no luck, phone call or otherwise. "Nothin'," she reported as we met. "I found a couple folks who said they been around their cabins yesterday evenin'. They woulda noticed her goin' by. I don't think she was here."

She handed me the cell phone, and I checked it. No sign of contact from Evan.

"She could've gone the other way around the lake." There were cabins on the opposite shore, but Lily Clarette's teeth were chattering, and I couldn't feel my fingers anymore. "Let's run into town and get what we need, and then we'll drive over there and knock on doors. If Hannah hasn't been found by then, I mean."

Lily Clarette didn't follow as I turned toward home but instead stood there shivering, looking over her shoulder, the blanket wrapped tightly to her head. With the muted morning light drifting through the trees, she looked like a child playing Mary in a church Christmas pageant.

"What?" I followed her line of sight toward the mountains.

"Nothin'." She turned to follow, bending against the wind so that I couldn't see her face as we walked back.

The cabin was warm and inviting, but my sister remained strangely quiet as we shed the soggy blankets, then climbed the hill to the car. I wondered what she was thinking. "Listen, it might be best if I drop you at the library or one of the coffee shops. Someplace where you won't have to worry about Craig or Daddy finding you. I know you must be tired after last night."

Wincing, she moved the seat belt off her shoulder. "Don't be fussin' over me, okay? I wanna help. I'm not some dumb little child."

"I know you're not."

We let the topic die on the way to Looking Glass Gap. Several sheriff's department vehicles sat parked outside the pharmacy when we arrived, and the tactical truck for a canine unit waited in the alley. Inside, Helen Hall and her workers were alternately supplying coffee and calling everyone they could think of who might've seen Hannah.

"Anything so far?" I asked as Helen hung up the phone at the pharmacy counter.

Her gray hair surrounded her head in a frazzled halo. She laid a hand over it, seeming lost as to what else to do. "Nothing. I just can't believe Hannah would run away on purpose. Something has to have happened to her."

"How's Violet doing?"

"The doctor gave her a sedative. She was beside herself when they figured out that Hannah was missing. Vi blames herself for not being able to look after Hannah and for Evan being gone so much to the doctor's appointments . . . and for being asleep yesterday . . . and for Jake getting himself in trouble again. She's just sure he's got problems because of something she did raising those two. I don't know what's wrong with that boy. He's always been so foolish. You know he hasn't even turned up again yet? He doesn't even know about Hannah." She blinked hard, holding back tears.

Lily Clarette stretched a hand across the counter and touched

Helen's arm. "I been prayin' we'll find her real quick. I just know we will."

Helen gave my sister a confused look, and I made introductions. Helen's gaze lingered on Lily Clarette's face as if she were discerning the bruises beneath the wind-reddened skin. This morning, a faint black-and-blue semicircle rimmed the cheek Lily Clarette claimed had been struck by the truck door.

"Thank you, sweetheart," Helen said finally, her face lifting as a sheriff's deputy came in the door, then falling when he obviously was only there to warm up and grab coffee. "It's so cold outside. I just don't know where that child could possibly be."

I thought of Lily Clarette when I'd picked her up at the Algers store—how chilled she'd been after only a short time outside. Would Hannah have any idea how to survive if she was lost in the woods? Worse yet, if someone had found her as it grew dark and the storm came in, would she have been naive or desperate enough to trust the wrong person?

There had to be something else I could do to help. Something more efficient than going from cabin to cabin around the lake looking for information. "Has anyone been to the Time Shifters camp to ask if she was seen down that way yesterday? The other day she was admiring some jewelry I bought there. Maybe she went to look." I was grasping at straws, and I knew it, but if Hannah had been there, Robin might have seen her.

Pushing her glasses up, Helen wiped her eyes. "It's worth a try, I guess. I hope Hannah didn't go all the way down there. What if one of those people followed her off into the woods?"

"Let's just take things a step at a time." But Helen had put horrible images in my mind. What if Hannah had been to the camp? What if people there knew who she was?

A crime that wasn't random hadn't even occurred to me until now. But Evan Hall had money . . .

Another sheriff's deputy came in, this time with a police dog in tow. Helen watched hopefully as he crossed to the counter to catch the deputy who was filling his thermos. The body language was easy enough to read even without the snatch of conversation that drifted across the store. ". . . luck in the snow."

The dog wasn't picking up anything.

Helen excused herself, and Lily Clarette and I turned toward the door. The need for coats and dry shoes was evident as we stepped onto the street again. "We can grab some coveralls and boots at the outfitter's store."

Lily Clarette caught my arm. "Jennia Beth, we need more than what we can pick up at the clothin' store." Her teeth worried the side of her lip. "We need to call Daddy and Roy and Levi. Get them to bring us mules and four-wheelers and the dogs. Daddy's coonhounds can find a mouse in a Christmas snow. You know they can. If there's anybody that can go from where that little girl started and maybe figure where she ended up, it's them."

My reaction was instant and visceral, my insides burning with revulsion and blinding resentment . . . and fear. "I'm not letting you anywhere *near* those people. No."

"You know I'm right."

"Lily Clarette, yesterday Daddy gave you away to the man who decided to knock you around. And now you want to *call* them? You think they're going to just *show up* here and help?"

"'Course they will." Lily Clarette had so much more confidence in our family than I did . . . and even that worried me a little. "They're upset at me, Jennia Beth, and they won't like what I've decided for myself, but they're not gonna let a child freeze to death in the woods."

# Chapter 27

The street outside Mountain Leaf Pharmacy was crowded with vehicles, ATVs, and searchers dressed in all-weather gear ranging from brightly colored ski clothes to faded, mud-covered camouflage. Over the mountains, the evening sky dimmed and promised another cold night. Portable floodlights created an unnatural glow above the street, giving the town the feeling of a snow globe, but the idyllic confectioner's coating was only a wicked illusion. Beyond the shelter of the buildings, the wind howled mercilessly, a knife against even the smallest bits of exposed skin.

Lily Clarette and I parked a few blocks from the pharmacy and limped toward the back alley, hoping to avoid the chaos in front. Word of the search had spread, bringing an onslaught of news crews during the time we'd been out combing the woods.

I couldn't imagine what Hannah must be going through as night fell, and now I realized how unprepared I'd been to still be looking for her. When my father, my brothers-in-law, and the men of Lane's Hill had arrived in the afternoon with their dogs and coon-hunting mules, I'd been convinced that we would find Hannah before dark. The mules could cover amazing amounts of ground in almost any terrain, and Lily Clarette was right—our dogs could sniff out a mouse in a blizzard. On Lane's Hill, hunting and tracking weren't only matters of pride but of providing sustenance and family income.

Now my father and the rest of the men had gone home, taking the dogs and the mules with them for the night. They'd found nothing. Hannah and Blackberry had literally disappeared off the face of the earth.

I thought of Evan and his family as we pushed our way through a mill of reporters and curiosity seekers who'd now staked out the back entrance of Mountain Leaf. Lily Clarette caught a breath when we finally closed the door behind us. She'd been clinging to my coat, letting me drag her through the crowd.

"Don't they know they're gettin' in the way? That there's a little girl lost out there someplace? I hadn't ever seen so many people in all my life." A weary, wide-eyed glance flicked toward the door as if she were afraid they'd push through any moment. We'd been stopped by news crews earlier while scouring the roadsides on two mules belonging to one of my father's neighbors.

"I'm used to it, I guess." A bone-rattling cold traveled through my body as I peeled back damp coveralls and threw them over a stack of boxes with my hat and gloves. "Crowds, I mean. Not circumstances like this."

"I don't know if I could live around so many . . . strangers. I can't even understand the way some a these people talk." Shivering, she shrugged out of the coat Coral Rebecca had sent from home and fingered a rip along the seam, looking uncertain.

Maybe she was second-guessing herself. When we'd turned the mules over to their owner, Lily Clarette had refused to leave with Craig and my father, but we both knew they'd be back again tomorrow with dogs and mules . . . and the expectation that Lily Clarette would come to her senses. If there hadn't been law enforcement personnel everywhere, they probably would have escorted her home already.

"Let's warm up and get something to eat." Weariness gnawed like a demon, determined to take possession of my body. I hadn't been on a horse or a mule in years, or out in the weather for so many hours at once. "You did the right thing tonight, Lily Clarette."

Anxiety lined her wind-reddened eyes. "I hope so. Craig was real upset, and now everybody in the church is gonna know . . ."

"Don't worry about them." I guided her through the storage area toward the hush of whispered conversation and the scents of hot coffee and food. "A girl who can break through thickets and climb down gullies on a mule can make her own choices."

"Anybody can ride a mule."

"Not the way you can." My sister was like a woodland sprite, like Sarra in the story, seeming to feel the forest in her very being, to sense its sheltered folds and hidden places. In her, there was much of those generations of Gibbs women who'd learned to live off this hard land, to gather the mountains' secret gifts and herbal remedies. How would she feel when all of this was far away, when she was surrounded by concrete and glass and a sky sectioned by the neatly geometric profile of buildings? "You can have whatever kind of life you want. Don't let anyone else tell you who to be."

"I'm just worried about that little girl right now," she said as we walked into the large storage room where folding tables held food, hot coffee, drinks, flashlight batteries, and other materials gathered for the search.

Helen was deep in a conversation about Violet's condition. ". . . to sleep. She's just too weak to handle the news that we haven't found Hannah yet."

She glanced my way as I reached for coffee. "You two are frozen through. Go out in the main room and sit by the woodstove once you get some food. We moved the shelves and put up some tables." A weary look followed. "Thank you for all you've done and for calling your family in. They've been a big help. I tried to get them to stay for food, but they wouldn't. They promised they'd be back at first light." She turned specifically to Lily Clarette. "Your fiancé said to call him when you're ready for a ride home. He'll come and take you to your daddy's house, no matter the time."

"Lily Clarette is staying with me," I answered quickly. Helen had enough to think about without our family drama playing into it.

"The dogs'll be fresh in the mornin'," Lily Clarette changed the subject. "They're always best when they're fresh."

Helen offered my sister a sad smile. "Goodness, you've got a nasty little cut there by your eye."

I craned to see, but Lily Clarette shrugged away. "Oh, it's nothin'. I was busy starin' at the ground, and the mule run me under a branch."

Slipping around the table, Helen caught my sister's arm. "I don't like the look of that. Come on in the pharmacy and let me doctor it up, hon."

Lily Clarette obediently followed Helen from the room, and I took a plate of chili and bread to the makeshift dining area out front. The store had emptied considerably since earlier that day, many of the searchers having gone somewhere else to rest. Residents of Looking Glass Gap had opened their spare rooms, and even those left in the Time Shifters camp had offered extra beds in their RVs and motor homes.

If the town had been of a divided spirit before, it was now united in the search for Hannah.

On a bench near the woodstove, Evan sat with his elbows on his knees, his head drooping forward, his hands and forearms crimson and raw. Once again, there was no sign of Hannah's father among the searchers. The last I'd heard, the police had been unable to locate him, but they didn't believe he had taken Hannah. After being seen at a drive-through beer barn the day he left the ranch, he'd simply fallen off the map.

Alone by the fire, Evan looked for all the world like a man who'd been crumbling for a while and was now breaking open, bits of mortar and stone falling away.

Setting my plate aside, I took the empty place beside him. "How are you holding up?"

He shook his head, his hair hanging in wet, dark curls, the last ice crystals still melting off. "Not so good, I think."

I laid a hand on his arm just below the damp cuff of a pushed-up sweatshirt sleeve. Cold skin against cold skin. "I'm sorry. I was so sure we'd find her before dark. My family's putting out the word, though. By tomorrow there'll be coon hunters and trackers from all over the area here. If anyone knows how to ferret out all the concealed places in these mountains, they do. They'll find her."

"I just can't picture . . . how she'll make it another night out there in this . . ." His voice broke, and I swallowed hard, blinking against the pressure of tears.

Words wouldn't come. I tightened my fingers around his arm instead.

"It's so cold," he muttered as if the temperature of my skin had reminded him.

*Don't cry. Be strong. Say something encouraging. That's what he needs to hear right now.* "But she comes from mountain folk. She'll make it the way people always have here. She'll find a place to shelter. Just like Rand and Sarra. They figured out how to survive with practically nothing. She will too."

"That's the difference between fiction and reality, Jen. In fiction, you can make sure people have the basic things they need. A field glass to start a fire, some dry tinder, a pouch full of hardtack or corn pone. Hannah didn't have any of those things." Cool droplets fell from his hair as he shook his head again. "I'd give anything if I could just go back and . . . do things differently with her. Stop waiting for Jake to step up." The muscles in his jaw tightened as he said the name.

I thought of my own family, of all the frustrations between us, of all the things I wished I could change and didn't know how to change. I thought of Rand, caught in the soul-splitting tug-of-war between the life his family expected him to live and the life his heart yearned for. Would he ever find a way to weave together the two? Would I?

Staring into the flames of the old stove, I tried to convince myself that there must be a way, that amid what seemed like impossible circumstances, there was a promise—the very one spoken of between Rand and Sarra in the kitchen house at Sagua Falls.

Even when we are lost, God has not lost us.

"You'll get that chance with her, Evan. You will."

"I hope so," he whispered. "I'm just ready for daylight to come so we can get back out there and keep looking."

# Chapter 28

The weather had turned clear again, at least, and warmer. The dusting of snow melted off by ten, other than the bits that lay hidden in moats of fall leaves. The sun had burned away the mist even in the valleys, allowing good visibility for searchers and helicopter pilots, yet half the day had rushed by and still there was nothing.

Even the beauty of the afternoon couldn't eclipse the growing horror of its reality. With each hour that passed, the chances of finding Hannah healthy and unharmed were waning.

"We're almost back to the road again." Lily Clarette pointed to the path ahead of us. We'd been following horseshoe imprints on a deer trail, but it was anyone's guess whether the single set of tracks had a thing to do with Hannah.

"I don't think it's her, anyhow." Lily Clarette pushed back her hood and squinted at the ground, leaning low over her mount's shoulder. "There's what looks like dog tracks here too. Sometimes the horse stepped over the dog track and sometimes the dog stepped over the horse track. They must've been made at the same time, and Hannah didn't have no dog with her."

Once again, we'd come up dry. Above, cars zoomed past as if it were another normal day. Did those people have any idea of the trauma of hope and disappointment playing out in the woods around Looking Glass Lake?

"Let's go on up to the road and I'll see if I can get cell service. We haven't checked in a while. Maybe . . ." My voice broke, and I couldn't say it again, even though I wanted to. *Maybe someone's found her by now. Maybe everything's fine.* The search force had nearly doubled this morning. They were moving even farther afield, checking areas that seemed too out-of-the-way for Hannah to have wandered . . . unless someone had taken her there. The more time that elapsed, the greater the assumption that she hadn't disappeared on her own . . . and that this might be a recovery operation, not a rescue.

Our mules lugged uphill until we cleared the trees. The phone reception looked unpromising, but I sent a text to Evan. **Anything?**

No answer.

I tried not to imagine what one more cold night might do if Hannah was still out there somewhere.

The phone emitted an electronic chime. Lily Clarette looked on expectantly, reading Evan's reply along with me. **Something found. Headed back to town now. Word is, good news.**

My sister caught a breath. "It's happenin'. I know it. How far from town d'you think we are?"

I looked back and forth, but all I could see was a mountain on one side and a mountain on the other, a ribbon of highway connecting them. "I have no idea, but there's one way to find out."

The mule snorted happily and leaned into the bit as I turned him toward Looking Glass Gap and let him have his head. "Let's go."

Lily Clarette urged her mount into a lope, and the mules ran side by side, covering ground until the roadside finally narrowed and we took to the woods again, working our way over a rocky crest. When we topped the hill, what remained of the Time Shifters encampment lay visible in the river valley below.

The buzz of excitement was evident even before we reached the edge of the field where the search volunteers' vehicles and stock trailers were parked.

Robin ran to meet us. "We heard that one of the dogs hit on somethin', and they followed the trail till it got away from them in a crick. Then one a them fellas smelt a fire burning and he climbed up a tree, and sure 'nuf, there was a little smoke comin' from the next holler over, but they couldn't get there. They sent in a helicopter and it was her. That's what we heard. Ray's headed to town to see what's goin' on, if you wanna hop in the back a his truck. I'll look after your mules." She pointed to a vehicle nearby, where Braveheart, in jeans and a jacket, his dreadlocks bound in a ponytail, was climbing into the cab. "Hey, Ray, wait a second! You got s'more passengers!" Robin yelled.

"Y'all come on." He lowered the tailgate to let us in with several other searchers who were already waiting to make the trip.

My pulse raced with anticipation as we ran to the vehicle. "Let me know when you find out if it's true, a'right?" Robin called after us. "I wanna be sure if that little girl's okay!"

The truck was abuzz with theories as we drove to Looking Glass Gap, but it was clear quickly enough that no one knew what was fact and what was fiction. Lily Clarette took my hand, held it between hers, and squeezed tight.

In town, news crews with cameras had begun to scramble into position on Main Street. Clearly they were preparing for some sort of event.

Evan's height made him visible among the sheriff's department personnel in front of the Mountain Leaf store. At the opposite end of the street, something else caught my eye—a black Appaloosa mule with a blaze and an unmistakable splash of white over the hindquarters. Beside it, my father stood among a nest of family members, Brethren Saints, and coon hunters controlling nervous dogs and livestock.

"There's Daddy." Lily Clarette seemed almost relieved to find a familiar face. "I'm gonna see what he's heard."

Instinctively, my arm snaked out, the motion like that of a mother protecting an unrestrained toddler from a sudden stop. "Let me talk to Evan and see."

A frown answered. "They're fam'ly, Jennia Beth, no matter how you feel about it." She was gone before I could protest again.

I pushed partway through the crowd before a policeman detained me, then decided to let me through. Evan looked my way as the sheriff issued a radio order for his deputies to clear the street. A National Guard helicopter was on its way.

Uncertainty was evident on Evan's face. Last night's worry lines remained deeply etched.

"Is she all right?"

"We don't have a lot of news yet. They say she's in fairly good shape, considering that she just spent two nights with practically no shelter."

"Where was she?"

"She and the horse took a fall down a canyon. That's why the helicopters couldn't find her. The horse couldn't climb out and Hannah has a broken leg." He scanned the horizon, watching.

370

"If it weren't for the coon dogs tracking so far over that way, it might've been another day or two before anyone covered the area on foot. And that would've been too late." His jaw clenched beneath wind-blistered skin, and he closed his eyes, struggling to hold himself together.

I waited for him to look at me. "But she's all right, Evan. She's okay."

"We came so close to . . ." The sentence hung unfinished.

"Hey . . . she's *okay*. She's coming home." The next thing I knew, I was wrapping my arms around him and holding on, weary with relief, with gratitude, with the slow building of a monumental joy I was afraid to let myself feel until we saw Hannah in person. Evan was right. It could've so easily gone the other way.

We clung to each other in shared relief, the din around us fading, time pausing until finally the whir of an approaching helicopter drummed the air. News crews went into coverage mode. Voices and electronic noises mingled with the shouts of sheriff's deputies, the clattering of hooves on pavement, and the nervous baying of hounds.

It wasn't until the swirl of debris from the updraft forced me to shield my eyes that I realized I was clutched in Evan's arms. For a moment, it had seemed as natural as breathing, and then suddenly I was aware of our nearness. He seemed to realize it in the same instant and loosened his hold, stepping away.

"She's home," I said, clearing my throat uncomfortably.

"Yes. She is." He was turning toward the chopper before the skids even touched the pavement. I stepped back, clearing the path.

"Come on," he yelled over the roar of the Army-green beast, holding his hand out for mine. An unexpected anticipation shivered through me as we formed the link and then ran through the empty space, ducking down even though the rotors were well above our heads.

The helicopter door slid open, and a guardsman jumped out as the engines slowly whined toward a stop. Inside, Hannah lay in a rescue basket, wrapped in a combination of silver insulator blankets and security straps.

"Hold on there," a medic was saying as he unbuckled the bindings, letting her wiggle her hands free.

Hannah stretched out her arms and tried to sit up. "Uncle Evan!"

Crawling into the helicopter, he embraced her so tightly that she disappeared from view, other than a pair of hands encased in camo mittens that were several sizes too large. Inside them, her fingers clutched Evan's jacket as his shoulders quaked over her.

I stood by the door, once again losing awareness of the noise of reporters, equipment, and officials holding the onlookers at bay. All seemed remote, unimportant. The only thing that mattered was that Hannah had come home alive. Alive, and able to speak and cry and hug. The fact that they hadn't rushed her straight to a hospital had to be a good sign.

I peered in as Evan held her face away, checking her over. Her cheeks and nose were blistered, the fringes of the sores slightly blue. Her lips were swollen and cracked, but the damage could have been so much worse.

She spotted me. Smiled as if it were any other day. "Hey, Jennia Beth! You're still here!"

"Are you kidding? There was no *way* I was leaving until we found you."

Pulling her hands into her lap, she studied her mittens. "I'm sorry I made so much trouble for everybody. Is Blackberry okay? Did they get him out yet?"

"They're working on it," the pilot answered, flipping a few switches in the cockpit before stepping out his door into the glow and flash of cameras.

"Don't worry, Hannah. They'll bring your horse back," the medic promised, checking some sort of monitor before backing away. He smiled at me on his way out. "That was all she could talk about on the ride here—whether the horse would be okay. She stayed curled in next to him to keep warm. That and knowing enough to den up in a layer of leaves are the only reasons she's in such good shape. Smart kid. You've got a minute or two with her, and then medevac will be here to take her on to the hospital." A concerned glance drifted over Hannah's feet before he left, and apprehension burrowed deep in the pit of my stomach.

Evan turned back to his niece. "Hannah, what were you *doing* way out there?"

Her dramatic sigh seemed to make light of all the hullabaloo. "I didn't mean to. I got lost. And then I was trying to find my way back, but it got, like, really dark after a while. I thought I was on the trail by the south gate, so I kicked Blackberry up into a lope, but I wasn't where I thought. All of a sudden the trail was just . . . gone, and dirt and leaves went everywhere. I couldn't see, and I couldn't breathe, and Blackberry rolled over the top of me and I thought maybe I was gonna die. I don't remember what happened after that, but then I woke up, and it was dark, and I could hear a creek, and I could hear Blackberry breathing, and I kept thinkin', *I'm just dreaming it all.* But I was so cold, and when I got up on my leg, I couldn't stand on it and there were, like, rocks all over the place. I started bawling and screaming, and then finally I crawled down to where Blackberry was and started thinkin' about what I needed to do—like getting leaves to make myself a nest and getting Blackberry to lay down so I could get close by him and . . ."

She hesitated then, peered around Evan's shoulder. A grown-up look of concern conflicted with the naively matter-of-fact recounting of her accident. "Where's my dad?"

Evan and I exchanged glances. His lips compressed into a thin, hard line.

"Oh." Hannah focused on the mittens in her lap. "He didn't come back. I thought he'd be lookin' for me with everybody else."

"He didn't know. . . ." The explanation was all I could think of, but it felt pathetically lame. A father who failed to realize that his daughter had been missing for two days wasn't a father.

Evan cleared his throat, the muscles in his neck holding position for a moment before they loosened to allow words. "Is that why you ran away, Hannah? Because you heard your dad and me fighting?"

Hannah blinked, startled. "I didn't run off. I just went to find Dad. He hangs out at that place down by the river sometimes and plays pool and stuff. There's some lady he knows there. I heard him on the phone the other day, talking about movin' back to Oklahoma with her. That's where she's from. I thought if I could catch him, I could tell him to come on home. That you didn't mean it when you said to move out."

"Hannah . . ." Evan's hand smoothed over her hair, swiped a tear as it trailed down her cheek. "All of that doesn't have a thing to do with you, and you can't fix it. Your dad's an adult, and he's just . . . not thinking like one. But you can't take that on. You need to worry about making smart choices . . . and about listening when we tell you not to do something."

"I know." She sighed. "I learned my lesson, okay? I almost got Blackberry killed. And me."

"You did a good job, Hannah," I interjected. For a girl who'd just survived an incredible ordeal, she looked monumentally sad now. "You did everything you needed to do to get out of there. You kept a cool head."

The praise won a halfhearted smile. "Well . . . at first, I wasn't a whole lot worried. I thought someone'd come find me right off. But then when the screaming didn't work and the *whole* night went by and I didn't hear any people or four-wheelers or anything, I told Blackberry, 'This is not lookin' good. We gotta be a *long* way from anyplace.' By the next day, I heard helicopters, but they just flew right over every time. So I told Blackberry, 'We are gonna have to figure a way outta here.' But of course, we couldn't climb out. So by then, I knew I had to figure how to get a fire. I had matches in my coat pocket because Granny Vi always says, when you go in the woods, a book of matches can be the difference between livin' and dyin'. But all the wood I could get to was, like, really wet. I used up most of the matches and couldn't get anything lit, and I figured I better save the last few.

"So then I cried for a while again. Then I started thinking about, how did they do it in the story? And I remembered how she put the little tinder bundle under her clothes when they walked all day so it'd get dry. I got some cedar bark and pine needles and stuff and put it up under my coat, and then I got Blackberry to lay down again, and I just squeezed up close to him as much as I could and piled the leaves back over us again. I knew I better not try the rest of the matches till I had some good dry stuff to burn, so I denned up and waited. Today, once the sun was up good and I figured people were looking for me, I made a fire." Turning her mittens palm up and flipping them through the air, she offered an incongruously impish *eureka*. "The tinder bundle worked, just like it did in the story."

My mind was racing now, scenes painting themselves in my head. "Wait a minute. What story?"

"The one about Rand and Sarra, of course. The one you came here for."

Evan drew back. "Hannah, how do you know about that?"

"I read it . . . last summer at Uncle Clive's place. He saves stuff, you know—outta people's trash cans around the cabins. I'm not s'posed to tell. It's a secret." A grin turned Evan's way, then she winced and touched the mitten to her cracked lips.

My thoughts raced through the connections like an electrical pulse moving from one end of a circuit to another, but Evan asked the question before I could form it. "Uncle Clive saved the *Story Keeper* manuscript from the cabin trash when we cleaned it out?"

Hannah turtled her chin into the collar of the coat. "Don't be mad, Uncle Evan. He can't help it. It's just . . . like . . . it's a *compell-shion* he's got. He wouldn't ever sell the story to anybody or anything. He loves all his junk, a *lot*. But then when Jennia Beth came here, I told Uncle Clive he oughta leave Uncle Ev's story at the cabin for her. Then nobody'd know Uncle Clive stole it and he wouldn't get in trouble, and she'd get the story, and she'd talk you into making it a book. The Time Shifters people wouldn't bug us anymore, and Granny Vi wouldn't be all upset, and you would be happy, and my dad wouldn't have to fix fences when people break in, so him and you wouldn't fight anymore. I didn't know Uncle Clive was gonna drop the pages off a little bit at a time, but he's kinda . . . *different*, if you didn't notice. I think he didn't wanna give away his stuff, really."

I stared at her, stunned. "So all week, it's been your uncle Clive leaving envelopes at my door?"

"Well, except this last time. This last time, it was me and Uncle Clive. I found some more of it the other day in my secret place, but it wasn't yours, Uncle Evan. It was somebody else's from a long time ago. I heard Jennia Beth tell you she was gonna go home, and I thought if we put some more of the story at her cabin, then she couldn't leave."

I was conscious of Evan's confused look. He turned from me to Hannah, his mouth hanging slightly slack. "What . . . what secret place, Hannah?"

"Down the hill by the old rock house."

"The old farmhouse? There's nothing in there. No one's lived there since Great-Grandma died when I was a kid."

Hannah leaned closer as the noise of an approaching helicopter crowded the air. "There's all *kinds* of stuff in the old milk barn down there. Dishes and pictures and trunks and chairs and a table and a bed. I made it my secret place. That's where I found the box with the papers stuffed in it. That's where I found more of Rand and Sarra's story."

# Chapter 29

"They built this thing right into the side of the mountain." Evan slipped a finger under the rusted hasp on the old barn I'd glimpsed on my first trip up the mountain. That seemed ages ago now, even though it wasn't. So much had happened since then.

The hasp swung open in his hand, padlock and all. "My family ran a dairy out of here for years. Rumor was, back in the day, more than butter and cheese was stored in the spring cave, but just about everyone around here claims to have a bootlegger somewhere in the woodpile. I remember my grandparents processing the milk in the front room and curing blue cheese near the spring, where the temperature and humidity were right. They locked the place up after they took over raising Jake and me. I always figured they did that because they were afraid it'd be a reminder. My mother liked it here. She used the space along the windows as a greenhouse before Dad's job took us to Florida. This was sort of her getaway."

A sudden sense of grief competed with the warmth of the Indian summer day that had dawned the morning after Hannah's rescue. Safe in the hospital now, she'd been given an IV of sedatives to combat the pain, but she was expected to recover completely, with time. Considering how bad things could have been, the prognosis seemed an incredible blessing.

Her hideout here at the farm had the feel of a place where cobwebs gathered and secrets waited. A cool, musty smell wafted out as Evan swung the door onto the weathered wooden porch. He smiled. "Leave it to Hannah to find her way down here."

"It's something I would've done at her age. I spent a lot of time sitting in the springhouse with stories in my head and books I wasn't supposed to read."

"Why does that not surprise me?"

"Don't laugh. Some of them were your books."

He rolled his eyes and held open the door, waving me through. "After you."

I peered into the cavernous barn. "You know what, I think I'm happy to let you go first." The dirty plate-glass windows allowed only muted interior light. I'd had enough close calls with copperheads, coons, and possums in my childhood.

"I thought you'd go anywhere for a book," he teased.

"*Almost* anywhere."

A flirtatious grin parted his lips. My mind flashed back to the afternoon we'd first met, and the little goat in the trailer. In the hospital, I'd promised Hannah that, once she was better, I'd find a bottle-baby goat for her. Coral Rebecca said she'd help. I hadn't confessed that plan to Evan yet.

Smirking, he led the way into the dairy house, and I followed. Inside, Hannah had created an imaginary kingdom of sorts, complete with an apple crate table and upturned buckets for chairs.

A tea service for two had been pieced together from mismatched cups and saucers. Old shelves along one wall displayed a throng of antique bottles that looked like they had probably been sifted from a dump somewhere on the property, and nearby, several creations fashioned from clay sat drying on a leaning Hoosier cabinet. The cedar chest Hannah had described to us in the hospital waited beneath the window near a tumbledown potting table. In the corner, a jumble of furniture sat draped in dust and spider silk—an iron bed, an antique high chair, a white metal cradle with ornate finials. Dilapidated moving boxes squatted along the wall. Mice had clearly enjoyed a field day there.

Evan took a few steps toward the strange conglomeration, his movements almost trancelike. If he noticed the cedar chest by the window, he didn't stop to look at it.

"I think this is the quilt box she was talking about," I said but Evan didn't respond. Instead, he stood gazing at the mess in the corner, mesmerized.

"Evan?"

"These were my parents' things. That was our baby bed. I remember my mother putting Jake in there." He moved toward the cradle, stretched out his hand, touched the milky railing, disturbing a gathering of dust, then wrapped his fingers around the metal and clung to it.

Standing back, I rubbed away the gooseflesh on my arms, not quite knowing what to do or say. Despite the artificial familiarity between us these past few desperate days, the truth was that I knew very little of Evan Hall, the man. Most of my knowledge was still confined to the myths invented by fans or produced by a crack publicity team. In reality, Evan kept everyone an arm's length away, including me.

"Would it be better if I left you alone?" It seemed the right thing to say. I couldn't imagine how he was feeling right now, finding these remnants of the family he'd lost, uncovering memories long put away.

He shook his head but didn't speak.

I waited as he skimmed the ornate metal scrollwork of roses and vines, swiping off the dust.

His voice was thin, shell-shocked. "My dad found this thing tangled in some debris along Sarra Creek. He brought it home and fixed it up for Mom before they had my sister. Mom told that story to us all the time. She called this her Moses basket."

Again, I was at a loss for words. It was wrong for something so precious to have been left here to decay, but I understood it. I could imagine the pain that must have caused the locking away of these heirlooms.

He laughed softly, the sound a memory mist. "She loved this thing. They had a fight over it when Dad got the engineering contract with NASA and we moved to Florida. The little house there was sleek and modern, and Jake was way too big for the cradle, but she insisted on taking it anyway. She said it was a piece of home."

I thought of the sewing basket I had kept tucked in my dresser drawer all these years, the memory of Wilda Culp and her big, book-filled house hidden inside. "Sometimes those are the things that matter most."

"She'd be disappointed in where we are now."

I wondered if he was thinking aloud or talking to me.

"Evan, life turns blind corners sometimes. We do the best we can." How would my mother feel about where I'd ended up? Did she have dreams for me? Did she nurture hopes as she stood over our beds at night?

"Mom always told me I'd be a writer."

"Well, she was right, wasn't she?" What did my mother think I would be? Could she ever have guessed I'd end up in New York, bringing books into the world?

"I don't think Time Shifters was what she had in mind."

I closed the distance between us, laid a hand on his shoulder. "You know, you may be surprised at what your mother would think about Time Shifters. I understand it differently since coming here—why all these people want to see Looking Glass Gap, why they want to experience a bit of what you created. They're here because what you wrote touched something human in them. It makes them believe in things we've almost lost hope in these days."

He straightened, turned to look at me, surprised. No doubt he thought I'd be the last one defending the enduring value of Time Shifters, yet it was true.

"There's a magic in the way Nathaniel loves Anna—not in a way that's trying to gain anything from her, but in a way that's selfless and sacrificial. He gives up *everything* for her—his world, his military career, his chances of ever returning home. He's willing to forfeit it all to run with her through time, to try to find a place where they can be together. That's the thing we all want to believe in, the kind of love we still need to see as possible between people. I see it in what you wrote about Rand and Sarra, too."

Had he ever thought of it that way? Did he realize that he wasn't just creating stories, but the thing that underlies the very best stories? Hope. "If your mother were here, if she could see fathers taking their teenage daughters on trips for the first time ever, grandmothers and mothers and twelve-year-old girls reading together and talking about what the story means, whole families coming here to spend time and dress up in crazy costumes, grown-ups playing *let's pretend* just like they're kids again . . . I think if your mother could see that, she'd be proud. I think she'd tell you to embrace it, not let a few crazy people spoil it. If you're done with Nathaniel and Anna, if you're finished with their story, then be finished, but *find* another story, Evan. You have a gift. A gift for showing what we're really capable of, a gift for touching people in the ways that matter, for making them believe in the best version of themselves."

He sent a wry look my way. "You make it sound so much more noble than a college kid trying to make a quick buck."

"I think it *was* more noble than that."

"Maybe."

"Evan, if your mother were here, she'd just want you to be happy." Somehow, in spite of everything, I'd always told myself my mother wanted that for me, but happiness isn't always within a mother's control. In the end, Evan's mother hadn't lived long enough and my mother had lacked the strength to take six kids and leave. I needed to believe that she'd wanted to. That she hadn't just walked away and forgotten us.

"I based Nathaniel and Anna on them, you know. My parents. They were so completely in love. It was as if they'd always been connected on some level, the way Nathaniel and Anna are in the story. I know that's a simplistic view of it. A child's memory. I'm sure they had their problems just like anyone else."

His description fell over me like warm water, comforting and tempting. "I think it's nice the way you remember it." How would it be to have a memory like that? Even one? To know for certain that love didn't have to be a cycle of breaking and destroying and surviving and controlling?

"Yeah, it is." A mixture of emotions played on his face—awe, disbelief, sadness, grief. "No one ever told me they'd saved my parents' things. Maybe Paps even kept it a secret from Granny Vi."

He moved to the table by the window, tested the dusty plywood with his fingers, and smiled slightly. "When Mom was pregnant with Jake, round like a watermelon, she had all her spring plants growing here. I guess my sister was gone that afternoon, because it was just Mom and me, carrying pots up the hill to the garden. My dad kept trying to get her to stop working. He said it was too hot, but she was determined to put those seedlings in the soil."

"It sounds like a good day."

"Yeah, it was."

Sunlight pressed through the window, scattered over the desk, and dappled the warped cedar chest on the floor. His head tilted as he followed the trail. "She loved that old chest. Her family had been through a tornado when she was a teenager, and that was one of the few things that survived."

"Hannah said that's where she found the other pages." I'd forgotten, for a moment, why we were here.

"I don't understand what my mother would've been doing with someone's manuscript. She told me the story about Randolph and Sarra, but I never knew her to write or proofread or anything like that. Dad did, but just professional stuff for engineering journals and so forth." Already he was leaning over the chest, lifting the lid. The time-rusted hinges squealed in protest. Rather than the scents of must and old fabric, the smell of cedar salted the air.

I peered in, my gaze settling first on a quilt and a baby's christening gown. Had it once been Evan's or his mother's? A ragged teddy bear lay beside it, a single button eye staring vacantly upward.

"That was Jake's." Evan turned the bear over, then set it aside on the table, shaking his head. "Mom tried every way in the world to get him to give it up so he could start preschool."

"Sounds like my little brother, Joey." It was the first time I'd thought of him without sadness.

Evan thumbed through the trunk, checked under blankets, baby clothes, what looked like an old dresser scarf. "There's nothing here." Pushing aside the fabric, he drew something from beneath. A scrap of paper. The edge of a page, moth-eaten and yellowed. The impressions left behind by typewriter keys were visible even before he turned the scrap over to reveal words.

"That's from the manuscript. It looks just like the last chapter that showed up at the cabin. The part Hannah found here." I tilted my head to read the text. *Her* on one line and *the mountain* on the next. "What was in this space when Hannah opened the chest, I wonder." I outlined a hollow area in the contents, then turned to scan the room. "Maybe she moved whatever came from there and forgot she did it or didn't think to tell us. She was so groggy at the hospital and . . ."

I saw it then. A wooden silverware box, seemingly out of place among shelves of dirt-encrusted mason jars. Fresh screwdriver marks marred the wood around the old skeleton locks. "Evan, look. Over there."

Angling a glance, he drew back in surprise. "That was my mother's. She kept it in the cedar chest." Four quick strides and he'd crossed the room to retrieve the box. A sense of anticipation hung in the air as he brought it back to the window table. "She always said the family silver was in here, but I never saw her get it out or use it." Pinching the tiny knob on the bottom drawer, he attempted to wiggle it open. The warped slides surrendered only a fraction at a time.

There was something inside: papers—old, damaged, mildewed around the edges . . .

The drawer gave way, nearly catapulting to the floor before Evan caught it. Inside, the pages fluttered, whispered softly, then settled, the stack lying facedown. "I think this is what we've been looking for." Evan's thumb traced a missing corner on the top sheet, the empty space a match for the scrap he'd unearthed in the hope chest. "Look familiar?"

"Yes, it does."

Setting the discovery in my hands, he tugged at the second drawer, but the tiny knob came loose, obviously having been torn off before and tucked back in place. He tried the lid next, but the box seemed determined to keep its secrets. "Pretty sure these two are actually locked. Looks like Hannah tried to pry them open but didn't have any luck. Maybe she was afraid she'd get in trouble if she destroyed the thing."

I thumbed through the pages in the drawer. "I'm guessing there are about thirty pages or so here. With the fifteen that showed up at the cabin three days ago, that would only be around forty-five, total. The numbers are random. They're out of order." I wanted to sneak off to some quiet place, rearrange them, discover the lives that lay in ink and paper.

But the box called to me as well. What else waited inside?

Evan measured its weight, then set it down again. "There's more in here. More of something, anyway. I can hear it moving around." He scanned the room. "Let's see what we can find to get it open." He spotted a screwdriver on the shelf and moved toward it.

"You're going to *destroy* it?" I was horrified.

"I'm going to either spring the lock or skillfully pry it open. There's a difference." He cast a one-sided smirk my way, blue eyes twinkling against dark curls.

"Ohhh . . . kay . . ." Doubt thinned the word. The antique lover in me hated the idea of damaging anything that had survived so long. "But promise me you won't wreck the box."

"I don't make promises I can't keep."

If I'd needed further motivation to ransack the dairy barn

for potential surgical equipment, that was enough. The search yielded a paint scraper, an old-fashioned ice pick, the wedge-shaped metal pin from a trailer hitch, a ball hammer, and a tire iron, along with the screwdriver.

"Please don't use that," I begged, motioning to the tire iron. "We can take this thing to a locksmith. I'll pay for it. Seriously."

"*Pppffff! Locksmith?* Just watch me work." He bent over the box, tools in hand. He attempted the drawer lock first, sprang it almost expertly.

"Now you're scaring me," I confessed as he moved the screwdriver from one end of the drawer to the other, wiggling it loose like the cork on a champagne bottle. "It looks like you've done this before."

"Reruns of *Castle*."

"I love that show." One more thing we had in common.

The drawer released enough that he could wrap his fingers around the edges and work it free. "Bingo. I think we've got more of the manuscript. But . . . that's *not* what I heard rattling around in here."

Setting the find aside, he focused on the lid while I leafed carefully through the new pages, running a finger over the indentations of letters and imagining fingers pressing hard against typewriter keys. *Whose* fingers?

The answer lay on a simple, typed cover sheet, tucked upside down, halfway through the stack.

*Sarra Creek*, the original author had titled the work. The page gave the manuscript a date and an author, as well. "This was written in 1936 by a Louisa Anne Quinn. Was that a relative of yours? A grandmother maybe?"

"Not that I know of. There are no Quinns in the family, but if it's that old, obviously my mother didn't have anything to do with writing it. She had possession of it, though, and if she kept it in the cedar chest, it was important to her." He lined up an eyeball near the lock, trying to trip the lid with the ice pick. "I have a feeling the answer is . . . right . . . in . . . here."

The tool slipped and skittered across his finger, drawing blood. Grimacing, he shook his hand in the air. "That didn't go so well."

"Have you had a tetanus shot?"

He rolled a look my way.

"I was just asking." We leaned toward the box together this time, our faces so close the heat of his skin touched mine. "I could try."

"Do you know anything about skeleton locks?"

"Not really. Do you?"

"Only what I've seen on TV."

A puff of irreverent laughter chased the moment. I couldn't help it. "I'm sorry. It's not funny. Promise me you're not going to try to muscle it ope—"

There was a slight gap beneath the rim of the lid now. I'd been so busy looking at the damage, I hadn't even noticed. "Wait! I think you got it already." I hooked a fingernail in the crack, lifted upward, felt some sort of latch restrict the movement.

"Allow me." Peering through the gap, Evan slid the paint scraper in and tripped the hook. The lid yawned upward of its own volition, the box seeming to take on life, finally determined to tell its story. Dust fell inward, danced in the window light, swirled over the faded red satin interior and an assortment of old photographs—scenery shots for the most part. Someone had been cataloging them with rubber bands and envelopes that were far newer than the sepia images.

Evan leafed through the stacks quickly. "That's my mother's handwriting on the envelopes. She always ended her letters with big swirls like this." He paused, pulled something from one of the stacks. "Look at these." Three Polaroids rested in his hands, the top two a shot of Sarra Bridge and a shot of the creek with the words *Sarra Creek Mill Site* written beneath. The third photo had adhered itself to the back. Carefully prying it free, Evan revealed the blotched image of a carving in a tree. *Sarra*, the scars in the bark read. Below, a notation in the white space read, *His carving for her.*

Evan studied the writing, running a finger over the caption. "My mother may not have written this manuscript, but she was researching it." He scooped the photos from the box, set them aside, tapped a padded satin base that looked like it had been shaped to hold chalices and a plate. "And this isn't a silverware box either. It was made to hold a communion set. Give me that screwdriver. There's a compartment under here."

I didn't even bother begging him not to damage the container. Inside me, the voice of rampant curiosity was screaming, *Smash it on the floor if you have to!* Whatever secrets remained, I was desperate to know them, to find answers.

The warped wood again surrendered its hold in small increments, Evan working the screwdriver around the rim while I tried to help with the paint scraper. Something shifted and slid, rattling against the side of the box as he raised it to get a better angle.

Evan glanced up, his wide eyes finding mine.

"That's not paper." A pulse fluttered in my throat, a wild anticipation.

"No, it's not." Finessing the screwdriver into the gap, he worked the inset again. "It's . . . going to . . . be a real . . . disappointment if . . . those are the keys." A grin dimpled his cheek, and for a split second, I lost track of the operation.

The pressure against the paint scraper vanished, and my hand flew upward, flipping the satin-covered inset like an overweight pancake. It landed on the table with a clatter, but neither of us bothered to look.

Instead, we leaned over the box together. There were no words for what waited inside, yet what waited inside made all the words real. Partially hidden beneath a sheet of notebook paper lay the aged corner of a leather-bound book, the edge of a gold cross, and a stiffened leather cord with a knot tied in it.

Evan lifted the paper, exposing the rest. The proof of everything. Tangled around the journal lay an ancient leather string bearing carved, ivory-colored beads, wampum shell, and a bit of blue sea glass. At the end, a small, hand-carved locket box bore the timeworn etching of a Maltese cross.

I touched it carefully, opened the lid, exposing the images carved in relief. The Virgin Mary and, on the opposing side, the image of the Christ.

"Sarra's prayer box." I swallowed hard, pushed back the unexpected tears. "The story keeper's box."

Beside me, Evan gently lifted the worn leather book, parted the pages in a way that mirrored my own reverence. Long rows of faded script awaited—lines and upsweeps, the thin strings of ink left between characters as the pen rushed to capture thoughts on paper, the blots of pauses and stopping points as the writer contemplated words. Field notes and drawings—berries, stems, leaves, animals, mushrooms, a bird's feather with descriptions of the colors jotted in the margins.

And then suddenly . . . the image of a woman. Sarra as she sat on her knees, a reverent smile on her wide, full lips, her palms and eyes lifted heavenward. Above the sketch, a note waited in the long, carefully formed curves of an educated hand. *Sarra, a Melungeon girl, October 17, 1889.*

"That's the first sketch he drew of her. When he watched her offer her morning prayers." I scanned the opposite page, took in the description of the scene I had already envisioned from Evan's manuscript. This version was written in Rand's handwriting, in his own words. The ink had faded to little more than a shadow in places, almost gone altogether. On the opposite page, Rand had added a note:

Should this book be discovered not on my person, it is quite possible that I have perished in these mountains. I humbly ask that the recipient would contact my family in Charleston and give them to know that I have maintained the dearest love for them until the last. It was ever my intention to return from this journey, yet I must follow the course that any decent man should expect of himself. Where there is injustice, one must stand against it. Where there is suffering, one must be the hands and feet of our Lord. Where there is opportunity for good, one must seize it. As go our words, so must our acts.

It is my hope that, should my family receive this book, they will think upon me with pride and some measure of compassion for the wild ramblings of my body and soul. I have walked my path and prayed that I might find God upon it. He has, instead, found me and called me to a purpose.

Yours now and ever,
Randolph Augustus Champlain

My fingers trembled as I touched the signature, thought of the hand that had rested there so long ago, leaving a slight spread of ink as the writer paused, looked up, studied the strange young girl for whom he had risked everything.

"The story's true. It's all true," I whispered.

Evan's gaze met mine. "My mother never told me she had these things. She never indicated that Rand and Sarra were any more than a bedtime tale. A folk legend that gave Sarra Creek its name and Sagua Falls its rainbow."

I studied the bone box and the beads. Their smooth surfaces and carved indentations touched a familiar place in me, reached for something I couldn't frame into words or pictures or thoughts. "Rand and Sarra weren't someone's invention. They really lived. What happened to them after the winter was over? Did he go home or did he stay?"

"My mother never told us the end of the story. It was always just this romantic tale of star-crossed lovers who jumped over Sagua together rather than being separated. That's where Nathaniel and Anna's escape scene in *Time Shifters: The Reckoning* came from. Of course, Nathaniel had the benefit of a time portal . . . and near water, the burst of quantum light from the portal going into hyper-phase would create a rainbow, giving birth to the legend of the lovers at the falls."

"Now you're scaring me again."

A shrug and a grin answered as he reached for the manuscript with the mysterious name typed on the title page. "But someone took the time to write this story in 1936, long before my mother ever heard of it. Based on the dates, this Louisa Quinn could have actually *known* Rand or Sarra, or both of them."

Carefully, he returned everything to the box, then stacked the manuscript drawers and handed them to me. "Here, take these."

"Where are we going?" Adrenaline raced through my body. I wanted to learn all that these pages and the journal would reveal.

Evan's face mirrored the wild need to discover, to finally know. "Up to my office . . . where we can spread all of this out and find the rest of the story you came here for."

# Epilogue

*I* move to the curtain, draw it aside just a sliver, and look out. The view both electrifies and terrifies me. It's so much to assimilate all at once. Life is changing in a thousand different ways, and I can't quite take it all in.

"You scared a little?" Lily Clarette asks, her hand resting on my shoulder. She looks so young in the simple, royal-blue dress that skims her slender form, her hair pulled away from her face, then left to spill down her back in loose curls. The style still feels strange to her. She fingers the fashionable silver clip with the tasteful smattering of rhinestones. *Here, this'll bling it up,* Jamie had said as she slipped the barrette in after arranging my sister's hair. It drives Jamie crazy that someone as naturally beautiful as Lily Clarette won't wear more than a touch of mascara and refuses to even think about heels.

"I'm scared . . . a lot," I admit. There's no point trying to hide it. My mind has been creating, re-creating, and worrying over this moment for months now. Lily Clarette knows. She's had her head bitten off about it more than once, poor kid. Her admin job at Vida House has become a baptism by fire. Now I'm sorry I got her into this. How in the world is she going to make it there without me? After a year in New York, she's still gobsmacked just trying to navigate the subway, and she doesn't understand that walking through the world looking like you're apologizing for your presence will get you into all kinds of trouble in the big city.

I should've answered the question differently when George Vida asked it. *No,* I should have said. A simple no would've avoided this whole mess, or at least the part that affects me.

"Look, there's Coral Rebecca and Evie Christine." Lily Clarette stretches a finger toward the audience but keeps it hidden behind the curtain. "They made it! They came! I wonder if they brought all the kids and everybody." Her face lights with excitement, and even that makes me feel guilty. It's unmistakable how much she misses the family, how she yearns for the Blue Ridge. I'm afraid she has stayed in New York this past year just to avoid telling me she doesn't want to be there. "Oh, and Marah Diane! They *all* came."

I stand slightly awed. A row near the back is slowly filling with the women of my family. Even Coral Rebecca's husband, Levi, has come along. When Lily Clarette suggested sending the tickets, I'd thought there was almost no possibility they'd ever be used. Now I feel it in the part of me that can't explain the events of this watershed year in any other way—the truth of infinite possibilities. No stretch of the imagination, no far-flung splinter of hope is too remote for God. If I've learned one thing, that is it.

In the end, this is what I have decided about my family, about the place I've come from, with all its beauty and tragedy. Yes, I can put my hands and my feet and my heart to work trying to remedy the things that are within my power, but so much of it isn't. What can't be understood and neatly sewn up must simply be let go, not in the way of giving up, but in the way of understanding who is really in control of it.

"I knew they'd be here. I knew it'd happen," Lily Clarette says, and I admire her blind faith, even as I realize that all faith is blind. We can never really know, except in hindsight, how prayers will be answered. "I'm gonna sneak out and say hi and tell them not to run off afterward. I'll take everybody out to eat, okay?"

"All right. If they want to." But there's a little pinprick inside me, a worry.

Lily Clarette sees it as I let the curtain fall. She's the wishbone in a tug-of-war between two worlds, and in all these small things, she feels the splitting apart of flesh and bone. "I'm just gonna say hi, Jennia Beth. I'm not gonna jump in the back of the truck and run off to home." Her bottom lip pooches out a little. I see the tiny sister I sat up with, watching an early snow drift downward outside the window as we rocked in my grandmother's chair, my mother curled in bed, not seeming to want anything to do with the baby yet.

"I know."

She hesitates then, the pout deepening, reaching her eyes. "But . . . ummm . . . I wanted to let you know somethin'. But never mind. It can wait. It's no big deal."

"What?" It is a big deal, I can tell.

She pulls in a breath, a monumental one, and straightens her slim shoulders. "Well . . . I was gonna tell you after we got home from church last Sunday, but when I went home for Labor Day vacation, y'know, and I stayed over with Mrs. Hall at the Mountain Leaf, and I told you I talked her into sellin' Marah Diane and Coral Rebecca's goat-milk soaps and creams in the store?"

"Yes . . ."

"Mrs. Hall said somethin' else, and I've been thinkin' about it." Her bottom teeth worry her lip, pull it inward. The next words take a minute to form. "She said maybe in a few years, she'll have to close the pharmacy in Lookin' Glass, because old Mace is gonna have to retire, and they can't hardly get pharmacists up there anymore. Lots of the drugstores have gone outta business already. Mountain Leaf is the only pharmacy still around for almost an hour's drive."

She pauses, and I'm left to wonder where she's going with this. Time is running short now if she wants to go say hi to the family before the event begins. "I've read that there's a lack of pharmacists everywhere," I agree hesitantly.

My sister nods with enthusiasm. "There is, and Mrs. Hall said, if I wanted to work there at the pharmacy and drive down to the community college, I could live in the apartment up above the shop, and she'd help me get my school paid for so I can get my basics toward my pharmacy tech. If I like it and think I wanna go for my pharmacy degree instead, she'd help me pay what it costs . . . whatever I can't get in scholarships, I mean."

My sister blinks up at me with my mother's wide, beautiful golden eyes, and I stagger back a step, trying not to openly react. There's a part of me that misses Lily Clarette already, and she isn't even gone yet. It's quickly at war with the part that knows this is probably the right thing for her. I think of her award-winning work in the high school science fair and how she soaked up every inch of the Museum of Natural History a couple months ago. She loves medical shows and the Discovery Channel and the science programs on PBS. She has even refined my grandmother's formulas for herbal goat-milk soaps and creams. She's working on creating an online store that will sell my sisters' wares far beyond the Blue Ridge.

I remember her in the woods when we were searching for Hannah, the way she knew the landscape in intimate detail, how marked she was and still is by those generations of Appalachian women who understood the hidden gathering spaces and the ancient study of healing roots and leaves.

I know she is her own person. She is not an extension of me.

Her gaze searches my face, the hopeful light slowly dimming . . . being purposely dimmed. She doesn't want to disappoint me. "I probably shouldn't've brought it up right now, but I been thinkin' about it, that's all." She scoots off to the side-stage exit of Clemson's Tillman Hall Auditorium and leaves me to contemplate all that she has just revealed.

I peek through the curtain again, watch her slip into the main hall and greet my sisters. She looks out of place among them now, in her fashionable blue dress. She's slightly embarrassed about it, I can tell, but the hugs they exchange say it all. They still love her.

I close the barrier, feeling like an outsider, a failure who somehow can't bridge the gap as my youngest sister does.

She reappears a few minutes later. "They can't stay after," she says, looking disappointed. "They don't wanna get home way after dark."

"We could book hotel rooms for them."

Lily Clarette returns a look that warns me not to be pushy. "Marah Diane says she's not much on restaurant food, anyhow. And they left all the littler kids back home with Aunt Sudie." She shrugs toward the door. "Come say hi a minute, at least, 'kay?"

I check my watch. We're ten minutes from go. "Come on," my sister insists. "They drove all this way." She waves toward the door again, and I notice an envelope in her hand. I ask her about it as we exit the stage.

"What's that?"

"Marah Diane carried it to me. I hadn't had a chance to open it yet. She's got somethin' for you, too."

I slow a bit, suspicious even though I don't want to be. My sisters and I have formed an uncomfortable peace over Lily Clarette, and I'm still afraid of anything that might tear it apart. Lily Clarette is the thread slowly binding us with haphazard, uneven stitches. We all love her, and we all want her to be happy.

I hesitate at the bottom of the steps, thinking that perhaps I should have my sister collect the envelope—whatever it is—for me. I can't let anything spoil this day. It's too important. A year of nonstop work has gone into it.

"Come on, Jennia Beth." Lily Clarette takes my hand, urges me through the second exit and into the corridor. Marah Diane, Coral Rebecca, and Evie Christine are there, looking uncertain and incongruous in their long cotton dresses, black Sunday stockings, and plaited hair.

We exchange greetings, talk about the drive. Coral Rebecca says, "So this is where you went to college."

"Well, here and then NYU for grad school," I answer without thinking.

Marah Diane puckers up a bit.

"Thank you for coming. It means a lot." I stretch out my arms. All of a sudden, I want to hug my sisters. I just . . . do. It feels as natural as breathing. I know their scents, how much each one holds on or doesn't, whether the hug will linger or be quick. We haven't changed so much in some ways.

Marah Diane's hug is quick. Stiff. Reserved.

"Clemson's a big place," Coral Rebecca chatters, trying to provide soothing background music, like the white noise at the dentist's office, intended to ensure that no one panics and bolts. "We like to never found the way."

"It took me quite a while to get used to it," I admit, reminding all of us of the eighteen-year-old girl who left home so long ago. The girl we've all almost forgotten.

"Well, it ain't Towash, that's for sure," Evie Christine pipes up, and we stifle irreverent laughter into our hands.

I ask them again if they can't stay afterward, and I make the hotel offer. *It doesn't hurt to try,* I tell myself. It would be nice to have the time together with my sisters and the older nieces they've brought along.

"You come on and see *us,*" Coral Rebecca interjects. "Whenever you can. You don't hafta just run home for book meetin's over in the Gap and then leave out right off, y'know. You can come just for visitin'."

"I will." Maybe there is a way forward for us. With all of our differences, we are still a family.

Silence threatens. I check my watch, glance toward the stage doors.

"I read that copy of the book you had Lily Clarette carry home to us," Marah Diane pipes up. "It was real good."

A glimmer sparks inside me, glows and flutters—a firefly light, an answered prayer. "Thank you. That means a lot."

"Daddy looked at it too." She punctuates that with a lemon-juice look, warning me not to read too much into it. "To make sure if it was okay for all a us to be readin'. I guess he thought it was. He give it back to me, anyhow. Didn't say much, 'cept not to be takin' what it says too serious." She nods toward my other sisters. "Evie Christine's got it now."

"It kep' me up half the night," Evie Christine admits with genuine enthusiasm. "Coral Rebecca told me it would. I wanted to load me a 30-gauge and go after that Brown Drigger and them other men myself."

We laugh together, and I ask them to at least stay around for a few minutes after so we can talk more. Lily Clarette and I have to go. We hug good-bye without really resolving the question. Marah Diane is already fretting about the trip home. Just before we part ways, she takes something from her skirt pocket and slips it into my hand—an envelope. It's nothing remarkable. Yet my other sisters watch me receive it. There's something inside. An object that feels cool and hard, like a small stone. Coral Rebecca and Evie Christine know what it is, I can see.

"This come from Daddy." Marah Diane's eyes avoid mine. She knows there hasn't been more than a word or two exchanged between my father and me during several visits home to meet with Evan while he was rewriting and filling in the gaps of *The Story Keeper*.

"Daddy sent it?" Some wounded part of me wants that to be true but doubts that it is. I consider just handing it back, saying I don't need it. I feel the envelope's thickness. There's a folded sheet of paper inside too. I see Lily Clarette clutching hers, still unopened. Was there one for each of us?

Marah Diane is giving me the death stare when I turn back—the sort that sharpens the knife between sisters but also cuts away the pretense that exists between friends. "You can ask a spotted mule to turn white on Monday, Jennia Beth, but it's still gonna be a spotted mule Tuesday." It's her way of telling me that Daddy is who he is and I'm only hurting myself by thinking things should be different.

"You're right."

She blinks, shocked by those two little words. Emboldened, she presses the case a bit further. "He let us come here. He's grateful about what you and Lily Clarette done to help fix up the house."

"I know." The bonus check George Vida threw my way for

402

the Evan Hall contract solved a number of short-term financial issues. I still wonder if George Vida was the one who put *The Story Keeper* partial on my desk in the first place, but he's never confessed. No one has. At times I wonder if Hollis might have been the culprit, or even old Russell, the cleaning guy. I caught him lingering over an advance copy of the manuscript months ago, but he wouldn't admit to anything.

The mystery remains, and maybe that's as it should be. It makes a better story that way.

I finger the envelope as I say good-bye to my sisters. I wonder what's inside, but at the same time I'm afraid to know. My name has been scrawled on the flap in uneven print that doesn't seem familiar. It's hard to form a mental image of my father taking time to write each of our names on envelopes, tuck something inside, close the seals. Perhaps one of my sisters is responsible.

*Think about it later,* I tell myself. *Right now, it's showtime.*

I walk up the stairs with Lily Clarette trailing behind, and there he is, Evan Hall in the flesh, whisking through a back-stage door, shaking hands and trying to move past a crowd of would-be sycophants. He is instantly swallowed by the activity, and all I can see is his head bent in conversation, his dark curls neatly slicked back against the collar of the black suit he must've worn to the fund-raiser luncheon prior to this event. I watch as he politely shakes hands with admirers important enough to be allowed behind the scenes. Cell phones are whipped out. Photos are snapped. A kid from the university newspaper moves in, brandishing his press pass.

I catch a glimpse of Evan's face. He seems remarkably calm, completely at ease. I try to decide whether I should hug him or slap him whenever I finally get close enough.

George Vida himself guides the knot of hangers-on toward

the side-stage door, where I now realize Lily Clarette has stopped beneath a light to open her envelope.

"He's all yours, Gibbs." It takes a moment for me to register the fact that George Vida is talking to me. The old lion grins ear to ear. He's in his glory. It's not every day the little publishing house celebrates the release of the book all the giants wanted. And one with this kind of story behind it happens less than once in a lifetime. Some people don't experience it in an entire career.

If I never buy another project that manages to make the lists, I'll have cred at Vida House from now until retirement. That today's event is happening here at Clemson, Wilda Culp's alma mater, makes it only that much more perfect.

That it involves Evan walking my way, wearing an annoyingly smug smile, is a slight drawback, but not enough to dull the magic.

"Seriously?" I say, and he knows, of course, exactly what I am talking about. He's trying to pretend that he doesn't, but the smile makes it obvious.

Stopping in front of me, he leans in and kisses me on the cheek, one of those things he always insists on doing, even though we've had the whole discussion time and time again. Work mixed with personal relationships—not a good thing. We both agree. We've both been down that road before. Not a pretty picture.

Aside from that, I don't want anyone in the business *ever* insinuating that I slept my way to the top.

A crackle of electricity passes through me as his lips move away, and that isn't *professional* either. It happens every time, and every time I pretend it's not there.

"What?" His lips form a smile that's as smooth as cream on fresh milk. For a man who was so determined to hole up on his mountain just a year ago, he's amazingly good at handling all this hoopla. The press ops all week have gone fabulously well. Evan Hall has managed to quickly light the world on fire. Again.

"You *know* what." I shift away, putting a safe distance between us, and cross my arms.

He responds with an impishly innocent look; however, he's anything but innocent here.

Once again I remind myself, as I have during many late nights of poring over last-minute edits on the manuscript together, that nothing good could come from Evan and me getting involved. We live in two different worlds. I'm finally standing at the pinnacle of mine. He has a twelve-year-old niece to raise, and with his granny Vi now gone, that in itself is a full-time job, especially with a book tour looming ahead. I wonder where Hannah is tonight—perhaps seated in the audience with Helen, ready to take in the unveiling of *The Story Keeper*. The book releases in stores at midnight. The ink on the movie options is already dry. We all knew it would happen fast.

"Talk to your boss. It was his call." Evan pulls a stack of note cards from his pocket, flicks the tip of his thumb across his tongue and leafs through them, only glancing at each one. His speech, undoubtedly. There's so much to tell about Rand and Sarra, about their life together in Appalachia—their years of helping to build Hudson's mill towns and then, later, years of fighting for decent living conditions for the impoverished workers who came to live in those company-owned communities. No children of their own, but countless mission schools founded, including one in Tennessee specifically for children of Melungeon blood. A lifetime of struggling against prejudice, bigotry, and the one-drop laws that classified people like Sarra as "colored" and deprived them of their rights, including the right to marry outside their own race. In many states, Rand and Sarra's marriage had been a prosecutable offense.

I can't help wondering how Evan will narrow the speech down to thirty minutes, plus time for questions.

I know I should wait to talk with him later, but the curtain hasn't opened yet. I'd like to catch George Vida before the presentation is over and tell him that Evan and I have resolved the matter.

"Evan, I'm an editor, not a handler," I point out, not quite looking at him. I've learned that it's easier to carry on these conversations if I don't.

"Good, because I don't need a handler."

Just this morning, George Vida called me into his office and dropped the bomb. I was being sent along on the book tour—at least the first half, maybe the whole thing.

Two months and a bazillion cities, six foreign countries. This was so far from my job description, it wasn't even in the realm.

I couldn't decide whether to be excited, embarrassed, or scared to death. Mostly I was just in shock and, yes, worried about how this would look within the industry.

And then there were all the personal issues. I'd been hoping this extended holiday from Evan Hall would help clear up the undercurrent of . . . whatever . . . that was tugging back and forth between us. With the rush schedule of the editing and production of *The Story Keeper* these past months, I've hardly worked on anything else. Even though Evan and I have put in many a late night together, the pressure to get the story right, combined with the depth of our investment in it, has made it easier to avoid letting the professional and personal lines blur.

But now this . . .

A quick wink and he slides the cards back into his pocket,

confidence radiating from him, and something more—a new enthusiasm, a passion that makes his blue eyes glow like the cool mountain waters of Looking Glass Lake. Telling the stories of Appalachia, the *real* stories, is something we both care deeply about, a way to bring attention to the peoples and the struggles that in some places haven't changed much in hundreds of years.

"Listen, I'm going to talk to George Vida and tell him I can't . . ." I stop as the dean of arts and humanities veers toward us, checking his watch on his way.

"Ready?" He pauses to shake Evan's hand and thank him for allowing Clemson to host this forum, the plate luncheon earlier, and the gala celebrating the book release. Later this evening, there will be a night of dining and dancing, to the tune of a thousand dollars a ticket—all for the benefit of charity. "We're starting off a bit late."

"Ready whenever you are," Evan answers. He leans close to me, angling his body toward the stage as the curtains sweep open and the dean crosses to the podium. "Don't bother. You won't get George Vida to change his mind about the tour."

"I can try. I just think it's best that . . ."

He smiles and shakes his head, indicating that, rather than discussing this, we should listen to the dean's introduction. When it finally winds toward an ending, Evan shifts so that his shoulder touches mine again. For a moment, I think he'll brush another kiss across my cheek. A prickle of anticipation tickles, feather-light, but rather than a kiss, a whisper touches my ear. "Don't bother. I had it put in the contract."

And then he is gone, striding toward his place at center stage, smiling as he crosses from darkness into light. I can only watch, openmouthed, while he shakes the dean's hand before taking the podium. Waiting for the applause to die, he casts a single, triumphant glance my way, then pulls the cards from his pocket, lays them next to the microphone, clears his throat, and begins.

"I'd like to thank all of you for coming out today to support what is, for me, a project of the heart—one that, like so much of the history of Appalachia's little races, came within a breath of being lost. If it weren't for a slush pile, an eleven-year-old girl, and an antique communion box discovered by my mother at a flea market, the real story of a young Melungeon woman and the son of one of Charleston's oldest families would probably have disappeared into history and local lore. Like so many family chronicles of the time, the truth of their story was whitewashed by future generations, the facts altered, the genealogies steered to more convenient paths.

"While the experts continue to debate genetic origins of the little races of the mountains, such as the Melungeons, and whether they are actually the descendants of native peoples inter-married with shipwrecked Portuguese or Turks, or descendants of survivors of Sir Walter Raleigh's mysterious Lost Colony on Roanoke Island, there's proof enough of these two lives. Rand and Sarra's story endured—not only in their own words but in the manuscript of Louisa Quinn, who remains an unknown entity to us. Who was she and why did she devote herself to document-ing this piece of personal history? Why is there no record of any further published work under her name? Hers is a mystery that endures, but in writing the *Story Keeper* novel, drawing from Louisa Quinn's unfinished manuscript and Rand's journal, I've tried to stay as close to attainable facts as possible. I've had one very determined, very talented editor making certain of it."

He casts another quick glance my way, and I feel it in every part of my body this time. For a moment, there is no one else in the theater. Just Evan and me. The pause seems endless, but it probably isn't.

Bit by bit I feel myself forgiving him for sneaking that clause about the tour into his contract. Okay, maybe I'm forgiving him more than just a bit. Maybe, all of a sudden, I'm glad. Filled with a giddy anticipation that eclipses all else.

"But before I get into that," he continues, "I'd like to share one more thing that pertains to all of you who've been so generous as to purchase tickets to come here today. You've been told that the proceeds from this event, as well as the luncheon and the evening gala, will be donated to charity, but you haven't been told in what way. I'm happy to be able to announce to you that these proceeds and my earnings from *The Story Keeper* will be given to fund the creation of Wilda's House, a foundation for the support, development, and encouragement of the young people of Appalachia.

"The first Wilda's House facility will be located on the property formerly owned by well-known writer and longtime Blue Ridge resident Wilda Culp. Over the years, her homes were places of respite and learning for the countless college students who grew under her tutelage at Clemson and later at several community colleges near her family farm on Honey Creek. Her effect on the lives of young people cannot be measured, but the desire is that the sense of shelter, encouragement, and expectation she offered can live on as her legacy and the legacy of all those who seek to combat the challenges created by geographic isolation, poverty, and lack of economic opportunity. Wilda's House, and the Violet Hall Village that will soon be under construction nearby, will offer retreat space for writers, artists, and musicians. It will also be a center for mentoring, tutoring, and story camp sessions for kids growing up in some of the mountains' most challenged areas.

"The telling, learning, and recording of our stories *is* Appalachia. It is my family's desire that Wilda's House provide a keeping place for those records, as well as a place for writers and storytellers to mingle and share. Rand and Sarra's life history, while a beautiful tale of love, survival, and devotion, is also in some ways a cautionary tale. But for a rediscovered manuscript, all would have been lost.

"Our stories are powerful. They teach, they speak, they inspire. They bring about change. But they are also fragile. Their threads are so easily broken by time, by lack of interest, by failure to understand the value that comes of knowing where we have been and *who* we have been. In this speed-of-light culture, our histories are fading more quickly than ever. Yet when we lose our stories, we lose ourselves. . . ."

A hand rises to my mouth, and I press fingers to my lips to ensure there's still air moving through my lungs. I imagine the place he's describing—Wilda's House. How could he possibly have kept all of this a secret until now? I feel as though I must have fallen asleep somewhere—perhaps with pages of *The Story Keeper* or Rand's original journal still on my lap—and slipped into a dream.

I feel Wilda here beside me, her hand on my shoulder. *So often it is our narrow focus that limits us,* she is saying. *When we look only at our own plans, we miss the infinite possibilities of a greater plan.*

Evan continues, giving the background of the manuscript, pulling a laugh from the audience as he tells of his first careless submissions to publishers and his dismay when no acceptance letters came.

Chuckling, I lean against the wall beside the curtain, shift, and look down when something crinkles under my foot. The envelope from my father. I've dropped it without even realizing. Silently I pick it up, feel its weight in my hand again. I realize

Wilda is right. I've limited the envelope with my own expectations, expunged the possibility that the contents are beyond my imagining.

I look around for Lily Clarette, knowing she has already opened hers. I'm searching for clues, I suppose. Or warnings.

But my sister has disappeared somewhere in the crowd or the darkness behind the stage. Even Wilda fades now, as do Evan and the chuckles of the audience, who are eating out of his hand.

This moment is for me alone. I focus on the envelope, quietly break the seal. Lifting the flap, I remember the very instant Evan sprang the lock on the communion box that we now know his mother came upon completely by accident. She had no relation to the people in the story, other than her desire to discover and record the rest of it. Using Rand's journal and his early-day photographs, she'd developed an obsession, something she pursued between housekeeping and child rearing, a quest she never had time to complete before time ran out.

Around me, all the world seems suspended in place now, breathless. Tipping up the envelope, I watch two sheets of folded paper slide into my hand—the yellow kind from a child's writing tablet. They have been wrapped over something, taped on both ends, as well as in the middle, forming a package. The tape is old enough to have dried and turned yellow, the adhesive almost gone.

It releases its hold easily as if it has been waiting for me a long time.

Unfolding the top flap, I read the beginning of a message written in the mixed print and cursive of a woman who'd dropped out of school in the eighth grade. Not long after, she would meet my father in a store in Towash and marry him to escape an unthinkable situation.

*Dear Jennia Beth,*
*Mama loves you . . .*

The letter begins. The one thing I've always hoped, always yearned for is *proof*. Proof that, even though she left, my mother still loved us—that she didn't just vanish one night without a word or a thought of what would become of her children.

*I know there's no explainin why I'm gone. Theres nothin in the whole big world you done to cause it or could do to stop it. Since the comin of Lily Clarette, the devil is whisperin things in me agin. Theres times I stood over her, the bad blood risin up, the voices sayin what a mama ought never to think. It come with Evie Christine and Joey, and now with this baby, its got worse by twice.*

*My goin is the only way I know to stop it.*

*Watch after the babies, my big girl. I hadnt got much to give you, but this was in my granny's family, and I always kep it with me. It's a old thing, from way far back. Granny hung it over my cradle when I was tiny, and I hung it over you till I found you with the string broke, just sittin there lookin at the pieces.*

*I thought I'd fix it back one day, but it's good it's broke still so I can leave one for each of y'all and take the middle piece myself. It ain't much to tie us all together in this big, wide world, but it's somethin.*

*I ain't much either, but I love you.*

*Mama*

412

Tears blur the words. I wipe my eyes impatiently, lift the top sheet, and stare down at my mother's gift taped to the second piece of paper—a single, oval-shaped bone bead etched with a cross, a star, and what looks like the oar of a boat. Carefully, I peel back the tape that secures it. I hold it in my hand.

It's so similar to the ones on Sarra's string. A piece of a heritage I never dreamed of. How would I? How could I have imagined this link to things still unknown, to questions yet unanswered?

This gift that was kept from me for so many years, and now has finally been released to me.

With it come both comfort and hope. A stirring. A rush of air and light and joy and tears of the kind that taste salty-sweet as they moisten skin.

As I gaze toward the stage and then into the auditorium, I see the path from the beginning to this moment as clearly as if it had been sketched on the paper and handed to me. The journey has led me here.

This time, I see the moment just as Wilda described it, not in hindsight, but in full and miraculous bloom. I experience it in a soul-deep way that is new and vibrant and all-encompassing.

This is the glory hour.

And this time, I step fully in.

# A Note from the Author

$\mathcal{D}$ear Reader,

I hope you've enjoyed *The Story Keeper*, and I hope Jen, Evan, Rand, and Sarra have made you at least a bit curious about Appalachia and its history. If you've never visited the area, please take the opportunity to plan a trip there. The peaks and hollows of the Blue Ridge and the Smoky Mountains whisper with history, with stories, with trickling brooks and teeming waterfalls waiting to be discovered by new eyes. While Lane's Hill, the Brethren Saints, Towash, and Looking Glass Gap are fictional, many of the places mentioned in *The Story Keeper* are real. Driving a loop along the Blue Ridge Parkway, you can visit Mount Pisgah, hike dozens of trails, and see incredible waterfalls (including Issaqueena, where Nathaniel and Anna disappeared through a time portal in Evan's book). You can marvel at the Stumphouse Tunnel, still frozen in time halfway through a mountain, and imagine yourself back in the days when men dug through mountains by hand. Appalachia offers so many incredible places to visit.

Go. Experience. Stay awhile and enjoy the slower pace.

You might also be wondering about the Melungeon people mentioned in the story and whether they are real. The answer to that question is yes. In 1654, the first English explorers to push into the Cumberland Plateau of Virginia, Kentucky, and the Carolinas reported the discovery of "blue-eyed, reddish-brown complexioned" people who referred to themselves as "Portyghee." The origin and meaning of that term and the word *Melungeon* have been long debated. *Portyghee* was thought to be a corruption of *Portuguese,* and *Melungeon* possibly a corruption of an African word meaning "friend" or "shipmate," but nobody really knows. In 1673, Englishmen James Needham and Gabriel Arthur, traveling with several Native American guides, reported meeting "hairy people . . . (who) have a bell which is six foot over which they ring morning and evening and at that time a great number of people congregate together and talks." The dialect used by these "hairy, white people which have long beards and whiskers and weares clothing" was neither English nor any Native American language the guides recognized.

The Melungeons and their origins remain one of the world's greatest cultural mysteries. Thought to be a tri-racial isolate of Anglo, African American, and Native American blood, they suffered under prejudice, discrimination, and misinformation. Their family stories were often lost or altered as later generations chose, in self-defense or shame, to hide their Melungeon roots. Both Abraham Lincoln and Elvis Presley were rumored to have been of Melungeon descent.

You can see, I suppose, why Evan Hall would have found these enigmatic, reclusive people a fascinating culture among which to set his novels . . . and why I have found them fascinating as well. Who were these people? Where did they come from? Were they the descendants of shipwreck survivors who, perhaps, pressed inland and intermarried with local indigenous populations? Does their presence in the Carolina mountains in some way solve the mystery of Sir Walter Raleigh's 117 Lost Colonists, who were left on the Outer Banks in 1584 and never seen again?

Much debate has been given to the question, and while the mystery might never be solved, it is fascinating fodder for a series of stories, don't you think? History's mysteries have a way of sweeping us up and transporting us into our own family origins, and also far beyond them into places we've never seen and lives that never were.

Or perhaps, lives that might have been . . . once upon a time.

Happy reading,

*Lisa Wingate*

TURN THE PAGE FOR

– *A PREVIEW FROM* –

## LISA WINGATE'S
UPCOMING NOVEL

# The Sea Keeper's Daughters

~ AVAILABLE SUMMER 2015 ~

# Chapter 1

Perhaps denial is the mind's way of protecting the spirit from a sucker punch it simply can't handle. Maybe some people are more prone to it than others. Maybe it's a function of a dreamy, impractical mind.

It could be simpler than that. Maybe denial in the face of overwhelming evidence is a mere byproduct of stubbornness.

Whatever the reason, all I could think as I stood in the doorway, one hand on the latch and the other trembling on the keys, was, *This simply can't be happening. This can't be how it ends. It's so . . . quiet.* A dream should make noise when it's dying. It should go out in a blaze of tragic glory. There should be a dramatic death scene, a gasping for breath . . . something.

Denise laid a hand on my shoulder, whispered, "Are you all right?" Her voice faded on the last word, cracked into several jagged pieces.

419

"No." The hard, bitter tone sharpened a cutting edge on the words. It wasn't aimed at Denise. She knew that. "Nothing about this is *all right*. Not one single thing."

"Yeah." Resting against the doorframe, she let her neck go slack until her cheek lay against the wood. "I'm not sure if it's better or worse to stand here looking at it, though. For the last time, I mean."

"We've put our hearts into this place. . . . " Denial reared its unreasonable head again. I would've called it *hope*, but if it was hope, it was the false and paper-thin kind. The kind that only teases you.

Denise's blonde hair fell like a silky curtain, dividing the two of us. Maybe it was easier for her to speak the truth that way. "Whitney, we have to let it go. If we don't, we'll end up losing both places."

"I know. I know you're right." But even as the words swirled into the frosty air of a Michigan spring, part of me rebelled. *All* of me rebelled. I couldn't stand the thought of being bullied one more time. "I know you're being logical. And on top of that, you have Maddie to think about. And your grandmother. We've got to cut the losses while we can still keep the first restaurant going."

With dependents, my cousin couldn't afford to take chances. She'd already gone further than she should have in this skirmish-by-skirmish war against crooked county commissioners, building inspectors taking backroom payoffs, deceptive construction contractors, and a fire marshal who belonged in jail. As nearly as I could tell, they were all in cahoots with local business owners who didn't want any more competition in this backwater town.

Denise and I should've been more careful to check out the kind of environment we were moving into before we fell in love with the old mill building and decided it would be perfect for our second Bella Tazza location and our first really high-end eatery. Positioned along a busy thoroughfare for tourists headed up north to ski or spend summer vacations in the Upper Peninsula, Bella Tazza #2 with its high, lighted granary tower was a beacon for passersby.

But in eleven months, we'd been closed more than we'd been open. Every time we thought we'd won the battle to get and *keep* our occupancy permit, some new and expensive edict came down and we were closed until we could comply. Then the local contractors did their part to slow the process and raise the bills as much as possible.

*You're not the one who needs to apologize,* I wanted to say to Denise, but I didn't. Instead, I surveyed the walls, with their beautiful painted murals and the fabulous archways over the booths and the frescoes Denise and I had worked on after spending long days at Bella Tazza #1.

I felt sick all over again.

"The minute we have to give up the lease, they'll move in here."" Denise echoed my thoughts the way only a cousin who's more like a big sister can. "Vultures."

"That's the worst part." But it wasn't, really. The worst part was that it was my fault we'd gone this far in trying to preserve Bella Tazza #2. Denise would've surrendered to Tagg Harper and his good ol' boy henchmen long ago. Denise would've played it safe if only I'd let her.

Yet even now, after transferring the remaining food inventory to the other restaurant and listing off the equipment and fixtures we could sell at auction, I still couldn't accept what was happening. Somehow, someway, Tagg and his cronies had managed to cause another month's postponement of our case with the State Code Commission. We couldn't hang on that long with

Bella Tazza #2 closed, but still racking up monthly bills. This was death.

"Let's just go." Denise flipped the light switch, casting our blood, sweat, and tears into darkness. "I can't look at it anymore."

The sound of the latch clicking held a finality, but my mind was churning, my heart still looking for a loophole . . . or a white knight to ride in, brandishing sword and shield.

Instead, there was Tagg Harper's four-wheel-drive truck, sitting in the ditch down the hill. Stalker. He was probably kicked back, sipping a brew, and smiling to himself.

"Whitney, don't get into it with him." Denise's hand snaked out protectively and snatched a fistful of my jacket. "I'm serious. I don't think you really know what he's capable of." A time or two, we'd wondered if Tagg might go a step further and do something drastic to come out on top in this war.

"That goes both ways." Fumes wafted from my skin, leaving behind a boiling, feverish anger, a seething hatred. I imagined the heat slowly rising upward, spinning through long, dark waves of hair, burning into my brain, turning brown eyes to glowing red. I imagined myself with some form of superpowers, the kind that could magically, miraculously vaporize Tagg Harper. Turn him to ashes right there in his truck.

Something superhuman was about the only remaining possibility at this point—that or a miracle—but Denise and her grandmother had been to church every Sunday for months, praying for our miracle. It hadn't come.

Denise's grip tightened. "I can't deal with any more of this today, okay? It's bad enough thinking about posting auction listings on eBay and parceling out whatever we can take away from this place."

"I'd just like to . . . walk down there and nail him with a

roundhouse kick to that great big gut of his." The past few months' drama had spooked me enough to prompt some refresher courses in Tang Soo Do karate, a pastime I'd given up after leaving the high-school bullying years behind. I hadn't told Denise, but someone had been prowling around outside my cabin at night, at least once lately and probably more than that.

Denise didn't need anything else to worry about. As usual, she was focused on the practical end of things. "We need to just concentrate on digging out financially and keeping Bella Tazza #1 alive."

"I know." The problem was, I'd been adding things up in my head as we moved through the mill building, making our auction list. What we'd get for the supplies and equipment wouldn't even take care of the legal bills we'd amassed, much less the final utility costs on the new building. With business slumping slightly at the other restaurant due to a flagging economy and an incredibly harsh winter, I wasn't even sure we could make payroll. And we had to make payroll. We had employees counting on the money.

Guilt fell hard and heavy, weighing me down stone by stone as I crossed the parking lot. If I hadn't come back to town five years ago and convinced my cousin to leave her teaching job and start a restaurant with me, she wouldn't be in this position now. But I'd been sailing off a big win, after starting a cozy little Italian place in Dallas, proving it out, and selling it for a nice chunk of change. With $300,000 in my pocket, I knew I had the perfect formula for success. I'd told myself I was doing a good thing for Denise, helping her escape the constant struggle to singlehandedly finance a household and pay for Maddie's emergency-room breathing treatments on a teacher's salary.

Denise, I had a feeling, had been hoping that the realization of the childhood mud-pie fantasy she played along with while babysitting me would somehow defeat the wanderlust that had taken me from culinary school to the far corners of the world and back.

"See you in the morning, Whit." She shoulder-hugged me before disappearing into her vehicle, starting the engine, and crunching across the layer of ice runoff from piles of leftover winter snow. Rather than disappearing down the driveway, she stopped at the exit. Through the dark, cold air, I could feel her watching, waiting to make sure I made it to the road without spiraling into a confrontation.

It was so like Denise to look after me. Since the days she'd picked me up after school while my mother worked late tutoring, she'd always been a caretaker. She'd understood all the things I couldn't tell my mom about—the bullying in the exclusive private school where Mom taught, the pain of not fitting in there, the lingering torment over my father's long-ago suicide. Denise had always been my private oasis of kindness and sage advice, the big sister I never had.

Passing by her car on the way out, I didn't even look at her. I couldn't. I just bumped down the winter-rutted driveway, turned onto the highway, and headed toward home, checking once in the rearview to make sure Denise was out of the parking lot too.

Tagg Harper's taillights came on just after she passed by his truck. The incredible, desperate hatred flared inside me again. I was turning around before I knew what was happening. By the time I made it back to the restaurant, Tagg had positioned his truck in the middle of the parking lot. *Our* parking lot. The driver's-side door was just swinging open.

I wheeled around and pulled close enough to prevent him from wallowing out. Cold air rushed in my window, a quick, hard, bracing force.

"You even set *one foot* on this parking lot, Tagg Harper, I'll call the police." Not that the county sheriff wasn't in Tagg's pocket too. Tagg's dumpy pizza place and convenience store was the spot where all the local boys gathered for coffee breaks . . . if they knew what was good for them.

Lowering his window, Tagg rested a meaty arm on the frame, drawing it inward a bit. The hinges groaned. "Public parking lot." An index finger whirled lazily in the air. "Heard a little rattle in my engine just now. Thought I'd pull in and check it out."

"I'll bet." Of course, he wouldn't admit that he couldn't wait to get his meat hooks on this place. He was probably afraid I'd have my cell phone on, recording. If I could ever get proof, I'd take it to the county DA so fast, it'd make heads spin. The DA was young and new and actually seemed like a decent guy, but without proof, he couldn't do a thing. Tagg knew that.

Which was why he was smiling and blinking at me like a ninny now.

"It's *my* parking lot, and it will be until the end of the month . . . and you're not welcome on it. We reserve the right to refuse service to anyone."

"Heard you were moving out early to save on the rent." His breath drew smoke curls in the frosted air. I smelled beer, as usual. "Expensive to keep a building for no reason."

I felt the pinpricks of my fist-locked fingers going numb. "Well, you heard wrong, because we've got a hearing with the State Code Commission in six weeks, and with that little bit of extra time to prepare, there's not a way in the world we won't win our case."

He drew back initially, his chin curling into wind-reddened rolls of fat before he relaxed in his seat, self-assured and smiling. He knew a bluff when he heard one. "Hmmm . . . well . . . that'd be a shame to drag yourself any farther under . . . what with your *other* business to think about and all."

There was a threat in there. I felt it. Fortunately Bella Tazza #1 was outside the county. There wasn't anything Tagg could do to affect it, other than posting negative reviews online, which he and his peeps had already been doing.

But he was *thinking* of something right now. That was clear enough even in the dim combination of moonlight and dashboard glow. His tongue snaked out and wet his lips, and then he had the gall to give the restaurant a leisurely assessment before turning his attention to me again. "Guess I'll wait until the carcass cools a little more."

Pulling the door closed, he rolled up his window, and then he was gone.

That confident look on his face haunted me as I left the parking lot and headed home. What else did he have in mind? What were the good ol' boys plotting as they kicked back together over doughnuts and coffee?

What other killing blow did Tagg have in his arsenal?

During the thirty-minute drive home, I couldn't decide whether to develop new theories, scream like a banshee, or just break down in tears. Rounding icy curves and watching the headlights glint against mounds of dirty snow, I had the urge to let go of the wheel, drive into a snow bank, close my eyes, and stay wherever the car came to rest, until the cold or carbon monoxide put an end to all this. In some logical part of my brain, I knew that was an overreaction, but the idea of going broke and taking my cousin with me was more than I could face.

There had to be a way out. There had to be something. . . .

But nothing came. Finally, the icebound shores of Lake Michigan glinted through the trees, and I looked toward the lake with hope, seeking the comfort it usually provided. This time, all I could see was a vision of myself, floating cold and silent beneath the ice.

*Stop. That.* The words in my head were a reprimand, strong and determined like my mother's voice. *You are not your father.*

But occasionally over the years, I had wondered . . . was there, inside me, the same demon that had taken him from us before I was six years old? Before I was even old enough to know him as more than a feeling, a snatch of sound, a mist of memory?

Could I, without even seeing it ahead of time, come to a place where giving up seemed like the best option?

How was that thought even possible for me, knowing first-hand the pain a decision like that left behind? Knowing what happened in the aftermath when someone you loved entered the cold waters and swam out to sea with no intention of ever coming back?

Someone should tell the dead that saving the living isn't as simple as leaving a note to say, *It's no one's fault.* For the living, it always feels like someone's fault.

Turning onto the cabin road, I cleared my head and felt the tears beginning to come, seeking to cleanse. Sometimes in help-lessness tears are the only thing you have left. They swelled and pounded in my throat, like the tide coming ashore, as I drew closer to the little lake cabin that had been home for over five years now. Fortunately, Mrs. Doyne, who lived in the house out front, kept her three rental cabins at 1950s prices. She was more interested in having responsible tenants who wouldn't turn the places into party pads than she was in making money off the property.

Dressed in her nightgown and probably just about ready to turn in, she waved from behind a picture window as I passed by the house. One of her ever-present crossword puzzles dangled in her hand.

I had the random realization that even Mrs. Doyne would be hurt if I walked out onto the softening ice however far it took to fall through into the water. *Get your act together, Whitney Monroe,* she'd probably say. *Life goes on.* Mrs. Doyne had survived the death of her husband of fifty years, her one true love. She worked in her gardens and volunteered all over the area and mentored a Girl Scout troop. She had the best attitude of any person I'd ever met.

There was a time when I was more like her—better able to take life as it came, to appreciate the subtle joys of an ordinary day, to let the future fend for itself. I'd worked in high-end kitchens, kept up with the pace, never let myself get rattled when an assistant on the hot line scorched a sauce or a waiter dropped a tray. I'd dealt with bosses who weren't much different from Tagg Harper—bloated, self-important personalities bent on showing the world how special they were.

I usually handled things well. I usually had things under control.

But what I'd never dealt with, what I'd avoided my entire adult life, was the very thing that had been squeezing me dry these past months. I'd never allowed someone else's well-being to depend on my own. I'd never had to live with the knowledge that my choices, my actions, my failure would destroy another person's life.

Turning off the car, I rested my head against the steering wheel as cold pressed through the windows and the engine's last gasps settled into dull metallic pings. A sob wrenched the air and I heard it before I felt it. The wheezing, hopeless sound seemed as though it must have come from someone else, but the hot moisture trails slowly tracing my skin said otherwise.

A breath heaved inward, stung my throat, and another sob

pressed out. I lifted my head, let it bump against the steering wheel, thought, *Stop, stop, stop!*

The knock on the window shot through me like an electrical pulse, making me jerk upright. Beyond the blurry haze, I made out Mrs. Doyne's silhouette against the security lamps, the fur-lined hood of her coat catching the light and giving her a halo.

My emotions scattered like rabbits, leaving behind only two that I could identify—horror and embarrassment. I didn't want *anyone* to see me like this, least of all Mrs. Doyne. She had been an angel about the rent the last several months, accepting it whenever we'd had an especially good day at Bella Tazza #1 and could spare the money from the till.

But like everyone else in town, Mrs. Doyne didn't know the whole story. All she knew was that we'd had some trouble with the inspections on the new restaurant. She may have been an angel, but she was also related to Tagg Harper, and she clearly thought a lot of him. Her deceased husband had been one of his ice-fishing buddies. In this county, the locals were closely connected.

Pretending to reach for my keys in the ignition, I wiped my eyes and then rolled down the window, hoping she wouldn't notice what a mess I was.

"Oh, honey." She touched my shoulder, and I gritted my teeth against another rush of tears. "I guess you heard."

I nodded, a rueful puff of laughter forcing itself past my throat and into the air. I watched it billow and disappear. She *knew*? Had she known all along? Had she been in on all of this, offering a good deal on the cabin, being so understanding when the rent was late, as a way of . . . what? Keeping an eye on me?

Was she just one more local helping to make sure that this county and everything in it continued to belong to people with ties to the Harper family?

"I'm sorry . . ." She seemed to leave the sentence unfinished. I wondered what that meant. What was she sorry for?

I hated myself for that question. Over the last eleven months, I'd come to think of her almost as a replacement for my mother. They liked all the same things. They even had the same Upper Peninsula accent. Being around Mrs. Doyne was almost like having my mother back again. Mrs. Doyne was even a breast cancer survivor. Someone strong enough to defeat the disease that had taken my mom five years ago. It was after her funeral that Denise and I reconnected and spent a long night talking about life, dreams, and Denise's struggle to pay Maddie's medical bills after her ex-husband refused to keep up the child support on a teacher's salary. Suddenly, the unexpected offer on my restaurant in Dallas seemed to make sense. All of it seemed meant to be.

"Come on inside." Mrs. Doyne's hand circled under my arm, as if she meant to forcibly lift me out the window. "You look like you need a spot of hot tea."

I didn't argue. I didn't have the energy. I just went along.

Inside, the house smelled of cats, baseboard heat, and the earth of plants in fresh pots. When spring finally came, Mrs. Doyne would have a garden half ready in her sunroom. How could anyone who understood growing things and loved them possibly be in on Tagg Harper's dirty dealings?

"Sit." She left me a sofa space between three curled-up cats. "Let me put the water on."

Sinking down with my cold fingers tucked between my knees, I let my head fall back, closed my eyes, tried to think. A cat crawled into my lap, nestled there and toyed with the zipper on my coat, its soft purring a strange comfort.

"I tried to call you earlier when I got the message." Mrs. Doyne's voice seemed far away.

*Another month . . . Can we hang on another month? There has to be some way to get the money. . . .*

My mind was racing again. Turning over options and options and options. Running into brick wall after brick wall after brick wall. And then the biggest one of all—the fact that if we went any further with all of this, we risked losing everything.

*You can't do that to* Denise. *You can't do that to* Denise, *and* Maddie, *and Grandma Daisy.*

"I say . . . I tried to call you on your cell phone when the message came."

Mrs. Doyne's words broke through the din.

"Message?"

The teapot whistled, the high, shrill sound causing the cats to stir.

The whistle died, a spoon clinked, the refrigerator door opened and closed. Cream and sugar. Mrs. Doyne knew. We'd shared a few cups of tea in the past months.

"It sounded as if the man had no idea where else to call. I would've just passed your mobile number along to him, but he phoned while I was out at the market. I didn't find the message on the recorder until I came back. You must've had the ringer off when I tried to get in touch with you. I suppose the man found your number and called you directly?"

Her slippers shuffled across the kitchen, and I sat up, opening my eyes as she reentered the living room and handed over my tea. I wrapped my hands around the cup, let its comforting warmth and chamomile scent sink in. "I'm sorry you couldn't reach me. I left my phone in the car all afternoon." The truth was, I couldn't deal with calls while we were facing the parceling up of Bella Tazza #2.

Mrs. Doyne gave me a perplexed look, settling into her

recliner, the mug balanced in her hands. "Well, I know it isn't the sort of news you need right now, what with your restaurant struggles. Are you close?" Her head inclined sympathetically. She leaned forward, her eyes compassionate behind her glasses. "

"Close?"

"To your stepfather." Frowning, she looked into her teacup, as if she might find the answers there. "I assumed not, given that the neighbor couldn't find the number to your cell phone in his home."

"My *stepfather*?" The words struck like a ricochet baseball drilling some unsuspecting fan in the head. I hadn't seen my mother's late-in-life husband since her funeral. It was no accident that my stepfather's neighbor couldn't find my new cell phone number among his belongings.

"Mrs. Doyne, I'm completely lost here. I haven't heard from my stepfather in almost five years. There's no reason he'd be getting in touch, believe me."

"Oh . . ." Pressing a hand to her chest, Mrs. Doyne blinked in surprise. "When I saw you crying in the car, I just assumed the message had gotten through to you. I'm sorry to be the deliverer of such news. The call was from your stepfather's neighbor in North Carolina . . . the Outer Banks, I believe he said. He thought you should know of the situation. Apparently your stepfather took a fall in the bathroom, and he lay there for nearly four days before anyone found him."

# Discussion Questions

1. In the beginning of the story, Jen feels as though she has finally achieved her dream, but the dream is about to take an unexpected turn. Have you ever stepped through an open door expecting one thing, then found something completely different?

2. Jen's adult life is in many ways a facade, in that it involves denying and concealing her past. Do you ever feel the need to conceal parts of yourself in order to fit in or advance in a career or social situation? What price do we pay for such choices?

3. When Jen finds the *Story Keeper* manuscript, she is compelled to read it, even though she knows it's both a personal and a professional risk. Why do you think she makes that choice? Describe a time when you were driven to take a risk personally or professionally. Did it pay off? What happened?

4. In Sarra's day, women were given far fewer options in life. Are there stories in your own family of women who faced difficult circumstances and survived or triumphed? How did they overcome their trials?

5. Faced with either helping Sarra or preserving his own safety, Rand chooses to take the risk. In the moment of crisis, he steps forward, even while imagining how a bullet would feel. Do you think we all have the capacity to become heroes? Have you had a heroic moment in your own life? Or can you identify a situation in your past for which you now regret not stepping up?

6. Evan finds himself limited by the persona that has been created by his success. Have others' expectations of you ever made you feel the need to "play a part"? How can we *get real* in front of the world?

7. In Helen Hall, Jen sees the "quiet festering of a dream" that was sacrificed in favor of family and business needs. Are there any dreams in your life that have been shelved by necessity? What would it take to go after those dreams? Will you be able to pursue them at some point in the future?

8. Evan Hall's fans have taken literary love to the point of borderline mania. Have you ever been so enthusiastic about a book that you wanted to visit the setting, contact the author, or "live the book" in some way? What characteristics captivate you and draw you into a story?

9. Because life among the Brethren Saints caused religion and abuse to become hopelessly tangled in Jen's mind, she has pushed faith aside. Have you dealt with "wounded believers" in your life or been one yourself? How can we separate what we've been told about God from authentic truth?

10. Sarra lives in a world that is limited by abuse and prejudice, yet she remains hopeful, determined, and faithful. Rather than blaming God, she looks to God. Where does this attitude come from? Do you think Rand's faith is "softer" because he has not been tested?

11. Despite the difficult history between Jen and her sisters, the ties of sisterhood still bind and tug. Are the bonds of siblings *always* lifelong bonds? When those bonds are broken and tattered, what are the results? Have you ever wished a relationship could be different from what it was?

12. The mountains are a touchstone to Jen's childhood. Where are the touchstones to your childhood? What do they mean to you?

# About the Author

$\mathcal{L}$isa Wingate is a former journalist, a speaker, and the author of twenty-one novels, including the national bestseller *Tending Roses*, now in its nineteenth printing. She is a seven-time ACFW Carol Award nominee, a Christy Award nominee, and a two-time Carol Award winner. Her novel *Blue Moon Bay* was a *Booklist* Top Ten of 2012 pick, and *The Prayer Box* was a 2013 *Booklist* Top Ten pick. Recently the group Americans for More Civility, a kindness watchdog organization, selected Lisa along with Bill Ford, Camille Cosby, and six others as recipients of the National Civies Award, which celebrates public figures who work to promote greater kindness and civility in American life. When not dreaming up stories, Lisa spends time on the road as a motivational speaker. Via Internet, she shares with readers as far away as India, where *Tending Roses* has been used to promote women's literacy, and as close to home as Tulsa, Oklahoma, where the county library system has used *Tending Roses* to help volunteers teach adults to read.

Lisa lives on a ranch in Texas, where she spoils the livestock, raises boys, and spends time consulting with Huckleberry, her faithful literary dog. She was inspired to become a writer by a first-grade teacher who said she expected to see Lisa's name in a magazine one day. Lisa also entertained childhood dreams of being an Olympic gymnast and winning the National Finals Rodeo but was stalled by the inability to do a backflip on the balance beam and parents who wouldn't finance a rodeo career. She was lucky enough to marry into a big family of cowboys and Southern storytellers who would inspire any lover of tall tales and interesting yet profound characters. She is a full-time writer and pens inspirational fiction for both the general and Christian markets. Of all the things she loves about her job, she loves connecting with people, both real and imaginary, the most. More information about Lisa's novels can be found at www.lisawingate. com or on the Lisa Wingate Reader's Circle Facebook page.